TYING THE KNOT

In today's divorce-torn society, marriage is no longer a given. There are many options for men and women who are involved in their careers and seeking personal fulfillment. Romance and sex are very much alive, but when the word commitment is heard many people head for the hills.

Here is a thought-provoking guide for lovers of all ages who are trying to decide if marriage is for them. Careful evaluation of the partner you want to have a long-term relationship with is crucial.

First Comes Love offers guidelines, case histories and quizzes to help you determine if this is the person you want to marry. There are suggestions for how to improve a relationship as well as discussions of many critical issues like childbearing, sexual roles, communication, patterns, stepparenting and maintaining your relationship.

If marriage is looming in the near or distant future . . .
If you've ever been in love and thought about getting married . . .
If you're currently in the middle of planning your wedding . . .
If you're divorced and wondering if you'll ever marry again . . .

First Comes Love

is for you.

With love to my parents, Stanley and Genevieve Edwards, married 40 years and still in love.

FIRST COMES LOVE
Deciding Whether or Not to Get Married

Diane C. Elvenstar, Ph. D.

PaperJacks LTD.

Toronto   New York

PaperJacks

FIRST COMES LOVE

PaperJacks LTD.
330 STEELCASE RD. E., MARKHAM, ONT. L3R 2M1
210 FIFTH AVE., NEW YORK, N.Y. 10010

Published by arrangement with the Bobbs-Merrill Company, Inc.

Bobbs-Merrill edition published 1983

PaperJacks edition published December 1984

Second Printing September 1985

Third printing February 1987

This PaperJacks edition is printed from brand-new plates. No part of this book may be reproduced or transmitted in any form or by any means, electronic or mechanical, including photography, recording or any information storage or retrieval system, without permission in writing from the Bobbs-Merrill Company, Inc.

ISBN 0-7701-0492-4
Copyright © 1983 by Diane C. Elvenstar
All rights reserved
Printed in Canada

Contents

Introduction   1

Section I Some Preliminaries   17
1. Getting Started   18
   Some Definitions / "Are We Meant to Marry?" / Some Skills to Sharpen
2. Why Get Married?   32
   Marriage Is Different from Living Together / Reasons for Getting Married / Drawbacks of Marriage / Reasons Why People Choose Marriage Over Living Together / Reasons Why People Live Together Rather Than Marry

Section II New Trends in Relationships   53
3. When to Marry?   54
   Why Later Marriages Are Increasingly Accepted / Why People Choose to Marry Later in Life / Can You Find the "Right" Person? / Assessing Your Personal Goals
4. Serial Marriages and Blended Families   71
   Why People Divorce / The "Former Entanglements" Questionnaire / Effects of Divorce / What Divorce Does To People's Views of Marriage / The Singles Scene / Why People Want to Remarry / Coming Together: Blended Families / Stepparenting Questionnaire
5. New Roles and Bargains   94
   The "Expectations Sentence Completion" Exercise / How Expectations Have Changed / How Social Changes Are Affecting New Relationships / New Choices, New Problems

Contents

Section III Bases for Marriage — 113
6. Personal History and Patterns — 114
   Patterns Weave Your Future / A Snapshot of Your Past / Building on Strengths / The Role You Assume
7. Patterns in Your Relationship — 133
   Your Communication Style / Power and Control / Problem-Solving / Resolving Conflicts in Your Relationship

Section IV Planning a Future — 171
8. Children — 172
   Problems of Parents of Younger Children / Concerns of Parents of Adult Children / Children: To Have or Have Not? / A Parenthood Questionnaire / Parenthood After 30 / Making It Work / Choosing to be Child-Free
9. Needs and Desires — 190
   Sexual Needs and Desires / Improving Your Sex Life / Determining Sexual Boundaries / Needs and Desires for Affection / Expressing Love
10. The Unthinkable — 211
    Divorce / Pondering the Unthinkable
11. Ten Guidelines for a Long and Happy Marriage — 219
    Make Sure You're Selecting the Right Partner / Make a Commitment / Balance the Giving and Taking of Support / Forget Fighting—Communicate / Enhance Each Other / Use Gestures of Affection / Encourage Independence and Individual Growth / Maintain Sexual Excitement—Exclusively and Creatively / Put Your Relationship First—And Your Kids Second / Put Effort into Maintaining a Good Relationship
12. The Wedding Ceremony — 244
    Imagining Your Wedding / Why Getting Married May Be Hazardous to Your Emotional Health / Fear of the Wedding Ceremony / The Ceremony as a Reflection of Your Personality / Studying for Her M.R.S.

Section V Putting It Together — 259
13. Rational Aspects of Commitment — 260
    Contracts for Coupling / Ingredients for a Contract / Goals for the Relationship

14. Emotional Aspects of Commitment: The Fear and Flutter of Love   273
   Motivations for Falling in Love / Desirable Characteristics / Natural Fears About Marriage
15. Making a Decision   285
   Using the Results of the "Benefits and Drawbacks" Questionnaire / Completing the "After" Questionnaire

Bibliography   311

Acknowledgments

My thanks first to all the participants in my First Comes Love workshops for allowing me to glimpse and learn from intimate and touching moments in their lives.

Thanks also to my warm and supportive editor and friend, Barbara Lagowski, who deserves all her present and future success.

My gratitude also to all public librarians, and especially for the Community Access Line of the Los Angeles County Public Library.

And finally, my love to Raccoon, who brings laughter amidst chaos, and to Mickey, the sweetest husband (and most accommodating proofreader) I could ever imagine.

Introduction

"Doris and Ralph, sitting in a tree. K-I-S-S-I-N-G! First comes love! Then comes marriage! Then comes Junior in a baby carriage!"

Remember the chorus of children chanting those words? Perhaps you were such a child, teasing a pal good-naturedly when it looked as if he or she was smitten with a playmate. It's an interesting poem, that jump-rope rhyme, because it was from just such innocuous sources that we all first learned that kissing, love, and marriage go together—well, like a horse and carriage.

Until recently, this simple progression of life toward marriage was accepted, with enthusiasm, by the majority of people in Western civilizations. Part of this cultural orientation was women's attitude that, with few exceptions, marriage was not just an ideal state but the *only* state that would make them complete. Conversely, men viewed marriage as a "ball and chain." Jokes about being stuck in marriage were plentiful ("Take my wife. Please!"). Yet divorce was rare. While much has changed, it's my hunch that in general, people were no more and no less happy then than they are now. However, with new options come new dilemmas, and that is what this book is about.

You are the product and the beneficiary of a new, exciting, and certainly tradition-breaking time. You're not latching onto a mate to make you complete; you're not getting married because if you don't, people will think you're peculiar. You're not contemplating a walk down the aisle because you've reached a certain age and the American script says that now you must attend to this life task. You're considering possibilities, weighing choices, and exploring as yet uncharted territory. There is little established wisdom to guide you.

Lately, researchers have been studying long-married couples in an effort to understand the secrets of connubial bliss. While the studies have yielded some interesting conclusions, which will be detailed later on, the assumption cannot be made that male-female relationships begun in the past are perfect models for the changed relationships of today. Many people who married ten, twenty, thirty, or fifty years ago were responding to the social pressures and the dictates of their time, their own marriage-oriented upbringings, and, in some cases, particular fads. Some of the "tricks" for staying together that were appropriate in the 1940s and 1950s may be outmoded now. You may realize from your own experience that certain standards, habits, bromides, and types of interactions that were applicable to your former relationships no longer apply. This moment in history—in *your* history and in the relationship in which you are involved—is unique. I hope this book will help you realize just *how* you are special.

This Book Is for You

This book is designed to be helpful to you whether you are very close to your prospective partner or just beginning your relationship. The ideas offered may also be useful in helping you to look back at past relationships, in order to analyze just what went wrong and determine how you might better approach the new relationship in which you are involved. A number of exercises will be offered; ideally, you should complete them simultaneously with your partner, so that together you can discuss your answers and reactions. But this isn't essential—in fact, some people prefer to evaluate their relationships privately in order to choose whether to continue their emotional investment or leave. They don't want to discuss this process with their partners because they first want to fully understand their own feling and perspectives to gain a basis for taking action.

There are four major types of situations in which this book can be most valuable.

1. *For couples engaged to be married.* You may know in your heart of hearts that you've made a perfect selection of a mate, and the wedding date may be set and invitations in the mail. In this context of strong certainty, it's often rewarding and even fun to confirm your feelings, and discover as much about your future spouse as possible. In this case, the goal is not to decide whether

to marry, but instead to enrich the foundation upon which your married life will rest. After completing the exercises in this book, you'll be able to tell your grandchildren (if you end up having them) that you made an informed decision and entered marriage well aware of the differences, similarities, likes, and dislikes of each party. What better way to begin a life together than on a firm footing?

Of course, the cliché "begin a life together" implies that you are a young couple, perhaps with stars in your eyes, collecting your first Corningware. Like most clichés, this phrase has grown tired and inadequate. Many engaged couples have been married before; they may have one or several children, and be skeptically mature enough not to plunge impulsively into so important a move. If this is your situation, this book can be especially useful because your past life experiences will give you a basis for realistically interpreting the ideas offered and the results of the exercises.

2. *For couples considering the options.* People in this group, unlike those who are already engaged, are still at a point of decision-making. You, if in this situation, are not seeking to confirm an existing choice but have strong tugs toward several possibilities and want to sort them out to determine which is most appropriate for you.

It's likely that you want to decide between simply living together (or continuing to live together) and marriage. Perhaps the choice facing you is whether to maintain your relationship or break it off completely. Or it could be that one partner is leaning heavily in one direction (for example, preferring marriage to living together) and the other, while preferring the status quo, is being pressured to respond with a decision. This book contains methods for looking at these possibilities, allowing you to compare your present relationship with the kind of relationship you really want.

Again, many people who are considering such options are experienced in love rather than optimistic teenagers embarking on a first romance. And individuals whose past morals would have forbidden the idea of living together are now changing their perspectives to consider this possibility. Conversely, many people who have previously lived with one or more partners may say "Enough!" and feel more comfortable about the prospect of marriage. These are new and often confusing choices to be considered, especially in a climate where ostensibly happy marriages are crumbling in startling numbers. That's why having the most significant considerations laid out in an orderly progression will provide you with a constructive approach to a satisfying decision.

3. *For couples in a developing relationship.* Differences between people are apparent to a greater or lesser degree depending on how long a couple has been involved. If long-married individuals constitute one end of the commitment continuum, then people who have just begun getting acquainted form the other end. This book can be extremely helpful to those eager to speed up the learning process, because it provides an expedient framework in which to bring up topics that are important but might otherwise not be approached until later in the relationship.

For some people, finding things out quickly may not seem a great boon. There is much to be said for a slow and easy courtship, free from pressure to know all in the shortest amount of time possible. Each person has his or her own style of getting to know a partner. On the other hand, isn't it nice to get some of the more important things out of the way, or simply to discover new facets of each other? Two people who work through the exercises in this book need not feel they are admitting that marriage is on their minds, though certainly those who are marriage-minded will gain from the evaluations. Instead, they are voting for efficiency, for convenience (provided by the structure), and probably also for fun. Discovering new things about each other *should* be fascinating and fun, and usually is.

4. *For individuals trying to sort out a past relationship.* As mentioned above, people who are coming out of a close relationship and are in some stage of the normal healing process might choose to reexamine their past relationship in order to gain insight. Many divorced people find that by reconstructing their thoughts at different phases in their marriage, they end much of the pain and bitterness that naturally follow a severe emotional trauma. They find a new set of emotional tools, gain renewed confidence in their ability to use them, and are fortified to attack their goals—whether these are in career, family, hobbies, or love—with anticipation and optimism.

A love relationship can be lost in ways other than divorce, of course. A widow, in reading this book, might be soothed by confirmation of the positive aspects of love she once experienced. Perhaps also, as she honestly completes the exercises in the book, she will see more clearly both good and bad sides of the past relationship, an experience that can help her to stop dwelling on fantasy and begin approaching life with more realistic expectations. As in the case of divorce, however, the main benefit of this book for widows or widowers is an assessment of the type of relationship desired for the future and a greater understanding of inner resources that can be rallied toward positive action.

Other people have just emerged from a noncommitted relationship in which they had high hopes for deeper commitment. These people's natural rebuilding process can be speeded up through use of the questionnaires and information provided here. Even when a person is still in the stage of experiencing tearful hours—perhaps tearful weeks—a frank evaluation of the past relationship can make the transition easier and facilitate the rejuvenation process.

Goals of This Book

First Comes Love is not meant to be an academic tome; it is primarily a format for you to use in evaluating your present relationship. The book can help you gain tools to:

1. Understand recent changes in societal and personal views of marriage and the family. We may have been fond of *Father Knows Best*, *The Waltons*, and other television classics, but do they fairly reflect a realistic ideal of family life today? In some people, the old ideal is well ingrained; these people may struggle throughout their lives to make their daily relationships live up to it. For most of us, though, emulation of Jim Anderson's or John Walton's character is impossible, given the new opportunities for "free love" and "open marriage," the sexual revolution that has occurred, feminism, and other radical changes in thinking. Not all people regard these changes as positive. In fact, there are some indications that the national mood is swinging back to past visions, and we need to evaluate whether some individuals have suffered from recent pressures toward greater unconventionality and experimentation.

2. Gauge how ready you are for marriage. What's *too* gun-shy? How do you know the difference between "commitmentphobia" and practicality? Questionnaires and case studies will help you to clarify your feelings about both your relationship and the timing of a possible commitment.

3. Evaluate your partner's suitability for you as a mate. Though you'll find questionnaires to fill out, they are not "tests"

that someone must pass in order to be worthy of you. The exercises are not designed to portray a partner as "suitable" or "unsuitable"; no value judgments are implied. The key is to look at your partner in terms of needed or desired similarities to you in important categories, as well as against your ideals and the characteristics you find acceptable. The *amount* of similarity is not the issue—rather the issue is whether enough relevant similarities exist for the relationship to work.

4. Examine existing patterns in your relationship to determine whether they form a solid basis for marriage. In other words, you'll assess your own values, expectations, and feelings; then think about those of your partner; and finally, look at the unique entity formed by the combination of the two of you. It's this unique entity, the "us-ness" you share, that makes up your relationship, and it's defined by the way you interact with each other.

You'll be thinking about how well you communicate with each other, how you divide up your emotional, spiritual, and day-to-day tasks; how each of you fits in with the other's important activities and dreams. The goal is to see how harmonious a partnership you can form, and how the partnership you have now would be altered by changing the nature of your relationship by either getting married or living together. In some cases, the signs will point to your breaking up. Those looking back on a past relationship can see how patterns at that time may be uncomfortably replicated by patterns existing now.

5. Sort out external influences on your decision about your relationship. It's usually difficult to separately identify all the pressures pushing you toward a decision (get married, live together, or break up), or even to figure out why you are attracted to a certain type of person in the first place. "Tall, dark, and handsome," "marry a doctor," "great bazooms," and other personal criteria have become clichés that some people have adopted without stopping to question them. It's essential to pause to sort out (a) whether you truly agree with the standards you were raised with or believed in at some time in the past; and (b) how important the opinions of others are to you regarding selection of a mate.

"Oh no, *I'm* not influenced by the fact my mother hates Harold." "*I'm* oblivious to the fact that my younger sister got married six years ago and has three lovely children." "*I'm* an independent thinker, sure in my values. So what if I just can't bring myself to break up with Angela? I don't want to hurt her feelings, that's all—I don't care what the other guys think!" People like to think they are not affected by the world around them—that they are truly independent thinkers—but the influence of others is always there.

6. Examine the ramifications of marrying your partner. Even if you're thinking about living together versus breaking up, using marriage as a model can be useful. The goal here is to project what your future together would be like, to arouse your true underlying feelings. After all, your feelings are the crucial determinant in the final decision you'll make. Romantic novels and fairy tales admonish that it's better to marry for love than for status, money, or power—and most people intuitively feel this is so.

For people engaged to be married, this will be a most valuable experience, because you'll be able to chart out your future together and speculate about contingencies that might occur. Using the premise that marriage is not a static state but a fluid, flexible entity, you can plan ways to weather the inevitable storms and anticipate how best to make your long-term fantasies come true.

7. Consider your ingrained expectations of marriage, husbands, and wives. Often a relationship breaks down primarily because of a difference between expectation and reality. If you expect John to pick up after himself, and he repeatedly leaves his shirts strewn across the living room floor, then you're going to be frustrated. Conversely, if John expects his wife to tend to household chores, he may be offended that you "nag" him to pick up his shirt after a hard day at work. Eventually an explosion can erupt, and John and his shirt may never return.

By laying out your visions of a "proper" husband and wife, and your view of what a marriage should be like, you can see the gaps between those views and reality. You can pinpoint potential trouble spots, negotiate differences, and rearrange your attitudes—perhaps separating out the ones that are based solely on the model your own parents provided for you. This thinking process may yield other outcomes as well: you may find that your expectations of *yourself*, not just your partner, are unrealistically high; or that your concept of a "wife" or "husband" does not jibe with the person you really are. You may then be able to relieve yourself of self-imposed psychological pressures, or choose to add to your responsibilities to create a more balanced, loving relationship.

8. Learn strategies for dealing with barriers to a satisfying relationship. Just as you once learned the ways in which you currently respond to situations, you can learn new ways to cope. When presented with a difficult circumstance, you can react in one of three ways: remain the same, change the situation, or change your attitude about the situation. There are infinite variations on these three themes, and the exercises in this book will give you ideas for more constructive versions of your present approaches and enable you to easily organize your options.

In fact, in trying out new coping skills, you might find carry-over benefits that favorably affect other relationships in your life. All you need is a sincere willingness to change your present patterns. The idea of trying something new and different sounds enticing at first, but we tend to get stuck in certain modes of responding. It may take some real—and at times unpleasant—effort to move toward long-term change. With the structure offered in this book, however, you'll have encouragement and tangible materials to lead you to the outcomes you desire.

9. Come to a final conclusion about the best course of action to take now. If you're confirming your decision to marry, you'll gain concrete evidence that this is the best step for you now, and will have new knowledge of yourself and your partner with which to confidently begin your wedded life together. If you're presently still weighing the options, you'll reach a decision that is right for you at the moment. If you're just entering a relationship, you will know much more about your partner than when you started, and be able to continue on a firmer foundation. And if you are analyzing a previous relationship, you'll have a better idea of its good and bad points, as well as a good footing for evaluating future relationships.

In general, anyone who completes the exercises in this book will come away with increased knowledge of himself or herself and of past patterns and desired future goals. By simply taking the time to carefully consider choices that many people make on impulse, you can dramatically improve the chance that your present relationship will become most satisfying to both you and your partner.

In reading this book, the above goals are what you can "get out of it"; but there is one thing you *won't* receive. That is, you will not be told what to decide. I have tried not to introduce any bias about what you should do with your life. Of course, I have opinions, but the forms, questionnaires, stories, and facts offered here are deliberately diverse—and, to the best of my ability, objective—in order to offer you the widest range of options available. One of the primary lessons I have learned in my university training, in my internships as both a school counselor and clinical psychologist, in 7 years of running workshops, and in private consultations is that there must be room for individual style. There's a long continuum of acceptable behavior, just as there is a continuum of commitment, and each degree along that continuum is deserving of respect.

While there are many benefits to finding out so much about yourself and your partner, there are also some drawbacks:

1. The process can be a bit time-consuming. Of course, you can skim the information and glance at the questionnaires, but to get the most out of this book, you should take time for careful thought and discussion. This book is quite different from a novel or romance that can be breezed through quickly, or the typical self-help book that gives you a pep talk and sends you on your way to blithely implement changes in your life. *First Comes Love* is basically a *workbook*, and your progress through it means real advancement toward your goals of improved understanding, strategy-planning, and decision-making. So, the more time you invest in it, the more you'll be rewarded.

2. The process of learning new things can be emotionally trying. You may realize facts about yourself, your family, or your partner that are deeply painful. If you touch on something that has remained buried because it was too sensitive, you might want to follow up your new insight with some short- or possibly long-term consultation with a counselor or therapist.

3. There's a possibility that your relationship could be affected in a way you do not prefer. Your partner may discover that he or she is not in love with you; you might have disagreements over some of the topics you discuss; you might end up having to do more chores or undertake more responsibility than you handled in the past. Any of these outcomes may be difficult in the short run, but they will probably help you avoid more serious problems later.

The above points can be drawbacks, to be sure, but I think that they are strongly outweighed by the many benefits you'll gain:

1. A structure in which to organize the many characteristics that make your relationship and take all important considerations into account.

2. A means to an end that can be achieved within a very limited time frame. In other words, working through the exercises will expedite your ability to reach a decision.

3. A format that can be used and then reused, either to evaluate other relationships you have in the future or to examine your current relationship at a different point in time.

4. A personalized, flexible method for exploring areas of particular interest and relevance to you. All of the materials are designed to be adapted to individual needs. Even the one questionnaire that is scored doesn't have an absolute scale by which to judge your answers, but rather offers a very personalized scoring system that lets you give most credit to the factors you value most.

5. A point of reference against which to compare your own values, expectations, and feelings. By reading the case studies of other couples, research reports, and the opinions of various experts, you will probably discover that your fears are common and your anxiety over conflicting feelings is normal. In each specific area, you can place yourself and your partner on a continuum and use this perspective to evaluate behavior.

6. A decrease in your degree of distress concerning the decision you're making now and those you'll face in the future. One of everyone's primary goals—and the purpose of most therapy—is to eliminate unnecessary distress. Naturally, we all want to maximize our good feelings and minimize our bad ones. Having a structure in which to make this important decision about your relationship can lift pressure. As you read along and complete the exercises, your growing insight will decrease your worry. Further, once you independently or in conjunction with your partner, have arrived at a satisfying plan for the future, you'll have the reassuring knowledge that the decision was made with as much care and concern as possible. You'll always be able to look back and say, "I made the choice that was best for me at the time, all factors considered."

How This Book Came About

Recall that the rhyme says—in this order—"love," "marriage," "baby carriage." While the importance of love is still in vogue, the idea that marriage and baby carriage necessarily follow has certainly come into question. Most people still strive for all three, but back in the late 1960s and early 1970s, many individuals started defying tradition in their belief that it was not necessary to be married or a parent to be whole and complete. And even in those days when cohabitation and free sex were most popular, it was still considered odd if a couple who bothered to legally tie the knot chose not to have children.

The process of decision-making has always fascinated me, perhaps because I've long wondered why it takes me forever to select my lunch from even the simplest menu. Because the subject interested me so greatly, for my doctoral research at U.C.L.A. I devised and tested a decision-making process for couples deciding whether or not to have children. The system I developed—called "Children: To Have or Have Not?"—contains the same kind of step-by-step structure, punctuated by readings and questionnaires, that is presented in this book.

In 1977, when I first began conducting "Children: To Have or Have Not?" workshops, most of the couples who enrolled were married. But over the next few years, an increasing number of the participants were living together or unmarried. For most of them, the decision to marry hinged on whether or not to have a child. Since cohabitation had become more socially acceptable, they reasoned, why bother complicating a great relationship needlessly with marriage unless they wanted to procreate? After all, no one is hurt by two people in love who share the same address. But a third person, the child, could be affected negatively if his parents weren't legally bound. Perhaps the child wouldn't be teased or asked embarrassing questions—many children are now raised by single parents and in other nontraditional environments—but institutions such as the government, school systems, and medical suppliers often won't include a child under the father's insurance coverage unless he's legally married to the mother. Many people in my seminars were also concerned about what last name to give the child.

These couples asked me to provide a method for assessing the pros and cons of marriage, one similar to the process by which they had tried to decide whether to have a child. I came up with the title *First Comes Love* because of my observation that the rules we were taught as children—expressed in the rhythmic phrases of this jump-rope song—are exactly the rules that couples currently are questioning when trying to decide whether to marry. Unfortunately, the sequence of events indicated by "First comes love! Then comes marriage!" often concludes nowadays with "Then comes divorce!" It is because all brides and grooms want their union to be a lasting one that I created my workshops and, stemming from them, this book.

When I started researching the existing materials on marriage decision-making, I was surprised at the dearth of assistance. Self-help books seem to be everywhere, and many do address issues pertaining to marriage. These books, however, primarily direct their attention to people who are not in a decision-making transition but rather in a state of marriage or bachelorhood. (Some topics that are commonly addressed are how to learn to live alone and like it, and how to communicate better within a marriage.) I did find several volumes that I consider useful to couples, among them *The Mirages of Marriage* by William Lederer and Don Jackson, *Marital Choices* by William Lederer, and *Stages* by Laura Singer. These books discuss different facets of being married and can help guard against some common traps and pitfalls. Three books that offer interesting discussions of recent developments in marital relationships are *New Rules* by Daniel Yankelovich, *The Marriage Premise* by Nena O'Neill and *Equal Time* by Genevieve Grafe Marcus and Robert Lee Smith.* I'll be discussing some of the findings of these writers later.

Unfortunately, in the course of my research I found few materials that offered specific methods for assessing whether or not to marry (or live with) a given person. The research was largely focused on existing relationships, not prospective ones. Some questionnaires existed that purported to predict a happy or unhappy future on the basis of personal characteristics or specific behaviors of each partner. "If you expect your mother-in-law to visit three times a week, watch out! You're in for trouble!" The problem is that such questionnaires tend to oversimplify and offer only generalizations. (Many couples, for example, are pleased to see their in-laws frequently and enjoy gaining the more extended family that comes with marriage.) Some useful strategies exist in the literature that have been known to work in the past. But there is such a diversity of healthy relationships that what works in one marriage may not be the best approach in another. In conducting

---

*Complete publication information on works by other authors that are mentioned in this book can be found in the Bibliography.

my research, what I found missing was a way to put together the best advice of the experts—the results of all their research and experience—in a way that took into account the idiosyncratic characteristics that make each of us, and each relationship, unique. This glaring need for a simple yet flexible organizing device was the impetus for my creating the exercises you are about to use.

Luckily, before beginning work on this book, I had several years of experience with my "Children: To Have or Have Not?" workshops on which to draw. The workshops consisted of reading assignments, discussions, and form completion by the participants. The focus was on the most salient issues faced by couples—either implicitly or explicitly, either early or later in a relationship. There are certain tasks that each partner completes in the process of getting to know the other and in setting rules for interaction. Early rules are renegotiated and restated as the relationship matures and the needs and desires of the partners change. But, if a groundwork is laid from the start, misunderstandings can be avoided and communication can be more direct, efficient, and rewarding.

When I began giving "First Comes Love" workshops, I was surprised in two ways. First, I was pleasantly shocked at the high amount of interest in a workshop for deciding what to do about an *affaire de couer*. Though participants in the childbearing decision-making workshops were enthusiastic about the "First Comes Love" workshops, I did not anticipate that the general public (the ones whose children chanted ". . . then comes marriage") would be interested to an equal or greater degree. The more striking surprise, however, was the diversity of the people who wanted to purposefully make a marriage decision. For example, there was:

- The older mother of five with her live-in lover of ten years.
- College freshmen, eager to begin their planned marriages on a strong footing.
- Two lawyers, each fresh from spoiled romances, wondering whether their new blush of ecstasy warranted their deciding to shack up.
- The up-and-coming medical intern whose partner was an older, experienced woman sailing out of her fourth divorce.
- The enthusiastic middle-aged man who wanted his partner to love him in the same way he loved her.

They were as heterogeneous a group as could be found anywhere, but they basically had the same questions: "Does our relationship have the necessary foundation to provide long-term happiness? Where do we go from here?"

I learned a lot from these people, about their needs and about ways to improve and expand my materials. After I had run several workshops, I began to see a commonality among certain subgroups making the marital choice. I was better able to succinctly troubleshoot their difficulties and to provide them with information that they seemed to need before they requested it.

I found discussions in workshops particularly fascinating. Often, the talk was fast-paced and charged with emotion. There were frequent tears, hugs, sighs, and jokes about "don't you come anywhere near me tonight." Some issues aroused much debate. For example, some group members insisted that all healthy relationships include arguing, while others believed just as strongly that constant serenity was essential. Some participants believed that individuals had to live alone and feel assured of independent competence before making a commitment; others responded that independent living had little connection with development of a healthy sense of self. These discussions reinforced my belief that there is no one set way for every family or couple to ideally behave. The gauge of whether or not a given behavior is "working" is the happiness of those involved.

So in this book you won't find absolute answers—no prescriptions about "right" or "wrong" ways to act. Instead, you'll discover that it might be wise to act one way in a given situation and a different way under other circumstances.

This book is broken into five major sections. In Section I, you'll assess your and your partner's positions now regarding marriage, and consider how marriage and living together differ. In Section II, "New Trends in Relationships," you'll use questionnaires to evaluate types of coupling that have become more generally accepted only in the past ten to twenty years. This section includes a chapter on living together—why, for many individuals, it's just not a good enough situation anymore, while for others, it is the answer to otherwise insurmountable problems. In this chapter you'll read about and ponder recent trends toward marrying later in life and toward serial relationships and blended families. And you'll find methods for comparing your present relationship with both the more traditional ideals of what constitutes a good marriage and the newest ideals. Section III of the book, "Bases for Marriage," focuses more on the characteristics of you and your partner. You'll have a structure for considering each of your personal histories, and probably will touch on some areas you've never thought about before. You'll also assess present patterns of behavior between the two of you. Through case studies (of both real people and composites of several real people), you'll be able to see that you're not unusual and will have a greater basis for comparison with your own situation.

In Section IV of the book, "Planning a Future," you'll continue to explore your relationship, this time using the patterns and personal histories that you've examined to rationally project your future together. You'll consider the question of how children (existing or potential) fit into your relationship; what your needs and desires are and will be; how you might handle some unpleasant but certainly possible future circumstances; and how to prolong the excitement and joy experienced by newlyweds into your later years. You'll also receive a framework for conceptualizing what kind of wedding you want. A wedding ceremony, of course, symbolizes far more than just your legal commitment—it reflects your personality and that of your partner.

The final section of the book, "Putting It Together," deals with *contracts* and *feelings*—seemingly contradictory subjects that in actuality can blend together to shape your ultimate decision. In the last chapter you'll complete a comprehensive questionnaire designed to pull together all your pondering so that you can gain a broader picture of whether a given decision is right for you. Once you have completed this questionnaire and the other exercises in the book, you'll always be able to look back and realize that getting married, living together, or breaking up—whatever you ultimately chose to do—was thoroughly explored and, to the best of your knowledge, the right thing for you to do at the time.

SECTION One

Some Preliminaries

/ 1
Getting Started

BEFORE YOU EMBARK on the process of questioning and analyzing, reading and pondering, take a few minutes to assess your position (and your perception of your partner's stance) right now. Completing the "before" questionnaire will give you an indication of:

1. How much *conflict* you're experiencing over the decision of whether or not to marry
2. How much *distress* you're feeling about the choice
3. The *interaction style* that you and your partner are using to deal with the marriage question
4. Your *inclination*, whether it is to marry or not, and when.

As with all the questionnaires in this book, complete this one independently of your partner. So that each of you can complete a form separately, you may want to use two copies of the book or photocopy pages on which the forms appear. Then compare your responses and discuss the reasons behind them. With this questionnaire and others, mark each answer with an X (or an XX if so directed).

Couples often have similar answers on many of the items, especially if they've been tossing about the idea of marriage for a long time. If you're completing the form by yourself, you won't have someone with whom to compare answers, but you *will* be able to compare your "before" responses with those you will make on an "after" questionnaire that appears at the end of this book. The major purpose of the "before" questionnaire is for you later to see how your thinking has been affected by the discussions and evaluations that will take place as you proceed. The "before" form is simply a baseline: just complete it, put it aside, and forget about it until later.

Items 3 and 4 on the questionnaire, about interaction style, are intended to give you an idea of how you and your partner presently deal with each other. (These questions are not included in the "after" questionnaire.) Shortly, you'll be receiving some simple guidelines for discussing the marriage decision that may not have occurred to you. These guidelines, incidentally, can be useful in approaching any discussion of a problematic topic. In answering items 3 and 4, you can get a clearer idea of how you now behave when talking and become aware of any idiosyncracies or habits that may not be constructive. If you and your partner both fill out copies of the questionnaire, you can discover differences in each person's perceptions of how the other behaves.

Some Definitions

In order to communicate intelligently about the decision you're considering, it helps to clarify meanings attached to certain words that are associated with wedlock. First, I suggest that you jot down (or at least pause to consider) the associations that arise in your mind in response to each of these terms: "marriage," "love," "intimacy," "fidelity," "equal partnership," and "marital disagreement." Then compare your associations with the definitions I propose below. Your definitions need not agree with mine; the purpose is simply to have you take a closer look at how you regard these central concepts.

1. *Marriage.* This term refers to a legal, public statement of commitment between a man and a woman. ("Marriage" is also used occasionally by people of the same gender in a homosexual relationship, but rarely is it *legally* solemnized or accepted). After a ceremony of some type, the bride and groom become husband and wife, with the understanding that each will be sexually faithful to the other until one of them dies. Usually, marriage brings with it a social expectation that the couple will have children. It is expected that the children will be raised (according to the words-between-the-lines on the marriage license) within the shelter of a nuclear family unit and will be instilled with values that are compatible with the laws and social norms of the surrounding culture.

Notice that in the above description of marriage, the concept of love is glaringly absent. Traditionally, marriage was primarily viewed as an institution whose purpose was to benefit society, ensure that an heir would be born, and provide economic benefit

"BEFORE" QUESTIONNAIRE

1. Conflict is evidenced by indecision, deciding back and forth or having a clash of ideas. How much conflict over getting married has there been over the past few weeks or months:

   a. Within yourself? ___None ___A little ___Some ___A lot
   b. Within your partner?
      (from what you can tell) ___None ___A little ___Some ___A lot
   c. Between the two of you? ___None ___A little ___Some ___A lot

2. Distress is anxiety — being upset or having negative emotions. How much has the decision about whether or not to get married been a source of distress over the past few weeks or months:

   a. For you? ___None ___A little ___Some ___A lot
   b. For your partner?
      (from what you can tell) ___None ___A little ___Some ___A lot
   c. Between the two of you? ___None ___A little ___Some ___A lot

3. When you and your partner discuss whether or not to get married, which of these things do *you* do? (Put an X for each thing that you do, but put *two* X's [XX] for the thing you do most often.)

   ___Argue strongly for my point
   ___Clam up or avoid the subject
   ___Become depressed or moody
   ___Become happy and enthusiastic
   ___Logically weigh the pros and cons
   ___Change my mind a lot

4. When you and your partner discuss whether or not to get married, which of these things does *your partner* do? (Use one X for each thing your partner does, *two X's* for the one thing he or she does most)

___ Argue strongly for his or her point
___ Clam up or avoid the subject
___ Become depressed or moody
___ Become happy and enthusiastic
___ Logically weigh the pros and cons
___ Change his or her mind a lot

5. What is the percentage that you lean *toward* marriage, and the percentage you lean against it?

a. *Right away?*
(within 6 months)

$\overline{\text{Toward}} + \overline{\text{Against}} = 100\%$

b. *In the future?* How long? _____

$\overline{\text{Toward}} + \overline{\text{Against}} = 100$

6. What is the percentage that *your partner* seems to lean toward and against marriage?

a. *Right away?*
(within 6 months)

$\overline{\text{Toward}} + \overline{\text{Against}} = 100\%$

b. *In the future?* How long? _____

$\overline{\text{Toward}} + \overline{\text{Against}} = 100\%$

7. Ten years from now, realistically, which of these do you foresee?
___ Married to my current partner   ___ Married to someone else
___ Unmarried but living with someone   ___ Unmarried and independent

to parents in terms of the work contributions that were expected from children. Love, as it is portrayed in the pages of Harlequin romances and fairy tales, was considered a lucky "extra" but not a necessity.

This definition of marriage may seem rather droll. Where is the passion, the excitement, the sparks that light the dreams of every adolescent in America? Where is the hope expressed in nearly every popular song? The music of youth carries with it the expectation that the ceremony will be the beginning of "living happily ever after." In recognition of its emotional aspect, the definition of marriage to be used here includes the acknowledgment of strong emotional investment and caring; it includes a vow between two people (whether or not the particular words are ever publicly spoken) to love, honor, and cherish each other. Through marriage, two individuals enter a unique relationship. They may have many friends and relatives, but between husband and wife is an exclusive bond—with regard to not only sexual fidelity but devotion.

So, marriage is a publicly recognized state in which two people pledge their faithfulness and their love. Marriage symbolizes a commitment to the other person: when arguments or hard times bring strain, a sincere effort will be made to overcome the hurdles and stay together rather than head for the nearest exit. People who do not recognize the enormity of their proposed commitment may find it easy to get married; later, they will find it more difficult to get divorced.

2. *Love.* Usually, love is considered an intangible—a flutter in the stomach, a warmth, a desire to be with your partner and exchange ideas, a caring that transcends daily concerns and forms a backdrop for everything you do and think. It may or may not include shared interests, shared values and backgrounds, and shared philosophical beliefs. Love does not necessarily include intimacy, though it is better when it does. Love is something you "know" you feel; no outsider can ascribe it to you. Being in love may feel different from one time to the next; it may even be redefined daily. Trying to quantify or define love is like trying to count the angels dancing on the head of a pin: both acts are based on faith in the existence of something invisible.

3. *Intimacy.* Though teenagers may snicker upon hearing that so-and-so is "intimate" with so-and-so, the primary definition that will be used here is concerned with *emotions* rather than sex. In

sexual intimacy—which may range from touching and holding each other to sexual intercourse—a couple communicates physically; in the more general use of the term "intimacy," a couple communicates in other ways. These may include words spoken, body language (such as glances), written notes, and deeds. Intimacy is openness, the free giving and accepting of feelings and beliefs, even when expression of these leaves the communicator vulnerable. Accompanying this communicativeness is a basic trust that the other person will not use any revelations against the partner; there is, as a result, a sense of safety and comfort and a deepening of the bonds between the couple.

Intimacy usually grows out of a shared history and common reference points. With partners who are intimate, each person generally understands what the other is saying because there is fundamental agreement on what words and signals mean. For example, a raised-eyebrow grin might always mean, "You sexy cutie! Let's rendezvous!" Another shared definition might be that when one partner comes home saying "I'm tired!" the other knows to respond with "I'm sorry, honey, what happened at work today that was so exhausting?" A different couple might not view the same cue as a lead-in to work tales, instead interpreting it as a signal to leave the fatigued person in restful privacy. The building of such a communication structure—as well as the free giving and receiving of feelings, a shared desire to exchange ideas, as well as affection and caring—constitutes intimacy.

4. *Fidelity*. Fidelity, like intimacy, has emotional as well as sexual components. It caused a national stir when President Carter revealed to *Playboy* magazine that he "lusted in his heart" for women other than his wife Rosalynn. Still, as long as Carter never acted on his lustful feelings, he was considered a faithful husband. Fidelity is traditionally interpreted to mean that sexual intercourse is reserved only for your spouse. In other words, the traditional definition is a sexual one.

To be faithful *emotionally* has another meaning: it entails saving your deepest feelings for your mate. Under this definition, you can remain faithful and yet be intimate emotionally with many other people, as long as your strongest feelings are for your partner.

This definition rests on the notion that intimacy involves a pledge to place your partner above all others. Some people do not intend such a commitment; for example, they may decide on an "open relationship" that includes each partner having a long-term lover on the side. So you can be faithful to your partner *as long as you uphold the terms of your agreement with each other*.

5. *Equal partnership*. Many couples nowadays claim to have this kind of relationship. But there is little consensus on just what "equal" means. In *Equal Time*, authors Genevieve Grafe Marcus and Robert Lee Smith define "equal" as meaning "you are like, the same as, or as great as your partner in *worth, quality, value and importance*" [italics theirs]. Marcus and Smith further explain equality in terms of the perceived power of each person in the relationship.

To me, the key is the word *perceived*. Even though chores may not be divided evenly, or one partner earns triple the salary of the other, a marriage is balanced and the partners "equal" if they both believe it is. Interestingly, many people with very traditional marital relationships say that they have an "equal partnership."

Betty, a long-married woman whom I interviewed, had been a homemaker throughout the thirty-six-year span of her marriage to Stanley. She had raised three children, now grown, and had gladly been the dutiful corporate wife. In turn, Stanley had been the provider, leaving child care to Betty. He relaxed at his weekly card games with "the boys" and handled the family finances. At one point Betty said jokingly, "Our relationship sounds like a rerun from *Father Knows Best*, but the facts don't express that we made decisions *together* and both contributed to the success of our family in our own ways. They may have been traditional ways, but I believe that in our dealings with each other, we had a liberated marriage, and certainly an equal one." You'll read a more complete discussion of traditional relationships versus newly defined marriages in a coming chapter.

6. *Marital disagreement*. Have you ever felt annoyed with your partner when you've wanted him or her to simmer down, and gotten the reply, "I'm not arguing with you, I'm just discussing this"?

By my definition, a "disagreement" involves differing opinions without an emotional clash. An "argument" begins when you stop listening to the comments of your partner or responding to the direct issue. And a "fight" flares when voices are raised.

These are important distinctions, because fighting and arguing usually don't resolve issues; they only let the other person know how impassioned you are. Disagreeing about something and discussing it, with options being explored and no taking of sides, can be constructive ways of ironing out problems and increasing intimacy. The value of venting negative feelings and arguing will be discussed later.

"Are We Meant to Marry?"

An implicit notion underlying society's elevation and sanctification of the institution of marriage is the idea that it's "natural" to get married. *That* idea, in turn, is founded on the idea that it's natural to be monogamous. Everyone who, in a flutter of love or otherwise, says "this is the one, my true love" is subscribing to the view that monogamy is the preferred state. But this view prompts some questions: If this one is your true love, then were all the others false? Were all the others just amusements along the way to the real thing? If this particular "true love" falls through, does that mean there will never be another? Such philosophical speculation may seem unnecessary, but your answers can tell you something about yourself: if you don't think people are meant to be monogamous, then why bother even considering marriage?

A feeling as to whether or not monogamy is "natural" is central in many people's choice to marry. For them, there is reassurance in the idea that they are following a natural scheme— perhaps even some grand design or divine plan. Though humans are able to set up their own conventions, even in the animal kingdom there are species that naturally mate for life, grieving at the death of a "spouse" and refusing to take another. Among these are ducks, eagles, foxes, geese, gibbons, linx, marmosets, mountain lions, swans, and wolves.

There are *more* examples, however, of nonmonogamous animals, paramount among them being "man's best friend." Similarly, there are many human cultures in which monogamy is not practiced. Polygamy is still accepted in some Muslim nations; under the Muslim religion, up to four wives are permitted any man. And Hindu law sets no limits on the number of women in one's harem. Polyandry, which means a woman taking more than one husband, is still practiced too, though on a more limited basis. In some Himalayan cultures, a woman may even be shared among her husband and several of his brothers. (Usually, the woman gets short shrift in these deals.) The point is that having one mate for life isn't the universal rule. Even in the United States until as late as 1890, Mormon men were allowed to let several women cleave unto them. In none of these instances is multiple mating considered immoral; in fact, it is given the legitimacy of religious approval.

The unfaithful husband who keeps a mistress on the side—one whom he says means as much to him as his wife—would readily attest to our ability to love more than one person at once. Of course, being able to love more than one person does not rule out a personal inclination to marry. I interviewed Doug, a wealthy vice president of an international liquor firm, to learn the reasons behind his dual relationships. These were his comments on having both a wife and mistress:

The old saw that my wife doesn't understand me is, of course partially true. But the important word in that sentence is *partially*. My wife is great in certain ways, which is why I would never leave her. She bore me two fabulous children, and I adore them. Part of the fun is adoring them with her, because she's an enthusiastic mother and is able to give lots of soothing and caring. She gives me soothing and caring too, and I truly enjoy making love with her. She's comfortable and familiar and safe, and she gives me a haven from the cruel world.

But Mandy [the mistress], she brings a spark into my life. I *like* the illicitness of our meetings. I *like* the fact that she puts on special perfume just for me and that we have our secret rendezvous. And Mandy's a fabulous woman. I tell her that she deserves better than me, but I'm always relieved when she says she likes me just fine. Mandy is an executive herself, and she understands the pressures I endure every day. I can bring her my work problems and she'll help me find creative solutions, all the while caressing my brow and blowing in my ear. How could I want more?

I asked Doug whether he thought he was "deviant," whether he felt he really should be content with his wife. He replied:

Deviant? No, I don't think so at all. If you listen to the guys in the locker room, you'd think it was deviant *not* to have a lover on the side. Sure, a lot of it is bragging, but I think that a lot is founded on fact. I don't say a thing, and many of the other guys don't either. And it wouldn't surprise me if all of them had a fling or two at one time or another. I think my wife knows what's going on and accepts it. Men are by nature on the prowl, but most men in our society have been conditioned to suppress these desires, or to channel them into harmless flirtations while killing each other on the football field. The only part about my affair that I regret is that I have to lie to my wife about it. I don't like to be dishonest. But, as I said earlier, the clandestine nature of my relationship with Mandy is part of the fun.

Doug claims that it's male nature, if not necessarily human nature, to have several relationships. Why did he get married, then?

I got married because it was the thing to do at age 22; because it was a rite of passage, and I wanted my friends and family to think of me as a man, a husband, and to give me respect. I've asked myself over and over why I got married, and I also have to conclude that I was in love with my wife. I still am. We have a great, solid relationship that grows deeper with time, and I truly believe in marriage. Otherwise I would call it quits.

"What?" I challenged him. "And give up two sets of daily strokes? You've got the best of both worlds."

At this, Doug's smile faded. He said: "I guess I *am* a good bullshitter. That's how I got where I am today. Sometimes I hate myself for it. I guess there are penalties as well as rewards in everything you do."

Part of Doug's justification for having two long-term relationships was that men are naturally on the prowl. And yet he swears by his wife, calling her a great mother and comforter, someone he loves dearly. His case shows that, for some people, having a rewarding marriage is not so naturally fulfilling that it precludes a desire for other liaisons.

Still, there are good arguments for both sides. Those who claim that mating for life is natural would say Doug has overridden his instincts in favor of serving his egotistical or other psychological needs. A "First Comes Love" workshop participant, Lloyd, who had been a seminary student several years before, was one person who strongly felt that the urge to marry was instinctive. Lloyd, who is now a counselor for drug-addicted teenagers, said that one reason why he made efforts to meet women at all was because he believed in the religious directive to marry, be fruitful, and multiply. He said:

Anyone who believes in the Bible must realize that we have a natural inclination to nest, to find a partner with whom to share life. If God doesn't know our nature, who does—and it was He who tells us through the Bible to marry.

But even if you're an atheist, you can plainly see it's natural to marry by simply observing the world. While it's true that in some cultures monogamy is not the custom, still most countries in the world practice it and make marriage an ideal. Almost universally, gays and spinsters or bachelors are looked down upon. I know that this started because we needed more hands to till the soil, but it's also because marriage provides positive benefits to all concerned. Think about this: Why is it that no matter where you look, men and women pair up? Why is intimacy something we want? Why even try for that one "perfect love" when nowadays you don't have to?

People still reach out because something inside them yearns for human companionship. They want love, and the only way you can be sure that the person you love will be there for you is to get some kind of vow that they will. And that vow is marriage. It makes sense to pledge that you love someone else and will be there for them, not because our culture says it's traditional, but because there's something basic in human beings to care for others and want love in return.

Lloyd had carefully thought through the evidence as he knew it and had decided that people were intended to get married and raise children. Interestingly, this belief was the impetus for him to start dating, and it finally led to his finding his prospective wife, a woman who shared his viewpoint. Their feelings for each other were strengthened by the underlying belief that they were meant to be together. Although Lloyd's perspective seems quite traditional, from his later comments I found out that he and his fiancée had a very egalitarian relationship.

So, two of the arguments suggesting that it is natural to marry are that religious writings say that marriage is desirable, and in most cultures monogamy is the norm. Further, some people who have repeatedly been divorced continue to be attracted to the idea of marriage. In fact, most people who get divorced remarry, usually within two years.

On the other hand, as noted earlier, there *is* some evidence that monogamy is not the "natural" state for everybody. Doug, the married executive with a mistress, is one of millions who respect marriage but still choose to break its rules. If we're meant to be married, why is it that according to 1980 U.S. Census Bureau statistics, the ratio of divorced persons per 1,000 married people more than doubled between 1970 and 1980?

The fact that we strive to perpetuate an institution is no proof that it comes naturally. Marriage, especially for the past fifteen or twenty years, has *not* necessarily meant monogamy. The idea of a married person having sexual freedom received widespread recognition in 1972, when Nena and George O'Neill wrote their much-publicized book *Open Marriage*. Unfortunately, their concept of open marriage was stretched by many people beyond its original meaning of *emotional* openness. Eventually, the term became associated with adultery that is tolerated or encouraged by both partners. In any case, most married people feel an occasional or frequent desire to "mate" with (or at least have sex with) another partner. While marriage may be a valuable state, there is no proof that it is a "natural" one.

Perhaps there is no specific way we're "meant" to be, but many people know the happiness that comes from creation of a stable refuge from life's turmoils—an environment of intimacy, in which even the most intense emotions can be shared.

Some Skills to Sharpen

If you're using this book to reach a decision with your partner (or confirm a decision already made), you'll be sharing new insights and making plans together. By now, the two of you probably have a particular communication style that has evolved. While it may seem to work well enough, your style may not be the most efficient or kind approach.

Refer to your answers to items 3 and 4 on the "before" questionnaire (p.   ) to analyze whether you are more emotionally or rationally oriented. If you checked that you usually "logically weigh pros and cons," or "argue strongly for my point," you tend to be more logical; if you most "clam up or avoid the subject," "become happy and enthusiastic," or "become depressed or moody," your style is more emotional. If you change your mind a lot, you may be responding to either rational *or* emotional influences. Neither style is "better" than the other; they're just different.

As you work through the exercises in this book, I recommend the common-sense communication guidelines below. These guidelines, incidentally, not only can assist you in your personal relationships but can be useful in any setting.

1. *Set aside a time to talk.* It's too easy to let crammed schedules interfere with a thorough exploration of ideas. In my practice, I've found that the most satisfied couples set aside a *regular* time for discussing the events in their lives. It may not be the same time each day, but both partners know that they'll be able to share thoughts with a sympathetic listener regularly. If finding time on a consistent basis is difficult for you, try making appointments with each other, and keeping them.

2. *Divide your communication time fairly.* Even though one of you may be more verbal, make an effort to allow each person a set amount of speaking time. Two to five minutes each, without interruption, can then lead to a general give-and-take discussion.

3. *Respect your partner's feelings.* Because your partner's current feelings and opinions are the outcome of a unique set of experiences and values, no feelings are "wrong" or "right"—they simply reflect an individual perspective. Instead of challenging your partner's feelings, respect them and perhaps acknowledge them by paraphrasing what he or she has said. This "mirroring" technique, made famous by humanistic psychologist Carl Rogers, assures your partner that you understand and are listening. If you strongly disagree with your partner's view, see an error in logic, or think your partner lacks certain information, provide input—but *calmly.*

This guideline is based on the idea that attacking feelings is counterproductive. Such an attack punishes your partner for honesty, and can make him or her retreat or become defensive.

4. *Realize and express your own feelings.* Instead of lashing out at your partner when you feel angry, realize that at times you're expressing something going on inside of you, not reacting to something that your partner has done. You may have heard good advice about "owning your feelings": try saying "I feel . . . ," rather than "You make me feel . . ." or "You are a. . . ." Whenever you have an urge to start an accusatory sentence with "You," pause and see if it can be rephrased to more accurately reflect *your own* emotions.

5. *Never assume.* These Sherlock Holmes watchwords are apropos anytime. Even if you and your partner are intimate to the degree of there sometimes being extrasensory perception between you, when making decisions or carrying on serious discussions, it's important to clarify the underlying basis for your statements. There are many interpretations of the same evidence, as the sleuth of Scotland Yard could tell you, so to avoid confusion or needless anger, spell out your own perceptions and *ask questions* whenever you're not sure of your partner's meaning.

6. *Recognize that problems may not be solved immediately.* It's not always possible to gain instant agreement, so realize that stalemates are bound to occur. Instead of becoming more stubborn or argumentative, just call a truce and drop the subject for a specified period of time (a few hours or until your next "appointment" together the following day). In the meantime, rate how strongly you

each feel about the issue on a scale from 1 to 10 (with 10 indicating the strongest feelings) and identify the factors that are most salient for each of you. Then write out ways in which each of you could change the situation or compromise. Writing down your feelings and beliefs gives you a chance to pause and think about their sources and consider whether your current stance is appropriate to the situation.

Some interesting research on anger by Carol Tavris, a social psychologist at the New School for Social Research in New York, suggests that it may be better to suppress anger than release it. Though this idea is contrary to the pop psychology of recent decades, Tavris found that releasing and rehashing hostility can just exacerbate negative feelings. That's why it's rarely constructive to simply "get it off your chest" when you're most volatile or distressed.

7. *Work toward a common goal.* When you and your partner are in separate corners, it's easy to forget that your main goals (I presume) are to resolve conflict and improve your relationship. Therefore it's wise to *look for* ways to compromise and cooperate. Too often, couples become adversaries because they forsake the health of the relationship for their personal preferences. A good marriage, according to the consensus of the thirty long-married women I interviewed, contains large amounts of tolerance. If every little habit or difference of opinion between you and your partner is irksome, pretty soon you're going to be fed up with the sum of these annoyances.

The guidelines above may appear too simple, as if you should be following them almost automatically. But most people have individual communication styles that are less then ideal. One's personal style often arises out of past experiences. If you were raised in a house where bickering was the norm, you may be assuming that *all* families bicker, and it may never have occurred to you to act any differently. If, in order to cope with your past family situation or current relationship, you've taken on a role (e.g., "provocateur," "failure," "problem," "success,") this orientation may have become a pattern you follow automatically. Adhering to the guidelines that I have outlined can take a bit of practice; you might even want to write them out and keep them handy during discussions. You'll have a chance to look further at your personal communication style in a subsequent chapter.

/ 2
Why Get Married?

BEFORE WE PROCEED FURTHER, take a few moments to respond intuitively to the items listed below. Without censoring any thoughts, check the reasons *you* might get married (or, if appropriate, why you got married before):

_____ Because I love him/her
_____ Because my beliefs are such that I'd just feel better married (at least at this point) than living together
_____ Because we've gotten so close that marriage just seems the next logical progression for us
_____ Because I'm feeling pressure from relatives or friends to get married
_____ Because we should either get married or break up entirely
_____ Because I have sexual needs to be fulfilled
_____ Because I want the security of marriage
_____ For financial reasons
_____ Because it would be more convenient to get married
_____ Because I think it would end my loneliness
_____ Because I want intellectual stimulation on a regular basis
_____ Because we're considering having a child
_____ Because we could use the wedding gifts
_____ Because my partner and/or I like to be the center of attention
_____ Because it would be good for career purposes
_____ Because my partner wants to get married
_____ (Write in anything else that comes to mind)_____

Marriage Is Different from Living Together

If you can have the same committed relationship without interference from the state, then why was the institution of marriage set up and, why was it tagged with the descriptor "honorable"? The answer has to be that somehow, marriage is different from living with someone you love. Recently I spoke to a man named Boris, who had been married twice before and had a total of four children from his previous marriages. He had become involved with a woman named Katy and, hesitant to get into another messy situation, had decided that he preferred to live with her. They were happy with the situation, grew closer, and purchased a home three years ago. They had one major area of difference—whether or not to have a child—which was finally resolved, and they got married.

I spoke with Boris just five days after his ceremony on Christmas Eve.

"Marriage has made a huge difference in the way Katy and I relate," he enthused. "I never thought it would be the case—in fact, it was because I knew that marriage could never make a difference between us that I didn't care to take the plunge."

Boris, a handsome man of 49, was a television executive who in his work regularly had to make hard decisions and take risks. But after two unpleasant divorces, he wanted to avoid further emotional upsets. He took the risk with Katy, however, and said, "After we were married we knew there was substance there, a total life commitment. Before, subconsciously, I'd reserved a part of myself; I couldn't totally let my hair down. Now I feel more responsible for Katy. I know she'll always be part of my life, and so I'm willing to really let out all of my feelings, and they've just poured out, stronger and stronger. It's just great!"

Boris's reaction is the one I hear more commonly from people who decide to marry after taking my "First Comes Love" workshops—the difference between marrying and living together isn't as much legal as psychological. Ironically, many people find that becoming tied to one person makes them feel more liberated than ever. Many living-together couples claim that their commitment couldn't be more real or deep than it is. And Boris would have agreed, prior to the little gathering in his living room on Christmas Eve. But now he says his reservations were *subconscious* and that it was only by marrying Katy that he knew they had existed.

On the other hand, many couples sadly report that marriage makes a difference in the opposite direction, harming their relationship. For example, Emily attended a "First Comes Love" workshop because she wanted to talk her partner out of making what she believed was a mistake. Speaking of a past relationship she said:

For me, marriage meant the end of a great relationship. Some people are naive enough to think that if they're happy before marriage, they'll continue to be that way afterwards. Not so. I got married to a man I'd lived with for two years. We thought it was the next logical step for us.

But the minute we put on those gold bands, life went downhill. My "ex" had a lot of subconscious expectations of his wife, and I just wouldn't fulfill them. It was okay for his girlfriend not to do his laundry, but his wife had to do the "family" chores. He didn't mind my separate checking account before the wedding, but afterwards he thought our money should be combined because, he said, now it was "half his"! He started to hem me in, just because he considered me his property. The passion went out of our lovemaking because sex was my duty rather than my pleasure. I felt stifled and he felt frustrated because I was "wild" and "unwilling to settle down." After three years of battling, we finally called it quits.

Marriage spelled the downfall of the best relationship I'd had, and while I know some people make it, the risk is too high. Nowadays, there's no reason to commit your life forever, and I believe you're unrealistic to think you should.

Emily was resolute, and insisted that it was because she valued her new relationship that she wanted to avoid the pitfalls of marriage.

Boris, Katy, and Emily all noted very identifiable *internal* or psychological differences that being married brought. However, it is also possible for marriage to result in only minor differences in a relationship. Whether there is much change depends on the personalities of the people involved. I remember one young bride who had dated her husband for four years before they took their vows. When asked afterward how it "felt" to be married, she shrugged, "It doesn't 'feel' like anything. After all, my husband's only Michael." For her, marriage wasn't a looming, scary unknown, because she so intimately knew the man she chose.

Another internal change that occurs with marriage, mentioned by Boris, is an increased sense of responsibility for the other person. This sense causes many couples who formerly led financially separate lives, knowledgable to the last penny about which expenses were "his" and which were "hers," to suddenly open up joint checking accounts. Whether or not you accept society's expectation that a married couple will support each other economically, marriage can bring with it a *desire* to see to the other person's needs. Even when couples keep bank accounts separate, each partner will usually have the compassion to help the other through tough times. A partner who treasures independence may, however, view the other person's desire to help as smothering.

Because marriage is a public proclamation, there are also some *external* differences in living together versus being married. One common difference is in how other people treat you. If you're cohabitating, then you're just, uh, "friends" when you're introduced. You are seen as disconnected from each other, not necessarily with any obligations. People are likely to regard you as dedicated solely to your personal ambitions, not to a special entity known as your relationship. When you have not made the "public promise" of marriage, people are often uncomfortable defining your relationship to each other. You may have moved a little furniture, but there's no legal record of your love, nothing to state that you intend to build a future together. So, how is Aunt Nellie supposed to react? Some couples are bothered by negative reactions from others; others simply dismiss such remarks by defining criticism as "Aunt Nellie's (or whomever's) problem."

There are also some external rules that society imposes on married but not cohabitating people. For example, laws state that you must financially support any children you have. You must, in states with community property laws, share ownership of your possessions with your spouse, unless you specifically exempt certain items. If you're living together, society (the government, people around you) have few expectations.

Living-together couples often take the attitude, "What do we care what 'society' thinks? Why can't we just announce that we're a stable couple to the people we care about?" That way you've make a proclamation to the public you care about, bringing little difference between marriage and cohabitation, aside from a piece of official-looking paper. There are two problems, though. First, as the highly publicized case of *Marvin* vs. *Marvin* illustrated, you may never be legally off the hook, piece of paper or no. There's also the problem that more traditionally minded friends and relatives won't believe that you intend a lifelong commitment. They see the open door, the chance for an easy exit. They envision you as never quite settled in; they're never entirely sure that you won't break up. They think, "If they mean it, why not make it official?"

Reasons for Getting Married

The decision to marry rather than simply live together is layered with many reasons. While some factors are emotional and difficult to verbalize, here are some motivations you might recognize in yourself.

1. *Legal benefits.* In cases where one partner is not working or makes a substantially smaller salary than the other, there are tax advantages to marriage. It was an urgent plea by their accountant that led Boris and Katy to tie the knot on Christmas Eve, just a week before the end of the year. Still, no amount of begging by their accountant could have nudged them to the *chupa*, if Boris and Katy hadn't already been emotionally committed and leaning toward marriage.

Another legal consideration (in some states) is community property. Some people feel that the equal ownership of all property acquired during a marriage is a disadvantage; others see the law as helping couples let go of possessiveness and share completely. This way, an item purchased is not "yours, mine, or ours" but simply "ours." Of course, community property laws can bring miseries when things have to be divided up at the time of a divorce, especially if the partners made unequal contributions toward their purchases.

There are also other situations in which having a legal bond can help. You can usually get in to see a spouse laid up in the hospital, but not necessarily to see your "significant other." As a lawfully married person, you can have your spouse covered by your health insurance. And you can receive an inheritance from your mate without question about your right to do so.

2. *Children.* Though it now sounds dated to lable any human child "illegitimate," the idea persists that having a child out of wedlock is immoral. Even people who appear completely "liberated" may feel that living together couples should not have a child—not because they distain unmarried mothers, but because they see the way society penalizes both mother and child in this situation.

Having married parents probably wouldn't mean much to a child who is being raised in a milieu where others have the same attitude as his or her parents. But there can be problems if, as is usually the case, the child is surrounded by other people who have differing beliefs. Some observers will accept unusual lifestyles;

others will not. It is to spare their child from needless taunting and embarrassment, and to provide reassurance that Mommy and Daddy intend to stay together, that both "liberated" and traditional thinkers usually seek legal recognition of their relationship. Incidentally, I was unable to find a law in any state that says the name of a child must have anything to do with the marital status or names of the parents.

In my "Children: To Have or Have Not?" workshops, I see many couples who would never consider getting married unless they wanted to have a child. Max and Sharon, both 33 and previously divorced, didn't want to complicate their lives any more than they had to. Max called a marriage license "that piece of paper," and Sharon kept repeating how she "never wants to get into *that* again!" They participated in the workshop because of their reluctance to marry despite a strong desire for a child.

One workshop member, frustrated by listening to Max and Sharon's merry-go-round arguing, said, "Then why not just have a child *without* getting married?" Max and Sharon looked at each other in near terror.

"And have a *bastard*?" asked a horrified Max. "That was the curse word my father used to shout at the worst scoundrels. I could never saddle my own child with such a degrading title!"

Eleanor, another workshop participant, was sympathetic. "It seems you're overreacting a bit," she told Max, "but I understand your concern. I would never be friends with people who might treat my child unfairly, but on the other hand, there's no way to control the cruel world. Even an occasional insult can damage a child's self-esteem for life. Why take that chance just because I'm selfish about my freedom or have hang-ups left over from a dead marriage? If I'm so stuck on my independence, then I shouldn't be having a child in the first place."

3. *Sexual benefits.* Probably one of the most attractive things about marriage fifteen to thirty years ago was the ability to roll over in bed and have sex. No putting your ego on the line trying to search out a partner in a bar, no worrying about "social diseases," no fumbling with the prophalactics in the back seat of a Chevy.

Perhaps the concept of sex on demand is an adolescent fantasy; a married partner may be no more willing than an unmarried one. But there *are* strong advantages to having someone you love available to meet your sexual needs on a regular basis. As love and communication grow, so can the meaning of sexual acts. In an atmosphere of familiarity, there is less risk that ignorance or insecurities will bring rejection, and often the desires of partners can be indulged with less risk of judgmental comments. Of course, it's quite possible to have an ongoing sexual relationship with someone outside of marriage that is equally good.

As part of my preparation for this book, I interviewed approximately thirty couples who had been married more than twenty-five years. Peggy, a 50-year-old public relations specialist, confided that—contrary to the myth that familiarity breeds boredom—sex with her husband had improved with time. She credited being married for this change:

> If we were only living together, I probably wouldn't have felt the tie, the cement, to Norm that let me bare my soul as well as my body.
>
> Of course, when we were married twenty-seven years ago, talking about sex was taboo. In the beginning, when we were dating, I didn't dare tell him that this movement was uncomfortable or that I preferred he put his hand "there." My focus was on pleasing him. As times changed and there was more fuss made about women's pleasure, I realized that there were more possibilities than I had tried. It was because of my underlying assurance that Norm wouldn't walk out, wouldn't criticize me, that I got up the nerve to show him an article [about sex] in a women's magazine. If we were just living together, I would've had the fear that he would rather just walk out the door than try to accommodate my needs."

Of course, the flip side to Peggy's experience is that sex in marriage can become stale with time unless spouses take deliberate steps to counteract this trend. Women's magazines, like the one Peggy showed Norm, *are* filled with articles on keeping the spark in marital sex; and the reason is that there is great demand for such guidance. For some people, making the effort to rekindle their feelings is more difficult than finding passion elsewhere.

4. *Convenience*. Despite major shifts in opinion about the propriety of living together, most people in this country still desire legal marriage. Even those who greatly dislike state interference in personal matters often anticipate more hassles fighting "the system" than riding with it. It takes a lot more breath to explain to relatives and acquaintances who this other person is, or why you haven't conformed to the rules by hitching up. It's more expensive to hire a lawyer to draw up contracts showing your connection than it is to simply announce it with a marriage license. And, it's a

lot easier to write thank-you notes for mounds of useful wedding gifts than it is to collect pots and pans, silver and crystal, on your own.

Not only is it more convenient to have your relationship out in the open, under conventional terms, but being married helps you to keep reassuring *yourself* that your partner is here to stay.

5. *Social benefits.* Avoidance of hassles is not the only reward you get from entering the mainstream and getting married. Even in our increasingly tolerant society, your marriage will probably bring relief to your relatives. When you get married, you assure them (a) that you'll no longer be "living in sin" if you had been; (b) that you're not gay, although this is not always true; and (c) that you won't go to your grave a spinster (or, more permissable but almost as pitied, a "confirmed bachelor").

You also inspire hope in the bosoms of your relatives and, perhaps, peers. The hope is that you'll have a harmonious marriage and be an example of happiness and tranquility. Some parents have visions of the glory that your exemplary behavior will shower on them. In a television commercial for extra-large photo prints, two older mothers are comparing snapshots. "Such a big son you have!" exclaims the mother with the regular-sized prints enviously. "Such a big house he has! Such a big baby he has!" (I always wait for her to squeal about the son's big wife, but she never goes that far.) The size of the photos is a symbol by which the women earn prestige for having raised successful children. If you, as the child, don't provide evidence of the good job your parents did when raising you (by conforming to the norm and getting married), *they* won't get the admiration of their friends. No big snapshots, no envious neighbors, no fodder for your parents' proud stories. Your folks give you strokes, your folks' listeners give you strokes. Everybody's happy.

Friends, in turn, may reward you for being a model of what they want to achieve: a happy marriage. By appearing content, you restore their faith in true love and marital bliss. Of course, you will lose this benefit—the pride in being a role model—if your marriage starts to crumble.

Another effect of marriage is that you automatically become accepted into the "couples club" when you say "I do." Acquaintances now sure of your status may send more social invitations addressed to the two of you than in the past. Friends may also mentally leap ahead to your next initiation—into the "parent club."

This phenomenon is mentioned as a benefit of marriage because many people enjoy this type of acceptance. Whether *you* consider it to be a benefit or drawback is, naturally, a personal matter.

Another benefit (if you regard it as one) is that when you're officially husband and wife, you're accepted by one and all as "normal." Even in our enlightened times, many people are uncomfortable about a person being single or divorced. They may feel you have a shortcoming that has prevented you from achieving the ideal of a happy married life. It's often a real social benefit to "fit in" with the majority of people (the ones who define what "normal" is). But if you surround yourself with friends who hold values like your own, general social acceptability may be of little consequence to you.

Another, and related, social benefit is that being married helps avoid negative social reactions from judgmental colleagues and relatives. In not-so-olden days, it was obligatory for up-and-coming executives to fit the clean-cut image, complete with wife who was mainly interested in creating the perfect meat loaf. Television situation comedies sometimes portrayed the elaborate schemes that men hatched to substantiate white lies they told ("of course I'm married, sir!") when they were hired. For them, saying that they were married avoided a negative reaction from a potential boss.

Advice columnists have devoted many paragraphs to the dilemma of how to introduce an unmarried partner without causing negative reactions. While "This is Susan" may be fine among good friends, it won't do in formal situations or with strangers. To call Susan "my cohabitator" would sound odd and would flaunt accepted morals, and bring distain or worse. Identifying Susan as "my wife" heads off such disapproval.

6. *Psychological benefits.* What other people do or say is certainly important, but of more consequence are your own feelings. What are the psychological benefits of marriage? Marian, married for twenty-six years, summarized it this way:

Marriage gives me the knowledge, the promise, that we will work out our problems rather than leave when times are tough. Our commitment means that through the classic "for better or worse," we're going to make an effort for the good of our relationship. It is a pledge that we won't be so selfish as to put ourselves above the other. Marriage is bedrock. Without it, we'd be just two people in love, with the option of becoming "just two people" with the turn of a door handle.

For Marian, the primary psychological benefit is *emotional* security. Other people gain peace of mind from *sexual* security—their partner has vowed to forsake all others and, in sexual terms, to be exclusively theirs. The important benefit here is that sex can become a personal expression of a special feeling reserved for only one person in the world. In a sense, your own pledge of fidelity is a gift you give. The gift you receive is the knowledge that your partner finds you just as worthy of exclusive sexual attention and expression.

Marriage can also boost self-esteem, as it is a constant reminder of your desirability. Being married proves that (at least once) another person chose you, from all others, to be his or her special lifetime mate.

Estelle, another of the long-married women I interviewed, said the main psychological benefit of her marriage is the availability of a companion who cares and with whom she has a shared history. She said:

I know that if I have a bad day teaching, if the principal yells at me or some first-grader throws up on another child, I can come home and Nick will patiently hear all about it. He's there; he's constant.

Because we view marriage as a permanent commitment, we never considered playing around or breaking up. Instead, the idea has always been to make the most of it, and that means getting unwavering emotional support from the other person. If I want to go to a movie, Nick will usually go with me. If he wants to see a basketball game, I'll be boosting our team beside him. We've developed complementary interests in most things, and we're tolerant of the interests that aren't shared. I think the best part of being married is this common orientation and experience—this coziness that for me is the definition of intimacy.

The phrase "lived happily ever after" suggests a gradually deepening closeness much like the one Estelle described. While people who live together without marriage can certainly have a deeply loving relationship, they may subconsciously have the same sorts of reservations that Boris (who was quoted earlier in this chapter) talked about. Boris said that until he was legally married to Katy, he had only *thought* he was giving himself totally. After the nuptials, he began to evision spending his entire life with Katy. He discovered then that he had more emotions to give.

You have just read about seven major benefits of marriage; of course, there are drawbacks too. Many of the drawbacks are simply the benefits turned inside out: social "rewards" to some can be social interference; legal consequences can be either positive or negative; "convenience" is in the mind of the beholder.

Drawbacks of Marriage

1. *Government interference.* Many people resent government regulation of their personal affairs. Most don't mind minor requirements like obtaining a marriage license, but people who wish to marry may be angered by laws that discriminate according to marital status. The "marriage tax," a disadvantage applying mainly to working couples, may cost a couple several thousand dollars annually (though Congress is moving to remove this inequity). Those on welfare can be denied benefits if they are married and the spouse has income (even if that spouse is absent from the home). The government makes certain assumptions about people just because they are married, and these may be inaccurate.

2. *Others' expectations.* Just as others have expectations of single people (i.e., that they should want to get married), they may hold expectations about married people. This becomes a problem if you break out of the stereotype and disappoint them. A major faux pas is not having children. Another no-no is an unconventional arrangement, such as an achieving wife with a househusband.

The fact that your lifestyle doesn't jibe with others' expectations is a drawback only if you're far out of line with the norm, or if you care a great deal about what others think. The point is that simply by getting married, you set yourself up for other people's expectation that you will continue with a typical life progression.

3. *Psychological drawbacks.* These are probably the most severe problems that can arise. If left to smolder and flame, they often lead to an eventual breakup.

One negative psychological response to marriage is *feeling trapped*. The same feeling of strong commitment that gave Estelle security can bring others claustrophobia. Eric, a "First Comes Love" workshop participant, put it this way: "I treasure my freedom, and I also see my life as an amorphous, growing organism. I expect to change, and I expect Pat to change too. By getting married, I'm supposed to love her even if she becomes a different person, even someone who is incompatible with me. It's like being chained to someone, and unlocking the chain means lots of unhappiness. I want to avoid feeling stuck together until we die."

Another drawback of many marriages is *lack of excitement*. In subsequent chapters, several partners who have kept the thrill in their relationships will discuss how they do it, and prove by example that time need not remove passion. However, you are probably more familiar with couples who have settled into a secure but lifeless sameness. (Sometimes one partner yearns for sparkle and flash, while the other displays no enthusiasm.) For such couples, the days slide on monotonously while the partners turn their energies toward the fulfillment of outside interests.

Many of my workshop participants said they had seen this phenomenon occur with their parents, and feared that they too could slip into a rut. There may be basic love and trust still strong in a relationship, but the daily luster of newness has long faded. Said Sally, a 41-year-old computer programmer, "My father calls my mother 'Mommy,' and she calls him nothing at all. They sit in the same room on the same sofa and don't see each other there. I feel so sad about this, even though individually they're warm and interesting people. It's as though they remain together out of habit rather than because they truly want to."

Another psychological drawback in some marriages is *deprivation*. This is the classic case of "What am I missing?" or "The grass is always greener on the other side of the fence." Many people fear that, when married, they'll miss the freedom and variety of relationships they experienced while single. While they may feel emotionally committed to their partner at the moment, they view marriage as almost a life sentence. What if they get that infamous "seven-year itch"? What if they crave attention from the opposite sex, despite a continued love of their mate?

Rowene, a 40-year-old friend of mine, had spent ten years with her partner before they finally got married. Jim had his problems, but Rowene was tolerant of most of them and gently encouraging about improving the rest. Jim was overdependent, was not physically expressive of his feelings toward Rowene, and was unwilling to let Rowene come near his possessions, (such as his stereo and typewriter). He would say he'd change and make a temporary effort, but then would soon lapse back into his old ways.

Shortly after Rowene got a visible position at a high-prestige company, a co-worker began flirting with her. At first she didn't even notice these attentions, but as time went on and her frustration with Jim's lack of progress grew, she did notice—and began reciprocating—what she considered to be harmless diversions.

The rest of the story is predictable: Rowene eventually became attracted to the co-worker, and the two became emotionally involved. Rowene felt it would be immoral to have sexual relations with another man while married ("I just couldn't cheat on Jim") but still found things in the romance that were not present in her marriage. She confronted Jim again about behaviors of his that were frustrating her and pleaded with him to work on changing himself through psychotherapy. When he refused, Rowene left him.

Once on her own, Rowene was flushed with the thrill of new excitement and sexual possibilities. Though her affair with the co-worker fizzled after a few weeks, she began to look at the world through new eyes, viewing every man as a potential lover. She reveled in several flirtations, and felt liberated. Soon she wondered if she could ever return to the confinements of marriage, even if Jim took her advice and sought therapy. I can't tell you the end of this story because it is still in process. But when married people hear it to this point, they often wonder aloud about whether, if suddenly released from marriage, they too might long for fresh blood.

A sense of being trapped, lack of excitement, and deprivation are related problems and can certainly occur in any marriage. But it's important to distinguish whether these occur because of the fact of being married or because of inertia on the part of the people involved. These types of situations can occur in *any* long-term relationship, with or without legal bonds. So consider whether these drawbacks might be the result of you and your partner's own behavior rather than arising from the constraints of being married.

Reasons Why People Choose Marriage Over Living Together

So why get married? Why not just live together? Below are the reasons that couples most often cite for their choice of marriage over cohabitation.

1. Living together provides no sense of permanence, no future. Marcy, a newspaper writer, married Sam after only a two-month courtship. Here is her thinking about the decision:

We'd both been married before. We knew what it was like to adjust to someone new; we knew the blush of infatuation; we knew what serious commitment was. So why futz around? What's the purpose of dating, anyway? To me, it'ts to find that one lifetime relationship, the port in the storm, not to have some transitory kicks.

I don't want to waste my time with men not up to my standards; I don't want the guys who want to use me for their gratification now and eventually move on to fresher meat. I knew right away that Sam was right for me, so what's the point in spending six months, a year, or whatever on the way to something we can begin right now?

Marcy's viewpoint is one shared by a growing number of self-confident women and men. These are mainly people who have enough life experience behind them to recognize a combination with potential, and to discard the rest immediately. They don't need to cling to anyone who provides flattery and admiration to boost their egoes. They'd rather be alone than in a languid relationship.

2. Living together makes it too easy to break up instead of confronting problems. Estelle, the older woman mentioned earlier, favors working through problems rather than ignoring them. She believes that a good relationship is worth rescuing, even if the effort involves a significant amount of pain and difficult changes in attitudes and behavior.

Not everyone agrees with Estelle, however. In fact, a strong unwillingness to admit fault or to bear uncomfortable emotions is the underlying reason for some people's decision to live together. Their attitude might be: When there's a conflict, separate. And, of course, the availability of a swift and easy exit is a perfect threat: "If you don't do it my way, I know the way out."

There's a sort of catch-22 here. If you're afraid that marriage might bring a trapped feeling, boredom, or deprivation, you might opt to simply shack up. But this might make it *too* easy to skip out before giving the relationship a chance.

3. Living together without marriage brings too much social pressure. As discussed earlier, you not only are subject to negative reactions from friends and family because you're living together ("fornicating"), but you also must deal with the urgings of others to "make it official."

4. Living together can bring fear of abandonment. Terror at the thought of abandonment is a very common feeling in children, and it lingers in the minds of many adults. With the living together exit sign ablaze, there's little to keep your partner with you except continued rewards—and constant efforts to make him or her happy can be a heavy load to bear. Also, since your partner

has not vowed to stay with you, you have to be on your toes to make sure that no outside lures take him or her away. Fear of abandonment may not be a conscious emotion, but it often lurks subconsciously to some degree.

There's also the fear of *sexual* abandonment. Even if you've agreed to be faithful to each other, without a written seal on that contract, there's generally more doubt than there is in a marriage. I won't forget the panicked look on workshop participant Edward's face when he confessed his worst vision: "I see Jackie coming home from work, thrusting open the front door of our apartment with a devilish grin, and announcing, 'I'm too sensual to love just one man. I think we need some sexual freedom to liven up our relationship.' I want a woman who is faithful to me; I'd go insanely jealous if Jackie started fooling around."

Jealously is, after all, a manifestation of fear of abandonment. When you're jealous, you worry that someone else will steal your lover away from you, leaving you alone and in pain. Needless to say, married people also face the possibility of abandonment, but many people whom I interviewed told me that they were remaining faithful simply *because* they made the marital pledge.

5. Some people have mixed emotions internally about the morality of living together. Even the most open-minded and liberal person can experience discontinuity between intellectual beliefs and gut feelings. Ronald, a 33-year-old veteran of the 1960s protest marches, found this schism distressing:

Here I am, bucking authority. I burned my draft card and I still contribute all my money to progressive causes. I refuse to drive a Mercedes, though I could well afford one; I live in a shack and plant my own vegetables rather than succumbing to materialistic city mores. That's why it troubles me to admit that I want to get married. Here I want to sink back into the traditions I've been rattling cages about. Marriage is a cop-out, totally incongruous with resisting the pressures of society.

Another workshop member—Donna, age 19 and engaged—was angered by Ronald's self-deprecation. She countered: "Why do you think that because you put down *some* of society's customs and traditions that you have to toss out *all* of them? Why do you think that it's all or nothing—that either you reject society or accept it? Obviously you've done well financially with your own company. . . ."

Donna had found Ronald's sore spot. He defended his company at some length, presenting it as an example of equality and fairness.

"You think you're outside the 'system'; that it's 'us versus them,' but you just can't see that you're part of 'them,' too!" Donna answered. "Why can't you accept that it's okay to take the best elements of the Old Guard and shape them into a new, workable alternative? When you and Pam get married, would you expect her to stay at home and forsake her career, barefoot and pregnant?"

Ronald was amused at the vision of a pregnant Pam surrounded by stacks of ironing. "Of course not," he replied.

Donna went on:

So, by getting married, you wouldn't be "copping out," you'd be redefining what marriage is. You'd be making it work for your benefit rather than conforming to old standards just for their sake. And besides, I can't believe that you're for restricting people's freedom. You should allow yourself the freedom of choice to decide what you'd like in a whole range of options. You should be tolerant of *every* point of view as long as it's chosen freely, and that includes people enjoying a conventional relationship as well as those who think marriage is bunk.

After a few minutes of silence, Ronald broke into a smile. He concluded that it was all right to feel conflicts, and that there was nothing hypocritical about his having an "old-fashioned" desire to marry Pam while continuing to lead his life in an iconoclastic way.

Ronald felt intellectually that he should oppose marriage, but emotionally he preferred it. To the question "Why not just live together?" he might have answered, "because I really don't want to." Your own gut feelings, whether they were influenced by your early socialization or by the last conversation you had in a tavern, are the most important factor in the decision of whether or not to get married. (This point will be discussed further later in the book.)

So, then, why do people choose to live together? What has lured thousands of people, young ones in a first relationship and old ones in their last, to eschew convention?

Reasons Why People Live Together Rather Than Marry

1. *Current entanglements.* Throughout this discussion it is assumed that both partners *want* to be together, that they share an attraction to each other and a sense of connection. Many people,

however, for legal or financial reasons simply *can't* get married. A slew of them are caught in a time warp between separation and final divorce decree. Other circumstances exist where it is illegal or immoral to get married, so living together is the next best option.

2. *Financial reasons.* A 1983 episode of the television situation comedy *Love Boat* showed an elderly couple who had lived together for three years battling to gain the approval of their grown children. It finally came out that Papa had tried repeatedly to win Mama's hand, but she staunchly refused on the grounds that she would lose her late husband's alimony payment if she remarried. Suddenly the formerly hostile children understood their parents' plight—they weren't defying morals but were simply trying to cope in a situation where both had low incomes.

The logic behind all the laws that end financial benefits at remarriage (or at marriage in the case of many inheritances) appears to be an assumption that a new spouse will assuredly have the wherewithal and inclination to support his or her partner. Many people circumvent the problem by cohabiting.

Some people live together to *avoid* financial entanglements with a partner. They may want to keep their property separate so that, if the relationship is dissolved, it cannot be confiscated by the other party. The fly in that ointment buzzed out of the *Marvin* v. *Marvin* decision, the well-publicized "palimony" case. Michelle Triolo Marvin claimed that Lee Marvin had welched on an oral contract, and she sued for half of all he had acquired during the six years they lived together. The California Supreme Court recognized Michelle Marvin's right to form a contract and made her an award. (For a comprehensive description of the case and its implications, I recommend *The Living Together Kit* by Toni Ihara and Ralph Warner.) So avoidance of marriage may not be a *sure* way to protect your income and possessions if your partner lays claim to them.

3. *Intentional avoidance of any commitment.* A new phenomenon that is receiving increasing attention lately is "commitmentphobia."* As the name implies, it's a fear of commitment. Why does this onerous-sounding emotion develop? Usually, an individual with commitmentphobia has had a negative experience with

---

*This is the name given to the phenomenon in a discussion in the May 1981 issue of *Savvy* magazine.

marriage or fears that the presently satisfying relationship will change if legally tied. People who are afraid of commitment frequently choose cohabitation as a means of having their cake and eating it too. They want the goodies of being married without the long-term commitment; perhaps they value having an open door, feeling they can always slip out the back, if necessary. Being afraid of commitment is actually an excellent reason not to marry: there is no sense in getting married if by doing so you bring on emotional distress.

A related attitude is the *carpe diem* philosophy, the preference to "live for today" rather than for the future. Bradley, 53, expressed this side of himself at one of the workshop meetings. Ironically, he is a lawyer who had to postpone gratification for three years while completing graduate school, and is now similarly exercising self-discipline whenever he becomes intensely involved in a case. He said:

I finally realized that life is not some long entity that you should "plan for." Life is a sequence of moments, and each day is the stuff of it. Marriage implies permanence, it suggests that we don't change. If somehow your "dearly beloved" becomes a witch, you're supposed to look back at your history, and forward to your future, and grit your teeth through what is not going right between you. I think that by living together you leave your options open so that you can act according to reality, moment to moment.

Some people avoid marriage because they don't feel ready to join or "become one" with someone else. They worry that if they marry, they'll be swallowed up by their partner's identity or will become lost in the conformist quagmire of "marriage." By remaining unmarried, these people feel independent.

Other people choose not to marry because of past negative experiences with a marriage. Barry explained his feelings: "I was married before, and getting a divorce was the worst time of my life. My ex-wife and I are now bitter enemies, and I never want to be connected by law to someone I hate."

His workshop partner, Helen, frowned as he spoke. At age 25, six years Barry's junior, she was filled with optimism and was pushing Barry to get married. "The trouble is, Barry," she objected, "that you assume our relationship is just like the one you had with your ex-wife. I'm practially her opposite! *I* would never do the insulting things she did. *I* insist on working, not sponging off you. I think it's totally unfair that because you had a bad experience once with an incompatible person, you think history would repeat itself with me!"

Perhaps Helen was right, but until Barry was able to deal with his reservations, he was not good marriage material. While living with Helen, he could work on changing his attitude and be supportive of her. In this case, by *not* getting married immediately, Barry and Helen gained time to sort out their values and perhaps avoid a costly blunder.

4. *Living together as a trial balloon for marriage.* Before the "sexual revolution" of the 1960s and 1970s, parents would disown their children if they "lived in sin." Today, some parents, upon learning of their child's engagement, ask, "Why don't you just live together for a while first?" Aware of the number of divorces among their friends, and perhaps themselves divorced, they want their children spared from the heartbreak of a failed marriage. Many previously conservative people still have conflicting feelings about the morality of living together but are coming to value "testing the waters" as a way of avoiding a regrettable mistake.

There are two main situations in which couples choose to live together as a test. In the first, there is an intention to get married, usually within a year if all goes smoothly. Living together is then reassurance that the partners' choice is correct. Unless some catastrophic blowup or series of annoyances queer the deal, this original agreement of "engagement" is executed and the couple marries.

In the second situation, couples move in together without any intention to marry. Each partner may feel a conflict over whether he or she *ever* wants to get married. Such couples, while they do view their cohabitation as a test, are mainly investigating whether or not they should pursue their relationship at all. Often these couples are together because of convenience as well as love.

So these are the major reasons that affect the decision of whether to get married or live together. To put all this together for yourself, check on the next page the reasons for and against marriage (both in your own case and in general) with which you agree.

Obviously, there's a lot more to making a lifetime commitment than just listing generalized pros and cons. Marriage affects every facet of your life; it isn't just a single compartment you can deal with rationally and then leave alone. In fact, one of my basic

Why Get Married?

Reasons to Get Married	In My Case	In General
Legal or financial benefits	_____	_____
Convenience	_____	_____
Sexual benefits	_____	_____
Social acceptance	_____	_____
Commitment of partner for life	_____	_____
Emotional support and companionship	_____	_____
"Love" (define): _____	_____	_____
_____	_____	_____
Children	_____	_____
Other: _____	_____	_____

Reasons Not to Get Married

	In My Case	In General
Legal or financial drawbacks	_____	_____
Feeling of being trapped	_____	_____
Deprivation: not enough new experiences	_____	_____
State interference	_____	_____
Boredom or monotony	_____	_____
Want to, but have other entanglements	_____	_____
Other: _____	_____	_____

Reasons to Live Together

	In My Case	In General
Convenience	_____	_____
"Love" (define): _____	_____	_____
_____	_____	_____

Marriage not possible because of:

	In My Case	In General
Current entanglements	_____	_____
High value placed on independence	_____	_____
Legal/financial reasons	_____	_____
To avoid making a mistake	_____	_____
To avoid a permanent commitment	_____	_____
As practice to judge compatibility	_____	_____
Other: _____	_____	_____

Reasons Not to Live Together

	In My Case	In General
No future in it	_____	_____
Not sure of feelings	_____	_____
Too easy to leave (if problems arise)	_____	_____
Social pressure against it	_____	_____
Fear of abandonment	_____	_____
Doesn't seem "right"	_____	_____
Legal/financial considerations	_____	_____
Other: _____	_____	_____

premises is that the decision to marry (or to live together or to break up) is essentially an *emotional* one. Still, you need to balance emotions and logic. How much weight you give the rational side of the choice depends on your own personal style—the patterns you have established in your past behavior.

The short lists that were just presented are far from exhaustive. In later chapters, you'll have an opportunity to explore other issues.

SECTION Two
New Trends in Relationships

/ 3
When to Marry?

NOT VERY LONG AGO, a woman unmarried at age 22 was considered an old maid. Her cronies often had two or more children by then, and it was by this badge of achievement that women were judged. Before the Industrial Revolution, it made sense for girls to marry early: their reproductive lives were relatively short, and more hands for the harvest were always needed.

With the twentieth century came improved medical treatment, which reduced infant and maternal mortality rates. Families gravitated toward the cities, where assembly-line jobs and other opportunities beckoned. Suddenly it was not so crucial to have a large brood. There was less of a need to marry young just to produce field hands; wealth came to be measured more by material goods than by offspring.

Of course, old beliefs and customs endure. And even when having a large family became detrimental to financial success, the social rewards for having such a family continued. Marriage was still idealized, but the compelling factor became an aura of romantic passion rather than simply expediency or procreation. Of course, love and chemistry always had their appeal. But commonly, love was regarded as a secondary benefit of marriage, coming after providing for each other's needs. "Do you love me?" Golda asks a startled Tevye in the play *Fiddler on the Roof*. Tevye, reluctant to consider that he might actually love the partner of his arranged marriage, finally concludes that yes, after so many years together, what he probably feels is love.

While American marriages weren't so likely to be arranged, strict social customs still guided the choice of a mate. After spoken and implied taboos were taken into account, the list of candidates considered appropriate for marriage was narrow. Parents were concerned about the continuation of their stock and their values, a fact that was often lamented in songs about love being ill-fated because of parental opposition. Some parental condemnations designed to direct an offspring's marital choice included, "He's from the wrong side of the tracks" (i.e., of a different social class), "He's not our kind" (i.e., of a different race), "She's not of the faith," and "She's no good" (i.e., she's not a virgin).

In the 1960s, with the civil rights movement and other protests of past values, came new morals. In terms of marriage, the most important influence was the feminist movement, which brought new respect for a majority rather than minority group.

It was against this vibrant backdrop of change that increasing numbers of people began postponing marriage. Historically, the median age at first marriage has hovered within a two-year range for both men and women. In 1920, men's median age at marriage was 24.6 years; women's was 21.2 years. The statistics for 1930 and 1940 are close to these figures for women, and identical for men. Marriage ages began to gradually decrease right after the end of World War II, and a major outcome of this time period is the "baby boom." Median first-marriage ages for men and women then held constant until the mid-1970s, after which time the figures steadily rose.*

Of course, these statistics reflect only medians for the country as a whole. Hidden within these encompassing numbers is a significant group, mainly women, who are postponing their first marriages many years beyond their early twenties. As these women have become more prevalent, greater social acceptance has followed.

Why Later Marriages Are Increasingly Accepted

Several factors seem to be responsible for the acceptance of later first marriage:

1. *Changes in women's roles.* With feminism came new opportunities, and while marriage and motherhood was still regarded as a desirable career, other options were increasingly encouraged. The advent of "affirmative action" brought the optimistic idea that women could earn prestige and wages far beyond traditional

*U.S. Department of Commerce, Bureau of the Census, *Statistical Abstract of the United States*, 1979.)

levels. And with the concurrent sexual revolution, unmarried women could now harbor the romantic ideal of finding "Mr. Right," and at the same time seek independence and personal development.

2. *Longer career preparation.* The value of having a high school diploma and a bachelor's degree has deflated. Now, the typical lament at college graduations is that a university sheepskin and fifty cents will get you a cup of coffee. People who are determined to rise above the herd and gain an employment advantage have increased their educational preparation. It's not unusual to find 30-year-old students in graduate school, still dreaming of their first full-time jobs. In my own graduate department, several students had hair whiter than that of their tenured professors.

They are stuck in an educational system geared for its own perpetuation rather than with the efficient imparting of useful professional skills. Still, it's the only system going. So, millions of marriage candidates postpone their nuptials until their educational ritual is completed. Stories of unsuccessful marriages begun before graduation scare away some wary would-be spouses. There's the classic case of the intelligent wife sacrificing her own training and career foothold to put hubby through medical school, only to be abandoned for a nurse by her philandering physician shortly thereafter. To avoid a similar fate, and allow themselves time for college and apprenticeship without excess responsibility, increasing numbers of men and women are choosing to remain single longer—even if it means that they eventually lose their chance of meeting Prince or Princess Charming.

3. *More time over a longer lifespan.* When life expectancy was only to age fifty or sixty, it made more sense to start young in the effort to accomplish life tasks. Now that medical science has allowed us a longer grace period, we no longer have to crunch so much into a short time. People are able to attend graduate school until they're thirty because at that point they have at least thirty more years of productivity—a figure that will rise as improved physical fitness, better nutrition, and further medical breakthroughs pay off. With these changes occurring, developmental tasks that traditionally were begun in childhood and continued through the teen years are now more likely to be tackled in the twenties or later. So marriage can now be postponed with confidence that there's plenty of time to enjoy it.

4. *New attitudes about children and the family.* We can again credit medical science and renewed attention to health for extend-

ing women's prime childbearing years. No longer is it imperative that a wife complete her family before her thirtieth birthday. With amniocentesis, new infant monitoring techniques, enhanced general health, and good nutrition, a woman can have strapping children right up until menopause. To be sure, the ticking of the biological clock is a distressing presence for many women, but at least the "what if" panic sets in at about age forty now, rather than by a woman's mid-twenties.

As a result of these advances, we've changed our beliefs about what constintutes a "proper" or "ideal" family. No longer do most people view a childless couple as deviant. It's no longer scandalous for an older woman to marry a younger man, or for a divorcée to marry a virgin. Other concepts that have been questioned in the past couple of decades are that a woman must be married in order to be fulfilled, and that a man "should" have a wife to iron his shirts, give him children, and wait breathlessly at the door with a welcoming martini.

Today, a single career woman is much more likely to be respected as an individual rather than regarded as simply half of a couple. Undeniably, old sexist attitudes remain, but now there is much more tolerance and room for variety. When it was found that just over a quarter of the nation's households contained the traditional nuclear family (a housewife and working father with their children), suddenly the remaining three-quarters felt the power of their numbers. So now it's considered all right to wait to marry. No longer is being single into your forties or fifties a disgrace or an implication of homosexuality.

With such choices, and with a dearth of partners (especially for women) who meet ever-soaring criteria, why then do postponers get married at all?

Why People Choose to Marry Later in Life

1. *A desire to procreate.* When single people approach their thirtieth, thirty-fifth, or fortieth birthday, they tend to assess the progress of their lives. "What's it all about?" Nigel despaired, his eyes heavenward. "There's that existential question." Nigel had worked for ten years in his father's insurance business, and at age 32 felt stifled. He said:

I really never realized how routine my life had become until a college classmate who'd moved out of state dropped by at Christmas time. His life seemed so alien to me, and yet I was jealous. He and his wife have four children. Four! Intellectually, choosing to have that much responsibility seems so stupid, but to see those kids and talk to them, it made me marvel at the potential of life. Each one had different likes and dislikes, and even at age four, one little guy was reading me Doctor Seuss! I've just let the years drift by, assuming that I'd accomplish my dreams later. I want a family, and so does Carolyn [his partner, whom he'd dated for seven years], and I finally realize that we've got to just *do something* to make it happen.

Of course, if you have no prospects for marriage, you have no recourse (except to have a child out of wedlock). If your relationship *is* going along well, barriers or reluctance to marry can be quickly overcome when you begin longing to have a child. And because women have a biologically restricted amount of time for childbearing, a sudden seriousness about finding a marriage partner can develop as the feared deadline nears.

2. *Psychological readiness to nest.* A friend of mine, an educational psychologist, is age 34 and has never been married. She theorizes that men as well as women hit a point when they "snap," and suddenly want marriage and family. She explains, "When that happens, often the man will leave the dating relationship he's had and then marry the next woman he finds." She's seen it happen repeatedly: the man gives up one woman, and within a month has married his assistant or boss (or whoever is most convenient). He then becomes a father, buys a house, and starts to "nest" in short order.

This was the case for Andy, age 33 and a college professor. After years of bachelorhood, he found Terry, was married in three months, and, true to my friend's theory, bought a house and now expects his first child. I asked him what had happened to precipitate such a dramatic change of lifestyle. He replied:

I guess that suddenly what had seemed so foreign and outside my realm just seemed right. If you had asked me just a year ago if all of this seemed likely, I would have been shocked. I was used to my independence, and other things were on my mind. I think that all people just come to a point when they realize that they're not young anymore. Not that I'm old; just that I figure that you have to get on with life, and not keep preparing for it.

Andy isn't the only man I know who reversed his life within a single year. Don, an independent film producer, did the same thing, and echoed Andy's comments. "It isn't that I couldn't have married before," Don noted. "I love my wife, but just finding someone to love is not all that difficult. The difference is that I suddenly became psychologically ready, and that readiness just dawned on me one day without warning or logic."

3. *A realization that relationships don't come any better.* Sometimes when you've believed the fairy tale of Prince Charming; when you've seen outwardly good marriages crumble unexplainedly; when you fear failure and keep a clamp on your emotions—it's difficult to admit that what you have is darn good. Sure, you know that every relationship has its ups and downs, but your ups are pretty consistent. You feel comfortable together and laugh a lot; you don't have the slightest urge to see how green the grass is out there. Yet something inside holds you back, as if you ought to wait for some divine signal to know that this is *it*.

Often these signals come with tragedy. Sharon realized it was time to marry Jack when her mother got cancer; Les decided to marry Bev when his brother's marriage broke up; Sandy and Marc tied the knot when their house was ransacked by robbers and her heirloom necklace was stolen. In each case, the jolt made the couple realize how fundamental marital ties are, how they can endure beyond the selfishness of everyday life and provide continuity over time. When Sharon, Les, and Sandy turned to their partners for support through a crisis, they realized that *what they had* was all they needed.

Sharing experiences and realizing how your personality interfaces with your partner's can suddenly click together so that marriage seems "right." Carol Tavris, the social psychologist mentioned earlier, explained why, at age 36, she got married for the first time: "We married to celebrate the culmination of years of difficulty that we endured to be together; and to make public our private delight that we, who are such an implausible pair on the face of it, have survived and thrived. . . ."*

4. *Finally finding the right partner.* The right partner is someone who meets your criteria, and in the "me decade," both men's and women's criteria escalated. Frequently there are close calls, such as broken engagements, that are later remembered with: "Thank heavens I didn't do it then." But often it just isn't that simple to find someone who matches your interests, temperament, and values. Selecting a mate can be the choice most determining

---

*Ms., March 1981.

of your future happiness and the direction your life will take. In my opinion, it's much better to be single than to rush into a relationship out of social expectation, dependency, or fear that you'll never find anyone else so devoted to you. Luckily, many people who remain single long into adulthood suddenly happen upon the "right" person to marry.

5. *An understanding of life's brevity.* I spoke in depth to Boris and Katy, introduced earlier. They had lived together several years before marrying, and had nearly split up over the issue of having a child. (Katy wanted the experience, but Boris, already the father of four, felt that that stage was behind him.) What reunited them was the realization of the preciousness of their love. Said Boris: "I got to thinking about how much time I have left. I'm no spring chicken [he was 49]. What's the likelihood that I'll be able to find what I have with Katy again? We have so much fun together; she gives me enthusiasm about life. I realized that I value that, and I don't want to start searching for someone to replace her. I just don't have time to waste in misery and loneliness."

How many people *want* to spend the rest of their lives searching? How many people would intentionally forgo marriage forever? When you're in your teens and twenties, it's easy to take your youth for granted. But once you have settled into a career, passed a landmark birthday, or experienced a significant loss or illness, you suddenly realize how quickly a day, week, and year go by. And you begin to feel that if you don't begin fulfilling your ambitions now, they'll never be fulfilled at all. Such is the stuff of "mid-life crises," whenever they occur.

To again quote Carol Tavris, "We married because ever since he had a heart attack three years ago, we have become aware of the great mischief-maker, time, and its bag of dirty tricks. That scare makes us grateful for each other and grateful for the time we have together, not fearing the 'ties that bind' but seizing them. . . ."*

6. *Self-reliance.* Those who marry late cite an important advantage: they know who they are (i.e., their likes, dislikes, limitations, and potentials) and have learned skills for survival. Self-reliance brings high self-esteem, and also prevents dependency on a partner. These older brides and gooms no longer fear losing themselves in another person. They already know they can get along by themselves, and so their spouse becomes a new dimen-

---

*Ms., March 1981.

sion to add onto a satisfying world. Some people overcome their hesitancy to marry only after they have established this high level of individual competence.

7. *The fact that marriage is coming back in style.* In recent years, trends in relationships have come in and out of fashion like hemlines. Signs are everywhere that marriage has come back into favor. *Ms.* magazine's March, 1981 cover story on late marriages touted the state of wedlock; *McCalls* magazine's April 1981 issue declared "The Big Wedding is Back"; churches are booked months in advance; and etiquette manuals are brisk movers. People who previously had not thought much about marrying are suddenly looking around them and seeing that in our dark economic doldrums, weddings symbolize a shinier future. The ceremony portends love, beginnings, birth, and trust in what's to come.

Why did the wedding of Lady Diana Spencer and Prince Charles become the highlight of recent British history? Because it drew attention away from severe unemployment, civil riots, trouble in the Falkland Islands, and the pound's demise. Similarly, as unemployment in the United States has crept upward and inflation, depression, and nuclear destruction crowd our concerns, more and more people are returning to safe, reassuring traditions as reminders that we *will* muddle through.

It's probably no coincidence that all this has come on the wing of a conservative political swing. "Baby boom" children born between 1947 and 1960, who represent a huge population bulge, are now reaching a mature, serious stage of life. In the 1960s they often were rebelling against their parents' social structures; now they're embracing many of them again.

8. *Achievement of a certain level of self-esteem.* Comedienne Joan Rivers has made lots of money and many guffaws by presenting shocking descriptions of events and people, and then commanding her aghast audience, "Oh, grow up!" The audience laughs because no one could be mature enough to accept her outrageous depictions of overly avant-garde mores.

One of the greatest myths is that at some point we definitively "grow up." The way I view it, life is a continual process of growing, changing, evolving, and struggling. It's often painful and tough, but for the most part it's pleasant and *interesting*. There are infinite directions in which to grow, but I think that everyone has one direction in common: the fundamental striving for greater self-esteem and self-confidence. At the root of almost all psychological problems is lack of self-esteem. Just about all negative behavior can be traced to feelings of insecurity about abilities or worth.

People with exceptionally low self-esteem usually relate to marriage in one of three ways. Some become "clingers," entering into marriage at an early age because they are dependent and want protection. Molly, 47, is a very accomplished middle-level manager in a large manufacturing corporation. She explained her situation this way:

> I went from the shelter of my father's house into my husband's. I served first my family, then my husband, and then my children. It was the traditional arrangement, and at the time, it felt comfortable. But as time went on and it dawned to me, through psychotherapy, that I was a competent person in my own right, I knew something had to change. Why couldn't I do the checkbook and pay the bills? Why couldn't I deal with the car repairman? What prevented me from expressing my opinion about our church's finances? I learned that what kept me from achievement was myself; believing that I wasn't smart enough to know about those things, or that it wasn't my place to interfere.

I asked Molly how this knowledge had affected her life. She laughed, tossing back her brunette mane, and replied:

> This was what I'd paid thousands of dollars to my therapist to find out, and it affected my life enormously. I finally realized that I didn't have to settle for things anyone else's way. Now, I didn't just go out and have an affair or divorce my husband like my girlfriend did. But I did confront him, and he really was hurt and angry. It was as if I was ungrateful to him for all the years he provided for me. It was as if he had suppressed fulfilling his own desires just so I wouldn't have to work, and our kids would get their orthodontia.

Here is Molly's description of the ultimate outcome:

> My husband ended up going into therapy himself. We *both* needed some self-confidence to do what we really wanted. He ended up chucking his position in the company to open a rare book store, cutting our income in half. Meanwhile, I went back to school, got my M.B.A. and am in the upward track toward a vice presidency in the company now. We've sort of reversed roles, and we're both the happier for it.

Molly's story is one of maturation. She "came to her senses" at age 43 and changed her life greatly. Her dependency and low self-esteem were replaced by self-reliance. Her marriage became a bonus to her life, not the reason for it.

When to Marry?

A second type of reaction to low self-esteem that occurs in marriage is dominance over the other person. Esther, age 55, is a client of mine. Her husband left her after twenty-five years of marriage, and she couldn't understand it. Gradually she revealed all the subtle and direct ways she had manipulated him because low self esteem kept her from directly asking for changes in his behavior. Her husband, mired in his own lack of self-confidence, fed on the manipulation and even encouraged it. But the time came when he became fed up and left Esther. Unfortunately, Esther did not think she ought to change. She thought her husband's latest action was simply a little stage he would soon pass through, something like "male menopause." After several sessions in which she resisted changing her domineering behavior, Esther returned in a stage of shock. Her husband had taken an apartment and was living there with a co-worker. "How dare he think he can get me jealous!" was Esther's angry response. But her husband didn't care at all how Esther felt. He was living it up, freed from the shackles that had bound him, and reveling in the new sense of importance that the co-worker was bestowing on him.

The third way people commonly deal with a lack of self-esteem is to develop "commitmentphobia," mentioned in the preceding chapter. They're gripped with panic when they feel hemmed in by another person. Any expression of affection is interpreted as an attempt to corral them. Such people try to assert their individuality apart from someone else, lest they get swallowed up in the identity of the couple. "I never want to be 'Mrs. Him,'" declared Beatrice, a 28-year-old secretary. "I could sure stand to be a 'kept woman' and get mink coats and a free penthouse apartment," she cracked. "But the minute a guy tries to get his meathooks into me, I'm off!" Beatrice prided herself in being a loner; she needed the constant reminder that she *could* stand on her own if she chose.

The overall point is that it often takes many years for people to acquire enough self-esteem to feel comfortable about marriage. In the past, independence wasn't valued as highly or mentioned quite as often as it is now. Today, there are a multitude of self-help books about saying no, putting yourself first, and looking out for number one. People who choose to postpone marriage until later in life often feel justified in spending time to develop themselves before taking on new responsibilities or commitments.

Can You Find the "Right" Person?

If by "right" you mean the *perfect* person, one who meets all your desired requirements, chances are pretty slim. People who want and value marriage, yet have no prospects, may find that their emotional distress is exacerbated by the gnawing questions, "Am I being too picky?" and "Is there really someone out there for me?"

Finding a suitable mate is often more difficult for women (especially upwardly mobile women) than it is for men. Statistically, there is a smaller number of men from which women can choose. For example, there are more gay men than gay women (13 versus 7 percent), and women comprise 52 percent of the population to begin with. There are fewer men willing to marry older women than vice versa; a man often wants to gain the prestige of having a nubile youth on his arm. Thus if you're a mature woman or one who is not regarded by all as attractive, you stand a greater chance of rejection. (Men, conversely, are often considered desirable even if overweight, graying, and sluggish.) In addition, women seem to value achievement and intelligence over appearance, while men often demean achievement and intelligence in favor of a Marilyn Monroe physique.

This is not to say that it's impossible to find an open-minded, nonthreatening man. But an informal survey I conducted, talking to forty single women in their thirties, suggests that they seldom meet the kind of men they desire for long-term relationships. And the ones who *do* find husbands sigh with relief that they are removed from the frustration of the search.

"I've asked men about their difficulty in finding women," Erica, a free-lance writer, says. "They say they're having a terrible time too. But if you look at the single men out there, and use careful standards to compare them to available women, you'll see that generally, the ones who aren't quickly snapped up after their divorces are qualitatively inferior to the women." Erica's sentiments were echoed by most of the women I met. The problem was detailed in a book by Marion Zola, *All the Good Ones Are Married*. The author polled many single women and found that since single men usually did not possess the qualities women desired, they often chose to have affairs with the plethora of married men available who did fulfill their needs.

William Novak, in his book *The Great American Man Shortage and Other Roadblocks to Romance*, suggests that women are restricting the number of men available to them by having unfair demands. Most of Novak's female interview subjects said they wanted men who were both shrewd in the marketplace and sensitive at home. This is a contradictory split difficult to integrate into a single personality, Novak's male interviewees assert. Novak also claims that women are hypocritical: "When faced with a choice between the new sensitive man the old-fashioned macho man, they choose the old-fashioned one. They may *talk* about a long-term relationship with a kind and nurturing guy, but they continue to be attracted to men of power and achievement. They're saying one thing and doing another."

Novak goes on to quote men's complaints about the shortage of *good women*. Most of the problems seemed to center around confusion of roles in the midst of changing societal expectations—and women's criticism of *them*.

A group of single women in their thirties whom I met with, who had read a portion of Novak's book, were angered by his findings. "Men complain that they can't be both agressive at work and tender at home," Noelle pointed out, "but how come women have been doing it for years? Look at all the women who raise families and still are climbing the success ladder. Look at all the *single* women who are achieving and yet yearning to settle down and be tender with a man!"

These women disagreed with Novak's idea that women now practice "selective liberation" by demanding respect yet expecting men to pay for dates and hold open doors. They feel that whoever invites the other out should pay for the meal, unless another arrangement has been agreed on beforehand. And they say that they hold doors open for *anyone*, male or female, who follows or accompanies them. "I don't know who Novak talked to," said Colleen, "but they seem to represent the defensive, inflexible, and insecure men who unfortunately seem to be our only choices."

Such clashing ends up causing much depression and loneliness among single men and women. Even the recollection of such struggles to meet "the right person" can be strong motivation to form a bond with whoever is around and even minimally seems compatible. People may feel that they are guaranteeing themselves lifetime companionship by grabbing onto a convenient and willing accomplice.

Women have an advantage in dealing with the "no-partner malaise." Because they have usually been raised to be more expressive of their emotions, they more easily form alliances with other women and platonic male friends. They therefore have an outlet for feelings and sources of emotional support that can carry them through tough moments. Men may have to develop ease in expressing themselves, or else face compounded frustration. There is an added benefit for the man who cultivates emotional openness: an increasing number of women are searching for men with just that ability.

It may be helpful to take the attitude of Jeanne, age 35 and divorced. "If you believe someone's out there, you'll tend to meet him. All you need is one. Despite having to look all these years, despite all the duds and dodos, all I have to do is click with one, and I can have a lifetime of happiness."

In trying to determine whether there is one "right" person for you, look at your criteria. If they are narrow and rigid, your chances are small of finding even one acceptable person. If your criteria are relatively open and flexible, it's likely that there are *many* people available who can nicely fit in with your life. Helping you to define your criteria is one purpose of this book.

Assessing Your Personal Goals

In order to determine whether now or later is the best time to get married, you need to have an overview of the direction in which you'd like to head. Of course, the experience of falling in love, and the characteristics of your particular partner both influence what you ultimately choose to do. But just to get in touch with your *independent* fantasies, remove yourself from the context of your relationship and focus on your own future possibilities.

The "Personal Goals and Expectations" form can help you to organize your thoughts. You may never have stopped to consider where you'd like to be in one, five, and ten years. The exercise may seem a little "off the wall," but give it a try. For each area of life that is listed to the left jot down your goal for within a year, within five years, and within ten years. There may be a discrepancy between the goals you write down and what you realistically expect to achieve. But don't censor yourself, even if you fear that your partner won't like what you write. This exercise is designed mainly to give you a private look at what you hope to accomplish.

When you finish writing down all of your goals, see how

Personal Goals and Expectations

For each area, write out your goals for the next year, next five years, and next ten years. Be as specific as possible. Then, in the right-hand columns, check how likely it is that each group of goals will be fulfilled by the target date.

Area	Within a Year	Within 5 Years	Within 10 Years	Very likely	Somewhat likely	Not very likely	An impossible dream
Career or education: Kind of work? Where?							
Physical condition							
Relationships with children							
Romantic relationship with opposite sex (mate, lovers)							
Living style: Homebody? Free spirit?							
Economic status— income							

Area	Within a Year	Within 5 Years	Within 10 Years	Very likely	Somewhat likely	Not very likely	An impossible dream
Residence (place, type)							
Friendships: How many of each gender? How close?							
Spiritual development							
External image							
Independence vs. reliance on others							
Conquering of fears or accomplishing tasks							
Acquiring goods							

close they are to what you actually expect to achieve. For each area, note whether the goals you have listed are "very likely," "somewhat likely," "not very likely," or "an impossible dream." Place a check mark in the column that best describes the chance of attaining the three goals you have listed.

The purpose of this questionnaire is to give you a visual overview of who you want to be. After one workshop in which couples completed this questionnaire, Nolan, a 25-year-old accountant, was depressed. He was gripped by claustrophobia over the life he was then creating for himself. He said:

I get horribly distressed at the thought of writing in my future in ten years, because I have few options but to continue in my present career. I went into accounting because I had a summer job assisting a bookkeeper. When she left to have a baby, I was promoted, and did such a good job that my company offered to pay my way through accounting school. Now I owe them years, though they never asked for any kind of commitment. I just feel trapped, like I never made any decisions for myself. My life was just laid out for me, and I'm watching it happen from the sidelines.

After the workshop ended, Nolan came to me for further counseling. He was engaged to Patti, an attractive 23-year-old kindergarten teacher. Her pep and warmth made him feel good, Nolan said, but he really wasn't sure he loved her. He said plaintively:

How can I discourage someone who is as considerate and supportive as Patti? She makes my life easier, and she's always there when I need her. I *think* I love her. There's certainly nothing *wrong* with her. I like to be with her, and everybody thinks I'm lucky to have such a cute girlfriend. I have no reason why I *shouldn't* get married, and our wedding date is just three months away. My mother is thrilled; she's always adored Patti. How come I'm such an idiot to question all this?

Nolan's "Personal Goals and Expectations" questionnaire helped provide an answer. When allowed to let his mind soar, Nolan wanted to be in show business—making films, engineering records, or being a radio disc jockey. He envisioned living in a little garret, a cozy hideaway—an idea that did not appeal to Patti. His ideal future didn't include a family and the competition of the business world. Yet Nolan was too afraid of spurning others' expectations to do what he fantasized would make him happy.

Perhaps your questionnaire confirms facts you already know: that your desires and reality don't coincide. You may not think you can afford to take time off from your present career to return to school or start your own business. You may have so many obligations that you see no way of getting out from under them. But what will your future be if you *don't* start to do something about your dissatisfactions now? This is just something to think about as you continue the process of self-exploration in this book.

/ 4
Serial Marriages and Blended Families

THIS CHAPTER IS ABOUT BEING SINGLE, married, divorced, and remarried. It's about pulling apart and joining together, about how a person's view of marriage can turn sour after divorce, and about the tenacity of the fairy tale that says someday, somehow, everyone lives happily ever after. I decided to include a chapter on divorce in this book because about two-thirds of the couples I see in "First Comes Love" workshops contain at least one divorced partner. Another reason for discussing divorce is the statistical fact that one out of every two marriages in this country will end in divorce. Gaining a better understanding of this common phenomenon and its precursors might even save *your* marriage someday.

Why People Divorce

Chapter 2 explored the various reasons why people live together or marry. The primary reason why people divorce is because they change. We wouldn't be human if we didn't constantly change. We can't be the same people we were yesterday, because we've gained experience with each new day. We learn facts, we interact with others. We suffer blows, and struggle to regain our self-esteem; we triumph and savor the moment while doing our best to see that it lasts. When I used to challenge my father at the dinner table, he dismissed me with the unarguable truth that he knew more than I did, simply because he had lived longer. I'm not convinced that sheer time on earth means more accumulated knowledge; ability and what a person does with his or her time are critical. But I do know that no one can remain untouched in a sterile vacuum; and this is bound to affect your marriage.

Unfortunately, many people enter marriage assuming that

neither they nor their spouses will change. They think along the lines of the trite phrases commonly inscribed in grammar-school autograph books: "stay as sweet as you are," "yours forever," "always." There is nothing wrong with wishful thinking, so long as you realize that wishes are not reality. But some people do confuse the two: satisfied with themselves and their partner at the time of their wedding they want everything to glide along, with no boat-rocking or other disturbances, until they sail into the sunset.

One of the main reasons you completed the questionnaire on goals and expectations in the preceeding chapter was so that you could map out the directions in which you might change. Interestingly, most people can easily envision themselves achieving and accomplishing in the future, but they may compartmentalize a love relationship into one rigid box, always expected to be sweet and mellow with the crush of infatuation or the bloom of newness. When the relationship takes on a new patina, they are easily distressed and wonder where the original excitement has gone.

Lawmakers are now acknowledging that there is usually no one cause of divorce but rather a mixture of events and changes on the part of both spouses. There may be a few cases of clear blame, as when one partner physically abuses the other, becomes drug- or alcohol-dependent, or simply vanishes. Under old definitions, these circumstances might be called "cruelty." Now, however, with "no fault" divorce becoming prevalent in many states, it is not always necessary to apply a label or give reasons for a split.

With legal name-calling less frequent, it becomes easier to examine reasons for divorce. Below are the reasons I've found to be most common. As you read them, consider how each one might have played a part in the dissolution of your past relationships, and how likely it is that each might interfere with your present alliance.

1. *A shattering of trust.* Trust is the foundation upon which marriages stand. It's security to be apart and to know that your commitment to each other will remain strong, no matter how long you're gone. Trust also includes belief in your partner's honesty; you trust him or her to tell you the truth and not omit or disguise negative feelings or events.

The most common way that trust is destroyed is through extramarital affairs. I spoke with a dozen divorced men and women, and all agreed that a partner's affair had or would undoubtedly alter their feelings toward their mates. Some said they could get over the pain, and understand the animal urges and emotional needs that might drive their partner into a liaison. But ever afterward there would be a nagging suspicion, a lack of ease, and doubt about the truthfulness of statements made by the partner who had "cheated." Several people admitted to having had affairs themselves, and they reported that the worst aspect of doing so was the deception and lack of honesty involved. Morris said he had felt torn when an opportunity arose to have sex with a visiting executive from a client's firm. He had begun a long-distance relationship that continued over a period of six months (until the woman cut it off, to Morris' chagrin). He regretted that the affair might negatively affect his marriage but the magnetism of the situation was so strong that he responded to its excitement.

Another case illustrates a second reaction to an affair, this time on the part of the wronged wife. Marilyn, a 50-year-old homemaker and part-time realtor, said:

When I found a pile of letters hidden in a shoebox in the back of John's closet, I thought I'd have a nervous breakdown. As I read them, I went from anger, to severe pain and depression, to pure hatred. I felt used, completely duped, as if John only wanted me for a maid and sex object, and for the status having a family brought him. The letters were passionate tomes from a girlfriend he had had for at least three years. I can't believe I could have been blind for so long. I instantly loathed John—my flagship, my pillar of strength for twenty-eight years—to the point that I just grabbed some of his clothes, stuffed them in a suitcase, and put them outside the front door. He called me and cried, and swore undying love, saying his mistress "meant nothing" to him, but I didn't care. You don't just snap back to normal when you've been run over by a bulldozer. I never let him back into the house. Our divorce will be final in another month.

Obviously, Marilyn was still in anguish over John's affair, even though it had ended five years ago and John had been faithful ever since. "I wouldn't even let him explain," she said, "because even if he had a good excuse, and there is absolutely none anyway, I still could never let him touch me. I could never enjoy being in the same room with him; I could never return to the easy days when I thought he honored our wedding vows." Severing her connection to John has been a tormenting ordeal for Marilyn, but she is single-minded. "There was nothing wrong with our relationship that I could see," she said slowly. Breaking into tears, she wispered, "but there must have been something terribly wrong. Terribly wrong."

2. *Lack of communication.* Lack of communication can cause a

host of maladies. Without communication, you can't give or receive support; you can't verify meanings or express feelings. No wonder some relationships stagnate; there's no stimulation to keep interest alive.

Couples sometimes get so involved with their own microcosms that they find it to bothersome to explain their activities and insecurities to their partners. They may be afraid that if they express vulnerability, even their own mate will confirm their worthlessness. That's what happened to Jim, Rowene's husband, who was mentioned in Chapter 2. As he faced problems in his business, he withdrew further and further into a shell, while at the same time Rowene expanded her self-confidence. She begged Jim to tell her his feelings, and she tried to be an example by revealing her innermost thoughts. All she received for her efforts were grunts—no comments or support. Soon she felt isolated. After getting a job, however, she was thrilled by the rewards of communication with others around her. It now appears that Rowene won't return to Jim until she gets her fill of praise from others and Jim has demonstrated his ability to fulfill her strong need for emotional expression.

Providing support may require effort—asking how your partner's day went, making loving gestures such as doing the other person's chores occasionally, and so on. Some long-married women whom I spoke with said they didn't need to hear their husbands tell them they cared; they "knew" it by his everyday behavior. After a couple spends many years together, their communication may become largely nonverbal, which is fine so long as both people understand that caring exists.

3. *A need to feel powerful in the relationship.* People certainly can feel powerless, and some may even think they deserve it, but *no one likes it*. People may take on roles (even passive ones like that of "doormat" or "shy one") in order to manipulate others and thus bring them the power they crave. A wife who is jealous of the time her husband spends with his mother might start belittling her. Suddenly there's "mother-in-law trouble" in the marriage. A husband who keeps reminding his unemployed wife that he makes the decisions because his paycheck supports the family may be shown up when his wife, as a way of asserting power, goes on wild spending sprees. Power plays can be enacted in the bedroom too. A wife may not reach orgasm, or a husband may ejaculate prematurely, as a means of denying the other pleasure or satisfaction.

Genevieve Grafe Marcus and Robert Lee Smith, in their book *Equal Time*, claim that balance of power is *the* crucial variable in marital happiness, and the determinant of whether or not a marriage is "equal." However, I've observed marriages in which the partners were so independent outside of the relationship that they were satisfied with what appeared to be very unbalanced roles in their mutual interactions. It didn't matter to Elaine that Jack expected her to prepare his meals and do the laundry in exchange for gifts of fur coats and expensive cars. She truly enjoyed cooking, just dropped the dirty bundle at the dry cleaners, and felt powerful away from home as president of a major charity. "I guess you wouldn't say we have a new, liberated marriage," Elaine sighed, a little embarrassed. "But just because I abdicate my power at home doesn't mean I don't feel adequate or important overall. I just prefer it this way."

4. *Incompatible rates of psychological growth.* Even when couples communicate, have a balance of power within the relationship, and trust each other completely, a marriage can go awry. Grant, 38, knew that by modern criteria, his relationship had been fine. He said, "It was one of those cases where the operation was a success but the patient died. I simply couldn't keep up with my liberated wife." I asked him what he meant.

When Shirl and I were first married, fifteen years ago, we shared all sorts of interests. I was about to enter engineering school, and she was teaching kindergarten. We seemed to be pulling for the same goal: my getting my degree and getting a job, and the raising of our family. We were pretty poor, but so what—we just ate grilled cheese sandwiches and on weekends had friends over to watch TV.

But after our three kids were born and I was getting successful in my work, we just drifted apart. Shirl got involved in the teachers' union and all her motherly duties, and I got caught up in the faster-paced world at work. While the kids were little it was fine; we worked together to give them a good start. But then Shirl took an extracurricular class at the university extension on consciousness-raising. Look, I'm all for equal pay for equal work, and I really respected my wife. But suddenly she had all these gripes.

We talked about them, and I willingly took on more household chores. But she decided to break our original bargain. No longer was she willing to follow the career *she'd* chosen, [as wife and mother] so she expected me to change *my* lifestyle. She wanted to go back to school, and I was behind her, but I thought she should go to our local college, and get a degree in a field our family could benefit from, at a reasonable pace.

She wanted to become a medical doctor! That would mean years of graduate school, an internship and residency, and most of her time away from home. She said that she'd denied herself a career all these years and that we should "understand" that it was "her turn." No way. She said I was "threatened" because she'd have more prestige and make more money than me. What a laugh. She couldn't understand that I was just *happy* with our lifestyle, and that I wanted a wife who put home and family above her selfish, off-the-wall career ideas.

Grant and Shirl were divorced, and Shirl left California to go to medical school in the East. The children, now teenagers, spend time both with their father (who is still in California) and with their mother under a joint custody arrangement. Shirl and Grant are not ogres, nor did they lack fundamental skills for communicating. They simply suffered from an inability to reconcile the changes associated with Shirl's new goals.

Dennie, a 24-year-old dental hygienist, had only been married to Mark for a year and a half when, she said, she "fell out of love with him." Before here marriage, she was "crazy" for Mark, a welder the same age as she. They had a lavish wedding, and settled down in a house they had just bought. Things quickly deteriorated. As Dennie explained:

He was critical of the way I kept the house, and when I asked him to pitch in, he refused. Instead of being loving and attentive, he just spent more time with his friends.

I got bored. I wanted to fix up the house and finish my bachelor's degree; he wanted to regress into being a teenager. It didn't take long for the ardor to die and for me to see what a mistake I'd made. Our relationship just cooled, that's all, and when I moved back home with my folks, Mark didn't even bother to come after me. We just quietly went our separate ways, as if our whole relationship had never existed.

Many men and women prefer to stick with traditional roles and conventional expectations of marriage. Even so, uneven rates of emotional development (or growth in a new direction) have become a common problem since feminism has blurred role distinctions. The women's movement has encouraged new, unfamiliar "rules" for interaction, and has opened up a plethora of new career directions for both sexes. Members of a couple often take to such changes at different paces, or one partner might soar developmentally while the other remains in a safe, comfortable position.

I believe that the major reasons for divorce are those summarized in the four points above. They are at the root of many more visible schisms, such as sexual dissatisfaction, in-law squabbles, and financial disputes. Reading about these trouble sources can be fascinating to divorced people who are reexamining what went wrong in their previous marriages. Engaged couples may find the discussion helpful for interpreting petty complaints—considering whether these represent deeper problems—and for identifying symptoms of severe marital strife that might occur in the future.

The "Former Entanglements" Questionnaire

Couples who are evaluating their relationship and the decision to marry need to consider how their former entanglements will shape their contemplated unions. The "Former Entanglements" form is designed to help you organize the likely effects. Independently, answer the questions in the left-hand column as they apply to each of the potential entanglement areas: parents, children, and so on. Naturally, not all these areas may apply to you.

Effects of Divorce

While getting divorced is emotionally painful even in the most amicable separations, along with universal discomfort comes unlimited opportunity. Yes, there *are* positives. A divorce marks the end of a usually messy process, letting you put aside an unpleasant chapter in your life. In many cases, a divorce frees you permanently from an unhappy relationship and presents you with more time and energy for goals you *want* to pursue. A divorce can be liberating.

When you are starting anew, you are able to envision an end to your pain and a chance to become an independent, self-reliant person. This challenge is often frightening, but it's exciting as well; it's stimulation to make the many changes in your life that you might have postponed. Suddenly you have to please no one but yourself; you can then get back in touch with your own desires and pleasures. This boosts your self-esteem and sends ripples of success throughout your life. You have few restrictions, and can enjoy the attentions of potential lovers without the albatross of a broken marriage hanging like dead weight around your neck.

The negative effects of divorce are better publicized. The healing process can be prolonged, and punctuated with questions

NEW TRENDS IN RELATIONSHIPS

FORMER ENTANGLEMENTS

Everyone has a past. Assess how yours and your partner's will affect you if and when you marry.

Question	Parents	Children	Former Partner(s)	Friends	Business/ Money-Making
What ties and commitments exist for myself and my partner?					
1. Time					
2. Financial					
3. Emotional					
How will our contemplated marriage affect each of these ties and commitments?					
What problems are created by these ties and commitments?					
How can each of these problems be handled?					
What benefits do each of us get from:					
1. My ties?					
2. My partner's?					
How will my partner's ties and commitments affect my own?					
What can we learn from past mistakes?					

about self-worth. There may be new hassles to deal with: shuffling children to babysitters or to the former spouse on visitation or joint-custody days; taking on more chores; changing residences; starting to work for newly needed dollars. Divorces can bring a lowered standard of living, as part of a person's income is diverted to a former spouse or children, whose love and/or presence now are denied. It's stressful to suddenly be saddled with financial responsibility, with none of its rewards. Newly divorced people also have to deal with the opinions of relatives and other outsiders, and perhaps with the difficulties of entering the dating scene.

What Divorce Does to People's Views of Marriage

There's no way to emerge unscathed from a divorce. I've heard many people boast that their "ex" is their best friend. But even so, being in a marriage, and coming out of one, leaves you greatly changed. Because marriage is supposed to be "for life," your emotional investment was, at least at one time, very strong. When this bond is broken, how can you avoid mourning the loss and feeling that somehow you've failed?

Different couples have different experiences in this regard. The only sure bet about how the divorce process will affect your opinion of marriage is that somehow, it *will*. Your perceptions of what marriage is and what it potentially can be will be colored by your experience, even if you vow never to let such a thing happen again. Typically, a divorce either propels a suddenly insecure person headlong into another commitment, or teaches caution about future marriage. At my workshops, I don't see many from the former group: they tend to walk down the aisle again the day the ink dries on their divorce papers.

After a divorce, a person's view of marriage varies according to where blame has been placed for the "failure." This phenomenon is related to the psychological literature on "locus of control," which says that behavior is determined by whether you credit the sources of problems as *internal* (i.e., yourself) or *external* (i.e., anyone or anything other than yourself).

If you blame the failure of your marriage on yourself, there are three likely reactions:

1. You might give up hope that you'll be able to find someone you can please. With this scenario, self-esteem is lowered to the

point where you don't want to risk another rejection, and so you simply consider yourself unavailable and busy yourself with other aspects of life.

2. You might keep looking for lasting love, but lower your standards regarding what constitutes an acceptable mate. "I deserve the dregs," said Ellen sadly. She'd been married to a well-to-do accountant, and when he left her for another woman, she assumed that he found her unexciting, unintelligent, and unsexy. "If my ex-husband was so disgusted with me that he had to have a mistress, how can I expect to make someone else happy?" Ellen whined. It took many therapy sessions to convince Ellen that she had plenty of desirable qualities going for her, and that perhaps her husband had taken a mistress to satisfy a lack inside himself rather than because he found fault with her.

3. You might go all out to change yourself in order to be more attractive to others. If the person you were couldn't even make a go of marriage, then, you may reason, it's time to become the sort of person who *can*. A beauty makeover or some new duds can give you confidence to reenter the world of being independent. A forced *personality* renovation is generally not a good idea, however. If you adopt artificial behaviors, the result might be that you turn off potential partners. As one of the divorced men I interviewed put it, "The front I put on for women turned out to be pretty transparent, and it was tiring for me too. I discovered that the women I got as the 'macho me' boosted my ego, but I was always afraid they'd discover the truth. I finally gave up the game and met my fiancée."

If you blame your partner for the divorce, there are two possible outcomes:

1. You might raise your criteria for potential partners. "I don't want to be stuck with another uncommunicative man," said Giselle, 66. After remaining single until age 55, she had finally married Daniel. They were divorced nine years later for reason number four: uneven psychological growth. At the beginning of their relationship, Giselle's expectations of a husband were traditional. It didn't bother her that Daniel rarely displayed affection, because few men she knew did so. But as her views expanded and she realized that some men *could* change, she demanded more from her marriage. "I learned that it's useless to try to change someone," Giselle shrugged, "so now I'm careful to make sure that my dates have all the qualities I value *first*."

2. You might isolate your experience in your mind and rationalize that "lightning can't strike twice." So you'd reenter the dating scene using your usual strategies and interaction style without modification, because your "ex" was an *ex*ception, and there's no way history can repeat itself.

These can be the proverbial famous last words. I repeatedly meet married people who had chosen new partners nearly identical to the ones they had divorced. Such behavior may have one of these underlying purposes: to resolve unfinished relationships with a father or mother by continuing to play out similar interaction patterns (often giving or receiving nurturant behavior); to confirm feelings of worthlessness in a masochistic way; or to take on a mission as provider or soul-saver in order to define one's value in life. "He needs a Mommy," one woman said of her new husband. "It seems I get myself into relationships where I am the caretaker. It sounds sick, but I guess we both get what we want out of it." Indeed, in some cases the situation *is* unhealthy, and counseling would help. Why settle for a marriage of enacted roles when honesty can bring greater rewards?

If you blame your divorce on the surrounding circumstances, you could react in two ways:

1. You might structure your life so that the particular circumstances cannot occur again. Theresa, age 30, saw marriage itself as something that ought not to be repeated. She told me:

I'm simply taking no chances. I have a daughter, and she suffered enough when her father and I got divorced. Sure, I miss having a man to do the household "dirty work," and I'd like an ongoing, caring relationship. But no more marriage. It's too risky. Even if you're deliriously happy in the beginning, something can go wrong. My daughter takes most of my attention, and I get plenty of love from her. We'll make it just fine without a man to complicate our lives.

Theresa was speaking defensively, and her position is extreme. More commonly, divorced people make external changes. They move to a new town, begin a new job, become involved with new people. They keep searching for a mate, but try to remove reminders of the past and any vestiges of the old relationship. By playing musical chairs with the components of their lives, they hope to prevent a recurrence of the events that led to divorce before.

2. You might just move on, looking for a new mate in the

way that comes most naturally. Placing blame for divorce on outside circumstances helps remove guilt (the idea that you somehow failed or did not do all you could to make the marriage work) and hostility toward your ex-spouse. "It was nobody's fault," said Vincent, age 60:

We just grew apart. We had been faithful to each other, yet noticed that our interests were away from home with others rather than as a couple. I got bored with marriage, and so did she. We don't hate each other, and there were no skeletons that came leaping out of either of our closets, which happened to two other couples we knew. We just decided it was time to try something new, because if we didn't we wouldn't have a chance to regain the excitement and new adventures we both wanted. I see her at least once a week, and we both get a kick out of describing our latest exploits. What we've become is good friends, and we value that a lot. We'll never lose our closeness, and we could still gain new romance if we find the right people.

This sounds so sensible, so easy. Somehow, I don't believe that Vincent escaped pain altogether. There's bound to be separation anxiety after a couple has spent many years together, as well as loneliness and a fear that the singles scene will bring rejection.

Placing blame outside the people involved seems to make the divorce process smoother and the recovery period shorter. Vincent takes the long view of life:

You go through stages, and for one stage of my life I was a meter reader with a wife and young children; for another I was a student and bachelor; for another I changed jobs and became a public relations man; and now I'm single, still in P.R. and enjoying the world. Why waste time being rueful and rehashing whose "fault" everything was? I just accept that everything that happens to me is at least partially my own doing, but that whatever comes along will be okay in the end.

The Singles Scene

What's the purpose of a singles scene? Why, to meet the "right" man or woman, fall in love, get married, and never have to walk into another bar or feel nervous on a blind date again. Getting married can bring some primary (and largely intangible) benefits, such as love, happiness, nurturance, comfort, companionship, support, and security. Secondary rewards might include sexual satisfaction, a parent for one's children, social standing, the pursuit of family traditions, and luxuries only money can buy.

For many, including myself, the main purpose of life is the experiencing and giving of love. Of course, marital love isn't the only kind, and unmarried people can have an abundance of love too. But we are taught to believe that the most sublime type of love is found within marriage, and so, despite distasteful encounters and the time and effort required, single and divorced people pursue this ideal.

And pursue it they do. Some people regard singles bars as useful for quick pick-ups for sexual relief. But I would wager that most people go into them hoping to find a long-term relationship.

It's both painful and humorous to hear some of the stories about divorced people who are anxious to find someone new. Barbie, a 37-year-old mother of two, is a caterer. As owner of her business, she divides her attention between wonton skins and other delicacies, order-taking, customer recruiting, and record-keeping. She was devastated when her husband left her a year and a half ago. I spent New Year's Eve with her; ironically, it was the day her divorce became final. She told me:

I was one of those people who went from my parents' protection right into marriage. So when Harold left, I was like a babe in the woods. Friends were so sympathetic that they started giving my number out to anything that wore pants. So about a month ago, I got my first phone call.

"Hey, Barb!" [she drawled, in imitation of a falsely slick come-on]. "Like, what's happenin', kid? Like, you and I could be real cool together, you know what I mean?" Here I am in my kitchen making crepes, and my mouth is dropping open in amazement. This had to be the biggest nerd in captivity. He thought he was so smooth: "Well, uh, Barb! So whaddaya look like, kid?" Can you believe him asking me this over the phone? Like an idiot I told him truthfully that I'm just a little overweight.

"A little overweight? That's gotta mean what? Forty or fifty pounds? Hey! That's okay, I like 'em big!" [Barbie was actually a very attractive woman whose plumpness was more in her mind than on her hips.] I ended up talking to this guy for an hour, and the whole time he kept making these horrible suggestive remarks and sounding like a caricature of the Marina swinger.

She was referring to residents of Marina del Rey, a Los Angeles oceanside community known for singles apartment buildings. Living there are male tenants who, when on the prowl, stereotypically wear open shirts revealing chest hair and gold chains.

Of course I was too dumb to say no when he wanted to arrange a meeting. "You like sushi, Barb?" he asks me. So we set it up for seven P.M. at this little sushi bar. I must say I looked pretty good that night.

I knew him right away. He was about four foot eight, had forests of curly chest hair and about three pounds of gold around his neck. Oh, yeah, and he was about 65 years old. The first thing I asked him was how he kept his voice sounding so young. He didn't even flinch: "Hey Barb! Dontcha know I work out?"

I thought of course that this would be it. We had nothing in common, and he was old enough to be my father. But that didn't stop him. After about two hours, I tactfully looked at my watch and feigned horror at how late it was getting. His reply? "Right, Barb, time to go! Your place or mine?" When I firmly said no thank you, he still wouldn't give up. Outside by my car, he grabbed me and tried to kiss me. He had only made it to my lower lip—after all, he practically had to jump up to reach it—when I managed to open the car door and slip in. Would you believe he called me the next day saying what a great time he had had, and wanting to know when he could "strike again"?

Does this experience sound familiar? It's all true, despite the fact that it sounds like the script for a *Saturday Night Live* skit. It is just one tale illustrating the lengths to which people will go in an effort to find love.

I also won't forget what Liz used to do. Her ploy was to frequent singles bars and assume different identities for each occasion. One time she'd be a secretary with a name like Patsy or Linda; another time she'd pretend she was an art collector named Genevieve (pronounced Jahn-vee-ehv). Liz was really a doctoral candidate in psychology, age 31. Her fantasies were not little "bar talk" games. She actually carried through with each deception, and sometimes got caught in her own lies. She, like the "Marina swinger," was trying to find love; she did not believe that truthfulness would work.

What kept Liz going was one success in which she magically had been attracted to a man whom she ended up dating for four years. She had seen him across the noisy bar, felt drawn to him, and crossed the smoky room to walk into his arms. (The drama was equivalent to that in the scene in *West Side Story* when Tony meets Maria.) This incident was enough on which to build a lifetime of fantasy.

I once appeared on a television talk show to discuss the tribulations of women who were in search of elusive true love. The staff had found two women to appear with me and discuss their own efforts to find a mate. One of them said she often makes connections on the freeways of Los Angeles. Her office overlooks an overpass, and she regularly displays her phone number when she can catch the eye of a prospective "hunk." Forget formalities, this is Hollywood.

Why People Want to Remarry

There's a lot of risk in meeting people at singles bars and similar places. But there seems to be general agreement that the possibility of a lasting relationship is worth it. When I asked divorced people whether they planned to remarry and why, the usual first reaction was surprise that I would ask a question with such an obvious answer. Here are some of the replies I received:

- From a 48-year-old man whose marriage of twenty years had broken up six years ago: "The question isn't 'whether,' but 'when.' I've had a succession of girlfriends over the past few years, and sometime soon I'll just be ready to settle down. I want to get married because I *believe* in marriage; I think that married people are generally happier."
- A 50-year-old author said: "I want to remarry because I'm lonely, and I want a companion. I've become capable of getting my own car fixed and painting my own kitchen, but it would be so much nicer to sometimes let someone else do them, or at least do them together." She had been married for two years in her twenties, and had dated on and off ever since. "It's depressing to spend Christmas at other people's homes. I want to roll over in bed and find someone there other than my dog."
- Said a 33-year-old high school administrator, divorced five years ago, "I want to remarry because I want to have a family. Being single is fine, but why should I miss out on the big stuff, raising children and having a loving husband?"
- "My first marriage was a bust; we were just too young," said a 29-year-old restaurant owner. "Now that I've found a career direction and matured a lot, I won't make the same mistakes I did before. All I need is a second chance, and I'll get it next Saturday!" (He and his fiancée planned a noon ceremony.)

This sampling of replies suggests that people often remarry for these reasons:

- A fantasy about finding the right person for "forever"
- The notion that divorced people have learned from their past mistakes, and now know better than to make them again
- A belief that a new partner will be unlike the first, second, or third partners
- The hope for a normal family life and children
- The need for support and companionship
- A fear of being alone.

Several of the divorced people I asked were non-commital about remarriage. Common responses were: "I'll see what comes along"; "It would be nice, but I'm not holding my breath"; and "I'm having a great time now, so I'll just take it a day at a time." One woman refused to comment, saying she might "jinx" her chances! That was certainly a response in itself.

I asked more than fifty people whether they planned to remarry, and only three said they probably never would. (The attitude that a lost spouse can never be replaced is more common among the widowed, especially those who are left alone later in life.

One reason people say that they don't know what will happen, or that they don't expect to remarry, is that this helps protect them from disappointment. By not pinning your hopes on the unknown, you can be pleasantly surprised if love waltzes into your life, and you won't be devastated or feel inadequate if it doesn't. Still, the one resounding message I keep receiving, over and over, from people of all statuses—married, single, divorced, or separated, of every age—is that they believe in marriage (or at least in long-term, committed love). If their lives are good, people wonder, at least in the more curious reaches of their minds, whether life wouldn't be *great* if only they had that one special relationship. They read about such a relationship in breathless romance novels, see it on television, and even know of real people who have found ideal matches. "If it can happen to them," they reason, "why not me?"

Coming Together: Blended Families

Remarriage often involves rearranging not only two lives but several. The image of the stepmother has traditionally been "wicked," and our sympathies extend to all poor Cinderellas. The term "blended family" (or "combined family") was created to help improve this undeserved image. Sometimes compensation for the old stereotype went overboard, as in the popular television series *The Brady Bunch*. (The smiling parents of three blond daughters and three brunette sons tackled one growing pain each week.) A different fantasy message has emerged: with the filter of romantic love, all will be right. However, as all parents know, life does not always live up to the standards set in a television sitcom.

How wonderous it is when Jill and George find each other. How romantic when they steal away for a weekend of bubble baths and moonlight dances. And what a comedown when they return to jelly stains on the carpet, outrageous bills for long-distance phone calls, feathers from a pillow fight caught in every crevice of the living room, and two children who are livid with each other. Accepting such chaos on a daily basis is what marriage of two parents is all about. My friend Melinda, age 42 and a school psychologist, summarized her experience in this way:

Mandy and Drew were 8 and 11 when Mark and I got married. He brought his two children, aged 14 and 8, when he moved into my house after the wedding. [Melinda and Mark have been married just a year and a half.] At first, right after the ceremony, we were amazed at how well the kids got along.

Then, as the novelty wore off, all hell broke loose. Screaming became a ritual, every night. The kids wouldn't obey us, and they were jealous of any attention we showed to one of them. Mark and I are rather quiet people, and we dislike raising our voices. But I found myself shouting at my daughter to just be quiet. All my energy was drained keeping them apart. And the kids would be very clever. We'd set rules and they'd manipulate us, and do anything they could to circumvent our intentions. It was as though they protested our finding each other. Before, they were the support system for their parents, and they got lots of attention out of it. Now that Mark and I have each other, the kids know they've lost their old role.

We spoke that time over dinner in an African restaurant. Several months later, I was at Melinda and Mark's home for a wine-tasting. The representative of a German wine company tried to explain the difference between Spatlese and Kabinett over the din of Mandy and Drew's screeches from the bedroom. Melinda smiled sweetly (though her ears were obviously trained toward the back of the house) and ignored the battle. Later, Mandy came out to snitch a handful of cheese. Melinda never said a word to her.

"We've really gotten regimented," Melinda explained.

"There's still too much noise for me, but they know that if they don't behave, their allowances will be docked." Each child is assigned chores, and loses change if he or she doesn't perform. Things have settled down to a general harmony, Melinda says, though she is bothered by the fact that Mark's son Tim, now 16, smokes in his bedroom. "We've asked him to stop, but he balks and says he shuts his door so no one else has to smell the fumes." Melinda and Mark's faces both show tension when they discuss their quandry about how to discourage Tim's smoking yet minimize alienation.

Of course, such problems are part of life for natural parents as well as stepparents. It seems, however, that the number of issues escalates in a blended family, as children vie for attention, test the limits of parental authority, and establish new, complex relationships with other family members. Many issues relating to jealousy, competition, fairness, and possession arise simply because the living arrangement is so new. Just as at summer camp, the pecking order must be set.

There are as many ways to react to the job of stepparenting as there are potential stepparents. One of the women I interviewed reported sadly that she had passed by an opportunity to marry a man she cared for simply because his daughter was so set against her joining the family. Another woman said that she had *only* married her husband when custody of his two children shifted to his ex-wife. A man claimed that if he had known the frustration he was to suffer as a stepfather, he would have reconsidered his decision to marry. And a colleague I met in my doctoral program, Marie, found that caring for children's emotions and welfare can detract from the primary relationship of a married couple.

Marie and Greg, both in their mid-forties, thought they had everything under control. When they married, he had four children and she had two. The children's ages spread from 5 to 18, and there were the usual squabbles. Marie's excitement about blended families, however, led her to make them the subject of her doctoral research. She developed a set of strategies for coping with typical adjustment problems, and put them to work in her own home.

There were several conflicts between her more relaxed parenting style and Greg's strictness, but her energy and apparent success were impressive. Between balancing her research, her motherly activities, and many extracurricular interests, Marie was quite busy. She thought that life was progressing swimmingly. "Even going out for a beer with Greg was a special event," she recalls. So she was floored and distraught when Greg, after five years of marriage, announced to her that he wanted a divorce. "My heart was broken," she says now, matter-of-factly. "Within a year after he left me he married an Asian woman, and a year and a half after his new marriage he told me: 'If it weren't for our conflicts over the kids, we'd still be together.'" Marie had to sell her home and move into smaller quarters. She has returned to graduate school, resolute upon finding another dissertation topic.

Before her divorce, Marie had done considerable research in the area of blended families, interviewing hundreds of stepparents. I asked her to boil down her advice for couples contemplating the creation of their own "conglomerate."

First of all, recognize that bringing together two families is a serious matter, and that kids are inevitably a strain on the relationship. If Greg and I didn't have any children, we'd still be together now. Be prepared for the stress, but know that there are lots of satisfactions too. I enjoyed the kids and had a great time. Single friends would say they wished they had my problems, because at least I was in love with a wonderful person. It was all worth it because I had a good relationship with their father.

All the stepparenting books say that after three years, the situation gets better, and it did in our case. We started compromising; at least I did. I don't think Greg believed I could sincerely compromise on so many things.

Another point is not to let it bother you if the stepchildren don't want to call you "Mom" or "Dad." Abandon the idea that being called "Mom" means you're a successful stepparent. Kids always have a need to have relationships with their original parents. You can still be the most important person in the child's life. Also, there's a tendency to want to keep the child away from the other parent, but don't do this because then the parent gets idealized. The more children see the other parent, the better, because then they know that person as she or he really is, warts and all, and they appreciate you. We always taught the kids that love is not limited. You can love two sets of parents, and by loving one, you don't take anything away from the other.

People try too hard to win over their spouse's children in the beginning. You have to remember that they haven't chosen you, nor you them. I never decided I wanted Greg's kids. The reason I got them was because I loved their father. It's best to just treat each other with respect.

Of course you have to be a parent; you can't be their friend. They'll break rules, and you'll have to step in and be a parent. My stepdaughter would scream at me, "You can't make me do that—you're not my mother!" I said, "I'm the mother *here!*"

I remember one book said "you have to have the hide of a rhinoceros." Kids feel guilty about being comfortable living with you. They get cruel and you just have to expect it. Even if they intend to hurt you, don't let them manipulate you. Just use common sense. Be firm, and use the skills you've used successfully with your own kids. If you've never been a parent before, read all the parenting books and get normative data on what kids are like.

If you're looking for some information and "normative data," Marie recommends the following books: *Living in Step* by Jeanette Loftas and Ruth Roosevelt, which Marie likes best; *Stepparenting* by Jean and Veryl Rosenbaum, and *The Half Parent: Living with Other People's Children* by Brenda Maddox. For a thorough reference that is more academically slanted, Marie suggests *Stepfamilies: A Guide to Working with Stepparents* by Emily B. Visher and John F. Visher.* Marie emphasizes that while it's often easier to describe the negative side of combining families, there are enough benefits that, with love and patience, all is well worth the effort.

Stepparenting Questionnaire

Though your love for your partner should be the main determinant of whether or not you marry, if children are involved you should definitely consider their potential effect on your relationship *before* you tie the knot. Answer the questions in the "Stepparenting Questionnaire" independently, then compare your responses with your partner's. Some of the questions simply help to clarify facts or possibilities; others pinpoint areas where trouble shooting may be necessary.

Custody/visitation/child care:

1. What are and will be the custody, visitation, and child-care arrangements for each child involved? _____
   _____
   _____

---

*Complete source information for the books cited can be found in the Bibliography.

2. Ideally, what percentage of the time would I like my own children to live with us? My partner's children?

Child's Name	Percentage
_____	_____
_____	_____
_____	_____

3. How well are my partner and I able to deal with my "ex," in terms of the children? With my partner's "ex"? (1 = very well; no problems. 2 = well; occasional hitches but generally okay. 3 = not so well; problems do crop up and are bothersome. 4 = poorly; a difficult situation. NA = not applicable.)
   How I relate to my "ex":_____
   How I relate to my partner's "ex":_____
   How my partner relates to my "ex":_____
   How my partner relates to his/her "ex":_____

4. How do my partner and I feel about the children seeing their other parent? (rate from 1 to 10: 1 = very negatively; 10 = very positively)
   Rating concerning my children:_____
   Rating concerning my partner's children:_____

Money

5. How do I feel about money that will be spent on the children? (Free associate your answer to this question, and fill in your response.)_
   _____

6. To what degree will child-support expenses affect our lifestyle? (1 = no effect; 10 = drastic effect) Rating:_____

Parenting

7. How would I rate each of our parenting styles? (1 = very permissive style; 10 = very strict style)
   Rating for self_____
   Rating for my partner_____

8. How flexible are we regarding the parenting approach the children will receive? (Rate on a scale from 1 to 10 with 1 = very flexible; 10 = very committed to a certain approach)
   Flexibility rating for self:_____
   Flexibility rating for partner:_____

9. How well are we able to cope with the children's misbehavior or insolence? (1 = very poorly; 10 = very well)
   Rating for self:_____
   Rating for partner:_____

10. How confident am I of my own and my partner's parenting skills? (1 = not at all confident; 10 = extremely confident)
    Confidence rating for self:_____
    Confidence rating for partner:_____

11. On the whole, how much enjoyment do I get from the children?
    (1 = no enjoyment; 10 = highest level of enjoyment)
    Enjoyment from my children_____
    Enjoyment from my partner's children_____
12. Describe how well the children now get along together, and how well you expect them to get along in the future: _____
    _____
    _____

Our relationship

13. How much do I like my partner's children? Briefly write out your feelings about each child: _____
    _____
    _____

14. Drawing on your knowledge of the children involved, note special problems that each one might bring. _____
    _____
    _____

15. How much strain do I think the necessity of dealing with the children will bring to our relationship? (1 = no strain; 10 = extreme strain) Rating:_____

Now that you have a better idea of the various ways in which the children can affect your life, you have the opportunity to change what you don't like. You might decide to wait a while to marry, to allow yourself more time to get to know your partner's children. Or you might plan alternatives for their care. Possibly, in looking over your completed questionnaire, you breathed a sigh of relief that you've already dealt with most problem areas and concluded that you have clear sailing ahead.

One common problem in blended families relates to who gets the most attention. Often, children who have survived their parents' divorces are used to attention—first during the parental separation stage, when energy formerly devoted to the marriage is refocused toward the child, then as the child becomes the center of a single parent's life. Now that you've found love, some share of your usual attention to the child has been usurped. It's no wonder that children attempt to regain what they've lost, even if they cause you distress in the process.

While coping with the changes may be difficult, don't forget to appreciate all the treats you receive as a parent that no nonparent can savor: those endearing moments when your child says something especially sweet; the excitement of watching a child master a new concept; the thrill of presenting a new idea to your teenager and watching him or her absorb the thought and mature. It can be delightful to share these experiences with someone you love.

/ 5
New Roles and Bargains

MARRIAGE. WIFE. HUSBAND. When you hear those words, you make instant assumptions. Just for a moment, try bringing your mental pictures into sharp focus. In response to "marriage," do you think of your partner or yourself first? When you think of a wife, what does she look like? What is her age? What is she doing? Try the same image-conjuring exercise with the word "husband." What view springs to mind? Again, note the age of the husband, his appearance, and the activity in which you picture him.

No one is free of all stereotypes or preconceptions. Stereotypes have gotten people into trouble throughout history: they may be simply false, or too negative and limiting as exceptions come along. But we wouldn't perform as well without them—and, for the most part, they *are* based on a kernel of truth. Thus, generalizations can sometimes be useful. If you have an idea of how something or someone is likely to be, then you have a head start on determining how you ought to behave or predicting what will transpire.

Some stereotypes are explicit, while others are vague. On the explicit side, the term "woman driver" might bring to mind a lady trying to commandeer a large vehicle, squinting over the steering wheel and cruising at a steady twenty miles per hour. Occasionally, she makes stupid moves right in front of *your* car. When you think of a "truck driver," the image might be of a burly guy in a grungy white T-shirt who needs a shave and has a sleeve rolled around a pack of cigarettes. The term "nun" conjures up ideas of a black-gowned woman, head bowed, walking piously into a chapel. Never mind that most nuns are now dressing in modern garb and actively working in the community; that truck drivers may be women who like Mozart; or that females drive race cars with precision and cause insurance agents to boast of their safety records. Our stereotypes persist because *somewhere* we've seen examples of them.

We have stereotypes of what marriage is too. These are more personal, less universal. They often reflect the marriage our parents had, or the marriages of couples around us. The important point is that we base our expectations of the future on our past observations of modeled behavior. We're slow to incorporate what we see in the *present* into those stereotypes.

So, in order to shape our futures, we should make an effort to differentiate out-of-date images from current reality. When it comes to marriage, this often means banishing sexist assumptions and experimenting with new roles. Phyllis Schlafly, and Helen Andelin's "Fascinating Womanhood" (advocating that women appear helpless and frilly to con their men into protecting and responding to them) provide examples of how tenaciously humans cling to mores that have proven detrimental to many. Often, people will use almost any rationalization that allows them to keep the status quo. It's hard and scary to break old habits and try something new.

Despite attitudinal barriers to change, people's concepts of marriage are shifting. Nowadays, the "ideal marriage" is much harder to define than it was even fifteen years ago. As popularized by television series in the 1950s and early 1960s (e.g., *Father Knows Best*, *Leave it to Beaver*, *Ozzie and Harriet*) and now romanticized in sitcoms about that era such as *Happy Days*, *Laverne and Shirley*, and *Joanie Loves Chachie*, marriage had a very specific character. The elements of a "traditional" marriage will be listed shortly. There are few television shows able to clearly portray present-day marriages, perhaps because there is no longer any single way to behave in a marriage. Our tolerance for divergent lifestyles, at least when they are under the umbrella of an acceptable marriage or "happy family," has expanded considerably.

The "Expectations Sentence Completion" Exercise

The "Expectations Sentence Completion" exercise offers an opportunity to use a tool—free association—that many psychologists find helpful. By completing the sentences quickly, you can bypass your usual censoring mechanisms and get more directly in touch with your underlying stereotypes and feelings.

New Trends in Relationships

For each "root," or beginning of a sentence, write in the first ending that comes to mind. Some roots are identical: for each one, try to quickly come up with a *different* ending.

Expectations Sentence Completion

1. A husband is _____
2. A husband is _____
3. A husband is _____
4. A husband is _____
5. A husband is _____
6. A wife is _____
7. A wife is _____
8. A wife is _____
9. A wife is _____
10. A wife is _____
11. I expect my spouse to _____
12. I expect my spouse to _____
13. I expect my spouse to _____
14. I wish my partner would _____
15. I wish my partner would _____
16. I wish my partner would _____
17. I wish my partner would _____
18. I wish my partner would _____
19. I think s/he wants me to _____
20. I think s/he wants me to _____
21. I think s/he wants me to _____
22. I think s/he wants me to _____
23. I think s/he wants me to _____
24. When people get married, they _____
25. When people get married, they _____
26. Marriage is _____
27. Marriage is _____
28. Marriage is _____

One goal of the exercise is to take a closer look at how you view a husband, a wife, and marriage generally. Another purpose is to expose some "wishes" you have regarding your partner and how you perceive your partner would like *you* to change.

As with the other exercises in this book, complete the sentences independently of your partner, and then discuss your answers together. Look at your answers generally to see whether there's a single overriding flavor or recurring theme. If you find such a theme, concentrate on it to see what emotion is aroused in you. The theme may be something you want very much to get or keep in your life, or it may be a source of discontent or disturbance. The themes that emerge are reflective of both your values and your experience.

It's often useful and fun to copy the sentence roots and redo them several times on other occasions. You may find that your mood affects your answers, or you may discover a surprising consistency in your responses. You might also find inaccurate perceptions and then, as you continue exploring your feelings about marriage, discover that they have been corrected.

When interpreting the sentences you've created, consider that everything you've written, even if it seems very general, pertains to you. If, for example, you're a man and you wrote, "A husband is *the breadwinner*," you might be saying that as a husband, you feel *you* should be the main source of income. Your answer may also reflect the marriages you have seen around you (notably that of your parents), in which the husband's role has been presented as that of primary financial supporter. If you're a woman, the sentence might mean that you want to be taken care of by your husband, or even that your husband has forbidden you to make more than he does, and you resent it!

Another helpful exercise involves taking a moment to see what your immediate reactions are to some rather new family combinations. Mentally picture a couple who have chosen never to have children. Or a single parent who has adopted a child. How about a divorced father with three children, or a gay couple bound in their own "marriage"? What do you think of a married couple who have a 15-year-old child—and a newborn? Or the family that includes a teenage daughter with *her* baby? (Extended families are increasingly common: perhaps you know one in which grandparents, parents, and children harmoniously reside.) Try picturing an elderly couple who live together—perhaps a man and a woman, but the "couple" could easily be two—or more—women making their own "family ties." I've known many such people who are unrelated by blood or marriage, but are united by voluntary bonds in their own support networks. Such bonds typically occur among graduate students who are living in housing for married students; or among neighbors on a closely knit street.

Conjuring up these mental pictures can help you to see that "family" or "marriage" need not have one narrow meaning. Also, you can evaluate whether your perspectives jibe with the nature of your present relationship. I remember one vehement reaction to this exercise. Matthew, 23, a college student who was engaged but nervous about it, said:

I thought of a husband as a stodgy old guy who comes home from work and hides behind a newspaper in his easy chair until dinner. A wife was a plain-looking woman in a housedress in the kitchen baking a roast, or tending a child in a high chair. I know I'm not ready to assume that guy's role, and I'm scared that my fiancée will become that boring woman.

The exercise made me nervous about getting married! It's funny, because my two best friends got married last year—I was even the best man—and they're both the same fun-loving guys I knew. They've always been striving for success and responsible and warm. None of them hides behind a newspaper at night while the "little woman" whips up a meat loaf. They're out to dinner and the movies and at political meetings just like they used to be. Still, I know I'll gag when I introduce Leslie as "my wife," because I'm afraid I'll turn around to find her wearing a zip-front housedress!

If you find your stereotypes at odds with the future you want for yourself, or with the reality you now know, don't worry. You've pinpointed an area of thought that is ripe for revision, and you may be relieved to see that your fears have been based on stereotypes rather than on anything you should realistically concern yourself with.

How Expectations Have Changed

Given that throughout history, attitudes about family life have been very slow to change, American perceptions of what constitutes an acceptable marriage have undergone lightning-speed metamorphoses. The list on the following page contrasts many of the radical changes that have occurred.

Of course, in reality most marriages, old or new, are mixtures of these two ideals. A couple may go through some phases in which adoption of traditional roles is more satisfying and practical, and other phases when new roles are more appropriate. Just be sure to evaluate consciously the options and *choose* the type of marriage you want, rather than having a stereotyped notion imposed upon you. I remember Christine, who became a feminist in

Traditional Ideal	New Marriages
Definition of marriage: A good marriage is sturdy, stable, and constant and static. Mate selection: The man should be slightly older, taller, and better educated than his wife. Either he is in a "better" career than his wife or she does not work. No mixing of religions, races, or social strata.	A good marriage is elastic and changing; the relationship is constantly being renegotiated. More tolerance for any combination of ages, appearances, stations, races, religions, and achievements, as long as the match is "simpatico."
Roles: The man is dominant and "wears the pants in the family." There is a strict division of labor: the man brings home the bacon (i.e., is the monetary provider) while the woman tends to children and home.	Marriage is a partnership or a balance with husband and wife dominant approximately equal amounts of the time. More eqalitarian task-sharing, or a division of labor based on competence and preference.
Sex: Sex is the husband's right and the wife's duty. Sex is assumed but not discussed. The sexual double standard regarding philandering is accepted. Men fool around; wives forgive.	Enjoyable sex is the wife's right, too. Sex is discussed more often, creativity is encouraged, and dysfunctions are corrected. Fidelity is still valued, but equally for men and women. A philanderer is as likely to be a wife as a husband.
Children: There is an assumption that children are part of marriage (love, marriage, baby carriage). There is a minimum of two, with a boy preferred first.	Parenthood is optional. Having just one child is fine; having more than two is considered detrimental to the environment.
Communication: There is serenity at all times; no arguing is permitted, since the man's wishes are law.	Free venting of emotions is a sign of emotional health; honesty about one's feelings is valued.

the early 1970s. She looked around her and observed that her mother-in-law, Sally, was a servant to her husband. Sally had no money of her own, took verbal abuse, and spent all her time cooking, cleaning, and waiting on her husband hand and foot. Christine didn't think this was fair, and wanted to point this out to Sally. She explained the women's movement and the option of being called "Ms." She suggested that perhaps Sally's husband might share in some of the household chores, given that both partners worked. She tried to open up new options for her mother-in-law in a loving way.

Christine was perplexed and frustrated when her efforts failed. Sally did not see that she was in a disadvantageous role—just that this was the way it was supposed to be. She felt there was no other option open to her, and was secure in knowing her place and duties. Although she did not like the insults her husband regularly directed at her, she had learned to expect them and to live with them. The point of this story is that while the components of "new marriages" listed earlier appear to be fairer and more humanitarian, many people who were raised to think traditionally prefer their own way. They may even encourage others to find the same rewards they have gained from a traditional lifestyle.

Some women, in contrast, feel somewhat ashamed that they have not adopted a feminist lifestyle. However, as we strive for greater respect for individuals, we should abandon any prescriptions based solely on sex or status. There's nothing "wrong" with a mother choosing to forsake her career and stay home with her newborn child, just as it is not automatically "right" for a father to do so. Betty, a 32-year-old mother of three, was adamant about her need for respect. She lived in the Midwest and was married to a college professor. Since her marriage eight years ago, she'd never held a paying job. Betty was well-read, articulate, and serious. She said:

I'm tired of answering the question "What do you do?" with "I'm just a housewife." I'm raising three individuals, and that takes lots of intelligence, creativity, attention, energy, devotion, and love. How many jobs call for that combination? Twenty years ago I would've been praised; now I'm "not fulfilled," "wasting my potential," "underutilized," "underpaid." Either that, or I'm put on a pedestal. Either way, other people are telling me what I feel, and they have no business doing that. Sometimes I feel frustrated; other times, I have the time of my life. Basically, I'm doing a job I love, and the payment isn't in dollars. So don't condemn me for staying home, and don't deify me either. I'm choosing my career, just like the female executive and the teacher, and don't you dare second-guess what I have to say.

Betty's is one reaction to the new options. She's not blind to what others are doing, and she knows that she's going against the trend. But because she is consciously choosing her path, she is illustrating the fact that after an evaluation of the options, some people can be comfortable and happy by intentionally choosing tradition.

Compare Betty with Addie, one of the long-married women I interviewed. Addie, age 69, was overweight and sad-faced, and was still married to her high school sweetheart. She reported:

I see all these young girls around me carting their babies with them to their yoga classes. I might have been born too soon, because I never had the freedom to do as I pleased. I married Herb because he was the first boy who showed any attention. I had our four kids before I was 25, while he started out as a young accountant. I never learned to drive, because Herb made me so nervous the first time I tried it that I ran into a tree. I wasn't hurt, but he said if he caught me behind a wheel again, he'd shoot me.

Addie's face brightened as she remembered her brief period of working for pay:

During the war, I worked on an assembly line in Chicago. But when the boys returned, I was a full-time mother again. Frankly, I was pretty bored. My life consisted of walking the kids to school, taking the bus to the store, cleaning house, and talking on the phone. No wonder I rewarded myself with a half-gallon of ice cream! I've never been able to take the weight off since. I often think that if I'd had some opportunities, my life would have been a lot happier. I was always interested in law, but there was nothing a woman could do in that field. I might have become a lawyer or even a judge. I guess a few women were pioneering the field at the time, but Herb wouldn't hear of it; and the kids came along so quickly that I didn't have time to think. By the time they were in school, it was just too late and I lost my nerve to do anything on my own initiative.

Nowadays, men encourage their wives to work, partly because they need the money, but also because they don't feel so much obligation to prove they can support the family. It used to be that if the wife worked, it meant the man couldn't make ends meet; it was a disgrace. Now women want to work because that's the way they want to spend their time. It's a completely different world, and, I think, a better one.

So Betty had *chosen* to take a traditional role; Addie lived the role, but not of her own volition. Where Betty felt liberated, Addie felt trapped. This is a central difference between marriages today and marriages in the past: formerly, a traditional role was adopted because of indoctrination and custom; nowadays, the choice of a marriage style is more likely to be freely decided upon by the participants.

You've read two case studies about women who were obviously affected by changes in marital roles. But what about the men? What did they say were the benefits and drawbacks of each marital style?

Ben, 63, is one of the long-married men whom I interviewed. He is a marketing director for a medium-sized manufacturing firm in the Midwest. He began carefully:

My wife Marjorie and I grew up never considering that there was any other way. I didn't even allow myself to dream about possibilities. I went into the army and luckily was able to serve as a training officer here in the States. When I came out we got married. I knew that I simply had to support her, no ifs, ands, or buts. It was just my place to go and find a job, and it wasn't easy at first. I actually sold encyclopedias door to door for a while, until I got started working in public relations, writing ad copy for household bleach.

Marjorie insisted on working for three years. We needed the money, and she was trained as a nurse, so it made sense. But I really felt guilty. In those days, a woman working was like taking a job away from a man. And it was a sign that I was too poor to support her. Guys at work would tease me when she'd drive by to pick me up. They were struggling along, but their big badge of success was that their wives sat at home making chocolate cakes. Their homes were cramped brownstones, but they had this need to be the sole means of support.

I think our marriage was better because Marjorie and I felt it was "us against them." We felt like we were pulling together. I think she liked working, especially where her skills were so needed. We weren't planning to have children just yet, but when she got pregnant, we thought it was fate. If we were doing it all over, we might not have had any children. We love our two girls, but we really cherished our freedom. We wanted to travel to Europe, but we never had the time or money. We hope to go next summer. The point is that we never even had the choice. We wanted children because that was what you did—you got married and had children. At least we'd had those years of both working, so Marjorie wasn't stuck at home her whole life.

Ben said there had been one stretch of estrangement between him and Marjorie, after he discovered she had had a lover for some time. Ben felt that Marjorie's straying was a result of her boredom with the traditional wifely role:

We talked about it at the marriage encounter, and Marjorie said that she had felt stifled at home. She wanted excitement. She said that she didn't want to hurt me or disrupt our marriage, but that she just wanted a diversion from life. So you see, I suffered because women couldn't fulfill themselves in the workplace. If Marjorie could've gotten rewards from work, she wouldn't have strayed. And if we could've communicated more directly, if I had been able to tell her that I hated the stress of making mortgage payments, and that I cried, then we could've been closer all these years.

Ben regrets the time he lost because of the standards of days past. He has now advanced to a point where he enjoys the more open and honest relationships bred by the 1960s.

Another person who has benefited from new options is Aaron, a 33-year-old minister. He has been married to Angela for nine years. Angela has just completed medical school, after spending several years before that as a journalist. She also had just given birth to a baby boy. Aaron said:

Angela is more radical than I am. She's always been deeply involved in politics and human rights. That's one of the things I admire about her.

I was raised with traditional values, but in the sixties, my eyes opened up. Angela and I wanted to live together instead of getting married, but it would've hurt both of our families. We have a semi-open marriage mainly at her insistence; we've had other partners but only as extensions of friendships, not just for sex. I feel some ambivalence about this due to my upbringing, but Angela has a convincing argument: why deny the physical aspect of friendship?

I plan to spend two years just taking care of my son, while Angela completes her residency. Right now she wants to stay home with little Jason a while, putting her training on hold. The church gave me six months' paternity leave, and I took three, just to get to know the little guy. The fact that they would even consider such a thing, and that I would want to be home, is a revolution, a sign that we'll never return to those medieval days when men weren't allowed to see a diaper, and women rarely were admitted to medical school. I also think that the quality of my relationship with Angela is much different than it would have been, and it's certainly much different than either of our parents had. They jokingly call us their "new age children," because we represent all the changes in society since their day.

My father, whose greatest pride in life was having a minister for a son, has started bragging *first* about his "doctor daughter" and *then* about his grandchild!

How Social Changes Are Affecting New Relationships

Probably the biggest effect of all the new options is confusion. When you first meet someone, what information do you have by which to judge the other person? At first, unless you've read the person's biography, all you have to go on is looks. Maybe the following scenario is familiar to you.

At a party, two people are introduced. What's going on inside their minds?

HE: Hmm, she's kind of cute. Brunette hair in a current style, clothes safe, but with a dash of flair from that red scarf. She's wearing makeup, and carries herself with authority, so she's probably a career gal, maybe in business. I wonder if she makes more money than I do? She's got a great body—she probably works out or maybe jogs. No low-cut clothes, but that silk kind of outlines her figure suggestively. I bet she's great in the sack; probably had lots of lovers. I'd better be careful or she'll show me up—better remember to ask what she likes, and spend just enough time kissing. . . .

SHE: Not bad. Love his hair—it's got some great sun streaks. I bet he's into outdoor sports, maybe tennis or softball. Nice body, too—broad shoulders. Maybe he's a swimmer. And those hazel eyes! He's wearing a nice sport jacket—he's got some taste and probably some money. I wonder if he makes more than me? Maybe he's a doctor or a lawyer. I wonder if he's married. You can't tell nowadays, but it doesn't look as if he's at the party with anyone else. Could he be gay?

If all you have to go on is looks, you'll make deductions based on limited clues. If you're male, these will probably tend to focus on a woman's physical attributes; if you're female, you'll probably estimate a man's occupation and financial status. As a reflection of recent social changes, men are now starting to think about occupation and wealth, and women are allowing themselves to focus on the physical. Both genders are more likely to question the degree to which their own position—traditional or "liberated"—will be acceptable to the other person. Because the range of perspectives and behaviors is now so large, there's much groping and testing as people try to maintain a prospective partner's interest while balancing self-assertion with courtesy.

There are three major ways in which new values are influencing how men and women interact. As you read the discussion on page 105, think about the importance of each trend in your own current or past relationship.

1. *People are open to a wider range of partners.* In just one "First Comes Love" workshop group, I remember seeing an older woman with a man fifteen years her junior; a racially mixed couple; a man divorced three times (father of six children) with a woman who anticipated starting her first family; a widowed couple in their sixties debating marriage versus cohabitation; and a pair of college freshmen (the woman was the mother of a two-year-old child). Each of these duos represented a type of coupling that many people would not have accepted even fifteen years ago. The fact that attitudes have changed does not mean that harassment of and discrimination against such couples have disappeared. But the situation has eased to the point where the automatic reaction in most locales is not open hostility. It's desensitization: once we tolerate a taste of variety, it's easier to accept the gamut of human combinations.

Melissa, 33, a real-estate developer, started revising her concept of what types of men were acceptable because she couldn't find a partner within her limited parameters.

For years, I searched for an unmarried Jewish man, about my age, living in the same city, who wouldn't be threatened by my achievements. Every man I found had a flaw. Either they were weak, were unambitious themselves, lacked self-confidence, or were afraid of commitment. I'd spend nights alone in my apartment wondering if I'd ever get married and have a family. It was as if my whole life was just completing itself without allowing me the experiences I wanted most.

So I just decided to widen my scope. I started dating older men and younger men. I was nervous at first, but I finally got over it and started judging each person as an individual. Then I decided to expand my geographical range. I met two men at a national conference, and had a fling with one and now commute about once a month to see the other. I won't give up my criterion on religion, though, because my Jewish identity is central to me, and I'd definitely want to share that with my husband. But I've even started dating men who are just separated from their wives, not divorced yet, and ones with more than one child. I want my *own* family, but if I don't start loosening up, I'll never have anyone to have it with.

Melissa's words were echoed by Sandra, 38, a striking black woman who headed the management training program of a national insurance firm. As an executive, she found that she was seldom exposed to people who met her criteria for the perfect match.

Frankly, I used to be into black pride and the civil rights movement. I felt I should find a strong black man and prove the stereotypes wrong. I wanted someone to stand up to society and succeed as fully as I have. Now, I still think it would be great to find someone like that, but do you have any idea how few really powerful black men there are?

After the two loves of my life ended, I finally let down my resistance, and went out to dinner with a white colleague from a competing firm. He had just gone through a divorce, and I suppose we each considered the other safe. We were first drawn together by common business interests, and slowly, over a six-month period of lunches, realized that we were attracted to each other. It was unsettling for both of us, because he had been brought up with the usual prejudices, and I had created so many. After we finally confronted our feelings and got together, it amused us to discover that our co-workers had considered us a pair for four months already! Just goes to show that public acceptance has come a long way.

Melissa and Sandra enlarged their vistas out of necessity, but I talked to a group of high school students who took for granted that anything—or anyone—goes. One 17-year-old boy said casually that his older cousin and he had dated when he was 14 (in fact, he had lost his virginity to her); one girl said snippishly that it was nobody's business but her own whom she dated; another girl claimed that she preferred men over 35; and a boy was actually embarrassed to admit that he'd only dated girls in his high school. There may be a 1950s fashion revival going on, but it's a whole new crowd beneath the mineral oil-slicked hair and wraparound sunglasses.

2. *Expectations about a partner's behavior have changed.* In some ways, we now expect more of our mates; in others, we expect less. We expect more emotional expression (of caring and love as well as feelings about what is happening in a partner's life). We expect more self-confidence and assertiveness, especially on the part of women. We expect more independence, a willingness to try new experiences, and greater tolerance of other people.

So much for commonly *raised* expectations. Other expectations have been lowered. Many women no longer expect a man to be chivalrous, opening doors and holding a woman's coat just because she's a woman. Many men no longer expect to pay for an entire evening out, unless they volunteer to do so (or the arrangement is understood because they did the inviting). The phrase "let's go dutch" is getting much heavier use. More significantly, men are no longer expected to put up a "macho" front, and women are no longer expected to cry at the slightest provocation. It's no longer required that the man be the social or sexual aggressor; women can now take the initiative.

Keep in mind that we're talking about *expectations*, not necessarily a greatly changed reality. Most women are still uncomfortable with making the first overture toward a man (such as asking him out for a date), and most men still prefer to be the sexual aggressor. Several of the people I interviewed stated emphatically that they are turned off when traditional roles are reversed. Still, they no longer make rigid assumptions about what will happen.

3. *Expectations of oneself have changed.* As expectations of the other person have shifted, so have personal expectations. In fact, raised standards have led to many divorces. Situations that might have been endured in the past "for the sake of the children," "because marriage means 'til death us do part,'" or "because of what the neighbors or my family would say," are no longer good enough. "Who cares what anybody else thinks?" said a 56-year-old woman, recently divorced. "Pretty soon you realize that you've got to please yourself."

To please themselves, lovers are, first of all, demanding intimacy—a real sharing of feelings and a strong sensitivity to what the other person is going through. Women are demanding sexual fulfillment—no more faked orgasms or unenjoyable maneuvers just to please the man. Another requisite for an acceptable relationship is independence. Many men *and women* are now demanding that they have enough freedom to continue outside friendships and have some private time. This change is a major departure from the days when "togetherness" was thought to be an unquestioned boon to a relationship, and women were expected to mold their schedules around their men.

Some people argue that these changes are simply reflections of the "me generation," and are narcissistic symbols of selfishness. I would reply that it's far better to understand what you want and work to get it, than to stew and suffer while continuing in a deprived state. One of the negatives of some old-fashioned relationships was an inherent unfairness. Some men expected everything from their relationship (love, emotional support, respect, obedience, sex, housecleaning, food preparation, personal hygiene) while their women expected very little (financial support mainly, with the hope of love and kindness and a small amount of fatherly participation). No wonder feminists often yearned for a wife of their own! The turnabout in values is not a pendulum effect (a reactionary swing) but rather an acknowledgment of individual needs, and an attempt to bring satisfaction to both partners.

All these changes stem from a redefinition of what a couple is. A couple is now less of a single unit that is melded into one entity. Instead, it's a combination of two separate individuals who are in a relationship because they love each other and continue to find satisfaction together. Ideally each person has confidence in himself or herself, so there's less reliance on a partner for status or identity. To most people, it's a relief to have these new choices; to others, it's heresy, a shredding of moral fiber. Fortunately, both attitudes are tolerated these days.

New Choices, New Problems

The "new couple" faces new questions concerning what behaviors are appropriate. Generally, the issues are more problematic for women then for men.

- "How much should I compromise myself to please a man?" Melissa, mentioned earlier, was in a real quandry. She wanted to find a mate but hated to misrepresent who she was in order to hook one. Instead, she broadened her circle to include a larger number of men, some of whom, she hoped, would want her just as she was. Other women, who had already found partners, wondered how much they should bend in order to keep their men. (In the past, women automatically tended to accommodate their partners, even if this meant sacrificing their identities.) While women now feel justified is asking men to respect their beliefs and desires, they are unsure of how far they can go before they cause alienation.

The solutions that women find are individual and seem to depend as much on the man as on the woman's values. "When I was with Bill, I would have sold my soul for him," commented a secretary in her twenties. "But now, with Peter, I refuse to cater to him. Bill, you see, was loving and warm, but Peter has a temper and is rather cool. He's got a lot going for him otherwise, but I find that if I demand more from him, I get a better response."

A stockbroker in her thirties admitted: "I'm confused over this one. I know I should stand up for my needs, and I make them known, but it's a lot easier and more comfortable for me to acquiesce. Why should I make myself nervous about confronting my boyfriend when I can let it all blow over and just relax?"

A department store clerk asked: "You know what happened when I was all gung-ho for women's liberation? I started demanding this and that, right and left, and pretty soon I'd lost my fiancé and couldn't get a date. People started calling me 'a dyke,' which really hurt even though I believe in lesbian rights. But I'm *not* a 'dyke,' nor do I like the connotation. For a long time I just said they were wrong and I was right, until one Saturday night, in about my fifth month without a real date, I decided it wasn't worth it. I started to 'soften up,' and finally learned that you have to give as well as take. I can't expect men to change overnight, and so I have to be patient and just try to educate them when I can."

- "My job's in New York, and my man's in L.A." How do women choose between the two? Traditionally, a man would follow his career, and his woman would follow him. Nowadays, many women are torn because they have invested so much in job preparation or have come to see greater potential for self-fulfillment. They cherish a good relationship, and don't want to damage it by causing a trailing spouse to resent them. Cynthia's marriage broke up because her husband refused to make the third career move in seven years. Cynthia made her difficult choice with the explanation, "There are many men who can love me, but if I stop my career momentum, I'll never regain it again."

More common is a woman's response that her relationship has first priority. "Joe makes me happy, it's as simple as that," said a 44-year-old middle manager. "I like my work, but I *love* my husband. My family life is the foundation for everything else I do. If I didn't have my career, I'd survive. In fact, there are days when I want a permanent vacation. But I love the weekends; I love traveling with my husband. We have a special communication. Work is stimulating, but I could be laid off tomorrow. With luck, my marriage will last a lifetime."

- "Why can't I have it all?" Women are told they can be achievers, super-moms, multi-orgasmic lovers, and beauties. They try for everything and soon feel like hamsters running on an endless wheel. They see magazine interviews with role models (many of whom have cash for full-time nannies) and feel guilty or incompetent for not matching those women's successes. Women can come to feel that each arena of performance is all-demanding. To be a great career person, you need to give your work sixty hours a week and constant thought. To be a super-mom, you need enough energy to spend "quality time" with your children. To reap the orgasms due you, you need to have the zip to contort in bed. And to look like a model you need three hours a day at the gym and in front of the makeup mirror. No way.

So women often stagger their successes. One week, they'll be super-mom; another they'll look like Jane Fonda. Either that or they accept the fact that they *can't* "have it all" at once. A woman may take three years off from her job to be a full-time mother (and overlap being a beauty and loving wife) and then return to the workplace, sacrificing part of her sex life and some porcelain fingernails. Even a woman who arrives at such a compromise may still have a nagging conflict about what she *could* be doing.

The problem originates with the wife, who feels simultaneously pulled to the success and status of the workplace, and the emotional rewards and pleasures of the home. Increasingly, however, the question of what to do is moot, because women's incomes are often a necessity rather than a luxury. They simply can't *afford* to give up their paychecks. Instead, they work and frequently feel guilty that they can't be with their children.

Naturally, men must deal with the problems mentioned above too. They may have to help a partner who is grappling with her need to develop a new identity, or decide whether to move if a partner finds a cross-country job. Overall, though, men appear to have it easier. They don't usually even *consider* compromising their values to please women; they are less likely to meet resistance when they contemplate a career move; and they enjoy advancement in the marketplace that is based on performance rather than ability to field flirtations well. Also, many men *do not care* a great deal about "having it all," because they get so many satisfactions from their work. There's an emerging group of men who value parenting, but most don't find staying with a child on a full-time basis attractive.

So, deciding to get married—or even to say hello to someone of the opposite sex—can be fraught with confusion, ambiguities, and conflicting desires. Fortunately, an increasing number of men and women are at least recognizing the pitfalls of rapid social change, and are attempting to cope with problems honestly.

There's no such thing as a perfectly liberated man—anymore than there is a completely liberated woman. We're all shaped by our upbringing, our developing consciousness of inequities, and our personal values, expectations, and feelings. By reading about common reactions in this era of flux, perhaps you can more easily work through difficulties in your own relationship.

SECTION *Three*

Bases for Marriage

IN SECTION II, "New Trends in Relationships," you did a lot of reading and thinking. The main purpose was information-gathering—helping you to gain ways of comparing your own perceptions and beliefs with those of others. Section III provides more participatory evaluation of your personal situation. You'll find questionnaires designed to help you understand how you cope with various aspects of your relationship. You'll also begin examining your feelings as a means for making (or confirming) your marital choice.

/ 6
Personal History and Patterns

TWO INDIVIDUALS are the raw materials of every relationship, so each person should have a sense of self apart from the other person. As discussed in Section II, this is a new development—today it is much less common to see a marital unit built around the man, with the woman only a "helpmeet." In this chapter, you'll focus on your own history in order to see how it affects the way you deal with your present partner (and, perhaps, how it affected your past relationships).

Patterns Weave Your Future

Some people think they need a crystal ball in order to view their futures. They fall in love and hope that the sheer intensity of their feelings will make for a lifetime of bliss. Caught up in a daze of infatuation, intimacy, planning, and excitement, they overlook an opportunity to improve their chances for happiness by working at their relationship.

Even though you don't have a crystal ball, or much inkling of events that will transpire in your future, you do have a potent tool for looking ahead: your past. Social scientists called "futurists" make their predictions about what's to come by projecting the continuation of certain key trends. They often suggest alternative futures, based on a series of "what if" questions. What if there's a huge oil glut? What if a cure for cancer is found? What if women decide not to have babies? Futurists play with these possibilities and put percentages of likelihood next to each scenario they create. You can do the same, in a simplified way.

All you have to do is discover the patterns in your life. Everybody has a repertoire of strategies for dealing with events.

These may, or may not, be the most efficient and constructive approaches at your disposal. They were developed because in your youth they worked. They've now become habit and have served you throughout your adult years. You may have purposefully changed some of the strategies; others may have been replaced out of expediency or because of repeated negative results. Still, by identifying general trends in your past behavior, you can more realistically project what your future with your mate will be like.

By pinpointing your habits and strategies, you'll also have a new opportunity to revise them—and to do so in harmony with your partner's desires. You may find that some coping methods you used in the past are ineffective in your present life. You also might find that your usual reactions are agreeable and "right," and can continue to serve you well.

A Snapshot of Your Past

Here's a chance to revisit your past. The "Personal History Questionnaire" (Part I) is designed to give you a perspective on events that shaped your present patterns.

As you can see, the first part of this exercise looks at "ancient history," your childhood. Important determinants of your present patterns include your parents' relationship, childhood social experiences, and school experiences. Most people look at a questionnaire like this and think, "What fun: time for some amusement!" But some of the questions may require some serious and perhaps painful thinking. The questionnaire probably touches on areas about which you are very sensitive or defensive. It might raise issues you'd like to explore with a professional counselor. The purpose of all this isn't to open up old wounds but to identify connections between what you experienced or learned in the past and what you do *now*.

For example, say you're nervous about getting married and have a history of getting close to someone and then, when the going gets serious, pulling away. Perhaps your family moved around a lot, and just as you were making friends, you'd have to uproot. The first time or two, you experienced emotional pain. You reacted by building a protective armor to avoid that happening again. Perhaps you would let people come only so close, and then would do something to alienate them or to convince yourself that the friendship wasn't really worth it. And now you're doing it

PERSONAL HISTORY QUESTIONNAIRE—Part I

Childhood

A. FAMILY

1. Describe your mother in three words. _____

2. How close were you to your mother:
   a. during early childhood?   very close   somewhat close   caring but not close   distant
   b. during late childhood?   very close   somewhat close   caring but not close   distant
   c. during your teens?   very close   somewhat close   caring but not close   distant

3. Describe your father in three words. _____

4. How close were you to your father:
   a. during early childhood?   very close   somewhat close   caring but not close   distant
   b. during late childhood?   very close   somewhat close   caring but not close   distant
   c. during your teens?   very close   somewhat close   caring but not close   distant

5. Choose one word to describe each of your sisters and brothers (use extra paper if needed).

   Sibling A   Sibling B   Sibling C
   name: _____   name: _____   name: _____
   word: _____   word: _____   word: _____

Personal History and Patterns 117

6. Choose a word to describe your *childhood relationship* with each sister or brother.
7. Choose three words to describe your parents' relationship (if both are at home).

8. How did your parents handle your sex education?

B. GROWING UP

	Person 1	Person 2	Person 3
9. Name three other important people in your childhood, and choose a word to describe your relationship with each.	name: _____ word: _____	name: _____ word: _____	name: _____ word: _____

10. Describe any health or physical problems of childhood.
11. Describe any special achievements of childhood.
12. Choose three words to describe your childhood.
13. Name two turning points for you during your childhood. 1. _____ 2. _____
14. What at-home chores did you do? What outside work experience did you have?
   a. ages 8–12

b. 13–17 _____
   c. ages 18–21 _____
15. "My largest concerns during each period below were:"
   a. in elementary school years _____
   b. in years 12–14: _____
   c. in years 14–18: _____
16. As a child, how many friends did you have? _____
   Who were the friends you remember best? _____
17. As a child, what did you want to be when you grew up? _____
   What influenced your eventual choice? _____
18. Describe your physical appearance at the ages below:
   a. age 10 _____
   b. age 14 _____
   c. age 18 _____

C. SCHOOL

19. "My school grades were generally:"
   a. elementary school   outstanding   good   average   below average   poor
   b. junior high / middle school   outstanding   good   average   below average   poor
   c. high school   outstanding   good   average   below average   poor
20. "If I were a teacher judging my school personality, I'd say I was" (one phrase or word per level):
   a. elementary school _____
   b. junior high / middle school _____
   c. high school _____
21. "The subjects I was good at were:" _____
22. "The subjects I was worst in were:" _____

Personal History and Patterns

with your prospective partner, even though you dearly want to find permanent love and hate the way you behave.

So what do you do about harmful behaviors that have persisted into the present? Here are some suggestions.

1. Just by realizing the source of your behavior, you've made a major advance. Such knowledge can help you to put your experience in its proper perspective and, perhaps, feel differently about the current situation. In the example about loss of friends, to overcome being overly "armored," you might try visualizing your friends missing you and making new friends.

2. You can use your daydreams to imagine a positive outcome of your present relationship. To continue with our example, you might think ahead and imagine you are married. Let yourself experience all your emotions, and then intentionally end the scenario with your partner reassurring you that he or she will always be there to provide love and support. This positive experience, even if it *is* only in your mind, can break the automatic reaction of withdrawing.

3. Discuss a problem with your partner to help dispell your fears. The process of discussing your revelations is a very significant way to overcome negative patterns, because you get the support of a "team member" who is rooting for you to change. Also, just by talking about your past and about your present behavior that relates to it, you have another opportunity to figure out connections. You can get some feedback from your partner as to the logic of your interpretations.

Often, people realize that their childhoods weren't very happy and that they've been dealing with unresolved feelings ever since. Tina, a 37-year-old divorced mother of two, was able to trace her compulsion to eat chocolate when under stress to her childhood role.

My mother would tell me to do the dishes, and my father would say, "No, that's too hard for Tina." Everything was too hard or I was too young or too dumb to do it. Now, I seem to ruin all my chances for a good relationship, and choose men who are really, for the most part, losers. And it struck me that perhaps I came to believe my father. I think I'm too dumb, or having a really great relationship is too hard for me. I give up on anything worthwhile because, underneath, I guess I don't think I deserve it. How could I? I'm just a child, incapable of doing even the simplest tasks! I flee to the solice of my Hershey bars because only when alone munching do I get sweet revenge and feel comforted.

I told Tina to just make one simple adjustment when she was tempted to give up. "Eliminate the word 'too,' " I said. "Maybe going back for your college degree *is* hard, but it's not *too* hard. You have to get yourself believing you can do it, or else you'll never try and will keep perpetuating the failure you set up for yourself." I could see Tina's brow furrowing with worry. She might have been thinking that changing her habit was "too hard."

Nevertheless, Tina made a bargain with me that she would consciously revise her thinking just for one week. The next time I saw her, she was beaming. "I repaired an old dresser that had been bugging me for years," she said, "and I saw a counselor at the local college about finishing my degree. You know what? It wasn't nearly as bad as I thought it would be. And now I have tangible evidence that I *can* accomplish things if I just *do* them."

The "Personal History Questionnaire" (Part II) is a continuation of the one you just completed. This time, you'll look at your adult history, in the areas of work, relationships, and personal characteristics. After you complete the questions about yourself, it's a good idea to ask your partner independently to make judgments about you on items 14 through 27. By comparing your ratings with those of your partner, you may be able to spot areas where your picture of yourself differs from the way your partner perceives you. You may also gain ideas for changing your behavior.

Here are highlights of Sam and Denise's experience. Under "work-related flaws" (item 5), Sam noted that he tended to procrastinate. As a free-lance writer, he had to set his own schedule. He'd do anything to avoid the blank page, including replanting the garden, writing thank-you notes, and getting his hair cut. He finally would get around to writing at the eleventh hour—literally.

Denise wrote down the same flaw and, in the discussion that followed, said that not only did his last-minute panics bother her—she was the receptacle for his anxiety—but he procrastinated in other areas as well. Whenever they had to get a wedding gift, for example, she'd have to go after it, or it wouldn't get to the church on time. If Sam had a cavity, Denise had to goad him into seeing a dentist before he reached the point of wailing in pain. Sam's pattern was to avoid unpleasantries, causing inconvenience to those around him. Sam admitted this and said he hated this characteristic; he explained, however, that putting tough tasks out of his mind minimized his anxiety. Denise suggested that his

PERSONAL HISTORY QUESTIONNAIRE—PART II

Adult Background

1. Summarize your feelings about your post–high school education. _____

2. Name three reasons why you liked whatever job was your favorite. _____, _____, _____

3. Name three reasons why you disliked whatever job was your least favorite. _____, _____, _____

4. What special skills do you have that make you a valuable employee? (give at least 3) _____

5. What bad habits or work-related flaws do you have? _____

6. If I could do anything I wanted as far as work is concerned, with no financial worries, I would: _____

7. Name the three most important rewards you're looking for in your work. _____, _____, _____

8. Summarize in one sentence how you got into the field in which you now work. _____

9. Compared with most people,
   my social life since my teens
   has been: Very full   somewhat full   feast or famine   dull

10. Over the years, I've found I
    like to:

    stick with   stick with   maintain   be by
    one partner   someone   several   myself
                        a while and then   relation-   usually
                        move on   ships

11. How have these others usually reacted to my relationships?
    a. family: _____
    b. friends: _____

12. Looking back over the people you've been involved with, what three characteristics did they all seem to have in common? _____ , _____ , _____

13. Name the two most important romantic relationships you've had, and why you feel each was significant.
    1. _____
    2. _____

14. What percentage of the time do I like to be with others, and what percentage do I prefer to be alone?
    _____ with others + _____ alone = 100%

15. When I'm under stress, these are the two things I usually do:
    1. _____ 2. _____ .

16. On a scale of 1 to 10, with 1 = boundless energy and 10 = constantly exhausted, I'd rate my energy level a _____.

17. Given a choice, I'd rather do a: (check one) _____ physical activity _____ intellectual activity

18. Given a choice, I'd rather: (check one) _____ travel _____ stay at home and relax

19. On a lazy Sunday, the three things I most enjoy doing are: _____ , _____ , _____ .

20. On a scale of 1 to 10, with 1 = a complete optimist and 10 = a total pessimist, I'd rate my outlook on life a _____

21. When annoying noises, inconveniences, or problems with people occur, I'd rate my tolerance (on a scale of 1 to 10, with 1 = extremely easygoing and 10 = very impatient) a _____.

22. Playfulness level: rate yourself on a scale of 1 to 10, with 1 = extremely playful and 10 = rigid._____
    Here are some more indicators:
    a. Do you gladly dress up in a costume on Halloween? yes _____ no _____
    b. Do you sing Christmas carols or the National Anthem with gusto? yes _____ no _____
    c. Do you like to wear flamboyant outfits and bright colors? yes _____ no _____
    d. Do you sometimes laugh uncontrollably in public? yes _____ no _____

23. Some people are workaholics and overachievers. Others choose to enjoy life through relaxation. Place yourself on this continuum:
    workaholic _____
    destructively lazy _____

24. Some people plan things in meticulous detail; others are spontaneous and willing to deal with unknowns. Place yourself on this continuum:
    cautious planner _____
    spontaneous _____

25. Name the two best features of your body: _____

26. Rate your physical activity on a scale from 1 to 10 (10 = extremely active; 1 = sedate)._____

worry could be replaced by *positive rewards* if he only broke down the steps to accomplishment and completed each step, one by one, at the earliest opportunity.

Denise, in answering item 12 on the questionnaire, had written that the people she had been involved with tended to be struggling in their careers and poor. Sam thought a moment and, putting this information together with the way Denise helped him through crises, suggested that maybe she liked to mother her men. He confessed that he didn't like it when she reminded him to get cracking on his work, or when she urged him to wear his sweater on a cold day. Sam also confessed that he liked many aspects of her mothering. He concluded that perhaps they should *both* try to be a little more independent and a little more expressive of their needs.

Denise and Sam found that they had given similar answers to many questions; on other items they differed but in ways they found agreeable. In answering item 18, Sam noted that he'd rather stay home than travel; Denise preferred the open road. Sam put himself toward the "lazy" side of the achievement-need continuum (item 23), while Denise said she was more of a "workaholic." Sam and Denise felt these differences were complementary and enhanced their relationship, helping to prevent monotony.

Working through the questionnaire also helped correct some misperceptions. Denise had the idea that she was quite serious and gave herself a low playfulness rating. Sam pointed out some of the zany, lighthearted antics she'd pulled over the past several months, and made Denise feel pleased that she was well-balanced. Sam indicated that he had a poor physical self-image, which Denise lovingly corrected.

Building on Strengths

Everybody has some areas in which they excel, and others in which they are weak. Here, the reference is not to innate characteristics but to learned skills or abilities that can be cultivated. You and your partner can *use* differences in strengths to help each other and solidify your relationship. The goal is for you to exchange talents by teaching your strengths to your partner and vice versa. On a separate sheet of paper, make two lists for each person: strengths and weaknesses.

Denise's strenghts included mechanical aptitude, cooking

skill, a musical background, and mathematical ability. Sam's were writing ability, organizational skills, a green thumb, travel experience, knowledge of history, and an ability to deal well with people. Sam and Denise decided to trade cooking for organizational skills, musical education for pointers on how to get along with others. They set aside time for instruction, and made an effort to compliment and assist the other as they practiced their fledgling skills.

Tom, a doctor, and his wife Diane, a psychologist, have put this to practice in their relationship. After all, they note, it was the magnetism of qualities they lacked in themselves that fired their initial passion. "I was an ivory tower researcher, and Diane was involved in a school," Tom explained. Diane felt lost in a setting of campus intellectuals, while Tom was less socially adroit in everyday situations. Their trade involved having Diane tutor Tom in communication skills while Tom initiated his wife into the wiles of academe. In the process, each admitted vulnerability in some areas. This helped to wipe away pretenses between them and bring them closer.

"Our model is climbing," Diane said, tugging an imaginary figure from the floor onto the chair beside her. "One person takes a step upward and pulls the other to that level, then the next progresses further, helping the other to new heights." This method of mutual assistance, they say, helps many of their clients, whose marriages have slid into compartmentalized corners.

In fact, the usual division of labor for couples actually prohibits the less competent partner from attempting to improve his or her skills. "Here, let me do that," said Gail, as her husband rather clumsily attempted to toss the salad. Instead of letting him practice harmlessly, or showing him a better way, Gail reinforced his feeling that he had better stay out of the kitchen. Then, of course, she complained that she was stuck doing all the cooking.

The Role You Assume

I never cease to be amazed at people's adaptability and flexibility. Many individuals, given a particular family setting or style that they must deal with, quickly discover the most painless and profitable way to survive. When you were a child, you found your role within the general parameters set by your parents (or, if your parents abdicated, as dictated by other members of the family). In other words, you cleverly found the best way to cope with your relatives and receive the most attention—or divert attention, if it tended to be negative. Sometimes, children are forced to develop patterns that work well in a certain family situation but are unconstructive in other settings. You imbed these behaviors in your character, and carry them with you (your "baggage") into your adult relationships.

This is no problem if you had an exemplary family that was characterized by an uncompetitive atmosphere, high self-esteem, and even temperaments. Few of us were that lucky. But even in the healthiest of families, people assume roles simply because they help the family to function more smoothly. If by implied or spoken consensus, one person is the leader, another the nurturer, and a third the dependent one, then there are fewer disputes and time is not wasted at every decision point. Everyone assumes roles throughout life; that, in itself, is normal and expedient. (For example, the role of "mother" comes with a set of duties and privileges, as do the roles "teacher," "uncle," "femme fatale," and "tennis expert.") Just make sure that the roles you take on now are voluntary rather than means of self-defense left over from childhood.

To help you make that determination, some commonly adopted roles are listed below. See which ones fit with your own behavior. Though some of them seem undesirable, remember that they were originally developed as part of a very desirable ability to cope with a given family environment. They are divided into two major categories: "rulers" and "the ruled." Most traditional families have at least one of each. In modern, balanced relationships, loving couples may alternate roles, or take on certain ones in certain circumstances. As you read, please keep in mind that there usually are no "cutoffs" where one role ends and another begins. The discussions are generalized: a particular relationship will lie somewhere on a *continuum*, and the only measure of its success is the happiness of the people involved.

Rulers

The boss is usually a dictator—sometimes benevolent, sometimes not. In traditional families, this may be the father who tells his questioning child, "You'll do it because I say so!" Whether male or female, the boss "wears the pants in the family"; this person's word is law. Often, the boss is someone who gets little respect outside of the family (e.g., has a low-prestige job) and so uses the home arena as a means of self-validation and a source of some control over an otherwise uncontrollable world. Most bosses come into their status by accident or birth rather than by earning their power. Men frequently expect to have such clout and assume it as their birthright.

Women may also assume this position automatically, or they may manipulate their way into it by making others feel incompetent. Some women become bosses by default, when their partners leave. The boss role involves considerable responsibility, but it has far more bountiful benefits to a person who likes having his or her will obeyed.

The achiever earns attention by living up to or exceeding expectations of performance. First-born children are classically achievers, because before their siblings were born, they learned to captivate their parents by pleasing them. Achievers belong in the "ruler" category because their accomplishments are usually worthy of universal respect. Typically, they are highly educated, rise to positions of authority in the workplace, and are outgoing and self-confident. With these qualities, they rule not only their younger siblings but everyone else in their environments. The downside of being an achiever is that this type of person tends to have a large need for love. Achievers' self-validation comes less from the control they have over others than from the praise and attention they earn via their achievements.

In an adult relationship, being an achiever can be a problem in instances where the person doesn't receive sufficient strokes from others. Also, any failure in the "cruel world" can cause an achiever to crash emotionally, with the result that more support is needed from a partner. Usually bosses, achievers, and the other types of "rulers" pair with "the ruled" because this enables them to command the responsiveness and caring they need. If taken to excess, this behavior—where partners feed off of each other so that the worst characteristics of each person are fueled—adds up to a symbiotic relationship.

The provider wins his or her rewards via tangible evidence of competence. The provider (who may also be a boss, though not necessarily) buys nonessentials and places great importance on these items being in abundance or of the finest quality made. Like achievers, providers need the admiration of others. But they attract it by what they *have* rather than by what they have *done*.

Jerry had never attended college, but even before he got a lucrative job in the entertainment industry, he had the aura of wealth. He stretched his credit to the limit to buy a $30,000 sports car, filled his house with original art, and took his friends to expensive restaurants, bribing the maître d' into deference. Once into some money, he bought his lover, Helene, spectacular jewels and a Mercedes. He needed to wow 'em for his ego's sake. He expected continual adulation in return, which his acquaintances provided. From his lover he expected humility and subservience; she also obliged.

The nurturer finds his or her niche in playing parent. Self-validation comes from the gratefulness of those being nurtured and the sense of competence earned from "doing" for others. Of course, parents play the primary nurturing role. They belong in the category of "ruler" because they generally have emotional control over their children, being able to instill guilt in them if they don't kneel in appreciation and awe. Also, since the nurturer's primary source of rewards is the child or partner, that other person feels a burden of responsibility for the nurturer's happiness. The child or partner has to behave dependently just to allow the nurturer the opportunity to feel needed and competent. This is symbiosis in action.

Edna was an only child, and her mother didn't work. She learned that to keep her mother's love, she had better give her something to do, someone to dote on. So whenever her mother started looking peaked, Edna caught a cold or the flu. The mother would perk up immediately, as she called her folk wisdom into action and valiantly nursed Edna back to health. Once healthy, Edna had to find another need for her mother to fill. She would have trouble with her mathematics or stop eating, and her mother would step in to help. When she was 17, in an effort to get out from under her mother's domination, Edna found a nurturer of her own to marry. She continues to be protected and fussed over.

The Ruled

The most common type of "ruled" personality is that of the *dependent person*. Edna is a clear example of this type. Just as her mother needed to nurture, Edna required taking care of. All of "the ruled" gain satisfying attention from their rulers, and in this respect, Edna was secure in her mother's devotion. She never wondered whether someone loved her, because her mother was giving her *life* for her! Being dependent has many other rewards too: protection from the world, avoidance of scary tasks, little external pressure. And dependent people control in their own way, by causing responses in their "rulers." Edna made Mother hop to it by getting the sniffles or a D on her math test. Dependent people have a sense of power, even if it is only over one other person.

Traditionally, women were taught to be dependent in their relationships with men. "Fascinating Womanhood," a philosophy advanced by Helen Andelin in a book of that name, urges women to be submissive and dependent as a manipulative tool. The idea is that if a woman needs protecting, her man will rise to the occasion. If she gives unconditional love, never asks for favors, remains uncritical, and acts very, very feminine, then her man will be appreciative and respond with the hugs and kisses she so desperately desires. Many women don't subscribe to the particulars of this approach but have incorporated some of its tenets, mainly because the feminine behavior is effective in getting them what they want.

A lot of men are dependent, too. These are the familiar Caspar Milquetoasts and doormats, the mild-mannered Clark Kents who never seem to find a phone booth. Some of these men, however, are Supermen at work and sink into submission only when they reach the front door. Perhaps they view their wives as mothers, and enjoy being taken care of as a contrast with the competitiveness and difficult decision-making they must deal with in the business world.

The victim invites criticism or sympathy by "letting" others treat him or her badly. Victims have very low self-esteem and often think they deserve punishment, so they accept verbal or physical abuse. As a child, the victim might be routinely ridiculed for having big ears, or for being stupid or clumsy. Instead of lashing out or trying to prove them wrong, the victim assumes that others are right and takes it.

Some victims have rich fantasy lives, escaping their torturers by envisioning situations of excitement and success. Others wear their deficiencies like a badge of honor, almost proclaiming to outsiders, "I'm the stupid one, so you'd better have sympathy for me!" Still others lead a two-faced existence, assuming the victim role only within the family context.

Katherine, for example, didn't even realize she was a victim until others in a "First Comes Love" workshop pointed it out to her. Everything she said in discussions about herself was an apology for innate worthlessness. Her partner, a "boss," criticized her publicly for her sloppiness; Katherine responded, "He knows me so well. I *am* slovenly. I don't know why I can't even learn how to keep house." Victims generally are not very introspective, perhaps because it would be painful to realize that they are responsible for keeping themselves down (as opposed to blaming their problems on natural inabilities).

You may ask why anyone would choose to live this way. One answer is that the victim is getting benefits and satisfactions out of the role. Also, being a victim may be the safest and most efficient way to cope in a difficult environment. If family members are looking for a scapegoat, why not just assume that role and please them all? When they're criticizing you, they're paying attention to you (albeit negative attention), and that's better than being ignored. And as long as you're denigrated as being powerless, you don't need to feel guilty for your transgressions, or for "getting away" with them. If you respect the opinions of family members, you may assume that they're right in criticizing you; it's your just due. Victims accept abuse because deep down, they believe that's the way things should be.

For every leader, there has to be someone who chooses to follow. *Followers* may simply be shy people who are unsure of themselves. Usually reasonable and compliant, they accept leadership intelligently, with rationalizations. They may feel that decision-making isn't their forte, and as long as they're accorded some respect from their boss, achiever, or provider, they're agreeable. They differ from dependent people in that they don't *need* their leader to survive. They just prefer the easiest resolution to problems, and that's to "let the buck stop *there*."

Jerry, the free-spending provider mentioned earlier, insisted on having his own ways in his relationship with Helene. She didn't mind—she got mink coats, a Mercedes, and a great place to live in exchange. When she had opinions, she gingerly suggested them, but in the end she usually went along with Jerry's decisions. One reason why the tradeoff seemed so reasonable to her was that, as a follower, she had a need to please. By deferring to Jerry, she won his affection. And because Jerry was a provider, she could afford other symbols that she "belonged." When everybody started wearing mini-skirts again, she could join the crowd, thanks to a shopping spree that Jerry was only too happy to finance. When the "in" crowd began lunching at a certain exclusive bistro, she could be included (and thus assured again that she was socially acceptable). Jerry and Helene trotted off blissfully, with five hundred of their closest friends, to the ritziest altar in town.

Unlike followers, *martyrs* feel they have no choice. They *must* sacrifice themselves for the good of the family. The ship is sinking? "I'll stay behind and use this tin can to bail!" says the martyr valiantly. Family members get great benefit from a martyr, because for the cost of some praise and attention, they get someone to serve them like a slave. The martyr is the mother who stays up night after sleepless night tending her child with the croup. The martyr eschews instant pudding because her family has to have the *best*, and then burns her hand in the process of making the real thing (just so they'll all know that the pudding had to *boil*).

Interestingly, the martyr usually suffers while doing tasks that don't really need to be done. She's going the extra distance, beyond the call of duty, because she's such a devoted, wonderful, loving mother or partner. The family would've eaten five-minute chocolate pudding. But then the thanks wouldn't be thick enough, even if the pudding's consistency is the same.

Being a martyr is a classic means of manipulation. A martyr, by being a stellar example of perfect love, demands respect and endless kudos. The martyr is under the category of "ruled" because she puts herself in the pseudo-position of servitude to her family. In reality, she usually has *them* writhing in the palm of *her* hand.

By the way, because of the prevalence of women who assume the role of martyr, I've used women as examples. Men can easily be martyrs, too, but they usually demonstrate their unbounded dedication to their loved ones via work or by pulling strings for their family. "I get up at 6:00 A.M. to bring in enough money to pay the rent," Victor told the workshop group. He and Lola, both 36, had lived together for two years. "I work my fingers to the bone in a job I hate [in an employment agency]; I have to put up with cigarette smoke and people's coughs eight hours a day. I drive an old Buick rather than a sports car I would have otherwise, just so Lola can go to the theater and get her hair done. The least she can do is give me some love and sex when I get home!"

In every relationship there is a ruler, as well as someone who is ruled. There is more flexibility in the healthiest relationships—the new egalitarian kind that seem so elusive. A person may take on one role with one partner, and a different role with the next. Or two people may assume their roles on the basis of competency. More often, however, I tend to see one person doing most of the ruling, and another being ruled. This isn't necessarily a problem. Problems arise when *both* people insist on ruling (rather than compromising) or following (so that decisions are never made). There is some truth in the adage that opposites attract—that two people choose each other because they can fill each other's needs. It sounds like a logical thing to do.

/ 7
Patterns in Your Relationship

So, you've discovered what roles you took on in order to make it in your original family. You've looked back over your history to discern typical patterns of behavior, some of which you might want to revise. If you discussed your findings with your partner, you have some practice in constructive interactions and some valuable feedback that can help clarify your future explorations.

Having identified the broad behavior patterns you developed early in life, you'll now look at the refined subset of them that you developed in this particular relationship. As you got to know your partner, you observed which behaviors in your repertoire brought certain reactions. You learned what your partner liked and didn't like; you learned what he or she expected and found shocking. Gradually, you wove the patterns you'd already established into a style that usually gets you what you want.

In this chapter, you'll focus on three major patterns you and your partner have established in your relationship: communication, power and control, and problem-solving. You'll be completing several questionnaires. Some of these are on the light side, using fun and humor to help you discover your values, expectations, and feelings. Other questionnaires may be difficult for you to complete: you may have to do some soul-searching and uncover cobwebbed crevices of your memory.

Your Communication Style

How you communicate is related to the role you take on. A boss might issue a command ("Go wash the dishes!") and expect an unquestioning response just because of his or her status. An achiever might make the request on the basis of fairness: "I did the dishes last night [i.e., I've achieved], now it's your turn." A provider might tell her or his mate: "I bought you the best dishwasher sold, so why don't you use it?" And a nurturer might croon, "Now, dear, you know that washing the dishes will make you feel good about the accomplishment, and will teach you about brands of liquid soap. I'll be right here to help you, so please start scrubbing."

A martyr wouldn't wait to be told to scour the dishes; she'd be checking on whether she could see her face on a freshly dried pan while the rest of the family still kibitzed around the table. A dependent family member, upon hearing the dishwashing command, would whine, "I can't do it, I need help. Do you use the powder or the liquid detergent? Do I put the glasses in with the silverware?" After this ritual goes on a few times, it's unlikely that the dependent one would be asked to do the dishes at all. A victim, on the other hand, would comply, perhaps in dejected silence. After all, he or she is used to being picked on, and is probably stuck with the chores all the time. A follower would wait for direction, and also for some rationale for the command. "Oh, yeah," the follower might respond, "*I* do the dishes, Mary does the laundry, and Martin does the shopping. I'm part of the team."

Naturally, "rulers" sometimes do dishes, and "the ruled" sometimes give commands. And, of course, communication consists of a lot more than simply commanding and responding. Think about the topics discussed in the course of your interactions with your partner over the last week. Would you say the two of you were mainly taking care of business (i.e., having interactions that were needed to make the household function smoothly), griping, or exchanging experiences? Would you characterize these interchanges as mainly pleasant, warm, and rewarding, or as uncomfortable, irritating, or hostile? All this thinking is a prelude to completing the next questionnaire.

The "Communication Questionnaire" gauges what your interaction styles are now. The purpose is to identify different components of your styles so that you can evaluate how satisfied you are with each of them. This tool can be used not only to measure the compatibility of your communication styles, but to pinpoint areas in which communication can be improved or enriched.

The questionnaire covers need for and frequency of communication; open- versus closed-mindedness; communication style (how you assert yourself, argue, discuss, and request); and your degree of satisfaction with each of these patterns. Admittedly, it's often difficult to generalize about your interactions, because they may vary with content. You might be aggressive about some subjects, complain about others. But if you take a step back and try to think of many interchanges over the past weeks and months, you'll get an overall view of what *typically* transpires. If you're coming up with all sorts of "ifs" and "buts," use *that* fact to discover why you may be avoiding a given topic. Avoidance is a communication style in itself.

I remember Calvin, a thirtyish workshop participant whose horn-rimmed glasses and pen-filled shirt pocket gave him the look of (as one participant put it) an intellectual nerd. He was bright and articulate, and took every opportunity to expound on why the questionnaires couldn't possibly be "valid" in the statistical sense. He harped on every ambiguity, every word without a clearly presented definition. The more time he took to sidetrack the group, the more irritated the rest of the participants became. And the closer to tears came his partner, Rene. Finally, I had to ask Calvin to save his objections until the break or after the session. Two or three workshop members jumped in to voice their support of my request, and Rene started to cry. Our attention turned to her.

"I'm so embarrassed and angry at Calvin," she sobbed. "He's always sabotaging our discussions like this. He can't deal with anything because he doesn't have *all* the facts. He can't say how he feels, because it depends on too many variables. He cuts off my complaints with 'I love you,' and expects that to be enough to make everything smoothed over. I feel like a complete idiot for even bringing up our differences."

Indeed, "idiocy" was the key to Rene's role in the relationship. Calvin was an achiever; his power lay in his intellectual superiority. Rene, believing she was stupid, was the dependent one, relying on Calvin's smarts to make up for her own alleged intellectual deficiency. In truth, however, Calvin was afraid of his feelings—afraid that if he acknowledged and gave importance to them, he would lose his power and become like the masses. He had every reason to stay "above" revealing his emotions, because by controlling them, he emphasized the difference (ability to intellectualize) that kept him superior to Rene.

This sounds somewhat diabolical, as if Calvin were secretly plotting to keep Rene in her place. But Calvin loved Rene, and never would have thought of belittling her. The above description

Communication Questionnaire

1. On a scale of 1 to 10, rate how much you hold in feelings. (1 = lets it all hang out; 10 = keeps almost all feelings inside). _____ Rate your partner. _____

2. On a scale of 1 to 10, rate how much *tolerance* you have for views of your partner that clash with yours (1 = no tolerance; 10 = completely at ease). _____ Rate your partner's tolerance of your views. _____

3. How much listening and support-giving do you give your partner daily? _____
   How much does he/she give you daily? _____

4. How satisfied are you with the amount of support you *receive?* _____
   How satisfied are you with the amount of support you *give?* _____

5. Arguing:
   How often do you argue?
   (circle one) Daily   Once every   Once every   Less
                         2–3 days   week   few weeks
   a. Who started each? _____
   b. What did each of you do? _____
   c. Was the outcome satisfying? Explain. _____

6. On a scale of 1 to 10, rate *my need* to get out my hostilities versus *my partner's need* to get them out (1 = very high need; 10 = very low need)

   _____ vs. _____
   Self   Partner

7. There are three types of statements: feelings, facts, and judgments (something is good or bad, right or wrong). To clarify the distinction between these three types, choose a topic that you and your partner discuss frequently and give an example of each of the following:
   Fact: _____
   Feeling: _____
   Judgment: _____
   What percentage of *your* arguing is: _____, _____, and _____ = 100%
                                           Fact   Feeling   Judgment
   What percentage of *your partner's* arguing is: _____, _____, and _____ = 100%
                                                    Fact   Feeling   Judgment

8. Are you satisfied with the way you work out differences? _____
   Is your partner satisfied? (your impression) _____

9. Fill in the blanks below, and then check whether the current situation is satisfactory or should change.

	This is satisfactory	I'd like this to change
a. "When I do something he/she doesn't like, I _____".		
b. "When he/she does something I don't like, I _____".		
c. "When he/she does something I don't like, he/she _____".		
d. "If I want him/her to do something, I _____ and he/she _____".		
e. "When he/she wants me to do something, he/she _____ and I _____".		
f. "When I don't want to be interrupted or bothered and he/she tries to, I _____ and he/she _____".		

g. "When he/she doesn't want to be interrupted or bothered, and I try to, I _____, and he/she _____."

h. "When he/she rambles on about an uninteresting subject, I _____ and then he/she _____."

i. "When I get very angry, I _____ and then he/she _____."

j. "When he/she gets very angry, he/she _____ and then I _____."

k. "When I disagree with him/her, I _____ and then he/she _____."

l. "When there's something I want, I _____."

m. "When there's something he/she wants, he/she _____."

of their relationship is simplified; people are extremely complex, and Calvin also had many good qualities that kept Rene with him. But in the area of emotional communication—an area that Rene considered important—he was incompetent. Rather than deal with this problem directly, Calvin turned on his intellectuality, which was his smokescreen for the real issue: fear of being exposed and vulnerable. He also used his intellectuality to seemingly best Rene at something akin to her own game (which was verbal expression).

The point is that you can learn about yourself if you accept and *use* your feelings about any of the questionnaires in this book. If you hesitate to complete any of them, are tempted to dismiss them, or worry about your partner's reaction to something you write or say, look for the message underyling those feelings. Sometimes people ask the intent of certain questionnaire items, saying that they can be answered in two or more ways. When they ask, "What exactly does this mean?" I turn the question around in true psychologist style: "What do *you* think it means?" They come up with an answer. "And what *else* do you think it could mean?" I query. They come up with another answer. "Okay, now put down your responses to *both* of these possibilities."

Once you've thought about your answers and shown them to your partner, what do you do with them? How can you tell whether your communication styles are sufficiently harmonious that you'll make beautiful conversations together for life? Here are some ways of evaluating your questionnaire responses.

1. *Open- versus closed-mindedness* is measured by items 2 and 7. In most cases, it's not "better" or "worse" to have any particular patterns. But with regard to these items, I'd have to say that there *is* a preferable position. In interviewing long-married couples, I found that one thing they shared was tolerence for their partner's views and idiosyncracies. These include the *feelings* and *judgments* you separated in Item 7. Facts are indisputable—arguments center on differences in feelings and judgments. Certainly there is a line where you simply cannot allow your partner to trespass on your wishes. But for the happiest of the people I interviewed, that line was distant and flexible. And there was seldom any need to draw it, since these partners were considerate and tried hard to accommodate each other while clearly stating their own desires.

2. *Need for the frequency of communication* would ideally be similar for both partners. (Item 4 and the statements in Item 9.) Sometimes opposites have attracted, however. If so, problems can arise.

Rowene, whom you met in the first chapter, was gregarious and outgoing. She had gotten little warmth from her mother as a child, and her stepfather was even more aloof. When, as an adult, she longed for compensation for this early deprivation, she reached out to others. The man she chose to marry met one of her main criteria (intelligence and wit) but not her need for openness and expression. He'd profess his love for her in private, but give her barely a nod, much less even a casual hug, in public. His lack of demonstrativeness bothered Rowene, but she was more distressed by his unwillingness to share any feelings or respond to her own outpourings. Rowene became more and more frustrated. Finally, her head was turned by the more expressive and loquacious co-worker who eventually stole her away.

If you're quiet and your partner is voluble, don't cancel the organist yet. To improve your speaking skills, or those of your partner, try practicing the art of skills exchange, discussed in the preceding chapter. The more articulate partner can lovingly assist and encourage the other to gain increased ease in speaking, simply by giving him or her a lot of practice discussing and responding. (The less articulate partner might reciprocate by teaching the other how to samba.) Rowene's problem occurred because her husband, Jim, *refused* to open up or change. Communication is fundamental to a resilient relationship. Even if you have little need to unload your *own* experiences and cares, try to be available and responsive when your partner shows a need to communicate. However, neither partner should be pressured to become someone he or she is not. While *some* communication is essential in marriage, only you and your partner can decide the exact amount needed to balance privacy with support.

Note that if you and your partner have very different needs in terms of frequency and intensity of communication, you may be satisfied with an unbalanced relationship. Maybe you "opposites" attracted because each of you added a complementary skill to the whole. If you're the articulate one, perhaps you should make all the phone calls. Your partner, in turn, may be the accounting wizard who keeps the checkbooks up-to-date. As long as both of you are pleased, and neither one feels deprived or frustrated, all is well. That's why the satisfaction ratings integrated into the "Communication Questionnaire" are crucial: if you're satisfied, there's no need to change.

3. Your *communication style* in serveral types of situations determines the mood of your marriage. In most "First Comes Love"

workshops, one of the most debated subjects is *arguing* (item 5 on the questionnaire). Here's a capsule of one recent discussion.

MONTY (a 29-year-old pilot): Jennifer and I never argue.

BRIAN (a 34-year-old private school owner): It's not healthy to hold in your anger; you really should learn to do some constructive fighting.

JENNIFER (27 years old and a professional violinist; engaged to Monty): We just don't have anything to fight over. We don't have any anger to let out.

BRIAN: Then you're *really* fooling yourselves! No two people can be in accord 100 percent of the time!

MONTY: Sometimes we disagree, but we never raise our voices. We just say our opinions and make a decision. Sometimes we go my way, sometimes hers. Why do we have to scream and yell in order to be sane? It just doesn't occur to us to fight.

BELINDA (a 52-year-old homemaker): Then you're taking out your hostilities in other ways. You're not trusting your relationship enough to let out your feelings there; you must have other outlets.

JENNIFER: I just don't get upset in general. I think we're just basically easygoing people. Sure, we get our share of frustrations, but they just blow away, they don't build up or require "letting out." Who cares about most of the petty issues couples fight about? Who cares about the minor inconveniences of the day? Occasionally, we come up against something that's patently unfair, and we get angry and fight it. But it's never something in our relationship.

MONTY: In fact, our relationship gives us strength to fight outside injustices fully. We're consistently warm and comforting for each other.

DAVE (Belinda's 55-year-old fiancé, an architect): I think you're living in Fantasyland. I love Belinda, but we're practically fighting every night. What would life be without some scrappiness? It would be boring! And how can you be an individual and assert yourself without disagreeing with your partner? I'd be afraid of your kind of relationship, Jennifer, because it sounds like you two are just blending into an amorphous, bland blob!

At this point, due to popular demand, I had to step in. "In my experience," I noted, "couples can have perfectly happy and healthy relationships if they squabble every five minutes—or if they *never* argue." It's a matter of style. Earlier, I mentioned that relationships can fall anywhere along a very wide continuum. Belinda and Dave are on one side, representing the more feisty set. Monty and Jennifer lie on the continuum's other, more tranquil end.

Each of these couples contains two of the same kind of people, and in both cases, the combination works just fine. Belinda was brought up in a household where self-defense required standing up for oneself. In contrast, Jennifer's family had emphasized politeness, calm, and relaxation. Put Jennifer with Dave, and she'd be horrified at his uncalled-for verbal brutality; Belinda, if with Monty, would be disgusted by his guileless lack of assertiveness. In their own contexts, though, each couple hums along contentedly. Moral of this story: There's no one way you "should" be. The frequency with which you argue, and the ways you argue, depends on your personal styles.

There *are* some common-sense pointers that can help you improve your communication when arguing, whether you happen to be mismatched or not. These guidelines were given on pages 00–00. Central to changing your style is setting rules. One rule might be to allow equal time to partners so that both sides of an issue are presented. Another rule might be to replace "you make me feel . . ." phrases with phrases beginning "I feel. . . ." One basic rule regarding arguing that recurred in the advice of long-married couples was the adage, "Don't go to bed angry." These people suggested that couples make a gesture to heal wounds in time for some nocturnal nuzzling.

I would add a rule to avoid arguing when emotions are at their peak. Strong feelings sometimes lead to "overkill venting," in which accusations and name-calling (born of internal anger rather than facts) can do irreversible harm. I urge hostile partners to express their negative energy, but *not to their partner*. I usually tell them to leave the room to (a) punch a pillow, (b) run around the block, (c) write a mean letter and then tear it up, (d) sit in their car with the windows rolled up and scream, or (e) find another way to physically release strong emotions. Then, when rationality and reason are possible, return for a calmer discussion of past feelings, present roadblocks, and solutions.

In "First Comes Love" workshops, participants complete written exercises every day between weekly meetings. One assignment is to take ten minutes each day to write out an answer to a "question of the day." In every workshop I've held, the members agreed that one communication-related question in particular reveals something profound about a relationship. Take a few moments now to write down *your* response to this question: "What are three things I've never said to my partner but I assume he/she knows."

Now, using all the guidelines you have read, and calling on

your speaking ability and capacity for honesty, share these special assumptions with your partner. One thing you'll learn from this experience is never to assume.

Another communication-related question can help couples see what keeps them together—what they have in common. Shared activities and concerns are almost always a source of dialogue. I said "almost" because I remember one man who said, in all seriousness, that "the main thing we have in common is that both of us hate to communicate or have anything to do with other people." He had come out of his den long enough to tell me this gem about why his thirty-five-year marriage was successful, then he returned to hibernation.

Take a few minutes now to write down, on a separate sheet you'll show to your partner later, "the most important topics, shared viewpoints, or issues in our relationship." Your list will probably include activities you pursue together, values or philosophies that you share, and issues over which you often clash. All of these are fodder for discussion.

Having your common interests and concerns written down on a list gives you an indication of how mutually involved you are. If you've only found one thing in common—say, "love of the finer things in life"—then you probably are aloof from each other and may not remain satisfied. If, on the other hand, your list is extensive, there's much to stimulate your thinking, and you should have an easier time communicating and feeling close. Also, note the length of your list of issues that involve conflict. Again, individual styles or needs will determine whether a relationship is working. If you and your partner are easygoing and have a "live and let live" orientation, you can disagree and continue in harmony. However, if you tend to hold firmly to your own viewpoints, or if divergent beliefs bother you a great deal, a long "issues" list could be a warning flag. Many couples are aware of differences at the outset but sweep them under the carpet while they're courting. Once the carpet is on the connubial floor, those dangerous dust bunnies somehow escape.

A partner may "find out too late" because of an unspoken expectation that the spouse will change, becoming closer to an "ideal." People do change, and marriage, as a major event, often brings about shifts in roles and behavior. But if you *expect* that you, or the state of marriage, can change a partner in a specific way, you're probably in for a disappointment. All real changes are voluntary.

Power and Control

Communication style is basic to the way you deal with every issue, problem, or discussion. It is a vehicle for the expression of underlying feelings, or a means toward completion of necessary business. Now, however, we get down to the nitty-gritty—the power and control issues that form the core of your relationship. Power over someone else gives you your relative status in life—the "boss" type may only have stature as the biggest fish in his little pond, but that pond is the only one that matters to him.

Important as these issues are, couples seldom talk about who controls their relationship. It is often taken for granted that the man will "wear the pants" and represent the couple to the outside world. Your early socialization probably taught you that men inherit their power. "Just wait till your father gets home!" says the mother to her errant child. She's saying that she's incapable of meting out punishment. Also, money talks in American society, and the person who makes the most is often handed the mantle of authority (never mind that a homemaker may work harder than her husband). Women may have been taught that they were incompetent to make decisions, or that their hormones made them susceptible to irrationality. More likely, they were silently shown that women, by playing dumb and allowing men to feel important, could manipulate in order to get their own say and make their dictators even more benevolent.

Most of the couples who participated in the "First Comes Love" workshops would not have willingly chosen a dictatorship in their relationships. But they were often blind to the specifics of their decision-making style, where a dictatorship might have existed. As with communication, there is a wide continuum of styles for decision-making. Some couples allocate major decisions to one partner, and minor ones to the other. In some cases, one partner or the other makes decisions independently, on all but the most major choices. Some couples abdicate decision-making, relying on relatives, and other advisers to "tell us what to do." Many decisions are made simply by inaction.

Critical to your decision-making style is the timing of your decisions. Preplanning may lead to certain behaviors, for example, extensive comparison-shopping. As the deadline nears, the style may shift, with a last-minute choice being made in a whirlwind of activity. In order to assess the decision-making style (timing and method) that is generally used by you and your partner, complete the "Decision-Making Style" questionnaire on page 148.

As you look at the column headings in the questionnaire, you may ask, "What is 'proper' timing? Where's the line between 'last-minute' and 'proper'?" I hope you had a lively discussion with your partner about that, because just *when* decisions are made is often a source of contention. People differ in what they consider to be the optimal time to act, but they are consistent in becoming irritated when that time passes. To avoid future petty arguments, you might proceed through the "Decision-Making Style" questionnaire with your partner, using a different-colored pencil from the first time, and specify the ideal time to respond to each of the situations posed.

You can also go through the list again, with the new pencil, noting how each decision should *ideally* be made (the "method" portion of the questionnaire). I can't tell you one or two "best" ways to handle decision-making, because there are so many acceptable points along the continuum. Also, couples usually have an individual decision-making *process*.

In the "First Comes Love" workshops, people differ in what they mean by a given answer. For example, most people say they "mull over pros and cons." The amount of mulling that goes on, however, varies greatly. Donald might mull for five minutes, standing at the wedding gift counter, debating the merits of a crystal serving bowl versus those of a silver nut dish. Darlene, on the other hand, might spend weeks comparing the crystal bowls at five stores and the nut dishes at five more. A *real* muller is the type who shops with a clipboard, on which he or she lists attributes, prices, information about warranties, and reactions to each item. This person takes *time* in decision-making, and has an emotional investment in making the best choice possible.

Jill was a real muller. She was a clothes horse, and each day, on her way home from work, she would spend at least two hours browsing through clothing stores. She knew her requirements: any purchase had to be a real bargain, had to fit with her existing wardrobe in at least three ways, and had to be the best quality (natural fibers only, good label, well-made). For her, making a decision was a challenge; her successes were triumphs that boosted her self-esteem.

Unfortunately, she was going with Reginald, a political lobbyist who cared little about material goods. Theoretical concepts and how they could be implemented were his domain. While he carefully evaluated each shopping choice, he made his decisions quickly. He didn't care if he paid 20 percent more than somewhere else; if he needed gray slacks and saw some that fit, he made a snap judgment and bought them. No looking back, no lingering. Reginald was a dynamo, and he had no time to quibble over details.

This difference wasn't usually much of a problem. Jill bought clothes for herself; she bought the stereo and redecorated the bedroom. Reginald barely looked at these trappings anyway. He did appreciate Jill's flare with colors and designs, and he was glad she was willing to make the effort for his benefit as well as hers. But when they decided to get married, they ran into some difficulties. (In reaching the decision to marry, Jill and Reginald's decision-making processes were typical: she said she'd been reading a lot about marriage and had talked to several friends; he gave it some thought and agreed five minutes later.)

"I wanted a big garden wedding, with six bridesmaids and three hundred guests," Jill said. At 29, she had never been married before, and looked upon the gala occasion as a chance to create a perfect atmosphere and setting. "*He* wanted a little gathering at our house, with a justice of the peace. We simply disagreed. But I dearly wanted this grand affair, and he just as vehemently wanted to keep it small." What happens when decision-making styles clash over an important issue? "I went for more consultation," Jill said. "I tried to see it Reginald's way, but I felt so frustrated! This was to be my big day. It meant so much to me to have a memorable wedding; it was a gift to my family and friends."

Finally, when Reginald observed how heartbroken Jill was, he changed his mind. Because trappings and ceremonies meant so little to him, he had far less investment in the decision than she did. So, because he cared for Jill, he deferred. Jill floated down a petal-strewn red carpet—a vision of voile, silk, and lace—in the garden of a Victorian mansion. Mine were two of six hundred moist eyes viewing the breathtaking scene. Reginald, by the way, joyfully basked in Jill's pride and their shared happiness. Once he had made up his mind, he was wholeheartedly elated.

The lesson in this story is that that when couples reach an impasse, *amount of investment* in the decision is usually the determinant of whose viewpoint "wins." Of course, Jill and Reginald could have compromised, and in many situations, they would

Decision-Making Style

Mark the timing and method of decision-making for each decision at left. Do this *twice*: (1) by putting an "S" (for "self") to indicate your own timing and method for each decision, and (2) by then putting a "P" (for "partner") to indicate the timing and method of decision-making you've observed or would predict for your partner.

Decision:	Timing:				Method:					
	In advance	Proper timing	Last-minute	Past due	Mull over pros and cons	Decide, then reverse	Decide, act, move on	Abdicate decision	Go by habit or custom	Decide but don't act
What to order in a restaurant										
What to wear in the morning										
What brand of toothpaste to buy										
How many old magazines to keep										
When to change the bed linens										
Whether or not to buy an article of clothing you like in a store										
What gift to buy a particular person										
Whether to use cash, check, or credit card										

	Decision:	*Timing:*				*Method:*					
		In advance	Proper timimg	Last-minute	Past due	Mull over pros and cons	Decide, then reverse	Decide, act, move on	Abdicate decision	Go by habit or custom	Decide but don't act
Whom to invite to a party											
What to serve at a party											
Where to go on vacation											
What to name a pet											
How to spend a free Sunday											
Which hairstyle to wear											
When and how much to exercise											
When you're sick enough to see a doctor											
What car to buy											
Whether you need professional counseling											
Whether you're in love											
Whether your salary is enough											
Whether to stay at your job											

	Timing:			*Method:*					
Decision:	In advance	Proper timimg	Last-minute	Past due	Mull over pros and cons	Decide, then reverse	Decide, act, move on	Abdicate decision	Go by habit or custom	Decide but don't act
What career to actively pursue										
Whether or not to get married										
If/when to have a child										
How to invest life savings										
Whether or not to separate from a partner										

Patterns in Your Relationship

What are the patterns you see in your own decision-making? ___

How would you like to change any of these patterns? ___

What patterns do you believe exist in your partner's decision-making? ___

How would you like him/her to change any of these patterns? ___

have. But sometimes, when couples compromise on big decisions, no one is satisfied. And there are some issues on which there is no compromise.

Lois and Richard came to my office in a hostile state. Lois, 35, sat on one end of the couch; her husband of six years, age 39, sat on the other. Lois was clutching my book *Children: To Have or Have Not?* for help in this emergency situation. She was eight weeks pregnant, determined to carry the child that had been accidentally conceived. Richard was adamant that she have an abortion, citing their original bargain to remain child-free. It seemed that Lois's style was to avoid confronting a difficult situation, instead making a decision almost unconsciously. "When we got married," she explained, "I really couldn't see having a child. I wanted my freedom and was in the midst of preparing for my nursing career. I knew Richard was firm in his decision, and that swayed me, because I loved him, to agree to nonparenthood."

"It isn't like I twisted your arm or anything," Richard shot back. "I thought everything was going along fine, and then you suddenly say you want to keep this fetus. I feel totally betrayed. I got into this marriage with my eyes open, believing you were honest with me. Now, you've changed the rules. Why should I have to accept my whole life turned upside down against my will?"

"I've tried to tell you that I've been changing my mind about having a child, but you completely closed yourself off to it," Lois protested. "I've been hinting, like all the times I've ohhed and ahhed over babies. And last year, when Les and Ann had their baby, I specifically talked to you about how my feelings were changing. You just didn't want to face that we might have a conflict over this."

Richard replied, "You *think* you told me your feelings were changing, but all you said was 'wouldn't it be nice to have a baby like Les and Ann's?' And if you remember, I said 'no!' " Richard crossed his arms and turned his body farther away from Lois.

"All right, I was afraid you'd just get upset if I pursued it. And I wasn't *trying* to get pregnant. My diaphragm failed, that's all. . . ."

"I think you *wanted* it to fail!" Richard snarled. "And now I'm in a helpless position. *I* can't get the abortion for you!"

"You can always leave!" Lois retorted.

"Maybe I will!" Richard said, narrowing his eyes.

In the next chapter, you'll read much more about the decision to have a child, as well as learning the outcome of Richard and Lois's antagonism. Right now just notice Lois's devious means of gaining power in the relationship. She had decided, partly through unconscious processes, that she wanted to have a child. She knew she was bucking the spirit and letter of their nuptual agreement, but she wanted to keep Richard *and* have her way. She broached the subject with him, dropping heavy hints that he ignored. They both knew what was going on, but communicated indirectly. Lois's hints were her request for a child; his rebuffs were his answer. Unconsciously or consciously, Lois might have been careless with her diaphragm. In any case, blaming her pregnancy on its failure relieved her of blame and freed her from accusations that she had deliberately crossed Richard or broken her promise. When her pregnancy was confirmed, Lois was in control. Suddenly Richard would have to make the move, to either leave her (which Lois was confident he would never do) or resign himself to becoming a father. Sneaky, clever, and unfair.

Now, Lois would normally never deign to stoop so low. She knew what she was doing, and she knew that she deserved Richard's wrath. She figured that he would be angry, she would endure it for a while, and then things would blow over. Having a baby was worth the backlash. But Richard was especially upset over this issue, because the decision was a far-reaching one. Having a baby means a lifetime of responsibility, a total revamping of lifestyle. Richard was shocked by Lois's behavior because normally he felt that he had equal power in their relationship. He was always consulted, on everything from carpet color to what to have for dinner. He had given in to Lois on the house they finally bought (his second choice), and had decided against a sports car in favor of a Volvo because of Lois's arguments. On these more minor issues, he did not mind compromising. But on this most consequential one, he was furious that his wishes were being disregarded. Lois was acting out of character, Richard insisted.

Richard was naive. Lois had given him the illusion of power by always consulting him, but *she* actually wielded it. She had more definite and forceful opinions, and she knew how to use logic to convince Richard. It took a few days, but Richard finally came to see that he was more malleable than he'd realized, and that he gave Lois more power than he retained.

This case shows how roles, communication, and power interact, and how examining past patterns of behavior can bring a clearer picture of likely behavior in the future. Lois knew how to control Richard, and so could predict that when she told him about her decision to have the baby, he would squawk but then defer. (We'll leave this cliffhanger until the next chapter.) Perhaps there are subtle or hidden but tacitly accepted patterns in your relationship that would be recognized.

Here's your chance to find out. The "Controlling Decisions" questionnaire lets you realistically recall how decision-making power has been allocated in your relationship, or estimate how it will be allocated in the future. By noting all the areas in which you feel decision-making is unsatisfactory, you have a tool that can help you to improve the balance of responsibility.

Keep in mind that many couples are happiest with an *unequal* distribution of power.

Take it from this couple, graduates of "First Comes Love" who have been married two years. Walt is a 40-year-old mathematician; his wife, Lillian, is a flight attendant, aged 35. Walt said, "I get very absorbed in my work. It's very theoretical, and I sometimes stare at a computer screen for weeks on end. I love it; it's like another world. The figures take on lives of their own, and there's great excitement and challenge in working—or trying to work—these things out." Lillian smiled and commented:

People said we'd never make it, that we were an unmatched pair. That's why we took the workshop. But we *both* have our own worlds. Mine is a flying metal box with wings, where I work hard but get to meet hundreds of people every day. Our families also think our arrangement is crazy, but for us, it works. I run the household, almost completely. Walt is the romantic, the artist, who arranges the flowers and selects the wine. I'm so practiced in efficiency that I keep the finances, keep the car and appliances in working order, and oversee the housekeeper.

CONTROLLING DECISIONS

For each decision area at left, check who generally decides, and fill in the percentage of control each person has over joint decisions. Then check whether this situation is satisfactory to you

DECISION AREA "Who has, or will have, control regarding . . ."	Woman decides	Man decides	Joint percentages Man's % + Woman's % = 100%	Satisfactory	Not Satisfactory
Woman's work outside the home					
Man's work outside the home					
Budgeting of total income					
How to spend budgeted money					
Where to live					
Arranging and furnishing the house					
Woman's home-related tasks					
Man's home-related tasks					
Where and how to have sex					
Type of birth control					

Patterns in Your Relationship

DECISION AREA "Who has, or will have, control regarding . . ."	Woman decides	Man decides	Joint percentages Man's % + Woman's % = 100%	Satisfactory	Not Satisfactory
Whether to have a child					
Caring for children					
Disciplining children					
Activities of the family					
Activities of the two of us alone					
My activities during unscheduled time					
My partner's activities during unscheduled time					
How and when to entertain friends					
How and when to entertain members of the man's family					

BASES FOR MARRIAGE

DECISION AREA "Who has, or will have, control regarding..."	Woman decides	Man decides	Joint percentages ———— + ————— = 100% Man's % Woman's %	Satisfactory	Not Satisfactory
How and when to entertain members of the woman's family					
Church attendance					
Where and when to take vacations					

Now go back and fill in the decision-makers and percentages you would like (using a different-colored pencil for all areas that are not satisfactory.

SOURCE: Adapted from William J. Leherer, *Marital Choices* (W. W. Norton & Co.: New York, 1981), p. 164–5.

Walt admitted that there were problems with the arrangement:

The guys at the health club rib me about it. They say I must be weird not to make decisions. They're all liberated sorts, who claim to share everything with their wives 50/50. In truth, most of them exert more clout in decision-making than their wives do. They never see that there are certain benefits and pleasures in having someone who *prefers* to take responsibility. They don't see that making decisions takes their time—to weigh the alternatives and do research, and then to follow through. I don't have to do that, and so I'm more liberated than they are.

Lillian explained, "We've reversed roles, but only in one visible area. I'm still feminine, and Walt's pretty masculine, as you can see." She glanced approvingly toward her husband's brawny physique.

We don't feel at all threatened by the fact that one of us is more competent at some things than others. And we're so secure in our relationship that we can both go off to our own worlds for days at a time, and return to pick up right where we left off—only *better*. And now that I'm pregnant, we'll have a whole new set of roles to reverse!

Problem-Solving

Now that you know who has the most power in your relationship, find out how that allocation is used to deal with problems that arise—both minor and more serious ones. This section lets you look first at your values and problem-solving skills as individuals, and then as a duo.

Problem-solving is actually a *series of steps*. You don't just get hit with a propitious lightning bolt of inspiration and glean the best solution to a problem. Instead, you progress through a rational sequence of events that eventually brings you to resolution.

First, you'll *define the problem*. This may mean opening an envelope and discovering that Ma Bell has charged you for a telephone call to Guam, or it could require some digging, such as checking that your niece is *right* about termites flying out of your basement. Defining the problem means establishing what is going on, how serious it is, and whether it requires a response.

Next, you'll *define possible solutions* to your problem. Sometimes this is easy. For example, with the Guam phone call, you might decide to check with your family to be sure no one made the call. (Maybe your niece called the Guam Public Library because she was doing a book report on big lizards.) Your next move would be to talk to your customer service representative at the phone company about getting the erroneous charge off your bill. You might prioritize your options as Plan A, Plan B, Plan C, and so forth, in order of ease, likelihood of good results, cost, time involved, or other factors.

The third step in problem-solving is *fact-checking*. Here, you research which of your alternatives is most feasible, and reconsider the choices before acting. If you're buying a new blow dryer because your old one blew up, this step might involve deciding on desired features, comparing the various brands of blow dryers, testing them out, and price-shopping. Sometimes this step is bypassed, when only few moments' pondering is needed to determine what to do next.

Finally, problem-solvers select a course of action and *act*. Acting may involve serveral behaviors. For example, if it turns out that your niece made the Guam phone call, you may lecture her, elecit from her a solemn promise never to touch the phone without prior approval, and tell her mother what happened.

All well and good for most problems. Of course, you have the option to stop your problem-solving at any time, simply by ceasing to progress through the steps. By just putting your feet up, you're selecting one of the ever present options for behavior, and the result will be consequences that occur "by default." If you never protest about your niece having called Guam, she may do the same thing again. If you don't go apartment-hunting, you'll stay in your present abode. Doing nothing continues the status quo at best, and brings your downfall at worst. If you never lift a finger, you're controlled by other people or by "fate." While this may spare you from facing the problem, you may lose a sense of power and control.

The problems that a couple has to resolve fall into two basic categories: complex and simple. A simple problem may be any dilemma or decision that the two of you must address. Such problems include where to live, what to buy as a birthday gift, how to get a neighbor to pay back the $20 he owes you, where Granny will sleep when she comes to visit, how to get the microwave oven fixed, and the thousands of other hassles and quandries that make up the fabric of daily life. With simple problems, you and your partner face a dilemma as an undivided unit.

Patterns in Your Relationship 159

Simple problems become complex when the two of you disagree about what to do. You may have defined the problem and laid out possible solutions; while you're fact-checking, one fact you notice is that your partner thinks differently from you. Now the problem is complex, because you're still dealing with the first dilemma, and are also presented with a second: how to work with your partner to find the best solution.

In the "Conflict-Resolution Tactics" exercise, you'll get to play an advice columnist. As you read each letter from a perplexed reader, picture its writer in your mind, and provide what you think is the best answer. Write your answers on a separate sheet, starting each reply with "Dear Half," "Dear Movin'," and so forth.

CONFLICT-RESOLUTION TACTICS

1. I'm very neat and orderly, and my honey simply isn't. So I end up doing a lot of the picking up, which is all right.

   We've made bargains that my messy mate won't impede my efforts by leaving dirty clothes or dishes out, but often my otherwise cooperative spouse "forgets" and I end up angry. How can we both live in the same house?

   Half of The Odd Couple

2. My mate has many outstanding talents, especially in organizing successful events. I believe people should use their talents to advance, and I went to graduate school and have become a top professional in my field.

   But my talented partner just plods along in the same old job, wasting valuable time and skills. When I point this out and offer to help toward finding a new position or training, the reply is, "I'd like to move up," but there's never any action. I'm getting exasperated and don't want to live with a lazy underachiever forever. What to do?   *Movin' On Up*

3. I've been happily married to the sweetest person on earth for three years, and it's truly been heaven. But lately I've felt my mate's pressure to have a child. I don't see why we should disturb a good thing, and conversations about this leave us both upset.

   You can't compromise on this—either you have a child or you don't, so what are we to do?   *Three's A Crowd*

4. Our finances are carefully budgeted, and we have only a small amount of leeway. But my partner finds it hard to refrain from buying the "perfect" item to round out a bulging wardrobe, or an expensive birthday gift that supposedly fits a friend or relative to a T.

   We've been deeply in debt more than once due to these uncontrolled habits, and I'm tired of explaining why they can't go on. My spendthrift has rationalizations for every purchase. How can we stay together and out of the poorhouse?
   Penny-Watcher

5. I've been married only three months, and already my partner's mother is intruding too much. She calls twice a day with advice on our personal business. Neither of us likes her meddling, but we've tried to be tolerant and civil, discouraging Mom every way we know how.

   I get tired of the lack of privacy and complain. But my partner responds, "Mom is just trying to be helpful." I think we *do* need help—yours!
   Didn't Marry Mom

6. My partner's sexual desires are too much for me. Every night, there's pleading for me to have sex at least two or three times.

   I've told my mate I just can't keep up, but the reply is, "Then I might have to satisfy the urge elsewhere, and I wouldn't want to do that." I wouldn't like that either, but what can I do?
   Sore

7. My otherwise dear mate has awful table manners, and I'm often embarrassed by behaviors like chewing with an open mouth, leaving food and crumbs all over, or burping after a meal.

   I told my partner the correct way to behave. There's some effort, but lots of ignoring the problem, too. What can I do?
   Dreads Mealtime

8. My partner's 8-year-old daughter from a previous marriage is living with us, and now is coming between us. Susie expects to get what she wants, and usually gets it. My spouse tries to set rules, but the child pits us against each other to connive her own way. I feel as if I'm in a strange position, since she's only been here a year. I don't know how to resolve this—do you?
   Not Quite A Parent

Patterns in Your Relationship

9. I really like to spend Sundays at home just relaxing, but my partner likes to constantly go, go, go. We tried to compromise by alternating Sundays, but on our "off" weekends, we're both frustrated and angry. What's the solution?

    Never On Sunday

10. My partner's a very social, charming person, which is one reason I was attracted in the first place. We give a lot of parties, and, ever the good host, my partner gives our guests a lot of personal attention.

    But when the guest is the opposite sex, I can't tell if it's flirting or hosting that's going on, and I find myself getting hot under the collar. My partner denies there's anything going on, but what I see isn't just friendliness. Any suggestions?

    Hurt By A Flirt

11. My lover loves an adorable dog, which is okay, but after a pan is used to prepare food, or when dinner's over, the dog is allowed to lick the pan or plate out on the back porch. This disgusts me but my partner says dog germs are clean and I should get over it. What do *you* think?   *In The Doghouse*

12. I believe one should have respect for one's body, so I exercise and try to eat right. I wish my partner would too, because I truly care and would hate for us to be separated by sickness or (heaven forbid) death.

    But this otherwise wonderful person is overweight, can't stop smoking, and gets no real exercise. I'm worried and said so, but my lover admits to a lack of discipline. I feel it's a matter of life or death but I don't know how to help.

    Fit And Frustrated

13. We have a lovely 6-year-old son, Danny. My spouse and I agree on how to raise him; it's Grandma who completely disregards the rules. We hate to keep complaining when she gives Danny too many sweets or lets him have any toys he wants.

    But she's over here for hours at a time, several days a week, and we're afraid her influence is getting destructive— Danny runs to Grandma for anything he wants. She ignores our requests that she change, so what are we to do?

    Had It With Danny's Granny

It was a challenge to write letters that didn't reveal the gender of the writer. Note which gender you assigned in each instance. Then scan your replies again. Most of the situations represent "complex" problems because there is disagreement between partners. Complex problems have four major methods of solution. Consider your advice-columnist responses to see how you applied the four styles below.

1. *Compromise*. This time-honored problem-solving method is usually applied when there is a range of possible solutions. In order for this method to work, there has to be some middle ground—an intermediate answer that involves concessions on the part of both parties. If you told "Half of the Odd Couple" in Letter 1 to set aside an area where Messy Mate could throw shirts and shoes, you suggested a compromise. That way the neater person would be guaranteed a clean living room, while the slovenly one could drop garments with impunity in an off-limits haven.

If you recommended that Letter 7's uncouth eater abide by etiquette in restaurants but have the freedom to revert to boorishness at home, you found a compromise. You did the same thing if you told the penny-watcher of Letter 4 to choose two occasions per year to spend lavishly on, while abiding by budgetary limits the rest of the year. With compromises each partner is satisfied to a degree, but not fully. Often compromise involves negotiating exactly *which* points each side should yield.

The art of negotiation involves many maneuvers, such as bartering, offering small concessions, introducing facts selectively, showing emotion at critical points, distracting the other person from the issue, and using specific negotiation-ending (or "closing") techniques. The negotiating process is the subject of many books, intended for use in interpersonal relations or in business. Many of the techniques require practice and an ability to sense your "opponent's" motives and moods. In a relationship you get lots of practice, and have the advantage of knowing your partner well.

2. *Educate and convince*. Everybody likes to think he or she is a reasonable person, so most people claim to have weighed all the pros and cons of a decision before making it. That's why educating and convincing your partner is likely to be your first tactic in getting your way. If you can convince your partner of your view, then you won't have to compromise.

When Rhonda wanted to invite 200 people to the wedding,

she knew Lance would protest. Because her family could only afford 150, they'd have to either ask his family to pick up the rest of the tab or fork out the cash themselves. Money was unimportant to Rhonda, but she knew that Lance was sensitive about it. So her negotiation-planning began before she broached the subject with him. She looked over the wedding presents that had come in already, and noted that Aunt Hilda had sent a check for $300. She also knew that her brother had pledged $300. Being a free-lance writer, she knew that she could, in a pinch, submit a Sunday magazine story to her friend at the local newspaper and earn another $400.

With these resources clearly laid out, she also planned possible negotiations with Lance. Maybe she would not have to write the story, if he would approach his well-to-do parents. She figured that, from a strictly financial standpoint, the other 50 guests would "pay their way" by bringing gifts. Poor Lance was not prepared for these negotiation tactics, so he was at a distinct disadvantage.

Rhonda's approach mainly involved educating and covincing. In pleading her case, she pointed out that part of the family would be slighted if they were not invited to the wedding. She noted that the garden would accommodate the extra guests without crowding. And she added that since chair and table rental fees decreased as quantities rose, the cost for those items would be practically the same. All very logical and reasonable.

Lance came back with his own set of facts. Actually he had only one fact, but it was compelling: "My family can't afford it." Rhonda then had to add more points to her argument, so since she'd exhausted the rational ones, she began referring to her feelings. Emotions are potent because no one can doubt them. Lance might have caught her on one of the other points (saying for example, that having an additional 50 guests might obscure the roses in the garden.) But what can he say to: "I *want* the Hayneses at the wedding! I haven't seen Mrs. Haynes in seven years, and I miss her! It would mean so much to me to know she was there when we got married!" Lance might then revert to his financial argument.

On the other hand, Lance can resort to emotions too. "I'd feel so pressured if we had to come up with extra money, and that pressure would ruin my enjoyment of what should be the happiest day of my life!" Lance knows his stuff. "If I asked my family for money, I'd feel like I was groveling; I'd be subordinating myself, as if I couldn't make it on my own. I can't take that."

Rhonda, if she's a caring partner, will show respect for Lance's feelings, and perhaps present more feelings of her own. An article in *Psychology Today* (October 1982) discusses the findings of John M. Gottman of the University of Illinois. He compared the arguing strategies of 487 couples who were either satisfied or dissatisfied with their marriages. Satisfied couples used "validation sequences" to indicate understanding of a partner's points; dissatisfied couples "cross-complained" by ignoring the other person and harping only on their own concerns. Since Rhonda's purpose was to educate and convince Lance, she needed to be attentive and reasonable. She couldn't just harangue him with her feelings, because then he would have felt that the discussion was out of control and unfair.

Because Rhonda and Lance were in a deadlock of feelings and logic, Rhonda had to pull out one of her aces. She attacked Lance's no-money argument directly. "We have $600 in wedding gift money that will cover most of the additional expense," she said, feigning that this revolutionary idea had just struck her.

"From where?" Lance challenged. As we know, Rhonda was prepared.

"From Aunt Hilda and my brother. They've each given us $300. And the reason they gave us money in the first place is to spend it any way we want. As you know, I really want to have the 50 extra guests." Cleverly, she moved directly from the mention of the extra money to an assumption that it should be spent on the wedding. This blocked Lance's possible counterargument that the money should go to setting up their household.

Lance was stymied. He didn't know that it would cost $1,000 to feed the extra 50 people. So, believing his argument destroyed, he consented. Rhonda smiled, relieved that she wouldn't have to write a newspaper story in the weeks before her wedding. She knew that the extra $400 would have to be paid eventually, but she was confident that the generosity of Lance's parents, or their own credit cards, would fill the gap. The hard part was getting Lance's okay in time to send out the invitations.

So in educating and convincing, Rhonda only had to use *some* of her negotiating skills. Lance didn't ask for a compromise ("how about inviting only 25 extra guests?"), and Rhonda didn't have to promise him her own labor to earn what she wanted. She never had to pull rank or remind Lance that he was getting *his* way on other issues. She simply presented facts; he raised a potential roadblock, and she educated him as to how it might be overcome.

3. *Alternate preferences.* In some cases of disagreement, when neither party wants to compromise or it's a one-or-the-other choice, the solution is based on fairness. The idea is that partners should take turns getting what they want. "This time you can invite 50 more guests; next time we buy the make of car I long for." This strategy is usually only necessary when both partners have equal degrees of commitment to their choices. "I *really* want the sports car, despite its unspectacular gas mileage." "Well, I *really* think we ought to get that thrifty family car." Sure, you can flip a coin, but there's no justice in that. One person can have a run of bad coin tosses and end up resentful. Instead, on issues of comparable magnitude, you can take turns.

In the advice-columnist exercise, that's what "Never on Sunday," tried to do. This person's preferred leisure activities clashed with those of the other partner. Unfortunately, theirs was a grudging compromise, and neither was willing to enjoy spending Sundays the way the other person wanted. They might now try the next strategy:

4. *Change your attitude.* There are only three things you can do about any given situation: change the situation (either leave so you're not part of it, or take action to make it different); do nothing; or change your attitude about it. Once you decide to solve a problem, you might conclude that the best course of action is to do nothing. And yet, you're unhappy. Things are just not right.

The real problem may be your *attitude*—you feel distressed about something that you can't change.

So, forget it. Don't make the problem your concern any longer. In your advice-columnist answers, you might have told "Movin' On Up," whose unambitious mate was a source of distress, to just accept the underachiever and quit trying to change him or her. "Hurt by a Flirt," the person who couldn't stand party-time flirting by his or her partner, could definitely use this advice. As you free yourself from concern or responsibility, you become more tolerant. And as you recall from my interviews with long-married couples, tolerance is one of the main ingredients for a blissful marriage.

Resolving Conflicts in Your Relationship

Through your "Conflict-Resolution Tactics" advice-columnist answers, you practiced being objective in the solving of other people's problems. (These are the most common problems I hear from married couples, by the way.) Now you'll have an opportunity to apply all these concepts to your own situation. The difference is that instead of being detached, you're right in the thick of current disputes or see potential ones coming.

The "Potential for Conflict" questionnaire can help you put the sources of your discontent on paper. Classic areas of disagreement are listed in the left-hand column. Check off the ones that are sore spots now. Then, if you're contemplating marriage, are engaged, or want to develop a relationship, check off the likelihood that each could be a future bugaboo. In the right-hand column, list the factors that might contribute to disagreements. A factor is any influence on a partner's feelings or on the conflict itself—for example, a factor on "relationship with relatives" might be "My folks live next door," a factor relative to "personal hygiene" might be "husband refuses to bathe more than once a week." If you expect other areas to be problematic, jot them down on a separate sheet and respond in the same way.

As a means of troubleshooting, it's a good idea to thoroughly discuss each of these areas with your partner. One way to lay out the particulars as well as some possible solutions is to use the "Resolving Conflicts" format. Fill in each box. This approach acknowledges that both you and your partner have a role in each disagreement or conflict, and that both of you have opportunities to help resolve the problem. In coming up with solutions, consider the alternatives of compromising, educating and convincing, alternating preferences, and changing your or your partner's attitude.

Now that you've identified your conflicts, and determined each of your roles in causing and solving them, you're ready for the next stages of resolution: choosing tentative answers, fact-checking them, and coming to a final decision about what to do. The format titled "Steps Toward Successful Negotiation" can help you to organize a negotiating session with your partner. In fact, whenever you're in the heat of emotional turmoil, it may be helpful to call a momentary truce, run for this book, and use these tools. They will help you calm down, and the structure will keep you on the track to resolution.

POTENTIAL FOR CONFLICT

Area	Disagreement now — Strong	Some	Slight	None	Likely Disagreement after marriage — Very likely	Somewhat likely	Not very likely	Not at all likely	Factors contributing to the disagreement
Relationship with my relatives(s)									
Relationship with my partner's relative(s)									
Money									
Children									
Sloppiness/ Neatness									
Personal hygiene									
Differences in goals or energy									
Division of household chores									
My career									
My partner's career									
Personal philosophies									
Place of residence									

Resolving Conflicts

The conflict	My role in creating the conflict	My partner's role in creating the conflict	Three ways I could improve the situation	Three ways my partner could improve the situation

Patterns in Your Relationship

Steps Toward Successful Negotiation

Instructions: Choose a topic about which there is current disagreement, as a way of trying out the steps below with your partner.

1. What are the influences shaping each person's desire:
           SELF   PARTNER
   a. From the past?
   b. In the present?
2. Whose need to have his/her way is greater regarding this subject? _____
3. Which of us is better able to tolerate *not* getting his/her way? _____
4. Which of us got his/her way the last time we disagreed about something of about the same significance? _____
5. Whose turn is it to have his/her way? _____
6. Is there some trade we could make where one person "wins" this disagreement but allows the other to have his/her way on another issue? _____
   If so, what is the other issue? _____
7. Is there some way we could each get *part* of what we desire regarding this issue? _____
   If so, which parts do I want? _____
   Which parts can I allow my partner? _____
8. Given the alternative resolutions to this conflict, and an underlying sincere desire to resolve this issue, the best course to take is: _____

Practice using the negotiation format with both major and minor disagreements just a few times. You'll learn the strategies inherent in it (educating and convincing, taking turns, compromising, and attitude changing) and will gain a valuable resource that should serve you in a variety of contexts.

SECTION *Four*

Planning a Future

THE PRECEDING SECTIONS of this book helped you assess yourself, your partner, and the relationship you have. You looked at personal characteristics, communication style, and roles. All of the discussion was directed toward predicting the future, and it's that future you'll have the opportunity to study more carefully now.

/ 8
Children

IN "FIRST COMES LOVE" workshops, I see three types of concerns about children, relating to (1) the care of existing young children, (2) the reactions of grown children, and (3) the decision whether or not to have a child. Couples can have one, two, or all three of these concerns. (There's also a fourth subgroup in the workshop: people who want to avoid the issue altogether.)

Problems of Parents of Younger Children

A large number of participants, ranging from their twenties through their fifties, are concerned about the care of existing children. They may have primary or joint custody with an ex-spouse; they may have even chosen to be a single parent, and adopted or had a child on their own. Some of these people's most frequently mentioned concerns were expressed by Deborah, 38, a mother of 10-year-old twin boys, and her partner Elliot, 34, who shared joint custody of his 6-year-old daughter.

"We've gotten very close over the past six months," Deborah began, "but we really don't know if we should marry. Not because of *our* feelings, but more because we care so much about the kids."

Elliot went on to explain:

They don't really know what's going on between us, and that's mainly because we're a little afraid to tell them. We're both high school teachers at the same school, and we've been carrying on our relationship between 3 and 5 o'clock. We spend breaks together, eat lunch together, and you can get to know someone pretty well after days discussing the same principal, discipline problems, union issues, and students. We went away for a weekend to a conference, and the kids do know that we're together, but they just think we're colleagues, not lovers.

Deborah said that their main fear was that the boys would be jealous of Elliot.

They've had all my attention for three years now, and they expect it. Elliot has come over twice for dinner, and they seem to resent him—they were talking only to me and treating him as if he were invisible! It's understandable; they're just boys who need love and caring. But they were so torn apart by my divorce that I'd hate to interrupt their lives again. Their father left them and only comes by three or four times a year, and they're justifiably afraid that I'll leave them emotionally, too. Then they'd be stranded.

Elliot interjected some comments about how the children should be handled:

We've read all the parenting books, and we agree that we have to make them part of *our* life rather than catering to them constantly. We've both dealt with enough kids to know that they want rules set for them; they need an authority. We're experienced at that; what we're not prepared for is having our own loyalties to our children interfere with our feelings for each other.

Deborah defended the children, saying:

My boys are pretty mature for their age. They fight some, but handling the divorce has given them a scary sophistication. They joke with their friends about child-support payments, and that horrifies me. But they only do it because most of the other kids have been through a divorce too, or have a relative who's divorced. I'm worried about how they'll accept Nicole, Elliot's daughter. Having a new man in the house would be traumatic, but having another child—and especially a *girl*—would bring chaos and lots of acting out.

At this point in the workshop discussion, Candice, now 50, recalled an experience she had twenty years ago.

My first husband died, leaving me and my two preschoolers clinging desperately to each other. I immersed myself in them out of sheer terror of facing the world, and as a result, they became very dependent on me. When they were about the age of your twins, Deborah, I felt strong enough to consider a dear family friend something *more* than a friend. I was afraid of losing him, so I'd never allowed myself to see more than platonic possibilities. I don't know why some other woman didn't snap him up, but we finally got together.

The kids already knew Robert, so there was no problem of introducing him in the household. But they did put up a fuss when we started to let them know that Robert might come live with us. "What? And steal

Mommy?" they thought, rightfully. They did just as you said: they started throwing tantrums and causing trouble at school. I had to have conferences with the school psychologist and principal and their teacher at least a dozen times. They told me to give them more attention, to reassure them that even though Robert was around, they'd always have my love.

Looking back, I can tell you that that was the *worst* thing I could have done. Instead of calming down, they got the message that if they misbehaved I'd give them more attention! They became such a problem, and my devotion to them was so complete, that pretty soon Robert figured that he didn't want to drive a wedge in our family. He'd seen us less distressed before the romance began, so he backed off. I didn't even protest, because dealing with the kids was making me a nervous wreck. We both figured that it wasn't worth it.

Candice looked down and put her hand to her face as she fought back tears. She whispered, "Here I had a close, warm, supportive relationship with a man who proved he would be there through thick and thin. And I threw it away and made my kids brats, all at the same time." The other people in the room were silent, as Candice breathed deeply to regain her composure. She soon looked over at Deborah and Elliot. "Don't be foolish enough to put the children before yourselves," she admonished. "Your children will grow up and you'll wish you'd taught them to respect their own desires; and you'll wish you had each other to love for the following thirty years."

Candice's advice is important because it is based on the most crucial factor in whether any couple—parents or not—should marry: *feelings* about one's partner. Deborah and Elliot were about to push those feelings aside because of their children. Though they were psychologically sophisticated, they did not fully recognize the need to prepare their children for independence and to set an example by being involved in a loving, caring relationship. Still, they zeroed in on several legitimate concerns:

- Jealousy and competition for the parents' attention.
- The likelihood that parents feel torn about how to allocate their time and caring, and feel guilty that they're neglecting someone who needs them.
- The relationship between children and the stepparent, once the new partner joins an existing household.

Deborah and Elliot never mentioned some other concerns that commonly arise when two families join:

- What role the natural parents would take in mediating disputes and refereeing the relationship of stepparent and children.
- Worry about the expense of setting up a larger household.
- How the privacy of family members (in terms of both living space and time to be alone) can be guaranteed.
- How different parenting styles can be reconciled.

Refer to the discussion in Chapter 4 for several suggestions for handling these problems. I've found that an enthusiastic attitude seems to portend an easy transition more than any specific techniques or rules. Couples who wave off problems, make light of inconveniences, and are confident that they can overcome obstacles convey that feeling to their children, and everything seems to progress more smoothly. Well-meaning parents who become bogged down in their concern for their children sometimes imply that there's *reason* to be worried.

Naturally, you should enter into your marriage with a realistic sense of what problems are likely to develop. But if you plan strategies for coping with problems in advance, they won't loom as large and may be avoided completely. In order to confront your fears, look at the two lists of concerns that were just given, and check off those you'd like to address. Then discuss them with your partner. If you do decide to get married, when you announce this to your older children you might mention some of your concerns and plans, and ask for their cooperation in pulling together for a successful transition. Then, take it in your stride when the children disregard their pledges and act like kids.

Concerns of Parents of Adult Children

Just because children grow up is no reason to think they are out of your life. Many workshop participants have adult children whose opinions they value. They may have reservations about remarriage because of concern about how their offspring will react. Esther, 55, said:

I've always thought of myself as a mother first. When I was married, I felt that my kids couldn't function without me, but my husband, an adult, could. That was my mistake. He functioned *very* well without me. He left me to marry a woman who was married at the time too. They both got divorces, and now *they're* divorced.

I didn't realize it at the time, but I decided to be a model for my children. I quoted Benjamin Franklin and Thomas Jefferson, I played

Bach and Mozart, I had a positive mental attitude. I refused to sit around and mope, so we went to the museum, the movies, the beach. I was proud of myself. And little by little, as the kids went to college and became independent, I got more self-sufficient.

Sounds pretty good, doesn't it? The trouble is that I sill think of myself as a model for the kids, and they come to me for advice. To them, I'm the Rock of Gibraltar. Now Thomas, my beau, wants me to live with him, and I'm really up in the air. I've got my youngest's college tuition to pay, and I'm just building a nest egg. I have a great job heading the counseling center at the community college. But I'm confused and afraid. I have been so straight-laced, I feel conflicted about living with someone, and yet it's the most logical thing to do. I keep rationalizing why I shouldn't do it. But the theme that keeps running through my head is: "What will the kids think?"

Esther couldn't get out of the role of "mother" and into the role of friend to her children. Admittedly, most mothers never do. People who are totally wrapped up in their parental role can't stop protecting their children long enough to respect them as competent individuals.

Some mothers feel their protective function should never end. They might say: "What do you mean, I should be a friend to my adult child? That's unnatural! I care about my child, so why shouldn't I be protective? I gave my life childrearing, made it my career. You can't just let go like that. You can't just treat your own flesh and blood like a stranger off the street!" Mothers with this attitude often have children who are in their thirties and forties (who have teenage children of their own). These "children" may have been divorced and remarried; they run companies and have at-home computers. They love their mothers, but wouldn't be caught dead with them in a trendy bistro. In fact, because values are so different for the two generations, they try to share little of their personal lives with their mothers in order to avoid aggravation all around.

I also know mothers whose attitudes are entirely different. I met some of them at my workshop, admitting their fears and being emotionally vulnerable. "I'm proud of my son," said Maggie, near 55 but with the body and panache of youth. "He's been married ten years and is a lawyer. His wife, also a lawyer, just had their first child, delivered by a midwife at our home. It was the most exciting experience of my life; they'd knocked me out for my own delivery." Maggie's excitement about new medical advances, travel, politics, and fitness was contagious. "I'm at this workshop because I believe in making informed choices. Bill and I have been living together for three years, and we suddenly just looked at each other and said, 'Why not?' " She laughed. "It was the same way we decided to take our trip around the world!"

For most people, however, it's difficult to make the change from protective mother to caring but independent friend. Still, I strongly recommend that parents of adults "let go." If this transition is accomplished, adult children's opinions become valuable information but not the driving factor in one's personal decisions.

Children: To Have or Have Not?

Earlier in this book, I mentioned that the "First Comes Love" workshops started because people in my childbearing decision workshops clamored for them. It may seem backward for couples to make the childbearing decision *before* they get married, but this is a growing trend. Perhaps a fourth of the couples I see in my "baby workshops" are considering marriage only *if* they decide to have a child. Otherwise, they feel more comfortable living together, perhaps as they've done for years.

Child-related concerns can make the decision to marry very complicated. One partner might have grown children, another might have younger children, and the pair might be considering having a child together. Most common, however, are the three types of decision-makers described below.

Now-or-Never Couples

These couples are in a bind. They're not sure they're quite ready to start a family (read, "become tied down, interrupt their careers, give up their wanderlust, lower their lifestyle, or bring a little person between the two of them"). But they're also racing the clock—feeling the ticks of time which signal that the woman is becoming too old for childbearing.

Rebecca and John are an illustration. "I'm perfectly content with my life as it is now," Rebecca lamented, "but I'm afraid that if I don't act soon I may end up regretting that I missed what's billed as life's ultimate experience." Married for six years, she and John enjoyed their jobs and their weekend outings to dog shows with their attentive shelties. "I'm not the kind of person who wants to come home and fuss with booties," Rebecca noted. "But who knows if I'd feel differently if those booties were on the feet of my *own* baby?"

Throughout Rebecca's pondering, John was supportive but noncommital. "I don't particularly long to have a child," he confessed, "but I want to see Rebecca happy, so I'd gladly go along with her decision. I kind of value my time alone, and like being able to come and go without much responsibility. I'm with Rebecca because I *want* to be. But I'd *have* to help with the baby; there's no choice." Still, he shared Rebecca's fear that he might later regret his decision. And because they were both on the cusp of 40, he knew that they could not just let the issue slide.

Conflicted Couples

These couples disagree about the children issue. They may also be facing a time deadline, but their overriding problem is that their inclinations clash. Lois and Richard, whom you met in Chapter 7, had this problem. As you recall, they'd come to me in an acute state of anxiety. Lois, two months pregnant, refused to get an abortion, though Richard was adamantly against having any children. Talk about conflict—their case is the extreme.

"You want to leave? Go ahead!" Lois challenged. "I don't want you to. I want you to be happy with me, to be excited about this new phase of our life together."

"You thought I'd be mad for a little while, and then I'd calm down, didn't you?" Richard asked Lois. He was right: that had been exactly her plan. Lois sat motionlessly, and Richard continued: "But I don't like being bullied, and I don't like feeling helpless, as if you're running my life. I hope you're prepared to be a single parent. Are you?" he shot to her unexpectedly.

Lois didn't skip a beat. "If I have to, I will," she replied firmly. "Do you want to get a divorce?"

Richard stewed silently. "I didn't say *what* I was going to do," he finally replied. "I try to plan out my entire life, I finally get to a place where I'm happy with the way it's going, and then wham! she pulls this stunt. This isn't the way it's supposed to be. This is completely unfair! And now I'm expected to just get out my hostility and then forgive her like nothing happened. Well, a lot's happened. I can never trust her again. I'll resent the child. I'll always be thinking of what I *could've* done with my life, with all the time we'd spend on diapers and spit-up and teachers' meetings. It was because I disliked kids that I made Lois promise never to have them in the first place!"

"But you'd make such a good Daddy," Lois insisted. "Maybe now you feel that way, but once you saw the baby, your own child, you'd feel differently. It's very different when they're your own."

"I never cared to find out!" Richard protested. "You've duped me, conned me. How can I listen to your asinine coaxing? How can I stand to be with you ever again!" Richard was hissing the accusations forcefully, to hold back his anger and tears. His behavior was understandable, as he was boxed into a corner.

I instructed the couple to try to detach themselves from their strong emotions long enough to complete some questionnaires and do some role-playing. They were to put themselves in the other person's position, as well as project their life both with and without a child and with and without each other. Normally this process takes about three weeks, but I condensed it into a single week because Lois soon either had to see a prenatal counselor or obtain an abortion.

"I'm more determined than ever to have this baby," Lois stated at their next appointment. "I'm willing to do it alone if I have to, but I know I can't pass this opportunity by. The timing is great for me, and my health insurance would cover the expense. I love Richard, but no matter what the situation is, my first priority is to be a mother."

Lois's stubbornness and commitment to her objective were part of her strategy to force Richard to give in. She knew that he valued his relationship with her. If she wavered, he might seize the chance to point out her doubts. Instead, she made the pregnancy a take-it-or-leave-it proposition.

Richard knew what was happening, and as the week had gone on, the exercises he completed with Lois had confirmed that he was fighting a losing battle. "I don't like being jerked around," he said. "It isn't fair!" Gradually his objections became weaker and weaker, until his only threat was that he might resent the child. Lois's optimism never wavered; she kept insisting that Richard would have fun with his child, and they would discover all sorts of new diversions together.

Not all conflicts have a happy ending. About a third of the conflicted couples I see break up over this issue. Usually, one partner has never been a parent and really wants a child, while the other has been through it before and cherishes the child-free life.

Conflicted couples aren't always in such opposing corners, though. Often the partners have slightly different inclinations, or they agree on the outcome but differ on timing. One couple wanted children, but the wife wanted them *now* while the husband wanted to wait about three years until his career took off. Another couple was divided, but one partner was about 60 percent in favor of a child, and the other 60 percent against. A third conflicted couple included a man who strongly wanted to have a child soon, while his lover wasn't sure what she wanted to do.

Planners

Planners are couples who *do* know their minds. They've definitely decided one way or another and feel good about that choice. But before they plunge ahead (by getting pregnant or by being sterilized), they want to confirm their decision and look at its ramifications. They're called planners because they like to organize their lives and prepare well for what's to come. In fact, just by the fact that you're reading this book, you're probably a planner, too.

Jack and Judith were in this group. While other couples at my "children" workshop would bring up all sorts of scary possibilities, they were uniformly upbeat. A group member would say that she feared becoming a stay-at-home with a child; Jack would immediately pipe up about putting the child in a backpack and trundling off to Europe. A woman would voice her concern about body distortion during pregnancy, and Judith would cite cases of women's figures improving with the experience. There was no doubt that Jack and Judith were psychologically ready to be parents, yet after the workshop, they thanked me for helping them to gain new insight. "We always wanted to have children," Judy said, "but now we know *why*. We also know more about the changes to anticipate, as well as several ways we can cope with them."

A Parenthood Questionnaire

The "Deciding the Role of Parenthood in Your Life" checklist is designed to help you sort out the major factors in the decision to have a child. Interpret each factor as it would apply to you. This involves examining values, expectations, and feelings. For example, under "Effects of a Child on Career/Education," the third item is "effect of parenthood on present job and short-term goals."

Deciding the Role of Parenthood In Your Life

Fill out this checklist alone, then compare with your partner's responses.

	Need to consider	Satisfied in this area	Problem to work out
● **Effects of a Child on Career/Education**			
How pregnancy will affect wife's professional development and how she is perceived professionally			
Effect of parenthood on long-term career goals (for self and partner)			
Effect of parenthood on present job and short-term goals			
The priority given home responsibilities versus work			
Synchronization of child care with work: One partner at home—how long? Which partner at home during which stages of childrearing?			
Feasibility of each child-care option: live-in help, relatives, baby-sitters, play groups, preschools			
● **Effects of a Child on Family Finances**			
Type of housing required			
Child-care expenses, immediately and as the child grows			
Obstetrics, pregnancy-related costs			
Savings for the child's future			
Change in standard of living, now and in the future			
Effect of child-related expenses on material or recreational desires			

	Need to consider	Satisfied in this area	Problem to work out
• Effects of a Child on Relationship Between Partners			
Potential competition for attention between child and partner			
Having the child for my partner versus for myself			
Whether having the child will make partners feel bound in the relationship			
Similarity of my partner's and my parenting approaches			
• Effects of a Child on Relationships with Others			
Relationship between the new child and existing children or relatives			
Our parents' reactions and how that would affect each of us			
Our place in our circle of friends			
Our role in community activities			
• Personal Considerations			
My view of myself as parent (as different from present roles)			
My freedom to do as I please			
My feelings about responsibility and good parenting			
Spontaneity—for myself and our relationship			
My/our need for privacy: How important is this?			
Strength of my own and my partner's feelings about the benefits of parenthood.			

Being a Parent

	Need to consider	Satisfied in this area	Problem to work out
My/My partner's feelings about:			
Pregnancy and birth			
Babies			
Toddlers			
Young children			
Older children			
Younger teenagers			
Older teenagers and young adults			
My/my partner's projections about what our child will be like			
The kind of world my child might grow up in			

You need to decide exactly what these effects might be, taking into account such things as company maternity/paternity leave policies, the type of work each of you does, and your inclinations either to stay home or to return to work shortly. If you have an acceptable plan, check "satisfied in this area." If there's some kind of hitch—ranging from a disagreement with your partner to, say, no available child care—check "problem to work out." If you need more information, check "need to consider."

One of the best ways to gather information about topics you have marked "need to consider" is to talk to parents. Ask what their experience has been, what the biggest surprises of parenthood were, and what things they wished they'd known beforehand. If you know people who have decided not to have children, ask whether they ever regret their decision and whether they have a need to have children in their lives. I also recommend borrowing a child, especially one of the age you fear most. The more first-hand experience you have, the more fodder you have for making your choice.

But remember that the childbearing decision is like the decision to marry: it's an emotional choice. As you interview parents, spend time with children, and discuss the issue with your partner, try to get in touch with your gut feelings. If you find yourself avoiding the subject, that's a message in itself indicating that either you don't want children in your life now or you want to avoid conflict in your relationship. If you can't wait to discuss the subject with mothers, start talking baby talk at the sight of a Gerber's ad, and daydream about playgrounds, you obviously are in favor of parenthood. On the other hand, if kids make you nervous and you value both quiet and your glass figurine collection, realize that you've probably structured your life so that having children would be difficult. Whatever your deepest feelings are, *talk* about them with your partner—unless you want to risk ending up like Lois and Richard. Make a bargain to keep reassessing how you both feel as the years go by.

Parenthood After 30

Just as people are postponing marriage for various reasons (such as wanting more time to get started in a career), they are putting off having children. In the "Children: To Have or Have Not?" workshops, I see many couples who went through one or more marriages in their twenties, and never gave parenthood a serious thought. But now that they feel their personal deadlines approaching—whether that is age 30, 35, or 40—they feel a need to decide one way or the other. These people often realize that they have more time than they'd thought.

"I'm 29 and I'm in this workshop because my 30th birthday is next week," said Louise. "My mother always said that it's best to have your family young, so you can grow up with them, and so you'll have lots of energy to meet the challenges."

Danielle, 37, grimaced. "I don't exactly feel over the hill," she protested. "I don't believe that myth that you lose your spunk just because of the number of candles on the cake. First off, I keep in great shape: I run three miles every day and I take aerobics classes twice a week. I think I could outrun a toddler, don't you?" The group laughed.

"My mother had me when she was 43," said Ryan. "She kept up with me just fine. In fact, she said that having me around kept her young. It's easy to stagnate if you don't have some stimulation or reason to be active. People keep their health longer nowadays. At age 70, my mother is still going strong. In fact, she walks the links playing golf four times a week, and she hauls heavy bags of groceries up the fifty-eight steps to their front door. I don't think you can use the same standards now that were used even twenty years ago."

Enid, a nurse, spoke up. "That's definitely true when it comes to childbirth. Did you know that a woman of age 40 giving birth now runs the same risks as a 20-year-old did just twenty years ago? I heard that figure from Planned Parenthood, and it's stuck with me. As an obstetrical nurse, I see lots of older women having first babies—even those over 40. Sometimes it's a little more difficult, but with their strong interest and the prenatal training they get, they seem to do just fine."

"I never had a child before because I wasn't married until age 34," said Carol. "I always wanted a child, and it used to bother me that I was deprived just because I wasn't married." The room tittered with comments about marriage not being necessary for childbearing. "Maybe a million teenagers don't think they need a husband to raise a child, but I do," Carol responded. "Anyway, now I'm glad that I didn't have a child when I was younger. I was able to accomplish a lot more and establish myself professionally. Now, when I *do* have a child, I'll just be taking time out from an ongoing career rather than having to start again from the beginning when my child is older. And I'm also aware that I'm more mature now; I think I'll be more tolerant and patient with my child because of the lessons I've learned."

"The important criterion for having a child," I told all the participants, "is that the baby should be a *bonus* to an already satisfying life. Don't think that a child will solve your problems, patch up your marriage, or be a nice career to try because your present one isn't satisfying. Only have a child if, after completing all the questionnaires and role-playing, you have a basic feeling that you *want* the whole experience of parenthood (not just a baby or the experience of childbirth, for example). Sure, you can and will have conflicts. No matter what you decide, there will be ambivalence and regret at times. If you choose to be child-free, you'll wonder about the child you never had. If you have children, you'll think about how far you'd have gone in your career, or how quiet the house would be if the kids weren't there. But keep in touch with the *balance*, the sum of your moments of ecstasy and doubt. If you keep your long-term goals in sight, you'll move in the right direction."

Making it Work

Earlier you read about Supermom, that mythical beast who is able to combine a passionate marriage, a skyrocketing career, and the rearing of two perfect children. Perhaps you've read about her counterpart, Superdad, who carries Baby to the park in a sling across his chest, makes incredible homemade pasta, and grows sixty-five varieties of vegetables in the garden. He's voluntarily put his career "on hold" to enjoy the experience of raising his child. There *are* some Superdads around (though very few—most men don't even consider giving up or postponing their careers), but you'll notice that this new male model is *not* as super as his female counterpart. Interestingly, we often give him more credit than we do the millions of women who have to combine career and motherhood, usually out of economic necessity.

Among the couples I see, the question of juggling work and parenting is often central to the decision of whether or not to have a child. Even those women who are most "liberated" and dedicated to their careers also dearly want to *be there* when their child is developing. They want to see those first steps, and encourage those first words. Far fewer men feel this way.

Yet many women don't want to put their careers "on hold." Some talk about part-time jobs, or getting a computer terminal and working at home. Others hope to use "flextime," working at unusual hours to be with the children more. Still others embark on new types of work that can be done at home, such as baking, writing, or sewing handmade items to sell. A popular solution (though one that most couples can't afford) is to have a live-in nanny—someone who can be trusted to give loving care when Mom is too busy, so that "quality time" can be squeezed in more conveniently.

Many women are rediscovering the value of the extended family, and relying on grandparents and others for devoted care. Day-care facilities and other community-sponsored programs are making child care by outsiders more feasible and affordable. Women have also discovered another option: each other. They're forming care groups and networks so that they can trade services easily whenever one of the mothers must be away from home. If you truly want to have a child, you will eventually find some way to surmount the inevitable hurdles.

Choosing to be Child-Free

Some people never have to think about the child-related problems just discussed—they've chosen to be permanently child-free. Before the early 1970s, this stance was definitely out of favor. Alexander, 48 and a university professor, tells his story.

When I got married in the '50s, you didn't even question what would happen. You got married. You had children ("get them out of the way" was often the term), and you got on with your life. Your wife took time off, if she was working, or she gave up all career aspirations gladly to fulfill this new, supposedly rewarding role of "mother." This viewpoint was simple and yet demanding. When I was just starting out, I had too many financial worries. I was still finishing my doctorate when my first son was born, and was doing research part-time. It was really tough. When I finished my degree, I had to take the first job offered me just to make ends meet, even though it probably wasn't the best offer I would've gotten.

To be honest, if I had it to do all over again, I probably wouldn't have had children. I love my sons. They're great companions and I'm proud of them. But I could have been very happy without them, and I would have felt a lot freer, like there was a heavy responsibility lifted from my shoulders.

You may have read about the responses that advice columnist Ann Landers got when she asked readers whether they would have children if they had it to do over again. "No!" was the overwhelming reader reply. The sample was not systematic and may not have been representative of the general population, but the point is that children can bring sorrow as well as joy.

"Not having children is so *selfish*," many parents counter. But I've found that having children and choosing nonparenthood are *equally* selfish. A study by Judith Blake at U.C.L.A. found that parents have children for selfish reasons, primarily for the social rewards they bring. If you know you wouldn't be an enthusiastic parent and wish to spare a potential child from your resentment, this decision is as altruistic as having a child because you truly want one. Some people, upon thinking through their desires and separating out all the reasons to have children that are related solely to others' reactions, find that they have no strong parenting drive within themselves. If more people realized this in advance, child-abuse statistics would drop accordingly.

Many people who decide to have children are thinking only short-term. Teenagers, especially, tend not to look at the longer haul. They may love the warm cuddles of a baby, and think toddlers are adorable. They may relish the attention given pregnant women, and want to bask in the pride of new motherhood. But seldom do they look ahead to envision themselves as the young parents of teenagers.

Many wise people, employing more farsighted thinking, choose nonparenthood. They know they'd want to give a child a lot of attention and love; they know that this tie lasts a lifetime. And they also know that they're involved in other things, like teaching. Paul and Carrie are good examples. Paul said:

I don't want to have kids because I see first-hand, every day, how much love and time kids require. I teach third grade. I enjoy the kids; I wouldn't have spent fifteen years as a teacher if I didn't. But I also see how easily kids are neglected. Mothers don't come down to the school for conferences because they've got little ones at home, or because they have to work just to make the rent payment.

It's true that some parents just don't care. But some want us, the educators, to take their kids off their hands so that just occasionally, they can slip out from under their emotional load and have a two-hour rest. I can understand that completely. I give the kids my heart and soul. I spend hours after school tutoring them, and I act as their surrogate father if no one else is around. And then I come home and collapse. I turn on the stereo and rest in solitude a while, and then I go running, just to work out all the tensions the children engender. They drain you if you're really investing in them, and I need respite from that at home, not more of the same.

Carrie agreed, and said that she and Paul needed time to be together.

I teach junior high school music and English. At that age they can be like monkeys, so full of growth and energy. The girls are the worst. They're competitive and catty, trying to be grown-up. They wear clothes I could never afford and talk about birth control openly. They need a good role model—someone who is firm, honest, moral. So I don't want to slip; I want to show them what they can become as well as teach them skills to last a lifetime.

When I come home, I'm just like Paul. I need my privacy too for a while, and I go running. We run separately, though we're sometimes out at the same time. There's a definite need to unwind, and with kids around, that peace and privacy would never be there. Also, we'd have to spend a lot of time talking about our child rather than *not* talking about children. When you're married to a teacher, you tend to talk shop a lot anyway, even if you swear you won't. I want to spend the *rest* of our time together talking about the next trip we're taking to Europe!"

Paul and Carrie are typical of those who choose not to have children. They're alert, concerned people who work in careers in which they give their talents generously. They simply know themselves, and want to continue living in a way that is pleasing them. In that sense, yes, they are selfish. But remember that most decisions are made on selfish bases; every life choice is based on what's right for *you*.

Whatever you do, express your present feelings about children—existing or contemplated—with your partner *before* you get married. A surprising number of couples don't, and enter into a permanent relationship harboring assumptions that prove incorrect. Sometimes these "permanent" relationships have to be destroyed sorrowfully because of this sin of omission.

/ 9
Needs and Desires

Two kinds of needs and desires are explored in this chapter: sex and affection. Some people think of them synonymously, as if the term "making love" was accurate. But I'm sure you know couples who have fabulously satisfying sex and still lack warmth, closeness, and demonstrativeness. Conversely, a couple can be "in love" and enjoy endless outward tokens of affection, yet seldom have genital sex. So for purposes of analysis, I've separated the two.

Sexual Needs and Desires

Right now, imagine the most sensual, sexy get-together you could ever have with your partner. How would it begin? What would (or *wouldn't*) you wear? What would your partner look like? Think about the setting, the time of year, the time of day or night. How does your time together progress? What makes this mood so special? Savor this daydream for a few moments, languishing in the good feelings.

Has that occasion existed in reality? Could it ever be reality? If not, what ingredients separate your fantasy from what you now have with your partner? Do you think your partner would have a similar daydream, or a different one? How does this ideal sexual situation compare with your usual experience? Do you even want it to compare? Some people like their fantasies to remain just that, and enjoy having a secret pool of images from which to draw. Others choose not to fantasize very much at all, and may not easily create such a picture in their minds.

Still, if you're deciding about getting married, it is important to consider sexual compatibility. Some people reserve their sexual experience until after marriage, but it can still be helpful for them to articulate their expectations. Sex isn't the one crucial determinent of happiness, but without rewarding sex, frustration and resentment can erupt.

The idea that sex should be at all enjoyable, or serve any purpose beyond procreation, is a relatively new development. Under the authority of religious leaders (who used to be moral arbiters, but in the last twenty years have lost much of their power), sex was not to be discussed with young people except to explain about "the birds and the bees." Women clandestinely showed their growing daughters sanitary napkins, and fathers told their sons to avoid "social diseases." On the eve of the wedding ceremony, mothers resumed their educational role, explaining that their daughters' duty was intercourse on demand. The *real* education was to come on the wedding night, with the rest of married life being a series of gifts brought by the stork ("girls, hide your bump!" says one antiquated pregnancy manual) and secrets behind the locked bedroom door.

As you saw in Chapter 5, changes in how men and women relate to each other have brought confusion along with new options. The late 1960s and early 1970s spawned the "sexual revolution," which broke through barriers of earlier restriction and, most notably, taught women that they too deserved to be pleased via recreational sex. The sexual revolution coincided with the introduction of birth control pills, which allowed women to be completely in control of contraception without sexual spontaneity being interrupted. Soon mothers of teenagers weren't describing adult anatomy to their daughters; they were instead coping with their own inhibition when they were around sophisticated sexual experimenters.

While there was (and still is) concern about sexually precocious teenagers, adults wanted to benefit from newly condoned freedom. Tales of nightly orgies and casual nudity around the hot tub (whether true or false) sparked many to dabble in sensuality. Soon, large segments of the population disregarded conventional taboos, such as those against adultery and unusual sexual practices. Eventually, acts once deemed sexual experimentation became *de rigeur*. Instead of merely the obligatory good night kiss at the end of a first date, the frequent response became "your place or mine?" As sex role expectations have changed, women who fulfill their lust are no longer "bad girls" who get "reputations."

Women's need for sex was further legitimized when researchers William Masters and Virginia Johnson demystified the nature of sexual response and began using unmarried surrogates to assist patients in overcoming "dysfunctions." Suddenly, Masters and Johnson's work intimated, everyone is entitled to satisfying sex. Women who formerly were labeled "frigid" could often overcome hurdles to orgasm via sexual therapy. It was also a revelation that men, as well as women, were often to blame for sexual problems.

It's generally agreed that sexual adventures between single people are their own private business. Municipal laws about the personal activities of consenting adults have either been stricken or are unenforced. Just about anything goes for the unattached.

But when you enter into a liaison with another person, suddenly your behavior becomes his or her business as well. If it's clear that you have no obligation to each other, a variety of sexual experiences is fine. But when you start to date steadily, strings usually attach. Expectations of sexual exclusivity arise, sometimes at different times for each partner, and may cause severe rifts. Traditional expectations often reappear when a couple starts to "go steady," becomes engaged, and finally marries.

As part of the sexual revolution, however, even married couples reevaluated the idea of sexual exclusivity. Some seized on the idea of "open marriage," deciding that while they could pledge their emotional allegiance to their spouse, there was no reason why they needed to be otherwise faithful. Listen to what Angela and Aaron said about their relationship. You met them in Chapter 5, discussing how their relationship differed from that of their parents. Aaron is a minister, Angela, a journalist turned medical doctor. After nine years of marriage, they had a baby.

"I've never believed that monogamy, or even heterosexuality, is the natural way humans are meant to be," said Angela casually. She knew that her words were shocking, and waited for the reverberations.

"Why," you ask? Because humans are not limited in their capacity to love. For some animals, mating for life is instinctual; they have no desire to find mate after mate. That's not the case for people. We're curious, and we have the intellectual ability to inquire about others and care for them because of their unique qualities. If we were meant to only love one person, we wouldn't even *think* about adultery. We wouldn't have conflicts, and we wouldn't see sexual encounters as exciting or alluring. But we do."

Angela paused so that her words could sink in. She continued:

It's possible to love more than one person, that's clear. We love our friends. So why should we shut off the natural progression of that love, which is its physical expression? We allow ourselves to love spiritually—perhaps to hug occasionally or peck on the cheek under the right circumstances. *This* is unnatural. If you care for someone else, you should be allowed to show it. Marriage is simply the vow that you'll have consistency in your life—that you'll include one special other person in the realm of closest friendships you have. It might mean that your spouse is your *closest* friend, your *dearest* love. But why should having this wonderful relationship mean you have to nip others at a certain point? Our system is absurd.

Her husband was squirming. I asked about his views on the subject, and he responded:

What Angela says is perfectly rational and logical. I was against having outside relationships for many years. Having a religious background, I could not accept that we should give ourselves—*all* of ourselves—freely to those we care about. But the more Angela talked about it, the more I realized that it was inhibition and upbringing that kept me from accepting it, not some inherent truth about it. Here I am a minister, seeing lonely people daily. I'd put a barrier between myself and them, an invisible shield that said, "Don't come closer, we might love each other." It was artificial and strained.

Now don't think that I go to bed with every woman I come in contact with. Far from it. In fact, I've only had two very brief occasions in the entire thirteen years I've known Angela. I just couldn't and still can't bring myself to feel comfortable with it. And I refuse to force it for the sake of an intellectual argument. Feelings come first.

At this point Aaron turned to Angela and said, "I'm sorry, in a sense, that I can't be as 'liberated' as you are." She replied:

It doesn't matter that much. The important thing is that we're open with each other, and happy with our own conduct. I've had several more relationships than Aaron. But still, not that many. When Aaron and I are together, my needs are met. Just in the times when we're apart, I become closer with others, sort of to take his place. I never stop loving Aaron, but others are just physically with me more, and so our friendships progress. I think we're both the richer for having more love in our lives. We're not constrained by false boundaries.

Later, Angela expanded on the statement she had made about humans not naturally being heterosexual. She said she had had a few sexual experiences with women, "but I find my relationship with Aaron more satisfying. I know it bothers him that I'm more expansive in my implementation of our philosophy."

"No, it doesn't," Aaron shot back. But the swiftness of his response told the true story. While both are able to live with Angela's sexual rules, Aaron is uncomfortable with them and goes along to please her. However, the fact that they have persevered and both benefit from their marriage despite these differences is a testament to the fact that "open marriage," at least to the degree they practice it, can work for some people.

Sometimes. My observations have led me to conclude that few relationships can withstand such permissiveness. Intellectually, "open marriages" sound good; in practice, lack of trust, jealousy, insecurity, and dishonesty pervade, usually leading to their demise.

When I first began preparing the materials for my "First Comes Love" workshops, I interviewed spouses and experts to get their advice for couples planning to marry. Two of the experts were a couple whom I'd known for three years. David is a licensed clinical psychologist; Yvette is a marriage, family, and child counselor. I had always thought they had a workable, satisfying marriage, and looked forward to drawing on their expertise.

The three of us were casually lunching, discussing their guidelines for a long, happy relationship. Suddenly, between nibbles of fruit, Yvette blurted, "I've got a rule: You should never talk about your affairs."

A piece of pineapple caught in my throat. I looked at her husband, David, and then back as she rushed on, "It's okay to have affairs, of course. I certainly don't want just one sexual partner all my life."

David quickly interjected, "The issue is what's going on between the two of you, not that you have an affair."

Yvette sensed my amazement and amended, "If you sleep with someone else, it could just be because you feel like it. It doesn't take away from the marriage. Having sex with two people doesn't preclude a genuine commitment to the marriage." Yvette reasoned that because one-night stands are without emotional meaning, revealing outside attachments simply promotes needless grief and pain. So, there's no need to mention them.

Later, I spoke with David further about his wife's surprising attitude. He reminded me that one women's magazine survey found that 75 percent of wives who wrote in confessed to surreptitious liaisons. He estimated that half the patients who come to him for marriage counseling have had extramarital affairs. But David admitted feeling divided on the subject. In his practice, he's discovered that affairs are usually symptoms of deeper malaise. "Affairs do negative things to trust. If people understand the consequences and want to do it, fine, but usually it's painfully difficult to work out."

This first set of conversations took place three years ago. About two years ago, he and Yvette decided to chuck the ratrace and move to northern California, living in a sleepy but fashionable town surrounded by giant redwoods. David continued his Los Angeles practice, commuting by jet two days weekly. I thought all was well.

One day, however, David told me that he now had a new address in his northern California hamlet. "Did you and Yvette find a new house?" I inquired, making small talk.

"No, I've taken an apartment. One of Yvette's relationships turned serious, and she wants to be with him instead of me." Apparently Yvette had been courteously mum about her lover, and without giving a clue to David, had become deeply involved. "Ironic, isn't it?" David grinned, with just the faintest hint of sorrow. "Here we tell you how to create an enduring marriage, and Yvette's advice was what did us in."

Six months later, in a still more ironic twist, I talked to David about his impending divorce. "Yvette and I have to get married," he said.

"What?" I asked, perplexed.

"We never broadcast it, but Yvette and I were never legally married. Now our lawyers tell us that we have to get married in order to be divorced, so that we can divide our assets and set up child support. I'm getting married right now by proxy." Truth is stranger than fiction.

"I was right all along," David admitted. "I was never happy with Yvette's affairs, and I never had them myself. I believe more strongly than ever that if you want to get married, commit yourself fully. Otherwise, don't. Your life will just get too complicated. Eventually."

Interestingly in the two examples above, the women were the ones to endorse sexual freedom while the men acquiesced. Contrast this with the traditional marriage, in which the wife has suspicions about her husband's philandering but often says, "I don't want to know about it." In either case, having a separate compartment of life, shut off from the partner's knowledge, can be divisive.

But what about sex, pure and simple? What about the partners who seek recreational sex *without* emotional ties, just for the fun of it? Swingers, who answer newspaper ads placed by others "looking for a good time," sometimes say they have the best of both worlds. "Our bodies were made for it, weren't they?" asks one confessed sexual enthusiast. "Everybody knows what he's in for; there are no pretenses. If we were to run into our 'friends' elsewhere, we probably would pretend that we didn't know them." I've heard of this type of lifestyle lasting for years. Couples get together with similarly inclined others and play, then return to their neighborhoods, respectable jobs, and ongoing lives unscathed.

I question whether they are all that unharmed. "What we do is our own business," the enthusiast says. "We don't foist it on anyone else, and we find that it enhances the lovemaking we do in our own bed. These times are exciting, they're titillating, and they're at no one's expense. This is a little-publicized but natural way to experience sex. But only if you're ready for it, and do it of your own accord."

Dr. James Grold, M.D. of Los Angeles did a study describing one hundred nonswinging and swinging couples, He found that most swinging is initiated by men, and women are reluctant at first. But after a while, women come to enjoy it, and suddenly the men get jealous. Overall, most people find that this practice adds a great deal of complications to their relationships.

While some couples have benefited from the sexual revolution, especially as regards women's rights to sexual enjoyment, others have lost out in the way they are regarded by society. One group—virgins—might once have been venerated for their abstinence but now are often ridiculed.

"Sex is a gift I'm saving for my 'special person,' " says Dave Dismore, a 37-year-old businessman and social activist. He's also a Vietnam veteran who emerged from his wartime experience with his virginity intact. "The guys would go into these sleazy huts and have a few drinks in the front. Then, one by one, they'd disappear into the back room with one of the girls. I just stayed in front, and everyone assumed I'd gone back too. I remembered the words of a chaplain out there that our virginity was such a special thing, why waste it on someone you care nothing about? I started to realize that it was the one thing that I could save for the 'special person' I'll love."

Dismore is no religious zealot; in fact, he claims no religious affiliation. He thinks masturbation is fine for both virgins and the experienced. And he's not against premarital sex for others. "I think everyone should make his or her own choice," he says, "but I don't think it's fair thay *my* choice should be considered odd or undesirable. I don't like the fact that there's so much pressure on people to perform sexually. It's as bad as the days when we expected all brides to be virgins. There should be *equal* respect for all choices, as long as they're made by consciously evaluating options, and making the decision that's right for you at the time."

Dismore is so committed to ending discrimination among peers based on sexual conquests that he's spoken at many high schools and elsewhere to reveal his own status and get his message across. "After I give my talks at high schools, people always come up and say, 'Thank you—I was feeling like I was the only one out there who didn't want to have sex yet, and now I see that you're not a freak or inferior if you decide to wait.' " Students are amazed that a healthy, heterosexual male would spurn all the opportunities in our culture for easy, blameless sex. "I've had opportunities," Dismore confesses, "but I was able to talk to these sensitive women and explain that though I cared for them, they weren't my 'special person.' The women were gracious and supportive. Sure, I find women attractive, but because I have this conviction so thoroughly entrenched in my being, there's really no temptation."

Dave Dismore's case illustrates that people come to marriage with a variety of backgrounds and expectations about their partners. Few would assume from looking at him that he is a virgin; similarly, you shouldn't take your partner's viewpoint and feelings about sex for granted either. Even if you've had gloriously rewarding sex in sixteen positions and experienced ecstacy swinging on a chandelier, you may still have a lot to learn about your partner's preferences.

"We have sex on weekends only, in the morning, with the sun streaming in our bedroom window," confided Hillary, 26. "We are predictable: the missionary position. Sounds boring, doesn't it? But frankly, Martin and I *like* it this way. We have fabulous sex, and I almost always have an orgasm. We can cuddle and hug as much as we want first, because neither of us is rushing to run off somewhere, and we're not tired from working all day. I really look forward to our soirees—rolling over in our bed about ten o'clock and reaching over to take his hand."

Sounds great—so what's the problem? "The problem," Hillary continued, "is that I'm made to feel inadequate. Here we are a young couple, full of energy and surging with hormones, and we only want to have sex once a week? According to magazines and newspapers, we're abnormal. In fact, we're sexually retarded!" She laughed. "We're supposed to like pornography—I saw *Deep Throat* and it was funny. Not sexy, funny. As for sexual positions, we've tried several but find that the missionary position is more satisfying, mainly because we have more face-to-face contact and because, frankly, I find that more stimulating."

Hillary sighed. "I can say all this to you, because you're a therapist. But neither Martin nor I would ever let on to anyone else. Our friends would surely consider us unusual, if not 'out of it.' I think it's about time that some of that pressure to meet some post sexual revolution standard of performance be dropped. No, sex isn't dirty, and it should be equally pleasurable to both partners. But it's not life's panacea, either. What's so rewarding about grabbing a 'quickie' on a lunch break? You blink, and it's over."

Both Hillary and Dave Dismore were arguing for the same revision of expectations. It seems over the past decade or so, views about sex have divided into two camps. There are those who abide by religiously inspired mores, and those who cheer the sexual revolution. Each camp tends to denigrate the other. A more appropriate perspective would be to view the whole range of sexual activity with equal respect.

Improving Your Sex Life

Many people are dissatisfied with the quality or type of sexual experience they are having. They may want to revitalize a now-lagging sex life, or they may have problems like impotence, premature ejaculation, lack of orgasm, or anxiety about sex. They might *want* to change the situation with their partners, but have fears about how to approach this goal. Therefore, they may go to a sex therapist for reassurance or instruction.

When couples enter sex therapy, they are usually told that intercourse is banned. They're instructed to explore their sensuality and sexuality gradually, little by little. First might be visual appreciation; no touching. Next, they might caress or massage nonsexual areas of each other's bodies. Finally the couple progresses to non-intercourse genital touching, and to penetration. All the while, the couple keeps regular appointments with the therapist, who encourages them to express their feelings about each exercise. They may keep a log or journal as well. Central to the process is learning how to communicate to the partner about what feels good. Often, a partner discovers that what he or she thought was pleasurable was simply habit, and that the spouse prefers something altogether different.

Also important in sex therapy is understanding the value of novelty. Good sex is not simply "wham, bam, thank y', ma'am." Sex includes not only variations on the main event but imaginative touching, fondling, and kissing. These activities have the unfortunate name of "foreplay," a term implying that they are merely a necessary prelude to a more important act, intercourse. However, many people (women especially) feel that foreplay is the most satisfying aspect of their lovemaking, and an underestimated number of couples chooses to make such activities the sum of their sexual experience.

As with the guidelines for communication, when it comes to sex you should *never assume*. Take some time to discuss your needs and desires with your partner. Include such topics as:

- How often you prefer to have sex.
- The role of foreplay activities in your lovemaking.
- Actions your partner can do that will enhance your partner's experience.
- Positions and activities that are most comfortable or uncomfortable for you.
- The times of day or night that you most enjoy sex.
- Your feelings about noise during sex.
- Your feelings about using vibrators, oils, or other sexual aids.
- What you consider the "right" amount of spontaneity versus planning.
- How you can make your fantasy of the perfect lovemaking scene come true (if you choose).

Determining Sexual Boundaries

Most people have some basic standards and a repertoire of behaviors for sexually-oriented situations though they play the specifics of each encounter with a new partner by ear. You probably never sat down and defined particular behaviors that are acceptable and unacceptable for you, much less tried to spell these parameters out with your partner. And yet many couples have had seething "discussions" in their car on the way home from parties where flirting went on. Other people have suffered silently while suspicions of a partner's unfaithfulness festered.

This interchange illustrates how differing expectations about acceptable behavior can spark anger:

HE: You were sure out late last night with "the girls."
SHE: Yeah, we were having coffee when Sally's cousin Jim and a bunch of his friends ran into us and joined us. We just lost track of the time!
HE: You know I was worried about you. What makes you think it's okay to be spending the evening with strange men while I'm waiting at home for you?
SHE: What do you mean, "spending the evening"? We were only talking!
HE: Four attractive women out alone. Four guys join them. What am I to think?

Obviously, the man was not very trusting of his partner, and expected her to avoid contact with men when she was unescorted. The woman may have suspected that the situation was not quite kosher, because she defensively picked up on the man's "spending the evening" intimations.

This little vignette, however, is minor in the modern scheme of relationships. Here's a more recent possibility:

HE: How was your business trip, honey?
SHE: Great. I got the Miller account. That's another $30,000 in commissions!
HE: Fabulous! Now we can add the hot tub and take a few days off for a vacation. Where do you want to go?
SHE: You know Bill, my new associate? He's got a house in the mountains. He invited us up this weekend.
HE: He and his wife?
SHE: No, he's single. He said he'd invite someone for you, if you'd like.

Zing. This couple never *had* the expectation of faithfulness. Sexual experimentation is part of their contract with each other.

Needs and Desires

No jealousy, no inquiries, and a willingness to make sure the other partner gets to have a fling too.

This is probably not your style. But take a few minutes now to define just where the edges of acceptable sexual experience lie. For each behavior listed below, determine whether you would find it acceptable, unacceptable, or you would have doubts or conflicts about it if your partner did it with someone of the opposite sex. In the margin, mark an "A" for acceptable, a "U" for unacceptable, and a "D" for doubts or conflicts.

"What if my partner would . . ."

Flirt harmlessly with a co-worker
Flirt with someone at a party where you are present
Kiss hello or goodbye on the cheek
Use sexual allure or an implied promise to get ahead at work
Kiss hello or goodbye on the lips (a peck)
Have dinner alone with a work acquaintance
Stay out very late "working" with the person
Hold hands with the person in my presence
Go to an evening play or movie with someone I don't know
Masturbate alone
Go out of town with a person of the opposite sex and stay in separate rooms
Let the person put his or her arm around my partner
Hold hands with the person while *not* in my presence
Kiss hello or goodbye on the lips—more than a peck
Go out of town with the person and stay in the same room
Have a casual, one-night affair with someone my partner will never see again
Have a one-night sexual fling with a friend
Have a casual affair, lasting a few weeks, with someone I don't know
Have an affair lasting several months
Maintain several sexual relationships simultaneously
Have an ongoing, long-term affair

Examine your answers to get a clearer picture of where you would draw the line. Now go through the list again and consider which things you feel are all right for *you* to do. (Mark your answers in a different-colored pencil.) Do these coincide with permissible behaviors for your partner? How realistic do you think your parameters are? And finally, how comfortable do you feel thinking and talking about this subject? Do you feel that there are some things better left unsaid?

Needs and Desires for Affection

Below are descriptions of two couples.

Anita and Max have been married thirty years. They are secure in the knowledge that each loves the other. Max came home from work one evening and collapsed in his naugahyde chair in front of the TV set, which occupies a position of honor in the living room. Anita, who works part-time as a department store cashier, was busy in the kitchen making fish for dinner. She heard Max turn on the TV and called in a cheery hello. As soon as the fish was in the oven, she greeted Max in the living room, sitting down near him. "What's new today?" she asked.

"Not much; the usual," replied Max. "Joe, the other foreman, ratted on little Sammy for taking a typewriter ribbon out of the supply cupboard. And here Joe takes stuff all the time. By the way, my tuna sandwich was especially good today. Now let me get back to this show." Max never looked at Anita when recounting his day, gazing instead at a *M*A*S*H* rerun.

That didn't bother her. She started telling Max all about the author who came into the department store to autograph his latest book on photography; about the cousin of Teri Garr who bought two towels; about the daughter-in-law of the other saleslady's sister who had just had a hysterectomy. Max didn't budge. Anita didn't notice.

One of their grown children came home and sat down in the living room next to Dad. Anita came in and kissed him hello, then brought him some potato chips to munch. "I got these on sale at the market for only fifty-nine cents," she chirped. "Reminds me of last week, when they had Fritos for only two bags for a dollar." The men were soon served fish on TV trays, while viewing a second *M*A*S*H* rerun.

That evening, as Max and Anita undressed for bed, her concerns came out. "I'm worried about Al," she said, referring to their adult son. "I haven't seen him go out on a date in months, and then he only saw her twice, at Ernie's bar mitzvah and your birthday party. He ought to date, find a nice girl. I'm worried. He's 28 years old, and doesn't even seem interested."

"Don't push the boy," Max told her. "He'll find someone

when he's ready." Inwardly, Max didn't want Al to leave. He felt good supporting his son; he liked having him around. He also knew Anita's unspoken fear. "Look, we know he's not gay," Max said. "He took out that girl twice. We saw it. So he can't be homosexual."

Anita forced herself to dismiss her fears. "If you say so, Max," she sighed. Then she brightened. "I know. I'll set him up with Sophie's niece. She's a bright girl; has a master's degree. Al will like her."

They climbed into their twin beds. "Goodnight!" Anita called lovingly to Max. She blew him a kiss. He kissed the air in return.

"Goodnight," he growled sleepily.

This relationship appears pretty pathetic. Max prefers *M*A*S*H* reruns to talking to his wife. Anita doesn't notice Max is tuning her out. The TV set is the centerpiece of their life. They're out of touch with their son, and they never seem to touch each other. I interviewed Anita about her marriage.

"We have a great relationship," she said confidently. "Max is a good provider. Doesn't drink or run around. He's there when we need him. We've raised a family together. There's a real bond between us. And besides that," her eyes twinkled, "He's kind of cute."

Max's view was equally contented. "She's a good mother," he said of Anita. "She takes care of our home and even brings in a little extra money. She puts me and the boys first, like she should. We have a close family; we care about each other." From observing their typical evening, you'd never guess Max would be so positive. Yet his needs are met; he doesn't expect anything else from his marriage.

Here's another portrait of a couple.

"I'm home, honey," Tony cheerfully called out as he entered the front door. "Where's my baby?" Clair was in her studio, completing a sculpture.

"In here!" she yelled, rising from her stool, hands still gooey with clay. They met in the hallway, and Tony wrapped his arms around her; she pulled him close while holding her hands away from his sport jacket. After a warm kiss, they stood close to each other.

"How's my baby?" Tony asked, stroking Clair's clay-streaked cheek.

"Just fine, sweetie," she smiled, "especially now that you're home." They kissed again, and then Clair pulled away momentarily. "Let me just rinse off my hands," she said, scurrying to the bathroom. Meanwhile, Tony loosened his tie, hung up his jacket, and sat down on the living room sofa. Clair returned to the living room, where Tony had his arms extended for her to sit close to him on the couch.

They kissed once more, and Clair ran her fingers along the stiff hairs in Tony's beard. "How was your day?" he asked her, stroking her neck.

"This morning I had my workout at the club—I got Sonya, the good teacher," Clair began. "I saw Eleanor there, you know, the one with the consulting business. We're going to have lunch next week. Then I talked to Mr. Solter from the gallery. He sold two of Betty's pieces and none of mine this week, but he said that one customer expressed strong interest."

"Well, maybe he'll come back then," Tony said hopefully. "Did Solter get a good price for Betty's pieces?"

"Pretty good. They went to different people. Her stuff is less expensive than mine anyway."

They talked about the latest idea Clair had for a sculpture; about the article she'd read on acupuncture; about her dread of approaching a new gallery owner. Tony had several suggestions and offered much encouragement. When it was his turn, he explained about the new client he was wooing into his advertising business; his failure in collecting a long past-due bill; his idea for a slide-show presentation at an upcoming convention. They touched throughout, unthinkingly caressing a shoulder, patting a hand, and sharing a momentary peck on the lips.

Soon, they put some Mozart on the stereo, changed their clothes, and met in the kitchen to prepare dinner together. While Tony tossed a salad, Clair poached some salmon. Tony elaborated on his frustration in trying to collect from the reneging client. "Why don't I call him and say I'm a lawyer you've hired?" Clair suggested. "Maybe that'll scare him."

"You're all brains," Tony said, taken with the idea. "How'd I ever find such a sexy, intelligent woman?" He nuzzled her neck.

"It's because you're such a sexy, intelligent man," Clair replied. When she went into the bathroom to get ready for bed, she found a note Tony had taped to the mirror during the evening: "love your lips!" She giggled.

Later, they crawled into their king-sized bed and once again began the endearments. They hugged as closely as two people can, legs and arms entangled. They just laid there, entwined, for five minutes silently. Then they gave a final hug, rolled over to their own sides of the bed, and drifted off to sleep.

Where Max and Anita seemed sadly estranged, Clair and Tony seem too mushily gushy to be real. Yet they *are* a real couple, and this excerpt from their typical evening leaves out many other romantic moments and compliments. How do *they* assess their relationship?

"Tony's the sweetest thing on earth," Clair said earnestly. "He's so kind and gentle. He's always giving me compliments, always saying something nice. I know it sounds too good to be true."

"Don't you find that you become immune to all that affection?" I ask her.

Clair shook her head. "Not at all, because what he says is sincere. It's based in reality, not just habit. He'll notice a new scarf or compliment me on the way I've pulled my outfit together. He recalls details about my work, and follows up on things that happened to me last week. He remembers, and it is always genuine. Instead of being an effort for him, it's a labor of love. I couldn't ask for anyone better.

"Of course, I'm the same way," Clair noted. "I value warmth and verbal praise, and I tell him whenever there's something positive to remark about. I love him in his yellow sweater, for example, and so every time I looked across the room and felt proud of him, I said so. It was honest, and it makes both of us feel good."

"That's the theme of our relationship," Tony explained. "We like to feel good, and make the other person feel that way. Our friends say we're sickening, because we're always fawning over each other, and paying each other compliments. They just don't do it. Now, every person is different, but I think our relationship is richer and more satisfying because we take the time to point out everything positive we can."

"That doesn't mean we never have anything negative to say," Clair interjected. "Sometimes I *won't* like something Tony wears, and I'll say so, but in a gentle way. Or it could be that one of his business ideas is off the track, and I'll tell him. We're careful to give sincere feedback, both bad and good. But the important thing that makes us different from our friends is the amount of time we spend giving each other strokes."

"And it's automatic," Tony said. "We don't have to 'work' at our marriage at all. We very seldom have disagreements, because we *want* to please each other. We *enjoy* being together and making each other happy. We've been married fifteen years, and it just gets better by the minute." He looked over at Clair and they both smiled.

Clair and Tony have decided not to have children, in part because they don't want to be distracted from each other. They find their work lives very satisfying, so they don't come together with a large amount of pent-up hostility. Still, they have an interaction style that is fairly common. (Don't you know at least one "sickening" couple?) How do you feel about their style?

The Need For Attention

My observations have indicated that spouses do want attention from their partners. While many people get used to living without attention, if given a choice, they want clear and frequent demonstrations of love. Think, for a moment, about your own relationship. For most benefit, get a pencil and jot down the answers to these questions. How do you and your partner show each other affection? What does your partner do—perhaps unthinkingly—that gives you positive feelings? Have your partner answer these questions too, and then discuss your responses together.

One mode that is prevalent with many couples is for the man to show his devotion by providing security (usually financial) and being considerate during lovemaking. He may bring flowers on Valentine's Day and remember his wife's birthday with a bottle of cologne. Other than that, he takes no initiative in expressing affection. If the woman says, "Do you love me?" he'll say, "Of course." But rarely will he make a surprising move, or say casually, "Gee, you look gorgeous today! I sure love you!" Because of their upbringing, many men find it difficult to show affection. They were taught that this makes them appear weak and that it's more "manly" to keep feelings inside. Of course, their lack of demonstrativeness doesn't mean they feel nothing. But their partners don't always know what's going on, and need the validation that everyone craves.

A woman who has such a partner may become a model of the affectionate, demonstrative person she wishes her lover would be. She might send "I'm thinking of you" cards, freely give compliments, and say "I love you" so often that her partner starts thinking there is an echo in the room. She may *tell* him that she'd like to hear a few more "sweet nothings" whispered in her ear. But eventually, she gets frustrated and gives up. "You can't change someone," such a woman has been heard to mutter.

No, you can't change someone against his will, but if someone *wants* to change, even if it's just to please his partner, he can. A person is most likely to change if he gets some direct rewards from cooing and cuddling. He may, however, have a block inside that is keeping him from becoming a tantalizing romantic. That was the case for Patrick, who had been going with Erica for three years. Erica was near calling it all off when I saw her in my office.

"He says he's just quiet, that's all," she lamented. "That I should just know that he cares and not expect more of him than he can give. It's a monstrous effort for him to even remember my birthday on time, though ultimately he comes through with some trinket. I've tried cajoling, setting an example, dropping hints, nagging. Nothing's helped."

I thought that Patrick should have a chance to express his side, so he joined us at the next session. "It's really no big deal," he said, puffing on his pipe. "Erica knows I love her. I think the problem is all hers, because she just can't be satisfied. We've got so many important things to talk about, and we both are very busy with our careers and hobbies. My needs are fulfilled, and I wish hers could be."

Erica was barely holding back her fury. "Tell him what you're feeling," I encouraged.

"You say I 'know' that you love me, and yes, I believe you do. But you expect me to have mental telepathy, and live on what I intuitively 'know'! What if tomorrow you found someone else? Would I 'know' that too? And what *is* a relationship, if not a place where we both can get some kind of reassurance; where we can have warmth and caring that's right out in the open? You say I have a problem. I do, and it's in your unwillingness to care enough about me to please me, to give just a little bit. You're simply not the kind of person I need, Patrick. I think we should spend some time apart—not see each other—until I decide if I want to live my whole life never hearing you *choose* to say you love me!"

"Now wait a minute!" Patrick said sternly. "Do you think you're threatening me just because I find it difficult or forget to say silly compliments, or because I don't spend time bringing you nosegays? This seems like such a trivial issue! I can't understand why you're so worked up over this. Just calm down, and when you're rational, then you'll be able to see that words are not so important after all."

Erica reached for a tissue and pressed it over her eyes just in time to catch her tears. "Don't say any more," she squeaked as she cried. "The more you say, the more I realize that it can't work out, because you think my desire for a little love, just a little love, is silly."

Erica broke up with Patrick later that evening. They'd mentioned getting married in June, but now she said she felt relieved that she'd avoided a big mistake. I continued to see Erica, and she progressed well in adjusting to her new state of being "single"; she surrounded herself with women who were supportive and were verbal about caring for her.

The big suprise came three weeks later, when I got a call from Patrick. "I miss Erica," he told me. "I want her back. I didn't believe she'd actually leave for good over this. I've been a wreck these last three weeks. So I want lessons on how to please her." I told him to talk to Erica, not me, to see if she even *wanted* him back.

She did, and they came in for "lessons" that included learning direct communication skills, admitting fear of failure, and practicing listening and affection-showing. Patrick was resistant to change because he thought he would be rejected or viewed negatively if he exposed his innermost feelings. Erica, however rewarded him for even the slightest attempt to share. Slowly, he became more comfortable discussing feelings with her, though he remained guarded around other people. Erica was satisfied, and Patrick said that he felt more relaxed—less tense overall—knowing he had someone in his corner to weather daily crises with him. He even got in the habit of stopping off once a week at the flower shop next to his office to pick up a nosegay for Erica, received with love.

Expressing Love

Even though you may be generally satisfied with your relationship, chances are that increased expressions of love would improve it even more. Showing positive feelings is often more difficult than showing negative ones, as was illustrated by the case of

Patrick. He criticized Erica's strong need for affection, saying they had too many "important" things to do to waste time on froufrou.

When there's something wrong, people are quick to complain; when things are great, they assume this is the norm. But a great thing can be made even better if it is enriched by compliments and attentiveness. The "Expressing Love" questionnaire will give you a chance to determine just which symbols of love are most pleasing to you and your partner. The listed acts are simple gestures, easily accomplished. They don't demand a great deal of forethought or expense. All they require is intent to show continuing love through appreciation of your partner.

Expressing Love

Instructions: Put an "S" next to the five expressions of love you'd like most, and a "P" next to the five you think your partner would like most. Then check how easy it would be for you and your partner to do *every* item at left.

	"S" or "P"	Difficulty for Me — Easy	Would take effort	Difficult	Difficulty for My Partner — Easy	Would take effort	Difficult
Greet me with a hug and kiss before we get out of bed in the morning							
When you are out walking, bring me a flower or a leaf							
Look at me and smile							
Call me during the day and tell me something pleasant							
Turn off the lights and light a candle over dinner							
Ask me how I spent my day							
Pick me up at the bus or work as a surprise							
Tell me how much you enjoyed having breakfast with me							

	"S" or "P"	Difficulty for Me			Difficulty for My Partner		
		Easy	Would take effort	Difficult	Easy	Would take effort	Difficult
Tell the children (in front of me) what a good parent I am							
When we sit together, put your arm around me							
When we're together at home, ask me what record I'd like to hear and then play it							
Wash my back when I'm in the shower							
Have coffee with me in the morning alone with no distractions							
Hold me at night just before we go to sleep							
Ask my opinion about world affairs							
For no special reason, hug me and say you like me							
Hold my hand when we're out walking							
When you see me coming up the drive, come out and meet me							
Put a surprise note where I'll find it							
When we're together, call me "dear," "sweetheart," or an affectionate pet name							
When we part, blow me a kiss							
Others:							

SOURCE: This list is adapted from William J. Lederer, *Marital Choices* (W.W. Norton and Co.: New York, 1981), p. 63.

/ 10
The Unthinkable

HERE YOU ARE, ready to plan your future. You're optimistic. You're excited. You foresee good things happening. If you're engaged to be married, you envision many years of happiness with your present partner, punctuated by joyous events — anniversaries, births (perhaps), triumphs in your careers, and exploration of the world around you. If you're deciding whether and how to proceed with a relationship, you're anticipating taking control of your life—intentionally pointing it in the direction you choose, whether it's with this partner, with someone else, or independently. If you're reviewing a past relationship, you're trying to improve all those to come. Positive thinking does go a long way toward making your desires reality.

Unfortunately, reality sometimes includes hitting snags. The house you buy has a roof more like a sieve. Your car turns out to be a lemon. The health of one of your parents starts to fail, and you're forced to cope with the unpleasantries of nursing homes, management of finances, and problems of becoming a parent to someone you've always admired. Unexpected troubles can squelch your plans. Though there's no need to build your life pessimistically, you *should* have some idea of what problems you might have to face, and how you would handle them. Then, rather than feeling uneasy whenever a "what if" runs through your mind, you'll have considered constructive steps already, which should put you more at ease.

Divorce

One event to be pondered is divorce, which was discussed in Chapter 4. The divorce rate has escalated sharply, more than doubling in the last twenty years. As pointed out in *Newsweek* magazine (January 10, 1983), for every two marriages there is one divorce.* According to the Census Bureau, "One-third of the nation's children live in homes without at least one of their biological parents." The article also quotes the findings of University of Pennsylvania professor Frank Furstenberg, who notes that half the children of divorce have not seen their father in the last year.

Women fare particularly poorly as a result of divorce. Many "displaced homemakers" are suddenly thrust into the workforce without marketable skills. Others who may have spent time on rewarding pursuits without much remuneration (including volunteer work or low-paying jobs they enjoy) must develop new skills in order to financially squeak by. The *Newsweek* article cites sociologist Lenore Weitzman's finding that, on average, a woman's income declines by 73 percent after divorce, while a man's *increases* by 42 percent. Often, the most tangible and important reward women take away from marriage is children. However, with custody by men and joint custody becoming more common, many men will fight to win full or partial care of their children.

Men also have their headaches as a result of divorce: many are saddled with large monthly payments to ex-wives and children. This hampers them when they remarry and suddenly have two households to support. They may find that their standard of living is significantly reduced by this burden.

Many people who make an exit through divorce are unprepared for the accompanying emotional pain. Even the person who initiated the split will suffer. The degree of sorrow varies, but people who blithely say they are sailing through an amicable divorce have simply not confronted the brunt of their feelings yet. Divorce is loss; it's a symbol of failure; it's tearing apart dreams that were sealed with kisses years before; it's embarrassment and shame, and coping with attitudes that you are somehow a "misfit" because your marriage didn't work out. Everyone who has been divorced will concur: it's not easy.

And divorce is not just a private matter affecting the couple. Embittered interchanges between attorneys are characteristic. Children, already emotionally shaken, feel suddenly compelled to make judgments, even if Mommy and Daddy tell them repeatedly that the divorce is nobody's fault. In-laws are torn away from

---

*The 50 percent figure doesn't mean that every other married person gets divorced. The same people may have multiple marriages and divorces; counting them raises the total.

once-loved spouses of their daughters and sons, as loyalty requires them to keep a distance. Friends are placed in an awkward position, unable to invite ex-mates to the same gatherings. Even friendly divorces are viewed with confusion, since all suspect that lurking beneath the calm facade are unresolved emotions.

Joan Dasteel, Ph.D., instructor of the "Marriage, Loving and Lasting" course at U.C.L.A. Extension in Los Angeles, says that there are actually three stages of divorce. *Emotional divorce* happens first, as couples pull apart from each other. Symptoms include withdrawal, a cold war atmosphere, and a feeling of being unsettled. Spouses may begin to act differently, showing signs of stress, depression, and lack of energy. While they may attempt to hide these negative feelings, other people know there is a strain. Dr. Dasteel notes that most couples go through such rocky periods in their marriages, but reconnoiter. During this phase, spouses might seek out another person to soothe them through the distress; in this or other ways, they may commit actions they later regret. Once emotional divorce is firmly entrenched, it may be too late to save the marriage.

The second stage, *legal divorce*, finalizes the marriage's dissolution. Because facing court proceedings and adversarial actions between lawyers is so traumatic, a reconciliation at or beyond this point is unlikely.

Finally, in the stage of *psychological divorce*, connections with the ex-spouse are severed. The divorced person puts his or her energies elsewhere—back to self, to other activities, and to new relationships. Many couples never achieve this stage and continue to hang on, often through their children. For example, they may go to court repeatedly to fight each other over custody and alimony arrangements.

To prevent divorce, Dr. Dasteel suggests looking at the roots of problems you are having. Check whether you simply chose the wrong person, whether the two of you have developed in different directions, and whether your roles have changed in ways that are unacceptable. Then address the problems directly rather than dismissing them or turning to nonprofessionals for outside support. You'll be more guidelines for a long and happy marriage in the next chapter.

Sometimes considering the likelihood of divorce means "futuring," or projecting from the present. Make a list of your own five worst habits or faults that affect your relationship, either directly or indirectly. It is especially important to note habits that don't seem like problems to you but that you know bother your partner. You may decide either to work to eliminate these behaviors, or your partner may come to accept them as your idiosyncracies. But, as an exercise, try to imagine what will happen if these behaviors go unchecked. Could one or more of them eventually lead to a split from your partner? What can you do to stop them from interfering with your happiness?

Also, make a list of five of your partner's habits or behaviors that have the potential for negative consequences, and devise constructive ways of averting problems. Armed with these positive suggestions, you might diplomatically present them to your partner and discuss them calmly.

In the preceding chapter you read about Erica and Patrick, who separated for a while because of Patrick's lack of visible affection toward Erica. Patrick didn't perceive his undemonstrative nature as a problem, and ignored Erica's pleas and hints for him to change. Had he heeded her requests earlier, the quality of their relationship would have been enhanced, both would have been spared much grief, and their temporary breakup would have been avoided. So, even if it's embarrassing or humbling, try to identify those traits you *can* improve now, in order to prevent possible heartache later.

PREPARING FOR THE UNTHINKABLE

For each unpleasant yet possible situation below, write out on a separate sheet: (1) your likely reaction, and (2) strategies for how you would deal with the situation. Be realistic. This exercise is meant to help you recognize that these things *do* happen, and to help you prepare *now*.

1. Without warning, your partner announces that he or she is leaving you for another lover. (Write what you'd say to your partner, then how you'd pick up the pieces.)

2. A reliable friend presents overwhelming evidence that your partner has been having an affair behind your back for a year. (Write what you'd say to your partner and your next course of action.)

The Unthinkable 215

3. Your only child, age two, is hit by a car and dies. (What would you do to help yourself cope? What would this do to your relationship? If relevant, how would this affect your plans to have more children?)

4. Your partner leaves you and refuses to take responsibility for your two children, ages 6 and 8. (How would you support them? What kind of child care would you need? How would you help them to deal with the loss of their other parent?)

5. An emergency requires all your financial resources and you are left penniless. (How would you continue to live?)

6. Your partner is suddenly physically incapacitated, permanently, and needs constant care. (How would you react to living with a permanent invalid? How would you manage caring for him or her, *and* the rest of your responsibilities?)

7. Because of a medical problem, your partner can no longer have genital sexual intercourse. (What would be your attitude toward loss of sex, and toward your partner? How would you cope?)

8. You find yourself strongly attracted to a potential lover who is trying to seduce you. (Would you tell your partner? What would you do?)

9. You are offered the job of your dreams in another part of the country, and your partner is happily employed here. (How would you decide on what to do? What would be your decision-making criteria? What would ultimately happen?)

10. Over a period of a few months, your feelings change, and you "fall out of love" with your partner. (What would be your course of action?)

11. Through amniocentosis, you learn that you or your partner is expecting a Down's syndrome child. (Would you favor getting an abortion, or carrying the child to term? How would you care for a

severely handicapped child? How would such a child affect your lives?)

12. You and your partner are in your fifties and find yourselves expecting a child. (How would you react? What course would you take? How might you and your partner cope with a child at this time of life?)

13. Your partner becomes deeply enmeshed in a religion with strict rules. (How would you deal with your partner? How would you proceed?)

14. You deeply desire to make a career change in a particular direction, but your partner feels the change is ridiculous and staunchly opposes it. (How would you work it out? If there was no compromise possible, would you choose career happiness over your relationship?)

15. A close, elderly relative for whom you feel responsible is senile and needs constant care. (What would you do? And how would you cope with that decision?)

16. You are permanently injured and can no longer work. (What would you do with your time? How would this affect your self-image and your relationship?)

17. Your teenager becomes incorrigible and refuses to listen to you, then becomes involved with drugs and has brushes with the law. (How would you deal with your child? How would you react emotionally? How would this affect your relationship with your partner and with other family members?)

18. Your teenage daughter, age 15, tells you she is pregnant. Her boyriend refuses to take any responsibility. (How would you act toward her? What course of action would you take?)

19. Your partner dies suddenly and unexpectedly. (How would you handle this? What would you do with your life? Would you remarry, and if so, how soon?)

20. Despite your efforts to be supportive, your partner becomes an alcoholic. You have tried everything you know to help. (How would you cope? Would you stay? How would you manage day-to-day?)

21. Though you cannot understand how or why, your partner has slowly and surely become obese and unattractive. (What would your tactics be? How would you relate to your partner? How would you feel about this?)

Pondering the Unthinkable

The "Preparing for the Unthinkable" exercise lists twenty-one situations that would require major adjustment or action on your part. Some of the occurrences may be more likely than others to happen to you. And perhaps some that you consider unlikely are actually more possible than you realize. Some readers are tempted to say they'd just handle a problem at the time it arises, letting their feelings dictate a course of action. People are very flexible, and there's no doubt that you would somehow muddle through. But the whole purpose of this chapter is to enable you to confront frightening possibilities now.

Have your partner do the exercise too. This will help you to see how similarly the two of you would react. Then, if there are differences, you can work out a compromise plan of action, or at least note the difference in your styles for future reference.

As the exercise indicates, some tragedies are wrought by our own misjudgments or wrongs, while others are brought upon us by nature, happenstance, or the acts of outsiders. Scrambled in the exercise were six types of problems. One type had to do with *relationships:* your partner leaves you for a lover or has a long-term affair; you "fall out of love" or a potential lover tries to seduce you. *Money*, either being in debt or losing everything and having to start over, is a second problem.

Children can bring many worries—a child may die, your partner may leave you as a single parent, birth defects or other physical problems could strike, or a teenager might become incorrigible or pregnant. The *physical state* of you or your partner could be affected so that your functioning is impaired. *Work* changes might bring conflicts over where to live or how to proceed. Finally, there may be severe *philosophical differences*, as when one partner joins a cult.

"This is morbid," you may be thinking. "Why dwell on all the negative aspects of life? Why not just hope for the best and deal with these problems as they arise?" Again, you may not be able to predict accurately how you would handle these crises, but there is some comfort in knowing that you have considered them, and that at least now you have thought over their likely impact.

As you addressed these issues and events, a far more important message was that with love and compassion, the human spirit is resilient. You can survive. Formulating answers to the problems posed in the exercise shows you that you are resourceful, and that you have a large reserve of strength that can be tapped at will.

/ 11
Ten Guidelines for a Long and Happy Marriage

I HOPE THAT THE PRECEDING CHAPTER gave you renewed confidence in your ability to handle an uncertain future. The purpose of this book is to remove as many uncertainties from your relationship as possible. Nature may bring surprises, but with a creative spirit, you'll cope. Yes, divorce is prevalent, but it doesn't *have* to happen to you. With communication, understanding, and determination to confront rather than retreat from hurdles, you can prolong your bliss.

This chapter offers ten guidelines for a long and happy marriage. The guidelines emerged as a result of my interviews with thirty long-married couples, my interviews with experts, and my experiences in "First Comes Love" workshops and clinical practice. Add to that a dash of wisdom from other researchers, and you have the underpinnings of a satisfying, lifelong union. This chapter is necessarily more prescriptive than others in the book. But keep in mind that every recipe should allow for the cook's taste. There are *continua* of behavior, and while one point on a continuum may be perfect for some people, it may not be for you.

Make Sure You're Selecting the Right Partner

The process of making a good relationship should begin long before marriage vows. The selection of a mate is one of the most crucial decisions you can make, and will affect your lifestyle, your place in a family superstructure, whether and when you have children, and how you spend much of your time. In *Lasting Relationships: How to Recognize the Man or Woman Who's Right for You*, Myron Brenton posits, "The key to a rewarding, stable romance is knowing how to choose the right partner. Nothing can affect your happiness more than your choice of a lover or mate."

In reading this book, you've already spent much time exploring your degree of compatibility with your partner and variables that can affect your future. Once you have an idea of where your similarities and differences lie, two major questions are raised: Can you have a successful relationship with someone who is opposite to you in many ways? Or is it preferable to choose someone who is very much like you?

From my experience, I'd say "both" but would recommend choosing someone with whom you have the great majority of characteristics you value in common. The words "you value" are important. Perhaps you don't care about athletic ability, secretarial skills, or even the drive to achieve in career. What matter to you may be religious commitment, love of the arts, and a desire for a large family. As long as your partner possesses the qualities you value most, you'll have a range of interests in common.

Take a few minutes now to write down the values, interests, and skills you value most in a *fictitious* person you'd marry. If your partner has only a small number of them, but you overlook this fact because he or she is sexually attractive or has another trait that seems to overshadow the others, pause and decide whether that trait (1) is permanent, and (2) is enough on which to base a lifetime of communication.

Generally, the more interests you share, the better. In some cases, overlapping interests can lead to competition. But, as will be discussed later, you should be able to identify such circumstances and avoid competing in a negative way. Competition in a playful, inspirational context can be positive and bring motivation to achieve. It can make a game out of improvement. "You beat me last time with a better golf score, but this time mine was three points lower than your best!"

Being "opposite" from your partner can portend either a positive or a negative outcome. Nolan, the 25-year-old accountant you met in Chapter 3, was attracted to Patti because he admired her effervescence. Nolan felt dragged down by life; he had fallen into his career and envisioned his life as a movie that he watched progress. Patti, 23, loved her kindergarten teaching and bubbled about their future. Nolan needed her as a pick-me-up rather than a serious partner in life. He chose her hoping that her pep would somehow "rub off" or that people would consider him cheerful by association.

Eileen, 41, had always considered herself mentally dull. She knew she wasn't stupid, but because her mother had cruelly teased her about her memory as a child, she carried the idea that she was intellectually incompetent. She selected as a mate Conrad, a rare book dealer eight years her junior. She loved his quick wit and obvious education, and the impression he gave of being a connoisseur. In other words, she felt that Conrad compensated for her flaw. When Eileen went to parties, she loved watching Conrad excel. He knew about the latest trends and issues, and could expound on them amusingly and at length. "That shows everybody that I'm smart enough to get a guy like that," Eileen said proudly. She never had to reveal her own supposed lack of intelligence, because, she thought, people assumed she was worthy just because she was on Conrad's arm.

Is this so bad? Yes, if Eileen used Conrad as a shield from the world, or used her relationship with him as an excuse for not improving her low self-image. Eileen didn't really have a problem with her memory, but she was able to continue this negative belief because she relied on Conrad to be the couple's intellectual representative. If she'd found a lover who pointed out how unfounded her lack of self-confidence was and encouraged her to bloom in public, she would have been better served.

Being with someone who is your opposite can feed into low self-esteem, as was the case with Eileen. Or, finding an "opposite" can fill a real need in your life. Remember the term "symbiotic," referring to a relationship in which people become fused together and each requires the other in order to exist? Such relationships are generally unhealthy. On the other hand, if you've always made mistakes in your home accounts, finding a partner who enjoys record-keeping can be a real boon. And, you then have the opportunity to learn from your partner and expand your skills.

Another common question regarding mate selection is, "How long do I have to know my partner in order to know if we'd be good lifelong companions?" Opinions about this vary. Chicago psychologist Bernard I. Murstein, as quoted in a September 1981 article in the *Chicago Sun-Times*, says love at first sight is a myth. Happily married couples, he has found, only gained *intense* feelings with the passage of time. But Norman M. Lobsenz (writing in *Woman's Day* magazine, September 1982) interviewed couples who had been happily married for at least thirty years, and noted, "No ideal conditions for a long, rewarding relationship emerged. Some knew each other years before marrying, others had whirlwind courtships. Some were always financially secure while others went through hard times. Some experienced severe personal crises while the lives of others ran a placid course. Some never argued, others always did."

From my observations, I would say that length of courtship doesn't mean much in terms of predicting the future. I interviewed one couple who literally ran into each other on a street corner in Hong Kong, and were married the following week. Another marriage began when one partner spied the other across a crowded dance floor, and proposed the same evening. A third duo met on a blind date and were engaged within a few days. The members of each couple reported that they just "knew it felt right." There's a comfortable feeling, a realization that something "fits." Sometimes couples sense this immediately; other times they need years to grow into such a relaxed state. So I can't help you predict marital success by the calendar, but do pay close attention to your feelings when you're together. If you feel tense, or if afterwards you feel exhausted, don't ignore these messages.

Make a Commitment

Earlier, the term "commitmentphobia" was used to describe those who shy away from close allegiance with another. Some people even enter marriage muttering "there's always divorce" as they two-step down the aisle. There's a tinge of "just in case" hesitancy in every prenuptial agreement; it is realistic to admit this. And at some stages of life, it's appropriate to fear commitment, because the time is not right for marriage. Still, most people want intimacy, which has nothing to do with public displays, engraved announcements, and legalese documents. Deep bonds are formed internally—through vulnerability and risk-taking, and an investment of the soul.

"I'd lived with Dan for three years before I became disgusted with myself for not taking control of my love life," Carolyn told me. As assistant to a dress designer, she made a point of being creative in all facets of her life. "I adore organizing fashion shows, I keep myself svelte through dance and yoga, I eke out every bargain in fabrics and food in town," she said, shaking her head, "and I fooled myself into thinking I had everything I wanted. But in my need to be creative and spontaneous, I ran from the closeness I emotionally craved."

When Dan was temporarily assigned to an office in another city, Carolyn was jolted by loneliness. "After I realized the insanity of my attitude, I gave in to Dan's standing proposal for marriage. I think he visibly rocked when he made the usual request, embracing me from behind as I tossed a salad, and I turned and calmly replied 'yes.'

"I realized that living together was not good enough anymore. I'd held my emotions at bay thinking that if I never gave in, I'd never be hurt. But that left me with a void that I tried to fill with more hobbies, more fashion flair. Now that we're married, Dan and I have become a family, not just a couple. Commitment made the difference."

Perhaps you recall Boris and Katy, whose Christmas Eve wedding changed their view as well. They shortly were able to set long-term goals for their life (as you did in Chapter 3's "Personal Goals and Expectations" questionnaire) and proceed in confidence. They recently moved to follow an exciting job opportunity for Boris, and soon Katy will try for the baby she longs to have.

Floyd and Harriett Thatcher, themselves married over forty years, interviewed one hundred couples and summarized the results in their book *Long Term Marriage: A Search for the Ingredients of a Long Term Partnership*. In a story in the *Los Angeles Times* (February 8, 1981), they said that the happiest couples have a "commitment to each other and to the marriage. Commitment included a determination to stay married. 'Argue, yes, divorce, never,' one woman said. Couples who had divorced or might divorce were ones in which one or both spouses saw divorce as an option."

Dr. James A. Peterson of the University of Southern California's Andrus Gerontological Center, and family counselor Marcia Lasswell, contrasted two types of long-married couples. "Survivors" stay together in spite of the hardships of their lives; "golden sunset" couples find that their enthusiasm for the relationship has grown with time. Both types make a real commitment, but it seems that "survivors" are more committed to the institution than to the other person; "golden sunset" couples feel a strong bond to each other as individuals. Norman M. Lobsenz, summarizing his research with happily married couples in a September 1982 *Woman's Day* magazine article, says that "older couples value commitment as a mutual gift of love. . . . Almost every long-married couple mentioned the significance of commitment." A July 1981 *Newsweek* magazine feature story on marriage scanned research in the field and concurred, noting that the commitment needs to be renewed as people change. "The fantasy of making a commitment once and forever is nonsense," says interviewed psychiatrist Sam Klagsbrun. I came to the same conclusion.

Recall that in Chapter 2, Marian, married twenty-six years, said that a commitment to work out problems rather than head for the door was the most important benefit of marriage. She elaborated: "Our commitment means that through the classic 'for better or worse' we're going to make an effort for the good of our relationship. It is a pledge that we won't be so selfish as to put ourselves above the other. Marriage is bedrock." And in my "First Comes Love" workshops, the main reason cited by couples who choose marriage is "we're ready for the commitment."

A critical aspect of your commitment is reliability. You know the type of gripping panic that seizes you when you're waiting on a seedy street corner to be met by a friend who's late. You look at your watch, glance at the suspicious guy with the greasy hair standing behind you, then look back at your watch. You keep gazing down the street in the direction of your expected friend, alternately nervous about the suspicious stranger and angry at your friend for putting you in this situation. Avoiding this kind of discomfort is worth a lot. Being assured of your partner's reliability—knowing that he or she cares for you and won't leave you stranded on a street corner—is a strong basis for lasting love.

Sarah, a vivacious and energetic computer salesperson, left her first husband because that sense of security was missing. "My first marriage was a blur of sensual body oils, sexual experiments, and pecks on the cheek on the way to work the morning after. I couldn't count on Bob for much more, and eventually I felt alone and isolated. I would ask him to pick up a couple of game hens for dinner and he'd forget; I'd expect him to at least choose an appropriate card for his own mother's birthday. The only thing I *could* depend on was that he'd never come through."

Now, Sarah's confident that when her fiancé promises to bring game hens, he'll make sure the wild rice and asparagus are on the platter too. "I can finally relax," Sarah sighed, "because the surface gestures are symbols that Lou's love will always be there when it matters. They show his total commitment."

Balance the Giving and Taking of Support

Why do career women say ironically that what they want is a traditional, subservient "wife"? They would like to have someone do for them what women have been doing for men for centuries—supporting and caretaking. It's wearing for anyone to constantly reassure, comfort, and support. Interestingly, leaning on a spouse as an emotional prop has become a common trap for women who are advancing in their careers. Finally, these women reason, men are willing to let us struggle to the top, so they ought to understand when we unload our frustrations on them nightly. Feature articles in women's magazines that describe the difficulty of combining job and family life usually assume that women continue to give emotionally to the same degree as has been the case traditionally. Many do. But women with high career aspirations are increasingly demanding that their men listen and console. Unless both partners feel they are receiving as much understanding as they need, resentment and weariness can develop.

Traditional relationships, where the wife is dutiful, can also topple from one-sidedness. "Men feel clung to, sapped, and drained because they aren't getting their own needs to nurture met," said Nancy Robbins, a clincial social worker in Los Angeles.

Her husband, psychiatrist Jeffrey Robbins, sat nearby, cuddling the couple's toddler. He expanded, "Everyone needs to be comforted, too. If the expectation is that the man isn't supposed to be needy, a husband will stomp out those desires." The solution seems simple: just give as much caring as you accept. But achieving a satisfying balance may not come easily. "Sometimes things go wrong in childhood so people can't handle it," Dr. Robbins cautioned. "They're afraid of being devoured by the other person." The problem of not being able to ask for support often begins when a child is the victim of neglectful or cruel parents. He or she may develop a lifelong stoicism as a means of self-defense. Giving up that defense, which has provided protection for years, is often more frightening than maintaining an unbalanced status quo.

There is a risk in relying heavily on a partner's support: slipping into dependence. It's easy to make fun of the wimpy man who follows all of his portly wife's barked commands. But slipping into a subtle dependence is as simple as developing familiar (though unconstructive) patterns. He makes all the phone calls to strangers; he tends to the car; he computes the taxes and keeps the checkbooks from falling into disarray. She writes social correspondence, feeds the dog, and oversees a flourishing garden. The arrangement seems workable until it's discovered that the wife gets palpitations at the thought of dialing a repairman and hasn't heard of a dipstick; the husband can't tell a weed from a corn plant. An exercise that can help combat helpless dependence is an occasional switch of roles, to stretch atrophied muscles and reaffirm personal competence.

Rigid rules are particularly risky for women. Those who swear that their fulfillment comes from total devotion to husband and family can become so invested in nurturing that they ignore other stimulating aspects of life. These women are sacrificing personal development to some degree. There may be rewards from dispensing hugs and warm batches of cookies, but when the children leave home, mothers find they must change. These are the tenders of the much celebrated "empty nest," who often retool and pick up where prefamily life left off.

The ones who can't adjust—who can't separate themselves from their families and may even sabotage their grown children's strides to be independent—may have a dangerous symbiotic relationship, in which a parent's identity is fused with that of other family members. As much as these mothers insist that they're content, problems bubble under their placid facades. "They aren't feeling the whole range of human experience," Dr. Robbins says. "For a good marriage, you have to start with two healthy people" with well-rounded interests.

"They key issue is flexibility," Nancy Robbins concludes. "The person who is hurting should be able to receive solace from the other partner at the time it's required most."

Ability to give and receive support is intimately tied to one's ability to communicate. Often, women have had much more practice in the skills necessary to listen in an active way, express themselves, and offer encouragement. Men, who may have discovered that keeping their "cards close to the chest" in business is the best tactic, find it difficult to make the transition to full communication at home. Recall the discussion in Chapter 3 about women's thwarted attempts to find men who are shrewd in business yet tender at home. Author William Novak found men angry that women should expect these dual abilities; yet women combine these qualities frequently. With motivation and practice, men and women can cultivate their communication and support-giving skills, and feel their way toward the balance that suits their relationships.

Ideally, equity in giving and receiving is the rule. When

you're bushed and depressed, you deserve to bend my ear; when I'm similarly low, it's your shoulder's turn to absorb a few tears. And when all's right with the world, we'll both take great pleasure in acknowledging this. The division of words may not be tit for tat, but the important thing is for us each to be secure in the other's availability.

Forget Fighting—Communicate

"I thought it was *healthy* to let out my feelings," Elizabeth scowled. "When Jon ignores the miniscule requests I've made to pick up the dog's poop or drop by the cleaners' for my blazer, I turn livid. He's made an agreement to *do* those chores, and simply can't follow through." This pair, married eight months after three years of living together, constantly squabbled over trivialities, occasionally blasting each other into week-long whimpers and pouts. Elizabeth wasn't satisfied with this pattern, and craved serenity. She blamed Jon for their hostilities, since he chronically disregarded his promises to run errands, do chores, and end annoying habits.

"So what am I to do?" Elizabeth shrugged. "I just can't keep my anger inside and expect him to suddenly become Prince Charming." What she *could* expect was Jon's becoming defensive and retaliating by harping on flaws of hers. Predictably, he'd retort in anger, and they'd lapse into their familiar habit of quarreling, thinking they were constructively clearing the air.

"Anger is often a defense," points out Dr. Dennis Jaffe, a Los Angeles/San Francisco psychologist and author of *Healing from Within*. He tells clients to control their outbursts. Better to punch a pillow, scream in the shower, or furiously peddle an exercycle, and then, once drained, return to calmly face your spouse. Jaffe recommends that, rather than complaining, you ask yourself *why* your partner's transgressions seem so heinous. "Use your anger to see yourself and your own reactions first," Jaffe advises; otherwise you're doomed to an unsatisfying win/lose battle. "Blaming and judging stops anything new from happening," he adds.

Elizabeth's badgering originated in her rigid view of how Jon *ought* to react. If she could see Jon's lack of interest in specific chores, she might have either done them herself (in trade for equivalent chores) or put aside her need to have them immediately completed, and let him feel the consequences of his inaction.

Part of the problem might have been the way in which Elizabeth delivered her requests. Adages touting "the right place at the right time" are on the mark; they emphasize the importance of sleuthing your lover's mood before making demands. You invite snarls if you interrupt a favorite pastime for a favor; similarly, your partner is apt to "forget" your request if you nag or command rather than ask. "Forgetting" may consciously or unconsciously be a way of paying you back for your lack of consideration. If you want continued cooperation, apply the behaviorist principle of reinforcement after a desired act by verbally praising your partner for his or her efforts.

If regular bickering is your style, think about the benefits you must be getting from choosing this way to communicate. There's nothing wrong with a mildly combative style if you and your partner are not bothered by it. Some people find argumentativeness challenging and fun; others find it tiresome. If you're not sure whether your style is desired or is a carried-over form of self-defense, take a few minutes to *ask* your partner. Have him or her assess your communication style and identify aspects of it that might be changed. Be willing to listen, and respond to what your partner says.

Remember that people *let* others irritate them; you'll never get upset if you don't view a comment or situation as upsetting. How you view a given situation is a product of both your upbringing and your past experiences. Your partner cannot "make" you angry all by himself or herself.

While it may bring distress, a combative communication style does have the advantage of getting emotions out front; you're not engaged in passive aggression. (In pairs with a peace-at-all-cost motto, the partners might turn to sabotaging success or not acting when doing so could be helpful.) The immediate gratification gained from clearing the air and moving on keeps many people "contrary." And some people have so little excitement in their outside lives that ritual warfare within the confines of the family brings a welcome break in routine and a chance to unload frustration built up from nonfamily experiences.

The question remains: is it *better* to live in tranquility nearly all the time? It is if you don't enjoy your daily battles, or if you feel exhausted from always having to be on your toes. Tranquility is also better if you have fallen into a pattern where you have to pick an argument with your partner in order to get a reaction or opinion from him or her (a very common situation, by the way). A calmer style is also preferable if you feel nervous or under stress when in the company of your partner. Below are ways in which you can break the bickering habit.

What to do if you feel like provoking your partner: (1) Take a few deep breaths. Sending more oxygen to your brain may improve your disposition and distract you from picking a fight. (2) Force yourself to phrase criticism in the form of a question. For example: "Were you too busy last night to pick up the dog poop?" or "Did you know you forgot to bring home the game hens for dinner?" The object of your ire can then self-impose his or her own guilt and will probably apologize or come up with a reason and make restitution before a fight begins. (3) Express your feelings in an "I feel" phrase: "I feel hurt that you seemed to have ignored our need for the game hens for dinner" (note that you've brought your listener into a partnership working together to create dinner). Another example: "I feel so angry right now that I'm going to leave rather than say something I might regret." A powerful statement, but be careful with that one because you may pique your partner's curiosity about just *how* angry you are. (4) Refuse to let small incidents get you down. Say to yourself "so what?" about the fact that you'll have canned spaghetti with your asparagus instead of the game hens. "So what?" is a very useful phrase in general.

What NOT to do when you feel like provoking a fight: (1) Don't speak without thinking. Taking those deep breaths or the ever helpful counting to ten will stall your anger. (2) Don't play devil's advocate. In an attempt to make his daughters mentally astute, one father got in the habit of questioning their every assertion. Result: They picked up his style and became "contrary" adults, losing friends who soon tired of having their ideas torn apart. Instead of bringing up a "what if" that would blow a partner's concept to smithereens, make an effort to be supportive, even if this seems artificial at first. (3) Don't use absolutes like "never" or "always." Every discussion, every moment is different, and trying to generalize from past history or to an unknown future is counterproductive. Stick to the present tense.

(4) Try not to interrupt your partner. Interrupting proves you aren't listening to everything your partner is saying, and implies that what you have to say is more important. Interruptions also quicken the conversational pace; the discussion can soon esca-

late to hostility. Even if your partner is saying something erroneous, or is accusing you, just wait it out (with those deep breaths or silent counting). Couples with a calm ambience *do* interrupt occasionally, and this needn't be a problem in a context of peace. But in order to break free from a squabbling style, you need to deliberately change. Practice makes perfect.

What to do if you're provoked: (1) Use diffusive statements. These acknowledge what your partner has said but keep your attitude as uncombative as possible. Try: "Thanks for your perspective." "I understand that you feel . . ." (then mirror back what your partner just said). "I can see why you feel that way." (2) Monitor the direction of the conversation: "I'd like to stick to accomplishing our task now, please." "We seem to be getting off our original subject." "Can we address this other question another time?" (3) Make your opponent into an ally by soliciting help in ending a bickering style: "Sometimes I get too emotional and end up upset. Would you help me create a more tranquil atmosphere?" "It would be great if we could use all this energy on something fun instead of something that divides us." "I care about you and want to get along, so let's get our bearings for a few moments." "Perhaps we can turn our attention away from negative thoughts and focus on solving this problem so we can avoid conflict."

(4) Call a time out, either directly or through distraction if necessary. "We need a few seconds' pause now; please hold on." "I have to take a breather from this conversation." "Give me a moment to regain my composure." Or, if you really need time to calm down: "Excuse me, but I have to go the bathroom." (Go there and wash your face or do some deep breathing.) "I need a breath of fresh air." Use a distraction as a last resort to keep you from responding rashly, not as a means of discounting or ignoring something your partner has said. Stopping before an argument flares is not "chicken" (indicating you don't want to face the emotions of a fight) but instead keeps disagreements on a negotiable and rational level. Return to readdress the issue when you're calm.

(5) Do something to show you care. Few arguments can continue if one partner makes eye contact, smiles lovingly, reaches out and strokes the arm of the other, or simply stops and says, "I love you." These behaviors put most petty arguments in proper perspective, and help you realize that they're not worth your time.

Even if you seldom have fights, you still need tools in order to discuss issues calmly. Remember that communication requires a message, understanding of that message, and acknowledgement of it, either with or without a new message. Practice putting all three ingredients in every interchange, no matter how small, and eventually you'll be talking to each other rather than at each other.

Enhance Each Other

My client Samantha was a quiet, brown-haired escrow officer. "For some evil reason," she began, "it's so tempting to undercut Jerome when he announces the conquest of a new account or even a record bowling score. It's not fair that he should hog all the glory. I excel constantly, but just don't have his kind of milestones to praise. So I feel vindicated when I respond blankly or even nitpick about a flaw in his grand success." Samantha also felt guilty about this relished behavior, and wanted to know why it was so satisfying.

It was partly Samantha's low self-esteem that led to competitiveness and jealousy. She needed praise and was in a marathon against Jerome to see who could achieve most. When Jerome dared to one-up her, Samantha had to even the match by subtracting a few of his points. Even more fierce was their duel in areas they shared. "I was so fulfilled by my starring role in our church theater group," Samantha said. Then she frowned with irritation. "When Jerome joined the group, supposedly to be with me, his acting earned him some flattery, so he thought he could just steal the spotlight from me." Samantha was so threatened by possible damage to her ego resulting from comparison to her husband that she was considering separation.

One way Samantha and Jerome could end their jousting is through delegating separate areas of competence. For example, Samantha could just divulge her anger about the theater group and ask Jerome to find his own creative outlet. "Mom and Pop" businesses where Mom keeps the books and Pop tends the store—often asking Mom for even a thin wad of spending cash—are built on this arrangement. Neither partner dares invade the other's bounds; there can't be competition when lovers play separate games. This approach works for many couples, and though it may seem selfish, each person *does* need a sense of uniqueness.

Another way for Samantha to deal with her anger is to understand and express her need for recognition. If this need was being met, she would not feel overshadowed by Jerome when he gets compliments on his acting. He didn't mean to horn in on Samantha's territory to start with, and who can blame him for responding to praise? On the other hand, Jerome could be more sensitive to Samantha's needs. If the pair had been communicating properly about the importance of the little theater to Samantha, Jerome might have backed off when the limelight was first aimed his way. There's a tinge of unfairness about Jerome having to sacrifice his own glory so that Samantha has a place to shine. But if Jerome got his fulfillment elsewhere, he might willingly choose to let her have the attention—as a gesture of love, not as a sacrifice.

Both Samantha and Jerome have far to progress in their relationship. A July 1981 *Newsweek* magazine article on "How Marriages Can Last" notes that marriages move through four basic stages:

> In the first, spouses are typically self-centered, looking only at how the relationship can serve them. At the next level they negotiate quid pro quos—a service for a service, a concession for a concession. During the third stage they begin to appreciate each other's individuality and make accommodations for the good of the marriage and each other. By the fourth stage they have evolved a set of "rules of the relationship" by which they can avoid or deal with problems.

Samantha and Jerome seem to be caught between stages one and two. If neither is willing to change, the progression might stop there.

I don't agree that all relationships progress through each of these stages in order (with some people being "stuck" at certain plateaus). A strong marriage between two mature people, I've found from the "First Comes Love" workshops, can bypass steps one and two. Partners who have had experience in previous marriages and have strong egos may have learned to approach new lovers with a healthy respect for their identities, which negates the need to look only for personal reward. These older couples start off by appreciating each other's individuality and negotiating "rules of the relationship." Among the happiest of the long-married couples I interviewed, these rules were frequently reevaluated as partners changed and grew.

Another way Samantha and Jerome could have ended their competition is to adopt a model used by Tom and Diane, the sex and marriage counselors mentioned in Chapter 6. They first listed areas of independent and shared competence, and then vowed to teach the other skills that each had developed. For example, Samantha felt competent as an actress, and Jerome had never tried his hand at it. Before he joined her little theater group, he might have asked her to share her expertise. Then, when he excelled, the success would have been a triumph for them both (for Samantha as a good teacher; for Jerome as a good pupil as well as actor). In exchange, if Jerome was good at French, he might have helped Samantha brush up on it. The pair would increase the areas they had in common, improve their skills, and find pride in accomplishment.

What is the goal of a relationship, after all, if not to help each person to flourish? When this goal is put above selfish interests and material goals (buying a house, taking expensive vacations, eating at fancy restaurants, owning prestigeous cars), much jealousy and competetion can be avoided. If Jerome most wanted Samantha to shine, he'd do all he could to enhance her; if Samantha wanted Jerome to bloom, she'd work to support his development. With this underpinning, they would know that their own needs for ego boosts would be constantly met.

Use Gestures of Affection

As you found in Chapter 9, affectionate gestures are fundamental for keeping a marriage exciting. For example: That gentle caress on the knee under the restaurant table. A perfect crimson rose laid on the pillow. A teasing phrase scrawled in the mirror mist during your shower. A wink casually tossed across the table at a business meeting. Your business suit ironed while you catch extra moments of morning sleep. A new, beribboned comb tucked next to your hairbrush. And especially, words praising your style, your eyes, your wrinkles, and your smiles. I found, from my survey of long-married women, that it was these small, often daily images of affection that kept the happiest of them swooning over their husbands. And it was a lack of such remembrances that most frustrated women with otherwise acceptable mates.

Two characteristics of these gestures made them especially valuable. First, they were voluntary, originating in the partner's imagination (rather than being precipitated by nagging or hinting). Second, the gestures came as a surprise. After twenty years of marriage, Los Angeles social worker Mervyn Cooper thinks his unpredictable endearments have enhanced his relationship with his wife, Natalie. He's careful to know her clothes sizes, and sometimes has sexy nightgowns gift wrapped and sent to her. He loves to startle her with a corsage and an evening at one of her favorite restaurant retreats. And he's consistent about being tender toward her when they meet at the end of the day.

Those moments rejoining after the day apart are crucial to a loving ambience. "Plan that greeting at the door," he suggests. "Give a loving embrace. Don't just start dumping your troubles." Cooper recommends simple signs of caring such as scribbling an affectionate note while on the telephone or fluffing sofa pillows into a soft nest for a tired spouse.

When seeing each other at the end of the day, you should also take time to become sensitive to your partner's mood. Most people bring home their troubles and triumphs, even if they formally punched out at five o'clock. If you're elated because you've just won the "most valuable employee" award, but your partner got dumped on at 4:45, he or she is not going to tune into your elation very well. This will frustrate you, and the bickering may well begin. One important way in which couples demonstrate their caring is by being sympathetic to the most needy partner first, and then celebrating any achievements of the day. You might try viewing your relationship as a single entity of two creative and energetic people. If the efforts of one member pay off one day, the unit benefits. When the other person's efforts pay off on another occasion, the "whole" is enhanced by that much more. Even disappointments can enrich your relationship, by providing opportunities for problem-solving and the exchange of emotions.

Encourage Independence and Individual Growth

One hard-and-fast rule, according to psychiatrist Jeffrey Robbins, is that it takes two independently confident people to create a joyful marriage. If your career is lackluster, your outside friendships are boring, and your greatest passion is watching nightly sitcoms, then how can your marriage sparkle? Each of you needs a rich network of people, interests, fantasies, and accomplishments to enliven your half of the combination.

Jeffrey Robbins's wife Nancy, a social worker, remembered her ire when a rabbi at a friend's wedding negated this need for independence, "He blessed the couple by saying he hoped they'd fulfill each other totally—emotionally, spiritually, mentally and sexually," she said. "I winced—he was jinxing them!"

Ten Guidelines for a Long and Happy Marriage

As women and men fumble for postliberation boundaries, the right to assert one's independence within a relationship is often tested. As a reminder of the need for separateness, many couples incorporate Kahlil Gibran's words from *The Prophet* into their wedding vows: "But let there be spaces in your togetherness. . . . Sing and dance together and be joyous, but let each of you be alone, even as the strings of a lute are alone though they quiver with the same music. . . ."

Even when people are aware of the need for independence, they still don't know how much marriage should bind them. Monique and Keith were seething when they talked about their contemplated divorce.

"She refuses to even tell me where she's going," Keith fumed. "As if I had no right even knowing!"

Monique's eyes narrowed in anger. "You always put limits on me. Now, when I'm finally involved with my photography class, a women's action group, and my fitness regimen at the gym, you think I'm cheating on you!"

"Yes, you *are* cheating on me," Keith retorted. "You're spending time we could be together on selfish activities. Marriage is supposed to be needing each other, not needing a daily fix on a Nautilus machine!"

Keith was plainly jealous of Monique's independence. "I even encouraged him to come to the gym with me," she added, "but he whined that *he* felt obligated to spend time at home! Like *he* is the dutiful husband and I'm a wanton, flirtatious hussy!" Possessive of Monique's attentions, Keith couldn't let loose even a little when she enlarged her sphere.

The answer, with much counseling and discussion, turned out to be twofold: Monique included Keith more in her activities, scheduling time together as well as apart; and Keith became involved in new adventures, resuming his stance at first base on the company softball team. In order for Keith and Monique to accept these changes, each had to revise their expectations of what marriage meant. They negotiated a middle ground where each could develop independently and yet feel the relationship was solidly cemented.

Psychologist Dennis Jaffe emphasizes that reserving a private realm is essential to marital success. "It could be a journal in which you write your innermost secrets," he says, "it could be moments of masturbation alone; it might be as insignificant as where you get your coffee in the morning, where you sit in the window of the restaurant. The point is to have your own retreat. It's a way to proclaim to yourself that you're terrific and deserve respect for your idiosyncracies." As an exercise, think of the personal outlets you now have, and whether they would be affected if you were to marry or otherwise change your status with your partner.

Crucial in encouraging independence is each partner's ability to accept and expect growth and change in the other person. Why is it that the divorce rate peaks near the twentieth year of marriage? Perhaps because at that point, children have left home, and parenting roles have to be scrapped. Couples suddenly realize they're not married to the person they thought they knew. It is a fact of life that people change—constantly. Whether people change in compatible or clashing directions depends on the amount of communication that is present in a relationship and on the degree of tolerance each partner has for the other's interests and goals. Frequently, a man whose wife realizes that she is not fulfilled at home will resist change and further stifle his partner. The result: What should be joyous evolution is constrained by friction. In the best relationships, partners generally are honest in expressing feelings (either positive or negative) about what the other does, but if they see that the other person is extremely enthusiastic, will provide unqualified support. They do this knowing that support will be there for them, too, if they should choose to pursue a new direction.

Life can be viewed as a series of experiments. We try one career; if it doesn't work out, we try another. We discover our bodies, and try various means to achieve the goal of fitness. We hear new ideas about sexuality, and wonder how they can be implemented in our lives. Each day is a new challenge, a new experiment. Marriage, if characterized by tolerance and unqualified support, becomes a secure basis from which to try out new behaviors. It is the home base from which we venture out into that uncertain world.

Maintain Sexual Excitement— Exclusively and Creatively

There's one more part of yourself to attend to if you'd like a good marriage: your body. "You can't let yourself go and expect magic when your spouse comes to bed, "social worker Merv

Cooper says. Your partner may continue to love your values, wit, and spirit, but if he or she is turned off by your appearance, your marriage is likely to crack eventually. By taking pride in your appearance, you not only enhance your health and self-esteem, but you compliment your partner by implying that his or her admiration is worth working for.

Dr. Joyce Brothers, writing in the January 1982 issue of *Woman's Day* magazine, says physical appearance is much more important to men than it is to women. In fact, she asserts that "men are attracted first and most to good looks. A man doesn't need to know a woman for any length of time to know whether or not her looks appeal to him. The average man makes up his mind in seven short seconds whether or not he wants to know a woman better." If this is true, then no wonder women stay on the clothes/diet/makeup merry-go-round: if they're not vigilant, their men only need seven seconds to choose someone who is. While this sexist situation still exists, women are becoming more admiring of men's appearances, and both sexes are coming to appreciate fitness more than fashion. In any case, by becoming fat or slovenly, you are communicating to your partner that (perhaps for a complex set of reasons) you "vahnt to be alone." And you will be.

Whether or not you are successful at keeping your body attractive, there may be times when you want validation of your desirability from a person other than your partner. One way couples try to "have their cake and eat it too" is through open marriage. Remember Yvette and David from Chapter 9. They were the couple who swore that they could make open marriage work. They later were divorced (after a hasty proxy wedding) because Yvette took one of her flings a bit too seriously. Angela and Aaron, as you recall, view their rare sexual liaisons as extensions of deep friendships that happen to be with people of the opposite sex. They're still together, have just had a baby, and still believe that their outside relationships don't interfere with their love.

I hope Angela and Aaron don't end up like Yvette and David. Unfortunately, on the basis of my observations and the conclusions reached by numerous experts, the prognosis for their relationship is poor.

More frequently, people do recognize the value of exclusivity. Jane, a 59-year-old bookkeeper, ended a lusty past when she married Alan thirty-one years ago. "If I didn't find him the most attractive man around, I'd say to him, 'let me out,' [of our marriage]" she said. She's slightly annoyed that extramarital affairs have received such favorable press: "I remember overhearing my father caution my brother when he was getting married many years ago. He said, 'Many women may be attractive to you, but develop a sense of discipline, because your marriage is worth it.' "

Her husband, Alan, nodded and added, "When you're looking, you'll find an affair. Those things don't just happen."

And conversely, even the most seductive flirtation will hit a stone wall of non-response if directed toward someone not open to it. Have you ever been so much in love that your feelings blinded you to the advances of an otherwise stupefyingly attractive person? If you are consumed by abiding affection and strong dedication, an opportunity for momentary passions cannot distract you.

Reverend Peter Kreitler and Bill Bruns, authors of *Affair Prevention*, offer ten suggestions for couples who want to avert affairs: place your spouse first in your priorities ("numero uno" is their term); make the bedroom a special place for the two of you; set aside time to be together regularly, and synchronize watches so your free time coincides; know your energy limitations and don't allow yourself to come to your relationship drained; use vacations to relax and "re-create"; enjoy water (bathing with your partner); laugh easily and quickly at situations; let yourselves be childlike; pause periodically to consider your values and the status of your marriage; and foster communication skills. These actions prevent affairs by making your marriage strong, so that it fulfills all your romantic needs. These behaviors, of course, are useful to incorporate in your relationship whether or not an affair is on your mind.

An article on "Why Husbands Stray" in *Woman's Day* magazine (February 8, 1983) notes that people involved in affairs usually feel they have nothing to lose, and view their new relationships as arenas where, pastless, they can become a "dazzling new self." Possibly, they could have become dazzling within the context of their marriages. Men quoted who had had affairs all seemed to have given their wives signals that they were unhappy, only to be ignored. These men felt trapped in a hollow institution filled with obligations and few rewards.

In a course on marriage I attended, a classmate made a wise recommendation. When you have an opportunity for an affair, ask yourself two questions: "What harm will it do to my marriage?" and "what good will it do?" Both questions need to be asked, to keep the evaluation from being one-sided.

If an affair isn't on Thursday's agenda, electricity can still sizzle within a settled relationship. "Sexuality is bound to decline if couples don't work at it," Diane, the sex therapist, says. She encourages clients in sex therapy to "dare to be innovative with drastically different styles of sexually relating. Try sex at new times and in exciting positions. Describe conscious sexual fantasies and act them out. Adopting a different mind set or part in a fantasy may be difficult to do, but it's intensely rewarding. Even recalling previous enactments of fantasies can bring an extra dimension to lovemaking."

Diane related one case in which the husband was impotent. One night, his wife appeared at their bedroom door in a blond wig and sleazy cocktail gown, with a seductive glare, and told him, "I'm the girl you sent for." The man's problem vanished instantly. A playful attitude makes each encounter a discovery rather than a challenge to rigid expectations. Focus on the process rather than the orgasm as a goal of sex. All the time that a person spends worrying about orgasms is time away from enjoying the pleasure of the moment. Another guideline is to accept an unadventuresome sex life if you and your partner are satisfied with it. Remember Hillary and Martin, who did not feel they had to "swing from the chandeliers" and were happy with their conventional lovemaking. The point is to allow yourself to be as innovative and free as necessary to find mutual pleasure, but let your own desires rather than "shoulds" guide your behavior.

Put Your Relationship First— And Your Kids Second

Increasingly, couples are no longer enduring a tortuous marriage for the "good of the children." But an infant's wails, pony rides, and Girl Scout meetings can still become a daily focus. Pretty soon you're calling Robert "Daddy," and spending after-bedtime hours talking intensely about Junior's science award, a day camp decision, or the virtues of braces.

A child brings stress to even the closest marriage. Harold Feldman, of the New York State College of Human Ecology at Cornell University, studied parents' relationships at various stages of their children's development. He found that having a child almost invariably brought some sexual problems, competition with the child for attention, guilt over spending too much time on a career, and a feeling of being trapped. George Rowe of the University of Nebraska studied seventy-one couples who had been married for twenty-five to sixty-two years. He found that couples with fewer children have the most happiness in their marriages. Rowe, as quoted in the *Los Angeles Times* (June 21, 1982), said, "the study indicated a dip in marital happiness is almost always concurrent with the time the children are a heavy responsibility for parents."

Diana Burgwyn, in her book *Marriage Without Children*, notes, "Many scientific studies do support the view that children transform the nature of marriage—and not always positively. The first child, in particular, demands a big adjustment, with the mates having less time and energy for each other and the husband often feeling displaced by the child." Armed with the knowledge that children can disrupt a relationship, you can make a determined effort to make parenting a shared activity and to escape associated responsibilities on a regular and frequent basis.

After conducting my "Children: To Have or Have Not?" workshops for six years, I've seen many couples make the successful transition from cuddling twosome to caring parents. The decisive element is attitude. Resentful parents view the child as a burden, an obstacle around which to maneuver career, privacy, independence, and the marital relationship. These parents often want to "have it all," and while they love their children, they only feel satisfied if they can successfully juggle all the components of their life plan. In their juggling act, they sometimes put the children first, with career and marriage considered secondary. They feel stress, but have pride in being a role model of success for their children, an achiever. Unfortunately their partners, as understanding as they often are, don't like playing second fiddle. During the time periods when attention is focused on the children, the neglected partner may find other activities to engage in, and communication between the partners is minimized. Soon the spouses realize that they've "grown apart," and their marriage is in trouble.

Couples who successfully raise families have two characteristics: an ability to set priorities, and a consistently positive attitude. They effervesce confidence in themselves as ever-capable to innovate ways to accomplish things. To them, a child is a bonus, a delight enriching their lives, rather than a barrier to the life they desire. Pleased parents are careful not to let their children wrest attention away from the core of the family—their romantic bond. They are able to tell their children, "Please don't interrupt us now, we're having a private conversation," and they set rules that children are not to intrude on their special time together. They plan trips away and don't fret about the children left behind with another caretaker. Finally, they regard each other as romantic adults rather than solely as sharers of authority at home.

Because the happiest parents put their relationship before their children, they don't brush aside marital problems. They tend to them as they arise, and refuse to put up a facade—about the good *or* the bad feelings they're having. Because they're not overly sheltered, their children learn that sometimes adults get angry at each other, but that they find ways to work through a problem and make up. Children benefit from also seeing love and affection between their parents.

Dr. Dennis Jaffe, father of two, agrees that the best tactic to take with children is honesty. "There's no way to fool a kid," he says. "They always know what's happening between their parents." So focus your attention first on your relationship—and then worry about what to tell the kids.

Put Effort into Maintaining a Good Relationship

Too many people enter a marriage assuming that it'll automatically continue "happily ever after." They know the divorce statistics (and may be included in them), but somehow *this* marriage is *different*.

But life is a collage of daily events that can slide into a humdrum pattern unless you stay constantly attentive.

Pauline nearly lost Travis to his boss's secretary before she was stunned into earnest effort. "Sometimes I have to force myself to be patient, when I might have exploded before," she explained. "I have the rules for communication written on 3 × 5 cards, and I sometimes use the quotes written there rather than just go crazy like I used to." She also takes ten minutes when she gets home to talk with Travis free from interruptions. And she keeps a bottle of cologne on her nightstand to spritz on just before bed. "These extra touches are what Travis appreciates, because they show I do care about pleasing him," Pauline added. "I make these small gestures, and it opens the door for greater communication. In return, he's motivated to do sweet things for me. Yes, this is added work, but the rewards have made them fun rather than dutiful exercises to renew my marriage."

Keep tabs on how your partner is feeling toward you, day to day. Generally a regular time to talk will take care of it, but one wife uses another tactic as well. "Sometimes, when I suspect that something's wrong, or that my husband is slightly miffed at me, I use a little test. I say to him 'I love you' and watch his reaction. Normally, he'll smile, say he loves me, and give me a wonderful hug. In fact, we do this all the time. But if something's off, he'll make a little face and say 'I love you' in a grudging sort of way. This opens the door to a discussion of the problem, but precedes it always with 'I love you.' "

Many couples I interviewed said they "work" at their marriage. They consider the kinds of acts Pauline does for Travis part of their work; they also point to their willingness to be tolerant of a partner's idiosyncracies and to go along with a partner's point of view instead of their own. Most of all, they say that they touch base with their partners often, using communication to discern how they can help the other. "We're happy just being together, sitting in the same room silently reading," one wife of thirty-five years said. "We don't need to talk to communicate. I can just look up and know his mood. Sometimes I'll sense he wants a cookie and get up to get it. As I rise, he thanks me in advance. We're that close. And I want you to know that I *like* getting the cookie for him, I'm not at all subservient. In fact, he's usually up getting me my sweater before I notice my own goose bumps!"

The members of one couple I interviewed adamantly said that they *never* had to work at their marriage. Wed thirteen years, Randy and Priscilla were, in their home at least, one of those "sickening" couples always hugging and using pet names. Priscilla said: "I don't understand when people say they 'work' at their marriage. Being with Randy all these years has been sheer pleasure, not the slightest lick of work associated with it. We've even arranged our careers so we can be together, sharing our office and seeing some of our clients in our home." Randy was a consultant to businesses, teaching employees how to write proposals and reports; Priscilla advised on marketing and public relations. "We'll be in an important meeting and I'll run my leg up his under the table; we'll be in a supermarket checkout line and he'll surreptitiously touch the front of my sweater. We have these little secrets. And at home, we'll each be at our desks and suddenly one of us will send a paper airplane enclosing a big heart and a poem."

Randy smiled and said, "But we don't just play with each other. We do hash out concerns; we do have worldly problems to cope with. We both hate to hustle, but as consultants, we have to bring in business, so we console each other and try to be motivational. We evaluate each other's work and give constructive suggestions. We're a team, and we know that when one of us succeeds, we both do. Every minute is fun, and it just keeps getting better." Perhaps work and fun *can* be the same thing.

/ 12
The Wedding Ceremony

MARCIA SELIGSON, in *The Eternal Bliss Machine*, describes the lengths to which couples in American culture go in ritualizing and commercializing the wedding ceremony. This big to-do scares some would-be bridal couples away from getting married at all. They get nervous envisioning Aunt Matilda becoming tipsy enough to smack Uncle Henry. They cringe at the thought of having to pose for traditional photographs. They blush when they realize that for one day—and several weeks surrounding the event—they will be forced to be in the limelight. Getting married is always a big deal.

Imagining Your Wedding

Perhaps you and your partner are nowhere near getting married; perhaps your ceremony is next Sunday. In either case, before discussing the implications of this event, take a few moments to complete the "Imagining Your Wedding" exercise. Think about two types of weddings, with you as the bride or groom: your ideal wedding, and your most realistic vision of the wedding you probably will (or would) end up having. The purpose of this exercise is two-fold: (1) to get you thinking about the type of wedding that expresses your personality and what the ceremony means to you, and (2) to catch your *feelings* about the wedding ceremony. As you write down your realistic prediction, notice your immediate emotion, and assign it a number on a ten-point scale, with 10 = extremely positive (e.g., very happy or excited) and 1 = extremely negative (e.g., very depressed or angry).

Now consider these questions: How close to your ideal is your realistic wedding picture? If you were married before, how

IMAGINING YOUR WEDDING

	IDEAL	REALISTICALLY
Number of people attending		
Names of attendants I'll have		
Where the ceremony will take place		
Approximate date		
Person officiating		
Style of wedding		
Time of day		
Predominant color(s)		
What I will wear		
What my partner will wear		
Time and date of reception		
Place of reception		
Amount and type of food		
How food will be served		
Cost of the wedding and reception		
Percentage bride and groom will each take charge		
Type of rings, if any		
Destination after the wedding		

have your past weddings influenced your present ideals? Were there some aspects to your fantasies that made you feel more positively than others? Are there certain aspects about which you are more sensitive or stubborn than others? How would you reconcile differences with your partner in these areas? Compare your fantasies and realistic predictions with those of your partner.

Many people feel perfectly happy with their partners, and want to be married to them. But when the subject of wedding planning comes up, they begin to sweat, their mouths go dry, and they start seeing double. Their bodies are telling them that the intricacies of the ceremony raise unpleasant issues. "How 'bout hitting the courthouse at noon tomorrow?" might be the first words you can squeak out. In completing the "Imagining Your Wedding" questionnaire, you were able to note your feelings about the wedding ceremony that would realistically take place. Now you have an opportunity to pinpoint why you may be anxious. Keep in mind that it's completely normal to feel jittery or upset, as well as to have mixed feelings about the whole thing.

Why Getting Married May Be Hazardous to Your Emotional Health

Weddings bring tension because they force you to change suddenly to cope with a myriad of activities, decisions, and feelings. Here are eight likely sources of stress.

1. The *number of decisions* you have to make is staggering, and you have to decide not only what *you* want but what won't offend your in-laws, friends, and partner. "Here I was nearing my semester finals," said Julie, 21, married a year and recalling her engagement days. "We set a June date, and all spring I was like a chicken with its head cut off, jumping around from one decision to another. I was frantically deciding things that I'd have to live with for the rest of my life, decisions that I would've loved to give much time and consideration." I asked her for examples.

"Well, my china and crystal patterns," she said. "I went to one of those bridal fairs and looked at a few samples. My mother urged me to choose one design, and Douglas's mother pushed another one. They were trying to be helpful because I was confused. The decorations became blurs. And nowadays you're expected to pick out three or four patterns, one 'good' set of fine china, one intermediate set for company, a couple of stoneware sets for everyday, and maybe a Melmac throw-around set for loading into the dishwasher after a quick bite. I'll need a mansion just to hold all that pottery!"

"If you were so overwhelmed, why didn't you just tell your parents to back off?" I asked.

"Because I had this image of a perfect wedding, where everything was like a fairy tale. I was going to be the princess, floating down the aisle in my Cinderella ball gown. After the wedding, I was going to come home to a beautiful house with all the trimmings, and according to the bridal magazines, which I've read since I was ten years old, I had to have all these sets of china, a complete set of crystal, silver and flatware, a wok, an airless corn popper, a yoghurt maker, an electric ice cream freezer, and a pasta machine. Not to mention the obligatory Cuisinart, toaster, electric frypan, and blender." Julie started to laugh at her own ridiculousness. "Can you imagine taking this so seriously? I made the acquisition of gifts a tangle of burdens, because I had to evaluate all these brands and register for each item! And everything had to be in coordinated colors, or it was exchanged. There were times about a month before the wedding when I wanted to exchange my head!"

Decision-making causes stress. Making big decisions usually causes bigger stress. But when you're in the whirlwind of activity that Julie faced, every decision seems big, if only because you wish you could give it more attention. Then you start regretting, thinking over your options, and wondering whether you did enough comparison shopping. And in the case of a wedding, where the monetary stakes are high, you may feel much pressure from vendors, peers, relatives, and even your own partner.

In fact, because you and your partner have to come to so many consensuses, you have many more opportunities to disagree. I remember counseling more than one couple who had postponed getting married because of their conflicts over the ceremony itself. In one case, the problem occurred because the groom refused to back his bride's choices of gifts and wedding accoutrements when they clashed with those of his mother. Because he refused to get caught in the middle of their disagreements, he proved that he cleaved unto neither his mother nor his fiancée.

2. Getting married can be traumatic because you may have to develop or summon qualities of *assertiveness* that you seldom need in daily life. One shy bride, Catherine, 33, was sufficiently assertive with her partner, Glenn, but lacked confidence to stand her ground around others. Glenn's mother, Dorothy, had no daughters, so looked forward to her son's wedding as an event where she could use her party-planning skills. Dorothy wanted orange tiger lilies on all the tables at the reception, and on the posts leading up to the altar. Catherine, who didn't care for orange flowers, suggested orchids. Dorothy insisted, and Catherine relented. Over and over again. "Dorothy seemed to want the tiger lilies so much," Catherine shrugged. "I just didn't know how I could be firm without hurting her feelings."

If you're assertive by either nature or training, you'll have plenty of call for your skills. Even the most aggressive people, however, find it trying to be insistent after five or six battles. Skirmishes occur with caterers as well as family members, with people whom you feel comfortable with as well as near-strangers. Said one weary bride, "I walked down an aisle I didn't like, wearing a dress that made me look fat, carrying flowers that made me sneeze, and hobbling on shoes that matched my dress but not my shoe size. But still, I wrote my own vows and bought a ring I loved, despite its lack of diamonds. I found that if I'd pushed for my own way all the time, I would've been in a constant fight. So I just gave in as little as possible, depending on whom I had to contend with, and how much trouble it was to satisfy my own preferences."

Wedding plans are usually the purview of the bride. She may consult her partner, but he usually doesn't share her level of involvement. Ironically, brides are usually less experienced at assertiveness than their partners, and find themselves pitted against experienced salespeople. Many women find an ally in their mothers, no matter what their ages. With a unified voice, brides and their mothers can often conspire to create a wedding satisfying to both their dreams.

3. Assertiveness, however, is not enough to emerge from wedding planning unscathed. Also required is *diplomacy*. Whether you're creating an enormous spectacle or simply eloping, you're bound to hurt feelings along the way. Still, you have to put on your party-time smile, and break the news to Mrs. Watson that she can't be included, or tell Agnes, your friend since elementary school, that she can't be the maid of honor. When you are under the stress of endless decisions and standing up for yourself, expediency and directness sometimes take precedence over diplomacy. *Then* you feel guilty about the way you brushed over someone's feelings, or the offended party broadcasts your sin and very quickly your reputation is smirched.

"I hired a wedding consultant to be my buffer," said Rose, 40, married two years ago for the first time. "I'm a nurse, and at the end of the working day or week I'm too bushed to think about details. The person I hired took care of everything, including personal messages—she was like my secretary for two months. I gave her a guest list, and we had to trim it. Instead of leaving out forty people entirely, Edward and I threw a huge shower-type party before the invitations went out. At the party the consultant and I make a point of explaining to the people dropped from the wedding how sorry we were that there couldn't be enough space. The consultant took the whole rap, saying that she insisted we use a room that was, unfortunately, too small." Rose sighed. "So many headaches simply because we couldn't be all things to all people!"

4. Under any circumstances, *financial strain* brings tension. In planning a wedding, I know of few couples who don't stretch their own or their parents' budgets. Even those who slip away to city hall often throw lavish receptions afterward, usually at the strong request of family and friends. This is especially true if this is the first marriage for either partner or if the couple is relatively young (in their twenties).

Ironically, it seems that the more money and social standing a bride and/or groom has, the more obligated the couple is to throw themselves or their families into debt. It's unacceptable for the daughter of a wealthy town father to have a simple cake-and-punch reception. Marcia Seligson, in *The Eternal Bliss Machine*, writes about several such situations, such as the nuptials of an oil-wealthy family: "A mock Italian Renaissance court pageant, music by the Houston Symphony, costumes by Mr. John, who flew down from New York for last-minute nips and tucks." Or the "upper crust" but atypical wedding of Sharon Percy to John D. Rockefeller IV, "at which she wore a Mainbocher gown and the 1800 guests were serenaded by the Chicago Symphony Orchestra." Music, in wedding circles, seems rather important.

Because a wedding is one of the few occasions when families traditionally exhibit their standing in the community, they feel obligated to put on as grand a wedding as they can afford so others judge them favorably. Even if such pressures are not present, most bridal couples feel this is a once-in-a-lifetime event, and therefore *want* to make it as memorable and perfect as possible. Julie, the young bride above, felt the usual anticipation for her moment of glory dreamt about since childhood. Childhood dreams are not to be denied, even if they mean hocking the family heirlooms.

5. The symbolism and consequences of the wedding are also wrapped up in its preparation. At the ceremony the *joining of two families* is formalized. For many couples, the wedding is the first time groom and bride meet many of the relatives—who are bound to make judgments. Comments on physical features and demeanor are unavoidable. Christopher described how he felt at his reception, just six months ago:

I didn't think it would be such a big deal, but sitting at the head table I felt like six hundred eyes were scrutinizing my every pore. When I got up to dance, I was sure I had two left feet. I nearly crushed my mother-in-law's foot, and I wanted to make a good impression, of course. I think that I had blocked my fear of all these strangers until the actual night, which made things a lot easier. But my last impression of the wedding won't be the vision of my lovely bride but rather of Nancy's Aunt Judy's face when I called her Aunt Jennifer. Judy and Jennifer have had a feud for ten years, and we'd had to take Jennifer off our guest list to keep peace!

The discomfort of meeting many people at once is compounded by the realization that you are taking your place on their family tree. If you and your new family don't hit it off, you are still bound to them, and will have to deal with them for years to come. If they don't like you, they can make your life difficult by pitting your partner against you. If somehow your stock is considered inferior to theirs, they may not let you forget that fact. Of course, you can take steps to disassociate yourself from petty or snobbish people as much as possible. And many people in your new family will probably be delightful and add much to your life. The problem is the uncertainty of the situation, and the fact that once you are legally tied to this group of people, there is no escape except divorce.

6. Emotionally, however, the most significant symbolism of the wedding is your *personal role*. In vignettes of old, why did grooms jilt their brides as they waited at the altar? Because getting married *is* just the beginning—of lifetime responsibility. Your new role may be appealing, and you may love your partner with all your soul. But in taking this new direction, you leave behind your "old" self, the carefree, independent, mobile, youthful person you're clearly attached to. There's sadness as well as joy in this transition, not only because a phase of your life is ending but because you're headed for the unknown. You may have been miserable as a single person, but at least that was familiar. You may end up equally miserable as a married person, but then you have to contend with someone else's feelings as well as your own. Getting married makes life more complicated, even though it may also be much better. Or worse. And it's for better or worse that you're stuck, so it makes sense that you're jittery.

When I said in a "First Comes Love" workshop that role changes come with marriage, Martha, a 30-year-old manager with a large company, protested. "Maybe in the old days, when women were chattels. But come on, it's the 1980s!" she said. "I'm completely independent. I don't need my future husband's money or status; I don't want any children; I plan to come and go as I please. I'll be exactly the same person before and after the ceremony. I refuse to see myself as different just because there's a piece of paper on file at city hall."

Her fiancé, Marvin, wasn't too pleased. "I wouldn't want you to be a different person, but I *do* want you to acknowledge that you *are* my wife!" he said. "Otherwise, why are we at this class? Why bother to get married?"

Martha was startled, and somewhat embarrassed that her partner wouldn't support her. "What do you mean?" she asked, practically elbowing him. "We're doing this relationship *our* way, not according to anyone else's rules!"

"Yes, we are," Marvin acknowledged. "But that doesn't negate the fact that just by getting married, we're changed. I finally accepted that, Martha. I'm human, not some superperson who can flaunt all emotion and convention. I like the idea of being your husband, and I wish you wouldn't be so obstinately against being my wife."

Martha was speechless. She'd been denying that her commitment to Marvin would change her, rather than noting the ways it would *and* would not affect her roles and behaviors. Perhaps this was because she had (normal) fears about the loss of identity that can accompany any major change.

7. Preparing for a wedding also challenges your independence in that *people impose on you and make assumptions about your future*. Getting married is a symbol of your acceptance of cultural norms, and others expect further compliance with tradition. At a bridal shower, guests may make inquiries about personal matters: "When do you plan to have your first child?" "You're a modern girl so I supposed you're not *really* entitled to wear white." (tacky, tacky). "How long did you and Augustus know each other before you decided to get married?" "How does Fern compare to the other ladies you've known?" Because you've made your love a public fact, the public feels entitled to know details. Such questions would make anyone testy, but generally it is best to control your emotions and be diplomatic, per point number three.

Most couples take meddling in stride because they receive so many emotional boosts from the same people. Relatives gather from all points of the country to honor them. They are the center of attention at parties, in department stores, at the dressmaker. The bride, particularly, gets a lot of attention. In exchange, the bride and groom find themselves "living in a glass house." Couples who detest such attention usually choose a simplified ceremony and a quiet announcement.

8. Finally, weddings cause stress because *there's so much to do*. Your emotions and energy are taxed by organizing, making decisions, and setting up a new home (or, if you're living together, making room for gifts and visiting relatives). Again, it's possible to marry with little disruption in your life, but few couples choose that route. Most *want* a chance to stand out, as a highlight in the otherwise mundane passage of their lives. So they intentionally set up circumstances that require intense emotions and activities. And there's little difference in time invested between the most personal and innovative ceremony and the most lavish conventional one.

"I burned the candle at both ends," Julie said. "I was exhausted every day for weeks, and I lost twelve pounds. I forgot to eat because I was so busy writing thank-you notes, consulting with the caterer, and planning the honeymoon. The night before the wedding, after the rehearsal party, Douglas and I had an awful fight. We screamed in the car for forty-five minutes, never hearing each other. Afterward we were so tired, and so relieved, that we sat there laughing hysterically, tears in our eyes. We knew that we just had to get out all that tension and frustration, and it worked, because I felt completely relaxed at my wedding. It turned out just the way I wanted it to—the most wonderful day of my life!"

These eight sources of anxiety surrounding wedding ceremonies are not meant to shoo you away from getting married, but rather to help you understand what you may endure (and enjoy). No matter what obstacles precede it, a wedding is always symbolic of love between two people. Because of this appealing message, sentimental people are thrilled to witness couples formalizing their commitment. These "wedding freaks" cry at weddings, even weddings on TV and those of people they don't know. That two people love each other to the point where they want to spend their lives together, work through problems that arise, have children (maybe), and be constant sources of support, is miraculous. The visible symbols of this deepest of all feelings cause awe and reverence. A wedding reaffirms that life will go on, that people care and connect. Its power is intense and overwhelming, and so a wedding make peoples cry.

Fear of the Wedding Ceremony

For any or all of the eight reasons given above, you're likely to feel nervous about your wedding. Sometimes these feelings can go to an extreme. Gary and Kelly lived together for six years. They both wanted to get married, but Gary would go into a panic at the thought. His hand would get clammy, he'd perspire heavily, his heart would palpitate. He was immobilized, a basket case. He'd analyzed himself to death, and linked his present reaction to fears he had as a child. Still, this insight did him no good. He wasn't afraid of *marriage*, he explained, only of the act of *getting* married.

"I've lived with Gary's panic attacks for all these years," Kelly said. "But this is getting ridiculous. I'm beginning to think Gary deliberately brings these on to avoid the wedding."

"I can't control them, you know that," Gary replied helplessly. "I get so sick, so upset that I miss work. It's embarrassing and I feel awful. I'd do anything to avoid them." His doctor had prescribed medication that helped his symptoms somewhat, but Gary hated taking drugs and he never knew when the severe attacks would hit. "I want to get married. I really do," he reiterated.

We spent some time in counseling exploring whether Gary had a block to getting married. It turned out that he had experienced the same surges of panic when faced with major choices in the past. In fact, he had lost a prestigious corporate job because he had had these attacks when having to make job assignments and training decisions. This reaction to decision-making was a serious problem that Gary consciously wanted to overcome.

I tried desensitization techniques combined with relaxation. Deep breathing, visualization, and self-hypnosis were used. I told Gary to think of Kelly being with him, of entering the courthouse and walking up the steps. He started to get symptoms right away. We backed up, and I told him instead to imagine that he was going to the courthouse to pick up a copy of his house deed, on the occasion of paying off his mortgage (to associate the courthouse with a pleasant event). After he was able to do that, he was told to actually go with Kelly to the courthouse just to walk in the hallway. But he knew the purpose of this exercise, and again his symptoms returned. We backed up again, and I told him to simply drive by the courthouse with Kelly, then progress to standing across the street, and finally walking up the steps. Gary's progress was slow and painful, and Kelly was impatient.

The couple went on vacation, and while away, Gary got a great idea. Why not just send out announcements that they were already married? Then the pressure would be off. Everyone would think it was done and they could get on with life. Gary's goal was to fool himself into relaxing and then when they finally did go to the courthouse (for a mundane purpose) they could duck in and "remarry." Kelly immediately went to a stationery store, and bought and sent out announcements. I was surprised to receive one a week before they were due home.

When they returned, Gary explained, "We just told our families that our vacation was really a honeymoon. They congratulated us, hugged us, and I felt totally relieved." Gary still had to solve his original problem, eliminating the source of his debilitating fears. I referred him to a psychiatrist for long-term therapy. I also felt sad for Kelly, because she had accepted the position of martyr to Gary's weakness. But she could not be helped because she was content and did not want to change anything. Her singular goal was to get married, and now she had the world believing that this aim had been accomplished.

Most people wouldn't have Gary's problem, but early experiences and present circumstances can easily bring mini-panic attacks about getting married. Here's a free-association exercise you can try alone or with your partner to learn what fears you may have. Some anxiety, I repeat, is normal. But why not work to diffuse it? Write in the first word that comes to your mind:

wedding_____   bride_____
groom _____   veil_____
ring_____   license_____
church/temple _____   in-laws_____
invitation_____   honeymoon _____
reception_____   wedding cake_____

If most of your responses are neutral or positive, great; if you found some surprising replies, take a few minutes to explore their possible meaning. Think of all the weddings you've attended, and the stories about weddings you heard as a child. Are there certain activities in the ceremony that bother you, or do you need to ex-

The Ceremony as a Reflection of Your Personality

Ahh for the simple days, when just about *everybody* got married in a chapel, joined in the eyes of God, or had their guests gather 'round in the living room, with the bride two-stepping over her train as she descended the staircase. There wasn't much variety in weddings then, right up to the late 1960s, but somehow their uniformity was comforting, convincing us that a couple was doing it "right." Since the hippies emerged in Haight-Ashbury, however, tradition has been first stretched and then permanently changed. Marriage at dawn barefoot on a beach is a frequent California sight. Couplings in hot air balloons, on horseback, on a chartered yacht, or at the site of a first date don't even draw a feature page photographer anymore. And of course, garden and mountain weddings are *de rigueur*.

Most wedding ceremonies no longer include the word "obey," and poetry readings and guitar-accompanied soloists regularly punctuate the most sedate of gatherings. Think back to the fantasy exercise at the beginning of this chapter: did you envision a traditional, innovative, or quiet wedding? Here are a few ideas of what your vision could imply about you.

A large, festive *traditional* ceremony, held in a church, synagogue, home, or garden could mean:

- You (like most people) want to please your family and thereby earn their love.
- You believe in fairy tales, and think of a traditional wedding as something beautiful and magical. You want this dream to come true.
- Your life is rather bland—perfectly fine, mind you, but not studded with excitement—and you view your wedding as a chance to be the center of attention once and for all. If nothing else ever happens to you, you'll always have the memories of your wedding day.
- You like the sense of history, of being part of a ritual that connects you with the past and future.
- You don't want to bother with creating your own ritual, so you rely on established traditions. This is a major reason why people

belong to churches, by the way: it's helpful to have a source for rules and guidelines of conduct.

If your fantasy is more *innovative*, these could be among your motivations:

- You want to assert your own uniqueness and separate yourself from the rules of society.
- You think your unique location is more beautiful or appropriate than a place that has hosted countless other weddings, all similar to one another.
- You are deliberately rejecting the domination of your family.
- You want even more attention than the usual bride or groom gets (by being especially creative or tacky, or otherwise going to such lengths that you earn comment).
- You want to gain admiration from family members or others for your ability to organize an unusual event, your intelligence in writing your own vows, or your talent in performing your own music.
- You think large, formal weddings can be too commercial.

If you fantasized a *quiet or small* (under twenty-five people) wedding, it's possible that:

- You are shy.
- You are too busy to get involved with organizing a larger affair.
- You are getting married for the second (third, fourth, or more) time, or are pregnant.
- You feel large weddings are too commercial.
- You don't want to deal with your friends and family any more than is necessary.
- You treasure privacy, and feel that your marriage is a personal matter.

The type of wedding you want is important because it reflects the patterns of your life. Setting up a wedding is a microcosm of the larger decisions and activities you will face in your marriage. If you have the enthusiasm and courage to stage a huge gala, with flying doves and a champagne fountain, then you might be the type who later "keeps up with the Joneses" via an impressive house, vacations to all the right places, and clothes in the latest styles. Throwing a large traditional wedding suggests that you crave attention and have a need to please. You might have been a middle or younger child, and learned to thrive by conforming.

If you prefer a very innovative wedding, you obviously have a tendency to flaunt tradition and do things your way. I'd guess that you have a creative occupation, or one where you can be your own boss. You don't like taking orders in any part of your life, and you won't want to take them from your mate, either. You may be stubborn, but that doesn't mean you're necessarily combative; you may use logic to convince others that your thinking is correct. You are likely to be a first or only child, who learned to get your parents' approval by doing clever things; you may be an achiever now.

If you chose a quiet wedding, you have probably matured to where you have a long-range perspective. While you treasure the love and family closeness of a wedding, you don't need to broadcast your vows. You may be highly successful in the work world, but separate it from your home life. You give family high priority, and work to see that all goes smoothly and stays in harmony. Because you're probably older and/or celebrating your second or later marriage, you come to it seriously, aware of potential pitfalls and wary of repeating past mistakes.

These descriptions may sound like one-size-fits-all horoscopes, and indeed I have oversimplified to get the points across. You may have combined a traditional and innovative service, or been torn between two styles and chosen one capriciously. The point is to see how your fantasy of an ideal wedding corresponds to your patterns of behavior, and whether these are compatible with or at odds with your partner's patterns.

Studying for Her M.R.S.

In the days (not so long ago) when most women were enraptured by the myth of perpetual connubial bliss, a prevalent wisecrack on university campuses was to point to a girl enrolled in home economics and whisper "she's studying for her M.R.S." Since then most colleges have abandoned their home economics departments (and added women's studies), but that hasn't stopped women and some men from attending solely to find a mate. Once they find someone who is willing to get married, they feel "all's right with the world" because, they expect, now their life will have order. They assume that the wedding is a symbol of their triumph in finding a partner, and so direct their energy to the event. In effect, they are getting married just to have the wedding, and they push aside (make broad assumptions about) what life will be like afterward.

"Oh, come on," you may say. "That doesn't happen anymore." Granted, people with this orientation probably wouldn't read this book, but they are out there, hiding their true motivations for relationships, cruising singles bars, answering "personals" ads, dropping books in law libraries, and tripping qualified feet on health club jogging tracks. These young women (usually aged 18–25) want the glory of a wedding, and will stage one to their parents' financial limit, complete with six bridal showers. Underneath their single-minded aim is low self-confidence and, often, insecurity about a direction in life. They don't know what career to pursue, and they may not like the range of jobs their station and inclinations most likely allow. So they grasp for a time out, a grandiose event, to make everything right. On your wedding day, all things are possible. All dreams come true.

So the wedding ceremony is far from just another day in your life. It represents a major source of stress, the beginning of extensive change in your life, and has far-reaching symbolic implications. Contemplating these effects has given you an opportunity to further explore your relationship and improve your future.

SECTION *Five*

Putting It Together

PREVIOUS SECTIONS OF THIS BOOK combined inner evaluation with discussions of societal trends and other external issues. The purpose of this section is to help you weigh all factors and come to a satisfying personal decision.

/ 13
Rational Aspects of Commitment

THE MARRIAGE DECISION CAN BE made in two ways: rationally and emotionally. Historically, marriages were arranged, presumably on rational grounds, by parents for their own benefit. Nowadays we are barraged with messages that all important decisions should be made rationally, but at the same time we're told that love transcends all logic, and can make the most sober businesspeople into blithering idiots. Their feet aren't supposed to touch the ground; their heads are ostensibly in the clouds; they're reportedly consumed by passion to the point of starvation and muddleheadedness. Hardly conducive to a rational decision.

Psychological literature recently has endeavored to identify *stages* of love. A sort of pre love stage is "infatuation," where physical features or a stunning first impression inspires immediate sexual or emotional attraction. The next stage is often called being *in love*. The physical symptoms described above accompany obsession and ecstacy. The delerium of being "in" love is replaced gradually by a less consuming but weightier state, *abiding love*, where intimacy deepens with time. Another state of emotions might be called *kinship love*. Recent research reveals that many long-married couples grow apart eventually, staying in noncommunicative marriages just because they're commited to them. Kinship love is certainly a connection "thicker than water," but not really one of choice, romance, or, perhaps, even friendship. Kinship love can be a negative outgrowth of abiding love, but this progression does not always occur.

So, it appears that when under the heady influence of infatuation or first-stage love, humans are in no condition to make such a consequential and complex decision as the one to marry. Many people believe that a couple cannot possibly have the wits or the information to choose marriage until their feelings have settled into a more rational mode (i.e., in the abiding love stage). Do you agree? What about all those doves and champagne fountains discussed in the preceding chapter? If couples wait until their love quiets down, what happens to the extravagance of romance, the passion of unfulfilled longing?

But marriage is *not* a rational decision; it is based on a balance of rational and emotional factors. As mentioned before, the balance is weighted heavily in favor of emotions. Still, it's necessary to clear your head of swirling feelings, and get down to grimy basics. You may have attempted this by drawing up elaborate lists of "pros and cons" to getting married. But if the lists added up to an answer inconsistent with your inclination, forget them. Lists can be useful but only if considered to be a small piece of a complex puzzle rather than the final word.

Contracts for Coupling

Throughout history, contracts have been used to validate marriages. Trades of cattle for brides are described in Peter Lacy's *The Wedding:* "Among the Kaffirs, six cattle is regarded as about the minimum price for a homely girl with a bad temper, and thirty cattle are enough for an energetic beauty. Among the egalitarian Togolese, at one time, a standard price for all brides prevailed: $16 in cash and $6 in goods." The contract here is like a sales receipt: you give me cattle, I give you chattel.

This kind of "purchase" contract has been common throughout history. Often, as in ancient Greece and Rome, the deals were made between parents of young children for future marriages at age 13 (girls) and age 18 (boys). The dowry was often of more importance than the betrothed woman in these arrangements, for a son and his parents stood to gain considerable wealth by taking a girl off her parents' hands. Judeo-Christian marriages introduced the concept of love between the partners, though often marriages under these auspices were arranged as well. ("Matchmaker, matchmaker, make me a match!") The Jewish *ketubah*, or wedding contract, includes a reference to love and sets up rules for the marriage (including that the man will support his wife).

While arranged marriages and purchased brides are still prevalent in some parts of the world today, in nineteenth- and twentieth-century America, women gained the protection of their fathers rather than their scorn. Daddy earned the right to tell Mr. Wrong to skeedaddle when he came on bended knee to ask for a daughter's hand. Women's sudden shift from pittance to pedestal status can be attributed in large part to the Victorian exultation of love, and also, in western America, to the shortage and subsequent value of women in populating the plains. The dowry was replaced by the trousseau, usually filled with handy items such as quilts and seductive lingerie.

As women came to be valued for their delicacy and tenderness (rather than being regarded as drains on family income, and used as vessels for future sons), the need for written bargains sealing their destiny diminished. Contracts were only necessary when one party, usually a well-heeled financier or country gentleman of advanced years, wanted to prevent the other (often a comely young thing from a less moneyed family) from acquiring wealth. "Golddigging," the unseemly practice of marrying a man for his money, was at one time a desirable pursuit. Soon the state stepped in where religion had once dominated, sanctioning and regulating unions via the marriage license. A legal marriage in our culture carried with it contractual elements, and both men and women easily knew their roles. In the first 150 years of American history, people hardly had a choice: women were taught domestic skills, and men learned reading and were apprenticed in order to secure means of support for their families.

Contracts remained in general disrepute or neglect until the "liberated '60s", when they returned to fashion, mainly as a result of feminist pressures. In their new incarnation, contracts have four major purposes:

1. To serve as a substitute for marriage. Some couples want to avoid governmental interference, and so draw up a private document specifying the permanence and rules of their relationship. These couples have the *intent* of marriage, and in their minds *are* married. Their contract is for their own reference (the act of writing it clarifies their positions) and, more importantly, for a legal record, should some brush with legality arise (e.g., birth of children, death of a partner). The contract is clear evidence of their union.

2. To protect property from outsiders. A marriage or relationship contract keeps personal property separate and prevents it from being appropriated by relatives or state representatives in the event of a split or death. Property acquired jointly can be spec-

ified, and its disposition noted. This type of contract may never be put to use and may not affect the relationship, but the couple feels more secure knowing legally, their own possessions will remain just that, safe from outside claims or from a division that they have not agreed on.

3. To provide preparation for a breakup. In this case, couples protect property and potential children from *each other* in the event of a breakup. These wise couples, unsure of their future together, prepare for an orderly withdrawal, so as to avoid arguments about who entered the relationship with what. They're able to end their alliance more smoothly by simply following their own written instructions.

4. To delineate duties, freedoms, and roles. Bernice Kohn Hunt, in her book *Marriage*, notes that in 1797 Mary Wollstonecraft and her husband agreed to maintain separate quarters; the same was true of Margaret Sanger in 1922. Lucy Stone and Henry Blackwell announced in 1855 that they wouldn't obey laws that "refuse to recognize the wife as an independent, rational being, while they confer upon the husband an injurious superiority." More recently, contracts have stipulated who will take time to raise children; who will control finances; how much separate time each partner is entitled to; means of making major decisions; and when and how to renegotiate the contract.

One of the primary benefits of writing a contract is the *process* of deciding on personal responsibilities as well as the more mundane dispersion of goods. Dean and Roberta, ages 34 and 35 respectively, both had been married before, sans contract. Since their early divorces, each had pursued a career and acquired property. I asked them why they wanted a contract this time.

Roberta explained, "I wanted a contract because I learned that people change, and sometimes things don't work out. I don't want to divide my property under those circumstances, and neither does Dean. A contract saves many headaches if you have to break up."

"I agree," Dean said. "But more than that, I want to spell out our unusual relationship. We only agreed to marry under the conditions that we could take yearly separate vacations, invest our private resources separately, and even live apart for up to a year if required by our careers." Dean and Roberta are both in business, and want to be mobile to follow corporate leads. Dean went on: "These are not included in the standard marriage contract bought with your $10 marriage license. We needed to open up the rigid institution to suit our needs and help us relax about what we're getting into."

"It would be horrible if we entered marriage with a conflicting set of expectations," Roberta said. "By writing our contract, we're forced to discuss how we want to lead our lives. It's like combining all the questionnaires from the 'First Comes Love' workshop into a binding agreement. I think that every couple should at least *write* a contract, even if they tear it up afterward, because then they summarize all their assumptions and get set for their life together. If they can't come to terms on a contract, they shouldn't get married."

I find that most of the workshop participants agree in principle that a wedding contract is useful and practical, but in fact, few go to the trouble of drawing one up. Many people sense that there are major *drawbacks* to contract-making. "It sounds great," Jay conceded, "but why should we plan for a tidy divorce when we expect to be together for the rest of our lives? Writing a contract is like allowing an escape hatch, an admission that you may not stick around to work out all your problems. I think that doing these questionnaires is the perfect way to organize and explore your relationship. A contract can soon feel like bars keeping you in a prison, because you have to think of your relationship within the confines of clauses and paragraphs." Jay refused to write a marriage contract because, as a lawyer, he'd seen couples part bitterly because of differences in how they interpreted particular words and phrases. He didnt't want to be locked into arrangements that were made before he married (and really got to know) his wife.

Jay fears the phenomenon of the self-fulfilling prophecy: if you bank on breaking up, you will. By writing a "just in case" contract, you draw divisive lines, and rather than combining, put borders on your separateness by stamping possessions with ownership labels. "If you think about breaking up, you will," was the way Isaac, a veteran of divorce with a contract, put it.

When my wife and I were married, every time we'd fight, one or both of us would allude to the contract. When we finally decided to split, the first thing we did was use that contract as proof that the other always was selfish and wanted out in the first place. I'm convinced that if we didn't have that stupid contract, we would have emerged from the divorce as friends, but we couldn't because we had to play out the script, splitting hairs over the meaning of every line. I think it's better to have a soft agreement, a flexible plan. So what if you owned the stereo when you got together? After six years of use by both of you, the damn thing's worn out anyway.

Ingredients for a Contract

You and your partner may have no intention of drawing up a formal contract, but considering the ingredients of a hypothetical personal contract can help you see clearly your demands and expectations concerning marriage. Few real contracts would go into the detail these questions cover, but negotiating them with your partner will help in spelling out your respective duties and privileges.

In the next two sections, check off the privileges you'd like to reserve in your relationship. Items are phrased as if you are speaking to your partner.

How I Spend My Time: "I Want to Be Able To:"

Choose to be alone when we both are available to be together
Accept invitations on behalf of both of us
Work overtime frequently
Go out with friends without you whenever I want
Go alone to parties to which you're not invited
Make spur-of-the-moment reservations to go out of town (alone or with you)
Spend as much time as I want with my family
Stay up or sleep on a different schedule from you

Money: "I Want to Be Able To:"

Decide on my career or jobs that I hold
Choose to return to school
Make far less money than you do (not for the purpose of sponging off of you)
Veto proposals to spend large amounts of joint money on items of which I disapprove
Maintain a separate bank account if I choose
Buy whatever personal items (such as clothes) I want
Plan independent vactions or trips
Be consulted about joint vacations or trips

Invest my own money any way I want

Gamble my own money

Be responsible for my own debts

Consult with you on large items purchased with joint income

Go over budget to buy birthday or holiday gifts for you

Stash away "a little something" secretly

Use joint credit cards without your approval

Buy luxuries without consulting you

Eat out whenever I please

Make a long-term financial commitment (e.g., pledging money to a charity) without your consent

Borrow from a friend or relative without consulting you

Choose a new residence by myself when presented with a take-it-or-leave-it deal

Defining Financial Contributions

Pretend that you are married. In the blanks below, write your realistic estimate of the *percentages* of each expense to be paid by each partner. (Remember that the sum of Partner A's percentage and Partner B's percentage has to be 100.) If the situation with your current partner is temporary and does not reflect your ideal division of expenses, complete the percentages twice, once for your realistic short-term future, and another time for what you regard as ideal divisions of payment.

	Partner A's %	Partner B's %=100%
Food	____	____
Shelter	____	____
Utilities	____	____
Medical care	____	____
Children	____	____
Clothes	____	____
Recreation	____	____
Gifts	____	____
Education	____	____
Car(s)	____	____
Insurance	____	____
Business expenses	____	____
Credit or loan payments	____	____
Other: _____	____	____

Write briefly how each task will be handled:
Balancing the checkbook _____
Paying monthly bills _____
When one of us wants to make other than an incidental purchase, the other: (check most feasible plan) ___ Will trust the other's judgment ___ Must give concent ___ Need not be consulted if cost is under $____ ___ Has the power to veto before or after the fact ___ Other:_____

Housework

The usual arrangement will be that each task at left will be assigned to: (use either checks or percentages of the time)

	Him	Her	Other
Cooking	___	___	___
Dishes	___	___	___
Cleaning of toilet	___	___	___
Cleaning of sink	___	___	___
Cleaning of bathtub	___	___	___
Taking out the trash	___	___	___
Laundry	___	___	___
Dusting	___	___	___
Vacuuming	___	___	___
Car care	___	___	___
Clothes shopping	___	___	___
Food shopping	___	___	___
Errands	___	___	___
Pet care	___	___	___
others:_____	___	___	___

Outside Relationships

(Answer these questions on a separate sheet of paper.)
How will religious practices be handled (if applicable)?
What stipulations would you include in a marital bargain regarding separate friends?

Emotional and Sexual Needs

On the basis of discussions you and your partner had in connection with Chapter 9, (Needs and Desires), write down the boundaries of acceptable behavior (sexual and emotional) in relationships with others of the opposite sex. Include rules for both yourself and your partner.

Plans Regarding Children

Write down your plans regarding existing and/or contemplated children.
How would child-care duties be divided (if applicable)?
If you had an unplanned pregnancy, would you approve of an abortion? Would you approve of abortion in the event that amniocentesis revealed a Down's Syndrome fetus?

Communication and Personal Factors

Complete each of the following sentences.
"When we have a disagreement, we each pledge to. . . ."
"Habits, interests, or people I plan to tolerate (though I may not particularly like them) are. . . ."
"Habits, interests, or people I hope you will tolerate for me are. . . ."
"Regarding appearance and fitness, I pledge to. . . ."
"Regarding appearance and fitness, I'd like you to pledge to. . . ."

Changes

Write down three habits or characteristics you would work to change and, for each, write how you would go about making the change.
Write down three habits or characteristics you would like your partner to work to change and, for each, ways you think he or she should go about making the change.
Name the three things you would most like to get from the relationship.
Name three things that you will try your best to give your partner in terms of the relationship.

You'll notice that the ingredients to the "contract" above are emotional and physical rather than legal. If you'd like advice on writing a contract to specify dispersion of goods, it's wise to consult a lawyer or such books as *The Living Together Kit* by Toni Ihara and Ralph Warner, and *The Marriage Contract: Spouses, Lovers and the Law* by Lenore Weitzman. Most contracts specify the disposal of possessions each partner brought into the relationship and of large items (house, car, appliances) that were acquired during a couple's time together.

One of the most controversial topics discussed in "First Comes Love" workshops is how spouses' funds are to be combined or separated after marriage. Here's a sample discussion:

FERNANDO: Olivia and I plan to keep our bank accounts separate after we marry. That way we're each responsible for ourselves, and we'll never argue over finances.

JODI: How will you run the household? Will you split everything down the middle?

FERNANDO: Well, right now I'm earning more than Olivia, so we've agreed that I'll pay 60 percent of everything and she'll pay 40 percent. When she gets her promotion, we'll even things up.

JODI: You may be okay for a while, but I think after a few months, your accounting will be such a headache that you'll break down and just do whatever's easiest at the moment. It's so hostile, so unloving to never treat your partner, or always *have* to pay your own way. And some things belong to both of you jointly. Or should I say some things are 60 percent Fernando's, 40 percent Olivia's? Everything split down to the last penny.

OLIVIA: You sound like you have a chip on your shoulder. We've made this work for a year already. No problem. This way we each feel better, like we're pulling our own weight. We know we're each contributing to the unit fairly.

JODI: I had a bad experience with this "you pay half, I'll pay half" scheme. The guy I was living with kept buying stuff for the apartment, like artwork and pots and sheets, and then billing me for half! He said we needed them. I even went out and bought a handmade quilt for $400 and billed *him* half, just to give him a taste of his own medicine. So we started an approval system where we both had to okay all purchases. This was restrictive, and my boyfriend felt controlled and hemmed in. When we finally split up, he made me buy out the other half of the quilt! It was a mess. And the problem was the fact that we set up these rules.

FERNANDO: So what's the solution?

JODI: Russ and I are just putting all our earnings in a single pot, except 15 percent of our incomes that we can save, spend, or do whatever we want with. This way we have separate spending money and flexibility to make purchases and pay bills. We made a pact not to let money issues become a big deal.

OLIVIA: That was your problem the first time. Your boyfriend used money as a symbol of his freedom and control over you. Fernando and I make our system work by being casual about it. We have the same values, too. Neither of us would buy a $400 quilt, it would never occur to us. We might pay $400 for a piece of furniture, but only after we'd shopped around and decided on something that pleased both of us.

GENE: I think all of you are too hung up about money. Eloise and I are just keeping one joint checking account, period. We can take from the account whenever we need money. Why set aside even 15 percent? Keeping separate stashes means you don't trust each other completely. It means you're so insecure your partner will leave you penniless that you've got to have a safety net.

The room exploded in anger. Nearly everyone assumed that *of course* it was healthy to want your own separate money. You earned it, didn't you? Why would anyone, in this age of women's separate incomes and easy divorce, want to create a spaghettilike mess in their finances? What would possess Gene to basically *give* all his money to Eloise?

The key is age and acquisitions. Gene was 24, Eloise 20. Neither had anything to lose. They were both just starting out, with meager incomes and no major possessions. Who cares whose paycheck pays for the hamburger meat? Who cares who buys the bricks and boards for the living room bookcase? When you're just out of college, in love, and living in poverty, you don't let other people's scary stories affect you. You take a chance.

Fernando and Olivia, on the other hand, had wisdom born of experience. At ages 47 and 50, they knew first-hand the importance of that "safety net." They knew that an emergency could leave them destitute, and they knew that relationships that are supposed to last forever rarely do. Also, they had more to protect: assets to be passed on to children, family heirlooms, higher incomes from jobs in ongoing careers. They had more responsibilities, too, and they needed to know that they'd have the resources to meet them.

Money is an inflammatory subject because it symbolizes so much. It can mean identity, freedom, security, achievement, status. It is territorial and personal. Though money is widely considered to be the root of all evil, most couples are not greedy. They simply want to work out a mutually satisfactory way of handling a touchy issue.

Goals for the Relationship

Now that you've negotiated the finer points of your short-term future with your partner, here's an opportunity to project what the relationship will be like in one, five, and ten years.

Goals for the Relationship

Individually, fill in goals for both of you as a unit for the next year, five years, and ten years.

	One Year	Five Years	Ten Years
1. Residence (where, what style)			
2. Finances (give desired annual incomes)			
3. Friendships (state desired number of friends)			
4. Children (ideally, number and spacing)			
5. Relationship with each other: Amount of time together; Amount of personal privacy; Habits to change			
6. Relationships with family			
7. Work/education goals that both can work toward (i.e., how each can assist the other; timing)			

8. Special achievements to strive for; milestones.			

Fill out the "Goals for the Relationship" questionnaire. Your future stretches out ahead of you. Think of your patterns: Are you likely to stay with a choice you make now, or has history shown you to be mercurial? Will events that will shape your future (e.g., graduation from a degree program, the birth of a child) cause major shifts? Or does your life move at an even pace, grounded in security? Relax and fantasize.

One purpose of setting long-term goals is to provide place markers against which you can compare the progress of your relationship. With articulated goals, you'll also be cooperating toward specific ends rather than flailing for direction. You may have fewer arguments, because there will be more agreement on why a certain move is to be made, and you'll have fewer decision points to approach cold. Of course, your goals, once written, are not indelible. Make regular appointments—say, every six months, or whatever time frame you choose—to check up on your progress and set strategies for meeting goals you still endorse. If changes are needed, you can deliberately re-chart your course, directly communicating with your partner about what the new goals should be rather than making assumptions or excluding him or her from your latest thoughts.

/ 14
Emotional Aspects of Commitment: The Fear and Flutter of Love

AHH, LOVE. Unquantifiable, inexplicable, irrational. Love is a feeling that overwhelms so that nothing else matters. More words have been written about love (I would guess) than any other subject; more songs have been composed with love-touting lyrics than any others. Love makes the world go 'round, causes the birds to sing, the flowers to bloom, the sun to shine. It makes darkness light, old folks young, the poor into millionaires. All you need is love.

According to popular conception, love is paradoxical, unreasonable, and very powerful. People speak of love in hyperbole, saying their love is higher than the highest peak, brighter than the brightest star. A Victorian valentine poet had a knack for expression:

> The rose will cease to blow,
> The eagle turn a dove,
> The stream will cease to flow,
> Ere I will cease to love.
> The sun will cease to shine,
> The world will cease to move,
> The stars their light resign,
> Ere I will cease to love*

Many people eagerly throw aside caution for love. They abdicate thrones (as Edward VI did for Wallis Simpson) and chuck careers with nary a second thought. Many of these decisions are made in the throes of infatuation or first-stage love, when reason is unlikely to dominate. But other love-based metamorphoses grow

---

*Quoted in Judith Holden, *Sweethearts and Valentines* (New York: A&W Publisher, Inc., 1980, p. 44.

out of abiding love, the kind people realize is the most precious commodity in the world.

Motivations for Falling in Love

Love is complex. While it is a feeling, it also reflects a range of rational motivations. These motivations are often selfish, and may reflect a present need to correct a negative aspect of life. Among the reasons for falling in love are:

1. Desire to escape a bad situation. The high school girl falls in love with the sailor and—dreaming of exotic ports, palm trees flexing in the breeze—she marries him. In so doing, she moves out of a crowded ghetto apartment, and away from the domination of her parents.

2. Desperation. The aging spinster latches onto the charming suitor, relieved that someone finally showed an interest before she shriveled into a prune.

3. Desire to show the world you're grown up. "I must be mature, I have an engagement ring," was the unspoken thought of the pimple-faced teenager as she showed off the diamond on her well-manicured hand. Across town, a dynamic woman executive of 33 also displayed her ringed left hand in order to keep her male luncheon companion from making a pass at her. She's using being married to signal to her colleague that "I'm beyond childish 'notice-me' games."

4. Desire to show the world that you're young. The couple in their 50's is pelted with rice, symbol of fertility, after their nuptials. When they kiss for the photographer, their celebrants cheer. The world is new again. Marriage symbolizes the new beginning, the clean slate everyone idealizes.

5. A wish to have something no one can take away. " 'Tis better to have loved and lost than ne'er to have loved at all." Remembering love's sweetness is almost as good as its first taste.

6. Loneliness. Love is the antidote to loneliness, an end to being isolated and alone. Being in love reaffirms your link with humanity and reminds you that you have feelings for others in the world.

7. Fear of aging alone. There's nothing more pitiful than the shadow of a withered lady staring from her nursing home window. Some people fall in love to have someone else to focus on, and to remove the ever-present fear of aging alone.

8. Boredom. Love is a stimulant, an upper. "I just hung

around the pool hall all day," said a workshop member who was recalling his youth. "So when Mary Lou blinked those seductive eyes, I followed her to the land of hot nights, steamy kisses, and thrilling passion. Sure beats losing nickles in a smoke-filled room."

9. A need to feel lovable. When you've gained ten pounds, your gray roots are showing, and you have crow's-feet that look more like tributaries to the Nile, it's comforting to know that someone thinks you have the warmest smile on earth. We all need to be loved and feel lovable, and reassurance that we're not ready for the wastebasket helps keep us going (to the diet doctor, hairdresser, plastic surgeon . . .)

10. A desire to re-create the past. To be young and in love, walking hand-in-hand along the Seine, the booksellers' stalls alive with browsers, and the buckets of flower-vendors ablaze with tulips and daffodils. . . . Though this scene may be from the pages of a story book, the *feeling* of being in love always recalls a more glorious past.

11. Need for a mother or father figure. "I want a girl, just like the girl that married dear old dad," says the old standard. In truth, he wants *Mom*, not some imitation. But given the limits of reality, he'll take someone who will care for him in the same way Mom did, making chicken soup when he's sick and taking unpleasant decisions off his hands. Similarly, young women often want "sugar daddies" who lavish gifts and penthouse suites on their sweeties in exchange for a little daughterly affection and servitude. Falling in love with a parental figure keeps apron strings in a tight knot.

12. Financial or emotional security. Being in love doesn't bring the kind of security that a wedding ring supposedly guarantees, but it's a step in the right direction. A woman can lay claim to a man simply by taking marriage vows and hissing, "He's mine." Men usually stand to gain a constant source of support and adoration; they may label their desire for such amenities "love."

13. Habit. Lina, a young woman of 26, had been going with the same man since high school. "I don't think I'm in love with him," she'll tell you, "but it sure is nice to be able to call him when I get home from a bum date!" After eight years of this fellow (who, by the way, sends weekly bouquets and serenades her with Spanish love songs), she conceded that she "cares" in a way that might be termed love.

14. As a distraction. "I had to make a big career decision about whether to return for my M.B.A. or take a promotion at my

humdrum company. Thank God I fell in love instead," chirped one 20-year-old woman. "Now I'm cheerful every morning, because soon we'll get married and board a plane for Tahiti!"

15. As an excuse why you can't do other things. The Tahiti-bound fiancée above could put off her dreaded decision because she was wild about her broad-shouldered lover. In another example, Noel got so wrapped up in courting Cheryl that he never did the charity work he had volunteered for, never washed his house windows, and never picked the abundant lemons off his tree. It was easy for him to believe that his mission of impressing Cheryl was more important than rotting lemons, needy orphans and window grime.

16. Validation that you can find someone and experience love. With all the hype about this ethereal and incomparable emotion, people sometimes *want* to be in love so badly that they find someone and convince themselves that this is it. Young teenagers are eager to feel love for the first time; those who have survived bad relationships yearn to know they can find true happiness after all. Sighed one bride to her distant aunt who had flown in for the wedding, "Sure, I love him, Aunt Winifred. I *guess* I love him. . . ." Uh-oh.

17. Sex. Love and sex aren't the same thing, as you well know. But many women can't give their bodies to an insistent, attractive man unless they at least *think* it's love. Sometimes after having sex, they try to rationalize their lust by calling it love. Either men or women who want regular and satisfying sex may justify their desire by emphasizing how much in love they are— even if their love isn't the abiding kind.

18. Admiration of another person. Why all the frenzy about rock musicians and sports figures? Why are people speechless with awe when they see Robert Redford on a Beverly Hills street corner? People admire public figures' displayed qualities of strength, skill, and talent. They also frequently find doctors, ministers, and professors attractive because these professionals hold a role of authority and wisdom, (traits that are parentlike). Admiring physical characteristics and personality (especially in combination with one or more of the motivations above) will hasten feelings of internal love.

Sometimes a love object is chosen not for intrinsic qualities but for what he or she can do for you:

- Nurture, heal, or parent you
- Give you someone to nurture, heal, or parent
- Be a backdrop so you can look good by comparison
- Provide fame, money, or some other status that extends to you
- Provide a moral framework and rules for conduct (if the person is religious or high-principled)
- Fill a gap in your skills or talents
- Provide support with room to grow (in certain relationships)

Yes, love is irrational, wild, and enthralling. But its foundation is in the needs of people—understandable needs that help us to survive and thrive.

While various motivations listed in this section don't seem to be very good ones in themselves, they often are the springboard for people to take the necessary risk to open themselves up to a partner. Why would anyone expose him/herself to pain, humiliation, embarrassment, and disappointment without *some* basis? Think about your past relationships and your current one. Which of the above motivations allowed you to come out of your personal shell and be freer with your partners?

Desirable Characteristics

Let's dwell a moment on love reason number 18, admiration. Love begins as a combination of attraction and personal motivations or needs. Some needs develop along with our earliest socialization; others arise later. How do you set your criteria for a mate? What characteristics of your partner make him or her appealing? Complete the "Desirable Characteristics" questionnaire.

Looking at a partner's desirable characteristics gives you one more handle on why you feel the flutter of love.

Exploring the criteria in the questionnaire can also be a means of troubleshooting for the future. If you or your partner possesses a large number of the qualities listed, there's a greater chance of being found attractive by *others*.

How it Feels to be in Love: Some Examples

"Huh?" asked Marcus, looking up from his tuna melt. "I didn't hear you." Marcus, 28, was in love, and I was trying to interview him on how it felt. His was first-stage love, the magical moments of rapture idealized in poetry and music. "Yes, I guess my head *is* in the clouds," he said.

Desirable Characteristics

On a scale of 1 to 10 (10 = most or highest amount of the characteristic; 1 = least amount), rate yourself and your partner. Then, in the right-hand column, rate the amount of this characteristic you *need*, and the amount of it you *desire* in a partner.

Characteristic	Rating for partner	Rating for self	Need Desire
1. Looks/attractiveness of face			
2. Looks/attractiveness of body			
3. Nice dresser			
4. Power over others			
5. Money/wealth			
6. Fame			
7. Charm			
8. Outgoingness			
9. Verbal articulateness			
10. Intellectuality			
11. Sophisticated style			
12. Significant professional achievements			
13. Demonstrative			
14. Associates with important people			
15. Talented			
16. Strong self-confidence			
17. Respected for high level of knowledge or expertise in a particular area			
18. Has secure and happy family made up of likeable people			
Other desirable characteristics:			

"When I first met Rita, I didn't think much of her," said the attractive dentist. "I'd just joined the dental group, and she was just another hygienist. I was so involved in making an impression, if you'll pardon the pun, that nothing else mattered. Little did I know that *she* noticed me. She started to do the craziest things," he smiled, "like hiding my instruments so she could find them for me, bringing me coffee, and even wiping my car windshield! I still didn't notice her. Then she invited me to go with her to a concert. I was taken aback, not because she asked me, but because I saw her as a woman for the first time. She's really a woman!" He gazed into space a moment too long before continuing.

"Rita is a doer. She goes out of her way to be sweet and considerate, and I mean all the time, in bed, at the office, even driving in the car. She's got the nicest hands; I love her hands." Marcus grinned in recollection.

On another occasion, I asked Rita, 30, how it felt to be in love. "Fabulous! We can't keep our hands off of each other! I knew from the moment I saw him that Marcus was the one. It was chemistry. Cupid shot one of his little arrows right at me!" I asked whether she'd ever felt this way before. "I've been in love before, sure," she replied. "Three times, in fact. But never like this—my head *is* in the clouds. Marcus and I don't need to even say anything; we just sit for an hour at a time holding each other. I'm an efficient person, but I find myself distracted, and I don't want to eat. I'd rather go out and buy a new outfit to wear for Marcus, or write a poem about Marcus, or brag to my girlfriends about Marcus. I've practiced writing my name with his a zillion times. This whole thing has made me a child again." That love makes one youthful was repeated by couples of all ages.

Love often justifies breaking social conventions, and in recent years, those traditions are less rigid anyway. Patricia, 68 and a widow, came to my workshop with Les, 40. They had not only an age difference but a racial one as well: Patricia was white, Les black. I asked how this factor influenced them. "It kept us apart for too many years," Les said, looking lovingly at Patricia. "I thought I couldn't possibly love this grandmotherly white woman. I thought I must be crazy to think about her all the time. I even went to a shrink who told me I wanted an authority figure. He didn't say that based on who we were as people but based solely on our demographics."

"How did you make the connection, then?" I asked.

"I made the move," Patricia said. "The sparks between us were unmistakable. I knew he was always hanging around; he'd show up at church and come by after work. Les had known my now-deceased husband through the university, and at faculty gatherings we'd talk. I denied the chemistry for a long time, too. But finally I couldn't stand it, and sat him down and told him how I felt."

"That was the most wonderful day of my life," Les said, smiling. "Everything turned around. No longer did I have to hide my feelings. No longer did I feel guilty, or think I was imposing on Patricia. No longer did we have to play games. We just decided to hell with the world. You've got to grab life as it comes, and live it to the fullest. I think that overcoming our obstacles made us treasure and enjoy each other all the more, because we're sure it's the real person we care about."

If it feels so great to be newly in love, how does it feel to love for a long time? As a journalist, I did a story on a couple celebrating their seventy-first wedding anniversary. Ben and Minnie Rabinowitz, 94 and 91, hugged and kissed each other shamelessly throughout the interview. Their sense of humor, excitement about life, and positive attitudes have made their love last. "The secret to staying happy is love and respect," Minnie Rabinowitz said. "I took good care of my husband. If all the people in the younger generation took care of their husbands like I do, there'd be no divorce!" By taking care, she meant that she was a partner: they worked side by side in their "momma-poppa" grocery store and later, garment store. "Don't stop [positive feelings toward each other] on little things," Minnie advises younger couples. "Be satisfied whatever happens."

Ben Rabinowitz added: "Tell the truth. The main thing in life is to be honest. That way you have nothing to hide."

Natural Fears About Marriage

Just as love is wondrous and joyful, its frequent result, marriage, brings many fears. Some of these are based on a distrust for the lore that exalts marriage, a distrust often well deserved. In their classic book *The Mirages of Marriage*, William Lederer and Don Jackson outline seven false assumptions about marriage: (1) that people marry because they love each other; (2) that most married people love each other (Lederer and Jackson claim that much destructive behavior goes under the guise of love); (3) that love is necessary for a satisfactory marriage; (4) that there are inherent behavioral and attitudinal differences between female and male, and that these differences cause most marital troubles; (5) that the advent of children automatically improves a potentially difficult marriage; (6) that loneliness will be cured by marriage; and (7) that if you can tell your spouse to go to hell, you have a poor marriage.

Lederer and Jackson's book, published in 1968 helped dispel many of these myths. The progress of the feminist movement, the onset of the "me decade," the prevalence of divorce and remarriage, and new insights by individual and marital counselors have destroyed others. But a few myths do persist, and it would be wise to check your own attitudes to see whether your assumptions or irrational feelings are interfering with the clarity of your thinking about marriage.

After reading about the pitfalls of marriage in this book, you may be even more nervous about plunging in. In the preceeding chapter, causes of distress about the marriage ceremony were outlined. Now you have an opportunity to acknowledge anxieties about the *state* of being married. Complete the "Marriage—Why Not?" questionnaire.

Having one or several of these fears is normal, but having a high amount of them signals important reservations about marriage. For items on which you rated yourself 7 or above, I'd suggest discussing the potential problem in detail with your partner and perhaps a professional counselor. Any items awarded level 10 intensity are warning flags. You may want to break off your engagement or relationship, but are so afraid of hurting your partner or disappointing others that you're unable to stop the momentum toward marriage. You need to, however. The distress you feel now is difficult to handle, but compare that to the continued distress and complications in untangling a more interwoven relationship, perhaps with the added factor of children. "This, too, shall pass," is a useful phrase for getting through difficult times. Think of moving on, of exploring new directions. As Ben Rabinowitz advises, "be honest in all things."

Acknowledging fears can bring you and your partner closer. You're entering scary and unknown territory together. Also, if your partner understands your fears about marriage, he or she can work to make them groundless. That's what Irma did:

MARRIAGE—WHY NOT?

Below is a list of natural feelings about marriage. On a scale from 1 to 10 (1 = least amount of feeling; 10 = most amount), put a number for yourself and for your partner.

	Amount I feel this	Amount my partner feels this
Fear of losing independence		
Scary notion of "forever"		
Wanting to resist the expectations of society		
Fear that the emotional investment won't last		
Dislike of the hassle of actually getting married		
Fear that a good relationship will be changed negatively		
Fear of having to face divorce in the future		
Fear of the responsibility of taking care of another person		
A desire not to face the question of whether or not to have a child		
A feeling that I should love the other person more or somehow feel more strongly about him/her		
Moving too quickly from one relationship into another		
Moving too quickly from one sort of dependence to another		
Needing to sort out career decisions first		
Needing to feel self-confident as an individual first		

	Amount I feel this	Amount my partner feels this
Tax or other monetary disadvantages of marriage		
Not wanting to be part of my prospective spouse's family		
A desire to "sow my wild oats" before settling down		
A doubt that monogomy is the proper way for me to spend my life		
A question about my sexual preference		
Fears about the impact of marriage on existing children		
Not wanting to be completely vulnerable to being hurt by another person		
Not being completely recovered from the loss of another partner		
Not wanting to settle for someone not quite up to my ideal		
Feeling that this isn't the right time to get married		
Feeling that I don't know the other person well enough to make a permanent commitment		

Sid was afraid of being hemmed in. He needed space, all kinds of space. He needed time alone, and physical space that would not be violated. I knew this from the beginning, and always accepted it. Marriage, in his view, was the ultimate shackle, so I bent over backward to prove that he could be married and free. Independence means a lot to me, too. So we got a four-bedroom house, and we each have our own wings. After three years together, Sid moved out of his bedroom and into mine so we could sleep together every night. He's changed his viewpoint and his needs because he truly *believes* that I'll never hem him in. It just took time for him to be convinced."

What do *you* need to be convinced of? Take a few moments to write out your major reservations about marriage, and what you'd need to feel more comfortable about them. Discussing these feelings with your partner is essential. As you poise to the first strains of the wedding march, don't you want to get started on the right foot?

/ 15
Making a Decision

THIS IS IT. You've looked at new trends in marriage and relationships, assessed yourself and your partner, planned your future, and dealt with emotions about getting married. The purpose of this final chapter is to pull it all together; to give you tangible evidence of your pondering and help you decide what course of action to pursue.

The "Benefits and Drawbacks Questionnaire" lists all the ingredients I've found that enter into the decision to marry. You'll be checking off whether these factors are benefits or drawbacks in marrying your partner. If you're reflecting on a past relationship or your relationship is in a fairly early stage, substitute "living together" or "dating" for the word "marriage" throughout.

There are seven broad areas to consider and under each one are several more specific items. Each item is simply a cue: use all the exploration you've already done to work from each cue to a complete picture of your situation. For example, the first item asks you to evaluate "the effect of marriage on career opportunities." To make your judgment, you have to interpret what these effects would be for both yourself and your partner. Perhaps your boss has been after you to marry in order to enhance the corporate image of employees being happy, family-oriented citizens. In this case, your marriage might bring you a promotion to a more visible post. You would probably rate this item as an important benefit of marriage. Perhaps yours is another situation. Soon after getting married, you might want to take time off from work to set up your new home. This might interfere with a big project you're involved with and affect your career opportunities adversely. This item would then probably be rated as an important drawback of marriage. Project the likely reality onto each statement listed.

For some items there will be both benefits and drawbacks.

Repeat items as many times as necessary with your varying interpretations to allow you to confront *all* benefits and drawbacks of marriage. This questionnaire is a tool for you to personalize. Discuss interpretations of items with your partner to see whether you view them similarly or differently. Probe why you interpret items in particular ways. This is an exercise to enhance your awareness; the more time, discussion, and thought you put into it, the more you will be rewarded.

Note that the "Benefits and Drawbacks Questionnaire" has a crucial middle column, labeled "not important to me either way." Having this column as an option allows you to sift out factors that are not affecting your decision, and score only those that have significance. Use this column also for items you consider important but feel neutral about.

There's no hard and fast scoring system, such that, say, "90–100 means you should be married, 80–90 means you should just go steady, and 70–80 means you should break up." There are no "shoulds" here. Generally, however, it's best to check the extremes whenever applicable. (Don't be one of those "safe" thinkers who avoid committing themselves. If you're like that, you may not be the type to make a *major* commitment, like marriage.) Since the purpose of this questionnaire is to give you clear evidence of your inclinations, checking extremes will more clearly illuminate what your true feelings are.

First, independently, go straight through the questionnaire alone, and, after giving careful thought to each item, check the appropriate column. Then score the items in each column, assigning points as indicated on the first page of the questionnaire. When scoring, add *bonus points* to any items that carry real significance to you, and which you feel deserve extra consideration. The number of bonus points is up to you—if one item is more crucial than anything else, you may want to award it, say, 50 bonus points, just to show that it's such a major determinant in your decision.

As an illustration of how bonus points are used, Katy, whom you met in the first chapter, added 12 extra points to the item "effect of marriage on the decision to have a child/children." She and Boris were happy living together, and they had no desire to marry *unless* they were going to have children. Once that decision was made, all hesitation vanished. Katy's score in favor of marriage was heavily weighted by the addition of her bonus points.

Benefits and Drawbacks Questionnaire

Check how important a benefit or drawback each item would be if you were to get married. Be sure to use your *feelings* as well as your logic.

	An important benefit of marriage	A benefit of marriage	Not important to me either way or neutral	An important drawback of marriage	A drawback of marriage
I. Career And Education					
Effect of marriage on how I'm viewed professionally					
Effect of marriage on career opportunities					
Ability to stop/start working					
Priority of home versus work responsibilities					
ADD TOTALS HERE:	2 pts.	1 pt.	✗	2 pts.	1 pt.

SCORING: 2 points for each "important benefit" and each "important drawback" checked. 1 point for each "benefit" and each "drawback." Add in as many *bonus points* as you feel are appropriate for any items that are especially meaningful in your decision. *Do not* add any points for items checked "not important to me either way."

	An important benefit of marriage	A benefit of marriage	Not important to me either way or neutral	An important drawback of marriage	A drawback of marriage
	2 pts.	1 pt.		2 pts.	1 pt.
Amount of time available to devote to partner versus work					
Effect of marriage on my long-range career decisions					
Effect of marriage on my short-range career decisions					
Effect of my partner's wishes on my career					
Effect of marriage on my present career					
ADD TOTALS HERE:			✕		

	An important benefit of marriage	A benefit of marriage	Not important to me either way or neutral	An important drawback of marriage	A drawback of marriage
	2 pts.	1 pt.		2 pts.	1 pt.
Effect of marriage on incentive to achieve					
II. *Finances/Lifestyle*					
Effect of marriage on type of housing					
Effect of marriage on standard of living					
How we manage the budget					
Effect of marriage on credit					
Effect of marriage on amount of income necessary					
ADD TOTALS HERE:			✕		

	An important benefit of marriage	A benefit of marriage	Not important to me either way or neutral	An important drawback of marriage	A drawback of marriage
Effect of marriage on feeling financially responsible					
Cost of the wedding					
Cost of setting up housekeeping					
Effect of marriage on home clutter and noise					
Cost of potential children					
Ability to save money					
Effect of marriage on desire to acquire goods					
ADD TOTALS HERE:	2 pts.	1 pt.		2 pts.	1 pt.

	An important benefit of marriage	A benefit of marriage	Not important to me either way or neutral	An important drawback of marriage	A drawback of marriage
	2 pts.	1 pt.		2 pts.	1 pt.

III. *Potential Parenthood*

- Effect of marriage on decision to have a child/children
- Marriage as a precursor to taking time off to have a child
- Effect of marriage on existing children
- My partner's feelings about having a child/children
- Being good parents
- My age at the birth of a child

ADD TOTALS HERE:

	An important benefit of marriage	A benefit of marriage	Not important to me either way or neutral	An important drawback of marriage	A drawback of marriage
My partner's age at the birth of a child					
IV *Relationships with Others*					
Being part of my partner's family					
Effect of marriage on our friendships with other couples					
ADD TOTALS HERE:	2 pts.	1 pt.	✕	2 pts.	1 pt.

	An important benefit of marriage	A benefit of marriage	Not important to me either way or neutral	An important drawback of marriage	A drawback of marriage
Effect of being married on my/our status in our circle of friends					
Effect of marriage on our relationships with family					
Effect of marriage on our relationships with friends					
Our role as a couple in community activities					
Competition between my spouse and my friends for my time					
ADD TOTALS HERE:	2 pts.	1 pt.		2 pts.	1 pt.

	An important benefit of marriage	A benefit of marriage	Not important to me either way or neutral	An important drawback of marriage	A drawback of marriage
	2 pts.	1 pt.		2 pts.	1 pt.
Effect of marriage on my closeness with same-sex friends					
Social pressure to be married					
Effect of marriage on our relationships with previous partners					
Effect of marriage on our relationships with in-laws					
Effect of marriage on our ability to entertain					
ADD TOTALS HERE:					

	An important benefit of marriage	A benefit of marriage	Not important to me either way or neutral	An important drawback of marriage	A drawback of marriage
V. *My Partner*					
My partner's age					
My partner's attitude toward new endeavors					
My partner's wishes about getting married					
My ability to influence my partner					
My partner's personality					
My partner's appearance					
Similarity of my partner to my ideal spouse					
How my partner treats me					
ADD TOTALS HERE:	2 pts.	1 pt.		2 pts.	1 pt.

VI. Personal Considerations	An important benefit of marriage	A benefit of marriage	Not important to me either way or neutral	An important drawback of marriage	A drawback of marriage
Getting married as part of growing and maturing					
My feelings about myself as a married person					
My view of my long-term future					
The names we each would go by					
My need to feel loved by one person					
My need to give love to one person					
ADD TOTALS HERE:	2 pts.	1 pt.		2 pts.	1 pt.

	An important benefit of marriage	A benefit of marriage	Not important to me either way or neutral	An important drawback of marriage	A drawback of marriage
Continuing a family name or traditions					
Effect of marriage on sexual satisfaction					
Effect of marriage on sexual relationships with others					
Effect of marriage on my freedom to do as I please					
Effect of marriage on my ability to travel					
My age					
Impact of marriage on my physical state					
ADD TOTALS HERE:	2 pts.	1 pt.	✗	2 pts.	1 pt.

	An important benefit of marriage	A benefit of marriage	Not important to me either way or neutral	An important drawback of marriage	A drawback of marriage
My partner as a helpmate to me					
My ability to continue alone should my partner depart the scene					
My status as an adjunct to my partner					
My independence from other sources of support					
VII. *Our Relationship*					
Opportunity for communication with partner					
ADD TOTALS HERE:	2 pts.	1 pt.	✕	2 pts.	1 pt.

	An important benefit of marriage	A benefit of marriage	Not important to me either way or neutral	An important drawback of marriage	A drawback of marriage
Effect of marriage in feeling bound to each other					
Effect of marriage on personal privacy					
Marriage as security					
Marriage as a cure for loneliness					
Having someone to always rely on					
Our ability to communicate with each other					
Sharing each other's achievements					
ADD TOTALS HERE:	2 pts.	1 pt.	✕	2 pts.	1 pt.

	An important benefit of marriage	A benefit of marriage	Not important to me either way or neutral	An important drawback of marriage	A drawback of marriage
	2 pts.	1 pt.	✕	2 pts.	1 pt.
Likelihood of divorce in our case					
Effect of marriage on being part of a "family"					
Fulfilling religious beliefs and teachings					
Being like other people					
Each partner's desired level of household neatness					
The amount of disagreements we have					
Each person's personal hygiene					
ADD TOTALS HERE:					

	An important benefit of marriage (2 pts.)	A benefit of marriage (1 pt.)	Not important to me either way or neutral	An important drawback of marriage (2 pts.)	A drawback of marriage (1 pt.)
Recreational interests and hobbies					
Spiritual considerations/religious similarities					
Personal outlooks or philosophies					
How well we know each other					
How I feel when we're together					
The way we make decisions					
The way we resolve problems					
ADD TOTALS HERE:			✗		

Score in favor of marriage: Add together scores in columns "An important benefit..." and "A benefit...."

Score against marriage: Add together scores in columns "An important drawback..." and "A drawback...."

Totals from first page
Totals from second page
Totals from third page
Totals from fourth page
Totals from fifth page
Totals from sixth page
Totals from seventh page
Totals from eighth page
Totals from ninth page
Totals from tenth page
Totals from eleventh page
Totals from twelfth page
Totals from thirteen page
Totals from fourteenth page
Totals from fifteenth page
Bonus points
ADD HERE THE GRAND TOTALS:

In favor of marriage	Against getting married

Using the Results of the "Benefits and Drawbacks" Questionnaire

After completing the exercise, take some time alone to think about your score, and the way you answered the questionnaire generally. Were there some items where it was difficult to project the future, or items where you could have answered in two or more ways? Mark such responses with a question mark, and note on a separate page what the problem in answering was. Then use the following guidelines to interpretate the results.

1. Note which items you did *not* score—that is, the things that were neutral or weren't important in your decision either way. These are the areas in which you can be flexible. If your partner does care about them, you may be willing to bend or compromise.

2. Note the items you felt strongly about (those earning two points each, but especially those which received bonus points). These are the areas least open to discussion or compromise on your part, and make up the core of your feelings for and against marriage.

Your current feelings, however, may change as you receive new information. Check with your partner to make sure that the assumptions on which you based your responses are accurate. For example, maybe you thought that your partner strongly wants to get married, so decided you would do it for him or her. If you find out that he or she actually doesn't care as much as you thought, you may want to change some of your answers.

Look over your bonus-point and two-point answers and judge which of them are most likely to continue to be reality, and which you're not sure about. Circle the ones you know won't change. (These may be important values or personal characteristics over which there is no control.) Recognize that if you're to marry, you'll just have to live with these things.

Look again at the bonus-point and two-point answers to see if they cluster under any one or two major areas. If so, decide whether these areas will be a continuing bone of contention or, on the positive side, will be an enjoyable theme of your relationship. Remember to look back at overall *patterns* in yourself and your relationship.

It often helps to think back to your childhood patterns that shaped the associations you carry about marriage and relationships (and thus affected your point assignments). Go back over previous questionnaires to see whether there are any topics that kept recurring.

3. Look at *how many* statements you felt strongly about (bonus points and two-pointers). If you have 60 or more as a score showing inclination for or against marriage, you know that the decision is highly emotional for you.

Next, after your partner has also completed the questionnaire, discuss the results with him or her. Use the "Partner Decision-Making Sheet" to organize your discussion.

Partner Decision-Making Sheet

Use this sheet with the results of your "Benefits and Drawbacks Questionnaire."

Write down the total points from each column in the questionnaire.

An important benefit of marriage	} Add together	Total in favor
A benefit of marriage		
A drawback of marriage	} Add together	Total against
An important drawback of marriage		

List the subheads or themes of items where your strongly felt answers clustered:

_____
_____

List the strongly felt answers you circled because they are likely to occur in the future or continue to be reality:

_____
_____

On a separate sheet, list alternatives for changing the future so you and your partner can live together more happily in marriage.

Decision Alternatives

"After considering my values, expectations, and feelings, and those of my partner, I believe the best course to take is . . ." (circle one only)

Get married within six months	Plan to get married within a year or _____ (write when)	Live together with no marriage plans	
Settle a personal issue, and then marry _____ (write the issue)	Enjoy now and don't think about marriage	See other people	Break up

If you and your partner disagree on the best course to follow, how do you propose to deal with this problem in the near future?

_____

1. Write the column scores from your questionnaires on the "Partner Decision-Making Sheet." First, discuss differences in *number of points*. Any wide differences are usually a warning, signaling differences in emotional investment in the relationship or disagreement about the importance of the decision. Be aware, though, that even though someone may have fewer concerns about the marriage decision (and therefore fewer points overall), he or she may still feel very strongly about the items that do receive two points or bonus points.

2. Compare and discuss *areas of importance*. Compare the headings under which you and your partner assigned bonus and two-point answers. Then discuss themes that you both feel are important, and areas where you seem to see the relationship differently. If you and your partner have a similar set of concerns, there are two possibilities: (a) you share a perspective and have a good idea of the core issues in your relationship; or (b) your view-

points are limited—concentrated in a few areas rather than offering an overall perspective on the relationship.

3. Compare and discuss *specific concerns*. List the questionnaire items you circled on the questionnaire (those likely to continue to be reality) in the appropriate space on the "Partner Decision-Making Sheet." Note whether these important values, expectations, or feelings are areas of contention. If they are, list on a separate sheet some ways of changing them. Drawing on what you have learned from this book and from observations of others, give as many alternatives as possible.

Remember to *state* the underlying assumptions you made when you were interpreting each item, to check whether they are shared with your partner. You might want to list the events or circumstances that must take place in order for your projections or assumptions to hold true.

4. Next, look at the "Decision Alternatives" listed on the "Partner Decisions-Making Sheet." Each of you should circle the choice that seems most realistic and satisfying at the present time. Discuss your reasons for your choices. If you and your partner strongly disagree, or are still uncertain about your choices, you can set aside the decision (therefore deciding to coast along with the status quo) and pick a date when you will work through the questionnaire again. If there is strong disagreement, it might be wise to consult an objective outsider (friend, relative, or counselor). In any case, do be open and honest about your feelings. Even if you're completely unassertive, *do not* just go along with your partner to please him or her. The decision must be a mutually satisfying one.

There may be some unfinished *personal* business one of you should take care of before plunging into marriage. For example, one woman had never completely found her independence apart from her family, and was about to leap from one type of dependence into another. She first had to find her self-confidence as an individual living alone, and then enter marriage with the knowledge that if she had to, she could stand on her own feet.

Another person was dissatisfied with his career, and thought that happiness with a wife could make up for a lack of rewards on the job. He needed career counseling and a new position before he was ready to get married. Otherwise, his wife would unknowingly be taking on the burden of being solely responsible for her husband's happiness.

Another woman dearly wanted to have a child, and unconsciously looked upon marriage as a means to that end rather than as an independent commitment. She cared for her potential partner, but refused to consider that someday they would *only* have each other, and that they had better be friends first and foremost. She also overlooked the possibility that one of them might be infertile and that adoption might be difficult. Before seriously considering marriage, she had to separate her feelings about having a child from her feelings for her partner.

The moral to the many stories in this book is that marriage should be a bonus to your life, the means to a sense of secure joy. When marrying, you are making a commitment to treasure your relationship above all else and to stick it out when times are rough (remember "for richer or poorer"?). Practically everyone enters marriage with the intention that it will be for life. But lurking in the back of many people's minds is the thought that there's always an out: divorce. Some think that divorces should be made more difficult to obtain, and marriage should only be entered into after couples pass a test, or perhaps complete a series of exercises like those in this book. What do you think?

Completing the "After" Questionnaire

You now have some numbers showing your inclinations and have tentatively reached a decision. The decision is not carved in granite, and should be reexamined and confirmed periodically. If working through this book has enabled you to strongly confirm your decision to marry, congratulations! You're embarking on your married life with as many guarantees as life allows.

Now that you've completed the decision-making process, see how far you've come. Complete the "after" questionnaire independently. Then discuss the results with your partner, and compare your responses with those on the "before" questionnaire on page 20.

"After" Questionnaire

1. Conflict is evidenced by indecision, deciding back and forth or having a clash of ideas. How much conflict over getting married do you note right now, at this point in time?

   a. Within yourself?   None A little Some A lot
   b. Within your partner?   None A little Some A lot
   (from what you can tell)
   c. Between the two of you?   None A little Some A lot

2. Distress is anxiety—being upset or having other negative emotions. How much is the decision about whether or not to get married a source of distress now?

   a. For you? None A little Some A lot
   b. For your partner?
      (from what you can tell) None A little Some A lot

3. What is the percentage that you lean *toward* marriage, and the percentage you lean *against* it?

   a. *Right away?* b. *In the future?* How long? _____
      (Within a year) _____ + _____ = 100%   _____ + _____ = 100%
                      Toward   Against   Toward   Against

4. What is the percentage that *your partner* seems to lean toward and against marriage?

   a. *Right away?* b. *In the future?* How long? _____
      (within a year _____ + _____ = 100%   _____ + _____ = 100%
                     Toward   Against   Toward   Against

5. Ten years from now, realistically, which of these do you foresee for yourself?

   _____ Married to my   _____ Married to   _____ Unmarried but
           current partner   someone else   living with someone

   _____ Unmarried and independent

6. At this point, when you and your partner discuss whether or not to get married, which of these things do you do?

   _____ Argue strongly for my point   _____ Become happy and enthusiastic
   _____ Clam up or avoid the subject _____ Logically weigh the pros
   _____ Become depressed or moody   and cons
                                         _____ Change my mind a lot

7. At this point, when you and your partner discuss whether or not to get married, which of these things does your partner do?

   _____ Argue strongly for his or   _____ Become happy and enthusiastic
           her point
   _____ Clam up or avoid the subject _____ Logically weigh the pros
   _____ Become depressed or moody   and cons
                                         _____ Change his or her mind a lot

8. What is the biggest change *in you* that has occurred as a result of working through the exercises in this book?

   _____

9. What is the biggest change *in your partner* that has occurred (from what you can tell)?

   _____

I hope that your conflict and distress about the marriage decision has decreased, and that you and your partner have developed a smoother communication style as a result of your exploration together.

Here are comments from graduates of the "First Comes Love" workshops about the knowledge they gained:

- "My partner and I are breaking up because of this experience, but it is with optimism and friendship. We finally understand why we shouldn't get married to each other, and we can go out in the world knowing what we should look for."
- "We weren't at the point of deciding marriage, and now we know that we have a lot to learn about ourselves before we latch onto someone else."
- "My partner and I started this workshop in love, but now we're *more deeply* in love because we discovered so much about each other."
- "The important result for me was learning how to communicate. This is a skill that will be valuable for the rest of my life in every kind of relationship I have."
- "Every teenager ought to take this course. I finally learned how to evaluate potential mates in terms of my own goals."
- "We've decided to be engaged. We'll be confident that our married life began on the best footing possible."
- "We had no surprises, though we gained a few new insights. Thank heaven, because we're getting married *tomorrow!*"

If you discovered that certain areas of your life need to be addressed before you decide the marriage question, you now have experience in pinpointing what your feelings are. You can always return to this book and reuse the questionnaires. If you marry happily, I hope you'll take out this dusty volume on your fiftieth wedding anniversary and redo the questionnaires to see how love and life have left their mark.

Laurence Shames was newly married when he wrote this eloquent answer to why people should marry:

... Marriage is, among other things, the adoption of a passionate morality, the decision never to disappoint someone. It is the election of a profoundly respected partner to be the keeper of one's character. It's the setting up and sharing of standards, the taking on of a fierce vigilance that fends off shabbiness and snarls at the notion of settling for less than one should. Marriage is a means of becoming unselfish yet of exalted value to oneself because of one's pact with another person. It's truly prizing something and taking the risk of trying with all one's strength not to mess it up. It's the incomparable adventure of not averting one's eyes . . . (*Savvy* magazine, March 1981).

Marriage in its best manifestation is beautiful and gentle. This outcome is the reward of careful discovery and courage to be vulnerable. You deserve praise for your bravery in viewing yourself and your partner through the mirror of the exercises and ideas in this book. Your prudence is shared by the anonymous Victorian writer who penned these words on a frilly valentine:

> Some wed for gold and some for pleasure,
> And some wed only at their leisure,
> But if you wish to wait and weep,
> When e'er you wed, look well before you leap.

Bibliography

Brenton, Myron, *Lasting Relationships: How to Recognize the Man or Woman Who's Right for You*, (New York: A & W, 1981).

Burgwyn, Diana, *Marriage Without Children* (New York: Harper and Row, Publishers, 1981).

Elvenstar, Diane, *Children: To Have or Have Not?* (San Francisco: Harbor Publishing, Inc., 1982).

Holder, Judith, *Sweethearts and Valentines* (New York: A & W Publishers, Inc., 1980).

Hunt, Bernice Kohn, *Marriage* (New York: Holt, 1976)

Ihara, Toni, and Warner, Ralph, *The Living Together Kit* (New York: Fawcett Columbine, 1980).

Jaffe, Dennis, *Healing From Within* (New York: Alfred A. Knopf, 1980).

Kreiter, Peter, and Bruns, Bill, *Affair Prevention* (New York: Macmillan Publishing Co., Inc., 1981).

Lacy, Peter, *The Wedding* (New York: Grosset and Dunlap, 1969).

Lederer, William J., *Marital Choices* (New York: W.W. Norton and Company, 1981).

Lederer, William J., and Jackson, Don D., *The Mirages of Marriage* (New York: Norton, 1968).

Loftas, Jeannette, and Roosevelt, Ruth, *Living in Step* (New York: Stein and Day, 1976).

Maddox, Brenda, *The Half Parent: Living With Other People's Children* (New York: M. Evans and Company, 1975).

Marcus, Genevieve Grafe, and Smith, Robert Lee, *Equal Time* (New York: Frederick Fell Publishers, Inc., 1982).

Novak, William, *The Great American Man Shortage and Other Roadblocks to Romance* (New York: Rawson Associates/Scribner Book Companies, Inc., 1983).

O'Neill, Nena, *The Marriage Premise* (New York: Bantam Books, Inc., 1977).

O'Neill, Nena, and O'Neill, George, *Open Marriage* (New York: Evans, 1972).

Rosenbaum, Jean, and Rosenbaum, Veryl, *Stepparenting* (Corte Madera, CA: Chandler and Sharp, 1977).

Seligson, Marcia, *The Eternal Bliss Machine* (New York: Morrow, 1973).

Singer, Laura J., *Stages* (New York: Grosset and Dunlap, 1980).

Thatcher, Floyd, and Thatcher, Harriett, *Long Term Marriage: A Search for the Ingredients of a Long Term Partnership* (Waco, TX: Word Books, 1980).

Visher, Emily B., and Visher, John F., *Stepfamilies: A Guide to Working with Stepparents* (New York: Brunner/Mazel, 1979).

Weitzman, Lenore, *The Marriage Contract: Spouses, Lovers and the Law* (Englewood Cliffs, NJ: Prentice-Hall, 1980).

Yankelovich, Daniel, *New Rules* (New York: Random House, 1981).

Zola, Marion, *All the Good Ones are Married* (New York: Times Books, 1981).